More Lakeside Love

LOVES OF LAKESIDE ROMANCES
THE COLLECTION - BOOKS 4-6

More Lakeside Love

MIMI FRANCIS

Table of Contents

RUNNING WILD 275

Can't Fight The Feelings

Dedication

Tiana, this one is for you. Your unwavering support, smiling face, and love keeps me going; your off-the-wall insanity keeps me smiling; and your advice never fails to be on point. Thank you for pushing me to be better. I love you.

Chapter 1

Natasha

"*N*ate!"

Natasha pounded on the thick wooden door, hard enough to make her hand ache. For a second, she wondered if she was in front of the wrong house; all of the homes in this area looked alike. It wasn't like she was thinking straight, either.

"Nate!"

She stepped back to check the house number, took a deep breath, counted to ten, and started pounding again with both fists.

"Nathaniel Boris Garin, open the goddamn door!" she screamed.

The door flew open so suddenly that she stumbled forward, landing on the hard wood floor of the small foyer on both knees with a startled "oof." Natasha's twin brother Nate stood at the door, wearing nothing but his boxers, his reddish-brown hair standing on end, and his blue eyes flashing. She'd always been jealous that Nate got their mother's deep blue eyes, while hers were gray like their father's.

"What the hell, Natasha?" he snapped. "Are you drunk?"

"Jesus, no!" She pushed herself to her feet and stalked past her brother, elbowing him in the gut as she passed him. "Why the hell would I be drunk? God, you're an insensitive asshole."

"Hey, you're the one beating the shit out of my door and barging into my house in the middle of the night!"

"Oh, god, why don't you just shut up?" Natasha shouted.

She entered the modest living room, dominated by a big screen TV and a sectional sofa. She dropped her backpack on the floor, threw herself on the sofa, put her hands over her face, and burst into tears. She'd been holding them back ever since she'd walked into her apartment and found her boyfriend, Brick, with that woman.

Natasha didn't know how she got to Nate's place; she remembered little after grabbing her backpack and storming out of the apartment she shared with Brick. It didn't surprise her that she ended up at Nate's house. Her brother was her rock, always there when she needed him. Going straight to his place for comfort was the only thing she could think to do.

Nate slammed the door shut, rested his head against it, and stared at the floor. "I repeat, what the hell, Tash? What are you doing here at two in the morning?"

Before she could answer, a door on the other side of the living room opened, and a giant of a man stepped out. Topping out at 6' 6", Mason, Nate's roommate and best friend, towered over both of them. Relief washed over her at the sight; Natasha hoped he'd be here. Her brother's best friend—her friend—would make everything better; he always did. Though it annoyed her that once again, Mason was witness to her bad taste in men.

"What is going on out here?" He pulled a shirt over his head then ran a hand through his shoulder length black hair, pushing it away from his face. He froze when he saw Natasha, and his eyes narrowed. "Why are you crying, Tasha?"

"Crying?" Nate vaulted over the back of the couch and landed beside her. "What happened?"

Natasha shook her head. "I don't want to talk about it." She hiccupped and wiped her nose with the back of her hand.

Nate scoffed. "You show up at our door at two in the morning, pounding loud enough to wake up the entire block, and you don't want to talk about it? I don't think so." He put his arm around Natasha and hugged her. "What did that asshole Brick do now?"

Natasha opened her mouth to tell her brother not to call her boyfriend an asshole, but instead, she lost it. She collapsed into her brother's arms, her head on his chest and tears pouring down her face. The story of finding her fiancé in their bed with another woman came out between her sobs and curses. Once it was all out, Natasha fell against the back of the couch, hiccupping sobs escaping her and with tears and snot all over her face. She was also bearing the hefty stares of one sympathetic friend and a pissed-off twin brother.

"I'm going to kill him," Nate growled. Once Natasha had the whole story out, Nate shot to his feet and paced back and forth in front of the couch, fists clenching and unclenching at his sides while his brow furrowed. Anger radiated off him in waves. "I am literally going to kill him."

"Nate—"

"When are you going to stop letting him treat you like crap?" her brother snapped. "When?"

Natasha sighed. "I don't *let* him treat me like crap. It just happens. And I don't want to have this discussion again."

"We won't have to if you tell me you're breaking up with him this time."

"He's my fiancé, Nate. I'm supposed to marry him." *Not like that's going to happen now.* The thought brought a fresh wave of tears. A reassuring hand settled on the small of her back, instantly soothing her. She glanced over her shoulder at Mason and gave him a grateful smile as her brother continued his tirade.

Nate rolled his eyes at her excuses. "He's your fiancé in name only. You've been engaged for almost a year, and you haven't set a date. He makes excuse after excuse to avoid making the commitment. Ever since he lost his job at the university, he's always drinking, he can't keep any other job, and he's making your life a living hell. And now, he cheated on you." Nate's voice got louder with every word. "What more does he need to do? How much shit is he going to put you through before you decide you've had enough? When are you going to figure out you deserve better?"

Natasha jumped to her feet. "Stop yelling at me!" she screamed. "I've had a terrible day!" She took a step toward her brother, the urge to slap his perfect face overwhelmed her.

Mason was on his feet in a second, stepping between them, with his arm going around Natasha's waist. He swung her off her feet, moving her away from her brother, and then put a hand on Nate's chest. "Alright, you two, that's enough. I think we've all had enough ... excitement for one night. Why don't we get some sleep, and we'll pick this up in the morning?"

Nate glared at Natasha, slapped Mason's hand away, and stalked across the room. The slam of his bedroom door echoed through the small house.

"He's a little grumpy when he first wakes up, especially in the middle of the night," Mason said.

"I know." Natasha sighed. "I'm sorry, Mason. I shouldn't have come here. I didn't know where else to go. Shit, I didn't have anywhere else to go." Another bout of tears threatened, thickening the back of her throat and making it difficult to talk. She closed her eyes and rested her forehead against Mason's muscled chest as he pulled her into a hug.

"You're always welcome here, Tasha; you know that." Mason kissed the top of her head and released her. Afterward, he opened a small closet next to the bathroom door, pulled out some mismatched, faded sheets, and tossed them on the couch. "There's a blanket in the cupboard under the coffee table if you need it."

"Thanks, Mace," she mumbled. Her brother's best friend was the consummate good guy. He was unbelievably nice, one of those guys who did stuff for other people without being asked, the guy who stepped up to help when no one else would. He was the good guy, to a fault. Whenever she needed him, he was there; sometimes she hated that about him, especially when she could only find the losers to date.

Mason smiled at her. "Get some sleep, Tasha. You can fight with Nate in the morning." He was almost to his room when he turned back to look at her. "Nate's right, you know. You deserve better."

—

The smell of coffee pulled Natasha from a restless sleep the next morning. She propped herself up on her elbows, squinting as the light hit her eyes. Across the room, thanks to the open floor plan of the small house, she could see Mason in the kitchen. He must have been out running because he wore basketball shorts, a zip-up hoodie with no shirt, and running shoes. There were a pair of earbuds in his ears, and his long, black hair was pulled into a tight bun at the back of his head. He had an odd look on his face as he pulled coffee cups from the dishwasher.

Natasha sat up and rubbed her gritty, puffy eyes. Her head pounded and her throat was raw from the emotional night. She shoved herself off the couch, wrapped one of the sheets around her waist, snatched her jeans off the floor, and stumbled into the bathroom to change. Ten minutes later, she emerged to find a cup of hot coffee sitting on the scuffed and marred coffee table, along with three sugar packets, a plastic spoon, and two of those little creamer cups. Mason sat on the couch, remote in his hand, while the other sheet and the blanket she'd used were bunched up beside him to form a barrier between them when she sat down.

"Thanks for the coffee."

"You're welcome." He glanced at her and smiled before he put the TV on some sports program, propped his feet on the table, and sipped his coffee.

Natasha poured the sugar packets and creamer in her coffee, stirring it with a plastic spoon. It was funny that Mason knew exactly how she took her coffee; she wasn't even sure if Brick knew how she took her coffee. Mason also knew she wasn't a morning person, and he knew when she needed to talk and when she didn't want to talk.

Natasha had known Mason since elementary school. He had lived three doors down from her family growing up and went to the same elementary school, junior high, and high school. She had known him when he was seventy-five pounds soaking wet, with unruly, black hair that stuck up in every direction, through junior high when he'd been awkward around girls, gangly, and unsure what to do with his changing body, and through high school, when he suddenly shot up in height and weight the summer between junior and senior year. The only person who knew Mason better than her was her brother.

Even though Mason was Nate's best friend, she and Mason had always been close. Mason was almost as important to Natasha as her brother was; he was the guy she could turn to when Nate became irrational or too brotherly. He kept both of them grounded and stood by them, no matter what. She hated that they'd grown apart since high school because of her stupid decisions, though they were still good friends.

Mason looked at her out of the corner of his eye. "Are you okay? Did you get any sleep?"

Natasha chortled, sounding a little like a sick chicken. "Yeah, I guess so. As good as one can sleep when their world is turned upside down, and they have nothing other than the clothes on their back."

She'd run out of her apartment with nothing but her back-pack—no clothes, no makeup, no money. It was uncomfortable sleeping in her tank top and underwear. She'd tossed and turned on the narrow couch, wondering if Mason would venture out and see her with little clothes on. Just the thought that he'd seen her sprawled across the couch in her underwear made heat rise in her chest and across her cheeks.

She shook off the thought and gave Mason a tight smile. "I am sorry you had to get in between Nate and me last night. We tend to get a little emotional."

Mason laughed. "It's not like it's the first time I've broken up a fight between you two. I'm sure it won't be the last." A grin spread across his face. He turned to face her, his arm propped on the back of the couch. "Do you remember that time in third grade when he switched lunches on you?"

Natasha thought back over the multitude of fights over the years between her and her twin brother. She giggled as the image of the three of them in grade school materialized in her head. Mason had weighed maybe forty pounds and looked like a string bean, she looked like Pippi Longstocking with her long red braids, and Nate had a bowl haircut she still teased him about.

"Oh my god, yes! He wanted my peanut butter-and-jelly sand-wich, right? So, he switched our lunch bags at home. I got his bologna sandwich. I hate bologna. Hate it."

Mason chuckled. "I remember you chasing him around the lunchroom. You almost caught him the third time around."

Natasha nodded. "That's right, I did! Except you jumped in front of me and shoved your lunch into my hands. It was a peanut butter-and-jelly sandwich."

Mason nodded. "And Nate lived to see another day." He cleared his throat. "You know, I hate bologna, too."

"Really? I didn't know that." She narrowed her eyes as she looked at Mason. "If I remember correctly, you ate Nate's lunch that day."

He shrugged. "Yeah, I did."

Nate's bedroom door flew open, interrupting their conversation. Her brother emerged, fully clothed this time, and made a beeline for his sister's side. He pushed the pile of blankets to the floor and sat down, elbowing Mason out of the way. Nate took Natasha's hands and held them tightly in his.

"I'm sorry I yelled, Tash," he said.

Natasha smiled and squeezed his hands; it was time for the inevitable apology. "It's okay. I get it. You're my big brother."

"By eight minutes," he reminded her.

"And you worry about me." Natasha glanced at Mason over her brother's shoulder. He was pretending not to listen. "You're right. Both you and Mason." She dragged in a deep breath. "I deserve better. So, I'm done. I'm leaving Brick, for good this time."

Nate released her hands and jumped to his feet, pumping his fist in the air. "Yes! It's about time. I'll help you move out. Both Mace and I will. In fact, we'll go tonight and get your stuff. I'll get Trista to watch the bar." He did an obnoxious little dance. "Wait? Are you ... are you going to move back to Great Falls? Live with Mom and Dad?"

The thought of living with her parents made her head hurt. She couldn't move home, not after living on her own for the last five years. Moving back into her childhood bedroom under the constant scrutiny of her overbearing parents was not appealing. Her entire life was here in Lakeside, more than four hours from her childhood home. She didn't want to go back to Great Falls, except she didn't have anywhere else to go.

"Well, shit."

Nate, always attuned to her feelings, knew what she was thinking. He kneeled in front of her. "You can stay here as long as you need to until you're back on your feet. Right, Mason?" He smacked his friend on the leg for confirmation.

Mason gave Natasha and Nate a weird look, mumbled something that sounded like "yeah" under his breath, and then he catapulted himself off the couch and into the bathroom. The shower could be heard turning on a few seconds later.

As soon as the door closed behind Mason, a huge grin spread across Nate's face, and he laughed. "This is gonna be fun."

Chapter 2

Mason

Nate might have been his best friend, but sometimes he seemed more like Mason's worst enemy. Letting Natasha stay with them for one night, maybe two, was one thing, but inviting her to *live* with them was something completely different. Nate was completely aware of Mason's crush on Natasha and the fact that he had been head over heels in love with his best friend's sister for years. Now he'd gone and invited the woman who held Mason's heart in her hands to live with them for some time.

I will not survive this.

Mason turned the shower to cold, trying to get the memory of the petite redhead sleeping on their couch out of his head. Every time he closed his eyes, he could see the sheet tangled around Natasha's muscular legs: her panties stark white against her tanned skin, her tank top pushed up beneath her breasts, and her hand splayed across her stomach. After seeing that, he had to run an extra two miles to calm down.

Fortunately, by the time he got home from his run, she'd rolled over and pulled the sheet over herself. Of course, five minutes later,

Natasha stood up, stretched—revealing more skin—then dragged the sheet around herself, and went into the bathroom. That was another sight that would fuel his fantasies for a while.

Shivering from the cold Montana water pouring down on him, Mason shut off the shower, grabbed the towel from the bar, and wiped off just enough of himself to keep from dripping on the hardwood floors. He wrapped the towel around his waist, threw open the bathroom door, and came face to face with Natasha. Startled, he took a step back, causing the corner of the towel to slip out of his hands and leaving him almost completely exposed, except for his dick, which was barely covered by the towel.

Natasha stared at him for at least thirty seconds, her mouth hanging open and her entire face so red, it matched her hair. Once she realized she was staring at Mason—or, more accurately, staring at Mason's dick—she spun around and, for good measure, put her hands over her eyes.

"Oh my god, Mace," she snapped. "Would you put some clothes on, please?"

"Shit," Mason mumbled. He scrambled to rearrange the towel around his waist. Once he'd secured it, he clutched it so tightly, his knuckles ached. "Sorry, Tash." He pushed past her, dove into his room, and kicked the door closed.

Yeah, this is gonna be fun.

———

Mason drove to work with the truck windows rolled down and the radio blaring country music. He thought it might help get Natasha out of his head, but it didn't work.

He was at the photography studio before anyone else, which didn't surprise him. Harry Ward, the owner of the studio, lost his enthusiasm for his job after his wife passed away six months ago. Mason suspected Mr. Ward would soon close up shop and move down to Missoula to be closer to his grandkids, so Mason figured it was time to look for a new job.

"Maybe Nate will hire me," he mumbled, as he unlocked the door and stepped inside the dark studio.

It wouldn't be the first time he'd worked for a Garin, which was Nate's last name. Back in high school, he'd worked for Nate's father, cleaning and detailing cars at Mr. Garin's three car dealerships in town. During college, both he and Nate worked at the Time Out Bar and Grill; when Mr. Garin helped his son purchase the popular hangout, Mason stayed on, working for Nate. The Garins were such a huge part of his life; he wasn't sure what he would do without them.

Thinking about the Garins naturally led his thoughts back to Natasha. Every time he thought he had that woman out of his head—and his heart—she somehow wormed her way back in.

Mason had been in love with Natasha Garin, in varying degrees, his entire life. He still remembered the first time he had seen her almost twenty years ago.

He and his mom had just moved into their new house— bought and paid for by his mom's ex-husband. She sent Mason outside to make friends while she unpacked the house. The minute he hit the sidewalk, he heard someone yelling. Since Mason was a naturally curious child and not afraid of the unknown, he'd followed the sound. To his surprise, he found a tiny red-haired girl, sitting on a boy in the middle of the lawn three houses down the street.

"What are you looking at, nerd?" the girl snapped when he stopped in front of them.

Mason crossed his arms over his chest. "What are you doing to him?"

"What does it look like I'm doing?" the little girl said. "I'm sitting on him."

"Why?" Mason asked.

The girl shrugged. "Because he's my brother and I can."

"Get off me, Nattie," the boy yelled.

"Or what, you'll tell Mom again?" She flicked him on the forehead. "Be quiet while I talk to the new kid." She turned back to Mason. "I'm Natasha, and this is my twin brother, Nathaniel."

Mason narrowed his eyes at the word "twin." "You're not twins," he said matter-of-factly.

"Uh, yeah we are, doofus." She poked Nathaniel in the back of the head. "We're the kind of twins that don't look like each other. Anyway, what's *your* name?"

"Mason. I live down there." He pointed toward his new house. "Mom sent me out here to make friends."

Quick as lightning, the boy—Nathaniel—grabbed Natasha by the waist, flipped her over, and shot to his feet. "You live here? Finally, another guy in the neighborhood." He glanced at his sister on the ground. "Now I won't have to hang out with my sister anymore."

Natasha jumped to her feet, tackled Nathaniel around the knees, and forced him to the ground. She was screaming and yelling something Mason couldn't understand, but at that moment his heart twisted in his chest, and Natasha Garin took up residence.

The three of them became best friends. They were always together, especially in elementary school. If the Garin twins were around, you could bet Mason Adler was there, too, and it stayed like that through junior high and their freshman year of high school.

Their sophomore year of high school, Natasha started going her own way and doing her own thing. When Mason and Nate tried to get her to hang out with them, she'd spout some line about three being a crowd and vanish with her friends. While they all remained friends, Natasha purposely separated herself from her brother and Mason, hell-bent on doing her own thing without their interference.

Even when they all went to Lakeside to attend school at the town's private college, she'd refused their offer to share a place to live. Instead, she moved in with Avery, a friend she met at school. Nate chalked it up to Natasha needing to separate herself from her twin and do something on her own; Mason was the collateral damage.

For the last eight years, he had watched Natasha get involved in one relationship after another, each of them ending in heartache for her. First had been Reggie, a football player and gigantic jerk. Not that Natasha had seen that side of him, because she didn't want to see it. After Reggie, she'd started dating some guy named Mike, a college sophomore she met on a trip to Missoula. Natasha couldn't be bothered to give Mason the time of day after Mike came along.

After Mike broke up with her, because she was too young, Natasha dated the captain of the basketball team, Dave. They broke up right before graduation—Mason never knew why—and Natasha retreated into herself, swearing off men. That lasted until the trio left for Lakeside, where she met a guy named Bobby. They dated off and on, and Natasha did her best to distance herself from her brother and Mason.

After every one of the breakups, Mason was there to pick up the pieces. Natasha would be heartbroken, and Mason would be there to take her out for chocolate ice cream with rainbow sprinkles and give her a shoulder to cry on. It was what he did; he was the good guy.

Mason didn't know Natasha was dating Brick until she breezed into Nate's bar one night, her new boyfriend in tow. Mason's dislike for him was instantaneous. Brick seemed nice enough, probably on his best behavior to impress Natasha's twin, but something about him didn't sit right with Mason. Or Nate.

He'd tried to be happy for Natasha when she started dating Brick, he really had, but that had quickly soured when he realized how awful Brick truly was. Mason couldn't understand why Natasha couldn't see it, but his and Nate's dislike of Brick only helped to push Natasha away.

The memories of Natasha's urge to separate herself from the people who cared about her weighed heavily on Mason's heart. Determined to get his mind off his best friend's sister, Mason made his way through the studio to the office in the back. He turned on the computer and opened the week's schedule. Summer was always busy—weddings, reunions, special events in the towns around Flathead Lake, even out-of-state visitors booking family photos while on vacation in order to take advantage of the lake's beauty. It looked like Mason's loaded schedule would go a long way toward getting his mind off Natasha.

On top of Mason's full photography schedule, he also worked part-time as an EMT for the small hospital in town, working two nights a week and on call on the weekends. It kept him busy and out of the house most days. He hadn't realized what a relief that schedule could be until Natasha landed on their doorstep in the middle of the night.

Maybe I'll add a couple nights to my rotation.

Avoiding Natasha might be the only way to maintain his sanity. That woman had him all twisted up inside—she had for years. However, living in the same house with her might push him over the edge, as having her in such close proximity would make it impossible to fight his feelings for her.

Mason shoved himself away from the desk, grabbed his camera, and stepped out of the back door onto a porch that stretched the length of the studio, overlooking Flathead Lake.

Without overthinking it, he snapped a photo of a robin pulling a worm from the dirt under a tree by the lake. Then he took another photo of a gull soaring over the water, looking for fish. The sun and the leaves from the tree created an interesting, dappled green pattern on the water, so Mason quickly took a shot before the sun shifted or the wind blew, changing it.

Three hundred yards down the road, Mason could just make out the back of the Time Out Bar and Grill. That, of course, just made him think of Natasha. Again.

Over the years, guys had come and gone from Natasha's life. Every one of them had left her heartbroken, and Mason had done his best to pick up the pieces, he and Nate.

Maybe this time, Natasha would notice that Mason was always there, waiting in the wings: ready to hold her hand like a good friend, console her with ice cream, and heal her broken heart. Except he was tired of being the friend who helped her get over her heartbreak and move on. He wanted more.

Not that he'd ever get more from her. Natasha would always see him as her brother's best friend, the skinny, gawky kid who lived down the street and monopolized her twin brother's time. She would never see Mason as anything beyond what he'd always been—a friend.

"Mason?"

He took a couple more photos before heading back inside to talk to the person who called him. His boss, Harry, sat at the computer, scrolling through the calendar.

"Hey, Mr. Ward. I thought you were going to Missoula today." Mason closed the door, set his camera down, and sat down across from Harry. "Did you want to take a couple shoots today?"

Harry shook his head. "No, you can do them. I am heading to Missoula, but I wanted to stop and talk to you." Harry sat back in the chair and crossed his arms. "Do you enjoy working here, Mason?"

He nodded. "Yes, sir. I love working here." He cleared his throat. "Why do you ask?"

"You do great work," Harry continued, as if Mason hadn't said anything. "Your photographs are on par with stuff I've seen in upper echelon magazines. Impressive."

"Thank you," Mason murmured.

"You've taken this studio to a whole new level. I can't remember a summer when our calendar was full like this." Harry pointed at the computer. "That's because of you, young man."

Mason shook his head, as heat flooded his cheeks. "No sir, you're exaggerating."

Harry laughed. "No, I'm not. I've still got people sitting in the studio or bunched up in awkward family poses. You don't do that; you have a knack for catching people looking natural, comfortable. They look like they're having fun and enjoying themselves. Those are the photos people want, not the stuff I do."

"Mr. Ward, are you closing up shop and moving to Missoula?" Mason asked.

Harry chuckled and shook his head. "Straight to the point, huh? I always liked that about you. To answer your question, yes, I *am* moving to Missoula. But I'm not closing the studio— I'm selling it. Hopefully, to you."

Mason sat back in stunned silence. It took him a few seconds to wrap his head around what Harry said. "You want to sell the business to me?"

"I'd like to," Harry said. "Give me a couple of days to come up with a number, and I'll present it to you. We'll go from there. And do me a favor; keep this to yourself until everything is completed, okay?"

"Um, yeah, okay." Mason's head spun with the possibilities. "I, uh, guess I can do that."

Harry nodded and pushed himself away from the computer. He clapped Mason on the back as he walked past him. "I'll talk to you later this week, Mason. In the meantime, get to work."

"Yes, sir," Mason replied. He wasn't sure how he could concentrate with all the thoughts spinning around his head. This took his hobby-turned-job to a whole new level. However, he wasn't even sure buying the studio was a possibility; it wasn't like he was rolling in money.

Mason took a deep breath to center himself. Too much had happened in the last twelve hours, so he needed to get out of his own head and get to work. That might be the only thing that would take his mind off his crazy life.

Chapter 3
Natasha

After the boys left for work, Natasha wandered around the small house. She had only been here two or three times since Nate moved in. A pang of regret hit her, as she realized how little time she'd spent with her twin brother during the last few years. Yet he hadn't hesitated to take her in when she needed help.

The house had two bedrooms, one bathroom, a large living room and kitchen, and a small backyard with a decent-sized patio. There was a small foyer by the front door that led directly into the living room.

If she was going to live in such a small house with two single men, they needed to establish some ground rules. Foremost, no one leaves the bathroom without clothes on their body; towels did not count. Her heart nearly stopped when Mason's towel slipped, and she got an eyeful of Mason's manhood. Damn, he grew up well.

Sometimes when she looked at Mason, she still saw the skinny kid who had been best friends with Nate since they were six. The skinny kid who had *always* been at their house, plotted pranks with her twin, and slept on couch cushions on Nate's bedroom floor. The skinny kid who sometimes took her brother away from her when she needed him most. Natasha forgot that the kid grew up to be a hulking 250 lb. giant, with muscles bursting from the seams of his shirt and an ass made for biting.

Natasha closed her eyes and took a deep breath. It was too easy to fantasize about Mason; the man was literally made for it. He could have graced the cover of any bodice-ripping romance novel. His flowing black locks and taut abdomen begged women to fawn over him; it had been like that since their senior year of high school. She still wasn't sure how she'd resisted his charms. The man was a walking romance ad.

But she shouldn't be thinking about Mason like that; she had Brick.

Except she didn't have Brick, not anymore. The realization was a slap to the face. That bitch with her legs in the air, moaning loud enough to rattle the glass in the window, while Natasha's fiancé pounded into her in every way imaginable, she was the one who had Brick. Natasha didn't have anyone.

Natasha dug her phone out of her backpack, called the theater, and told them she was sick. She couldn't face rehearsals and stage manager duties when she was an emotional wreck. After she hung up, she headed for the kitchen. Nate and Mason didn't have much to eat: a bunch of kids cereals, chips, dip, a couple of soup cans with dust on them, leftover pizza, and beer—lots and lots of beer.

"Doesn't Nate get enough to drink at the bar?" she muttered. Her brother owned and operated the Time Out Bar and Grill, one of the most popular bars in Lakeside, especially with the college students who attended Lakeside College.

Natasha grabbed a box of Lucky Charms, returned to the couch, found a Disney movie on one of the streaming channels, and buried herself under the covers on the couch. She would stay there until her brother got home, and maybe then she'd deal with the shambles her life had become. Until then, she intended to pretend everything was copacetic.

Except she couldn't stop replaying every minute of the last two years, wondering why she had been so blind to how truly awful Brick was to her.

Jason "Brick" Brickman came into her life her sophomore year of college. He wasn't the type of guy she normally dated—he was edgy, dangerous, a bad boy. The exact opposite of tooth-rotting nice guy, Mason Adler. She refused to acknowledge that her relationship with Brick began at the same time Mason started dating a pretty blonde waitress from the Time Out Bar and Grill. The two had *nothing* to do with each other.

Brick swept her off her feet. Everyone told her he was a jerk, a fact obvious to everyone who knew him. They tried to get Natasha to see it and she did, but she also swore there was a sweet side to Brick, something he kept hidden from others. Natasha dealt with him being an asshole because she believed he loved her, or maybe she *hoped* he loved her.

After they got engaged and moved in together, that sweet side of Brick seemed to disappear. Desperate to keep her relationship together, and unable to admit she made a mistake—again—Natasha turned a blind eye to Brick's lies, his late nights out, his constant drinking, and his inability to keep a job for longer than a few months. Even his refusal to set a wedding date almost a year into their engagement didn't deter her from staying with him. It was easier to ignore Brick's bullshit than it was to break up with him. Their entwined, tangled lives made it impossible to be apart; being with Brick was easier than being alone.

"God, I'm an idiot," she said out loud. Laying it all out in her head had Natasha wondering if she'd lost her mind. She couldn't believe she allowed Brick to treat her so shoddily. She deserved better. Hell, she wanted better.

The realization brought the tears with it. It wasn't long before she had the blanket pressed against her face, sobbing into it. The weight of everything that happened sat heavy on her chest, making it hard to breathe. Natasha couldn't keep giving all of herself to someone who gave her nothing in return.

Her sobs tapered off, and she closed her eyes in exhaustion. She must have fallen asleep because the next thing she knew, the front door slammed closed, and Nate's and Mason's voices echoed through the small house. She groaned and struggled to sit up. She'd been asleep for hours.

Nate stalked across the room, grabbed her ankle, and tugged her down the length of the couch until her ass hung off the edge. She kicked him with her free foot, barely missing his crotch and earning a laugh from Mason.

"Wake up, sunshine," Nate said. "We got Roselli's." He frowned at the half-eaten box of Lucky Charms on the coffee table. "You need some proper food. After we eat, we're going to get your stuff. I grabbed some empty boxes from the bar."

Natasha shook her head. "I don't want to go pick up my things. What if Brick is there? I don't know if I can handle seeing him right now."

Nate rolled his eyes. "If he's there, he's there. You'll tell him it's over. For good this time. It's time to put that jerk in his place. Confront him once and for all. You need the closure, sooner rather than later. The longer you wait, the more likely it is the asshole will think you'll take him back." He yanked on her leg again. "Don't argue with me; you know I'm right. Now, come eat so we can get going."

Natasha glared at her brother and prayed he would burst into flames. When he didn't, she sighed heavily, pushed herself off the couch, and followed Nate into the kitchen. Two boxes of Roselli's pizza sat in the middle of the table. Mason pulled paper plates from the cupboard and dropped them on the table. She slid into an empty chair.

Mason set a bottle of water in front of her. "Looks like you need this."

"Thanks." She could always count on him to look out for her.

The three of them ate in silence, her and Nate staring at each other across the table. Poor Mason—no stranger to their standoffs—tried to look anywhere but at the stewing brother and sister. After five minutes of uncomfortable silence, Natasha sat forward, her elbows on the table.

"Nate, listen to me—."

"I have listened to you," Nate interjected. "I have listened to you bitch about Brick for more than a year. I have dried your tears; I have turned the other cheek when that asshole has treated you like shit. I have held my tongue for too long. Not anymore. We're going over there, and you are telling him that the two of you are finished. Period."

Natasha took a deep breath and swallowed past the lump rising in her throat. She didn't want to cry. Again. "Nate, seriously, for once in your life, listen to the words coming out of my mouth. Please try to understand what I'm going through right now. I'm not … I can't see Brick. I just can't. Not yet, not with the image of him and that girl still fresh in my mind. Please, I'm begging you to understand."

She could feel the tickle at the back of her throat, and the tears pricking at her eyes. So much for not crying; the tears slid down her face. She plucked a napkin from the stack next to the pizza box and wiped her face. Her hands shook, and she couldn't talk above a whisper, fearful she would start sobbing again.

"I know what I need to do. I do," she continued. "Ending it with Brick is my only option. And I will, I swear. But I cannot do it tonight. I just can't. I need time to process everything. This is … this decision changes my whole life."

"You need a clean break, Tash," Nate argued. "You need to go over there and tell him to fuck off. You'll feel better once you do."

Natasha nodded. *God, that would feel good.* But just thinking about it made her stomach twist into uncomfortable knots. She took a deep breath to calm herself before she spoke. "I know, Nate. I know you're right. But … but I'm not like you; I can't turn off my emotions just like that." Natasha snapped her fingers.

"We're not talking about me, Tash. We're talking about you."

Natasha pinched the bridge of her nose. "Yes, we're talking about me, which is why you need to listen to what I'm saying. I am done with Brick. I swear. He and I are over. And I will tell him when I'm ready. Just don't make me see him today; it has been less than twenty-four hours since I found him naked in our bed with another woman. I cannot face him today. I can't listen to his excuses and his patronizing tone."

Nate opened his mouth, but before he could say anything, Mason interrupted them.

"Give her a break, Nate," he said. His eyes flashed with an emotion Natasha was afraid to analyze. "I know you want to watch her tear Brick a new one, but she's hurting. Let her stay here while we go get her things. She can destroy him later, and you can watch. Right, Tasha?"

Natasha nodded. "Yes. Th-that … that sounds—" Her voice cracked, and she swallowed thickly. She stared at the top of the table, the napkin pressed to her lips.

"Okay," Nate said. He reached across the table and squeezed her hand. "It's okay, sis. I'm sorry. I guess I didn't realize how you felt. Mace and I will go get all your stuff. Don't worry about it."

Natasha couldn't speak, so she nodded. She took a sip of her water as relief washed over her. When she caught Mason's eye a few minutes later, she mouthed "Thank you," to him. He nodded and shrugged one shoulder, a faint smile on his face.

Mason was a good guy.

Chapter 4

Mason

"Nate, you need to give Tasha a break," Mason said. "This can't be easy for her."

"Brick is an ass," Nate muttered. "She needs to tell him off, once and for all. You know I'm right."

Mason sighed. "I know, but it needs to be on her own terms. Not because her brother tells her to do it."

"You know, if you had just told her three or four years ago how you feel about her—"

"*Felt*," Mason interrupted. "How I *felt* about her. Past tense." He pulled into one of the parking spots in front of Natasha's place and put the truck in gear, shoving open the door and stepping out. Mason could feel Nate's eyes boring a hole into the back of his head as he left the truck.

Nate climbed out and shot his best friend a dirty look. "Uh huh, sure. Don't lie to me. You know damn well it isn't past tense." He shook his head. "I'm just saying, if you told Tasha how you felt in high school, or middle school, or elementary school, or at some point in our lives, we wouldn't be standing in front of her apartment, ready to move her shit out. She wouldn't be forced to live with us, and she wouldn't be crying herself to sleep at night on our couch. Instead, she'd be gladly living with us, sleeping in *your* bed, and a million times happier than she is now."

"Shut up," Mason grumbled.

Nate shook his head. "I think I'm done shutting up about this." He must have seen the terrified look on Mason's face because he chuckled. "Oh, don't worry, I won't out you to my sister. But I think it's time the two of you stopped this weird dance you've been doing for the last twenty years and figure out what you want. The two of you should be together. Problem is, neither of you knows it."

"Okay, you're right. I know how I feel about Tasha. I've always known how I feel about her." Mason snorted. "I have it more than figured out. I've tried to fight my feelings for her, and I can't. But I will not tell her when she is vulnerable and hurt."

"I think she deserves to know," Nate said. "So why won't you tell her?"

Mason pinched the bridge of his nose. "Because right now, knowing Tasha, she would feel obligated to let me down easy, which would just make everything worse. It can wait."

"If you wait too long, you'll lose her again," Nate said.

Nate was right; this was a familiar dance in their lives. Mason waited too long to make his move, and Natasha moved on to someone else.

Mason didn't want to talk about it, so he grunted, crossed his arms over his chest, and nodded at the door. "I don't want to discuss this anymore. Can we please get this over with?"

Nate dug Natasha's keys out of his pocket and headed upstairs. Mason followed him and leaned against the wall, while Nate pounded on the apartment door.

When no one answered, Nate waited thirty seconds and knocked again. Only then did he use Natasha's keys to unlock the door. The apartment was eerily quiet and obviously empty. Following the directions Natasha texted him, Nate ordered Mason to gather her stuff from the living room while he headed for the bedroom, with a box tucked under his arm.

Mason did as Nate asked. Before he looked for Natasha's things, he stood in the middle of the living room and took everything in. The apartment was dark and dreary, thanks to the drawn blinds. The stench of Brick's cigarette smoke, beer, and stale sweat permeated the air. Empty beer bottles laid on the floor and coffee table next to an overflowing ashtray, and an immense pile of dirty clothes dominated the floor next to a beat-up recliner. Mason couldn't imagine Natasha in this depressing place. She was such a bright person, bubbling with life. It hurt Mason's heart to think that Brick had slowly stolen that light from her, changing the girl Mason loved into a shadowy version of herself. Thank God she was getting away from him.

"Mason!"

"Yeah! Coming!" He followed the sound of Nate's voice to the back of the apartment.

Forty-five minutes later, Mason leaned against the truck while Nate made one more sweep of the apartment. They grabbed everything they could, calling Natasha several times to make sure they looked in all the right places. Nate was on his way out the door of the complex when a loud, drunk voice shouted from up the street.

"What the fuck you doin' here?" The words were slurred so badly, they were practically indecipherable.

Brick staggered up the street with a plastic bag filled with liquor bottles dangling from his fingers, his hair stuck up all over his head, and his t-shirt on backwards. He stopped a few feet from the truck and eyed the boxes stacked in the back. "What the hell are you doing? What's in those boxes?" He glared at them with red-rimmed eyes.

"What does it look like we're doing?" Mason asked.

Brick snarled. "It looks like you're robbing me blind."

Nate stalked the short distance from the apartment entrance to where Brick stood on the sidewalk. "We aren't robbing you, asshole. We're picking up my sister's things. She's done with you."

Brick snorted. "She'll be back. Nat always comes back to me. As soon as she stops pouting and answers her damn phone, I'll convince her to come back. She'll forgive me. She always does. So, you might as well put her stuff back."

Nate shook his head and clenched his fists. "Not this time. She won't come back."

Brick laughed, an ugly, thick, wicked laugh that made Mason's skin crawl. "Trust me, Nate, she'll be back. Nobody else will fuck her, so it's just a matter of time before she comes back to the only man who will."

Nate's face contorted into a mask of pure hatred, and he launched himself at Brick, connecting his fist with Brick's chin to make a resounding crack. Brick stumbled back and fell on his ass. Nate took a step toward him, but Mason lunged after him and grabbed his friend before Nate could jump on Brick and beat him into oblivion.

"Get in the truck, Nate. He's not worth it," Mason said.

"Did you hear what he said about my sister?" Nate bellowed, struggling to get away from Mason. "I'm going to fucking kill him."

"I heard what he said," Mason interjected. "Believe me, I heard it." He wanted to rip Brick's tongue out and make him eat it, but that wouldn't solve anything. Instead, he shoved Nate into the truck. "Stay put." He slammed the door harder than he intended, but he barely held his anger in check. Nate was right. Brick deserved a fist to the face, maybe more, but it wasn't their place to dole out his punishment; that was up to Natasha.

When Mason turned around, Brick had pushed himself to his feet. He wiped his hand across his lips and stared at the blood on his fingers. He wobbled unsteadily as he pointed at the truck.

"Get out of my way, Adler." He took a step toward Mason, headed toward the truck and Nate.

Mason shook his head. "Let it go, Brick. You're lucky I didn't let him kill you. You certainly deserve it."

"Fuck you," Brick snapped. "You love this. You've been mooning over Nat for years. Don't get too excited, though. She wants a real man. Like I said, she'll come crawling back to me."

"Stay away from Tasha," Mason ordered. "Or you'll regret it."

Mason marched around the truck, yanked open the door, and climbed inside. Brick screamed and cursed at him every step of the way. Mason swore he could still hear him, even as the truck rounded the corner.

—

Natasha stood at the door when they came back. "Well, how'd it go?" she asked.

"Your brother punched Brick, knocked him to the ground," Mason said.

Natasha put her hands on her hips and stared at the ceiling. "Please tell me you didn't?"

Nate grinned. "Oh, I did. The bastard deserved it, too. I would have done worse if Mace hadn't pulled me off him and forced me to leave."

Mason snorted. "I don't have the cash to bail you out of jail. Save it for another day."

"Did he … did Brick say anything?" Natasha interjected. "Did he seem sorry?"

Nate shook his head. "Honestly, he didn't seem to give a shit." He gave her a one-armed hug and kissed her temple. "He also said some really crappy things about you, Tash. That's why I decked him. He's lucky I didn't kill him."

A grimace marred Natasha's pretty face and her shoulders slumped. Before she dropped her head to stare at the floor, Mason saw tears glistening in her eyes. She extricated herself from her brother's grip, slipped her shoes on, pushed past Mason, and headed for his truck.

"I'm grabbing a beer before we unload," Nate said. "Do you want one?"

"Yeah, grab me one. I'm gonna go help Tasha bring her stuff in." He set the grocery bag in his hand on the table and headed outside.

Natasha had the tailgate down, yanking boxes off the truck while muttering under her breath the entire time. She stopped to open a couple of them and peer inside, which only seemed to make her more irritated. She grabbed the heaviest box and before Mason could rush to help her, it slipped from her hands and fell to the ground, spilling its contents across the driveway. Natasha kicked a shoe before leaning against the side of the truck with her head in her hands.

Mason walked down the sidewalk and stood beside her. He put a hand on the small of her back and rested his chin on top of her head. "Hey, it's okay," he whispered.

"It's not, though," she muttered, her voice catching on the last word. "Brick played me for a fool. I gave him everything and in return, I got shit. I was so stupid."

"You weren't stupid," Mason said. "You were in love."

Natasha scoffed. "No, I don't think I was. Maybe at first I thought I was in love, but I think over the last few months, I realized Brick wasn't the guy I'm supposed to be with. I chose him when I was really vulnerable and looking for somebody, anybody, to fill the hole in my heart. Brick was there; I thought he was the one. I was wrong."

Mason closed his eyes and hugged Natasha closer. "Who do you think you're meant to be with, if it's not Brick?" Deep down, he knew it wasn't him, but that didn't stop him from wishing it was.

Natasha stiffened in his arms and pulled away. "I ... I don't know. Maybe I'll never know." She grabbed a box off the ground and tucked it under her arm. "Let's get my stuff inside. We can shove it in the corner of Nate's room."

"I don't think so," Nate yelled from the front porch. He held up two bottles of beer. "Who wants a beer? I know I do!"

Natasha laughed and shook her head. "I hate beer. You know what I need?"

"Chocolate ice cream and rainbow sprinkles?" Mason replied.

She turned to look at Mason, a faint smile on her lips. "Yeah, that's exactly what I need."

"Good, because I stopped at the store and grabbed some. It's on the table."

Natasha smiled at him, and it broke his heart. "You're such a great guy, Mace. I knew I could count on you. Let's go drown my sorrows in ice cream."

Mason nodded and followed her inside. She'd piqued his curiosity; who did Natasha think she was meant to be with? Would she tell him? He certainly planned on getting some answers out of her.

Chapter 5

Natasha

Natasha sat in the large, overstuffed chair in the corner of the living room. She kept a wary eye on the slightly chaotic group of people surrounding her. Nate, Mason, and their friends Oscar and Gavin were in front of the big screen TV—a TV that was too big for their small house, in her opinion. Yelling and cursing filled the room as they watched a baseball game. She didn't know who was playing, or who was winning or losing, but she really didn't care. The noise and chaos helped keep her mind off the sorry state of her life.

She had lived with her brother and Mason for three weeks at that point. Three endless weeks. It wasn't like she wasn't grateful that her brother had given her a place to stay, because she was. But some days, she felt like they were back in junior high. Nate enjoyed teasing her and harassing her—as any older brother liked to do—and Mason tiptoed around her like he was afraid she would break down at any minute.

Natasha had to admit she had been emotional, off and on, during the last three weeks, but she was finally getting the tears and the "woe is me" attitude under control. It helped to remember how she had found Brick in bed with another woman, how he'd avoided setting an actual wedding date, and how he treated her like his maid and cook rather than his girlfriend or fiancée.

Sometimes things with Nate and especially Mason were awkward, but mostly it was good. Occasionally she caught one of them walking around in their underwear, though they'd gotten better at wearing pants around the apartment, even if they had a hard time finding a shirt. There had been no more glimpses of wet, naked bodies after a shower. She had to admit, with Mason, there may have been some regret that he kept himself covered up. Nate kept drinking her orange juice, stealing her frozen lunches, and eating her granola bars. Mason liked to drink her Coke Zeroes, and he'd eaten an entire box of cookies she'd bought. She couldn't stay mad at him, though; he'd replaced both of them for her.

Since moving in with her brother, she had learned—to her perpetual irritation—her brother was quite the ladies' man. There were phone calls, constant dates, and women she didn't know sneaking in and out of his bedroom at all hours of the night, women she inevitably got to see since her bed was the couch in the living room. Nate had been with so many women, she couldn't keep track of them all. When she asked him about it, he smiled, shrugged, kissed her cheek, and walked away happily whistling.

Mason didn't seem to have a girlfriend at the moment. He'd broken up with the pretty blonde waitress, Allison, more than a year ago and, as far as Natasha knew, he hadn't dated anyone since. This secretly pleased her, which didn't make sense, given her current dating situation, but she didn't want him to have a girlfriend. A hard knot of jealously formed in the pit of her stomach at the thought. She hated to call it jealousy, but she had to be honest with herself. She realized for years she had been jealous of any woman who got Mason's attention.

Her phone vibrated against her leg. Before she picked it up, she took another drink from the glass of wine in her hand. In the last ten minutes, five text messages had come from Brick. It brought the total for the day to roughly twenty, give or take a few. So far, she'd resisted the urge to answer him.

Vera, another friend of the boys, was perched on the arm of the chair. "Hey Tasha, how are things going? Are you settling in?"

Natasha shrugged. "I guess so. As much as one can when the couch in the living room is your bed, and you're living with two single men who sometimes still act like they're in junior high."

Vera laughed. "They're bachelors. They haven't had to answer to anyone but each other for a long time. There are no rules in this house."

Natasha snorted. "There are now. Rule number one is everybody wears pants." The sight of a very naked, well-endowed Mason flashed through her head.

Vera laughed. "Well, there you go. You're making rules, fitting right in. Are the boys adhering to rule number one?"

"Sometimes," Natasha replied. "They still don't clean up after themselves. The TV is always on something related to sports, and the only food in this house comes from a package or a restaurant."

"You'll get used to it," Vera said. "Besides, you won't be here for long, right? Nate said your stay here was temporary?"

"Hopefully, I'll just be here until I can get back on my feet. Only two or three months at the most."

"See? You only have to put up with it for a couple of months. Easy peasy." Vera patted her on the shoulder before she got up and marched into the middle of the chaotic men watching the game. She whispered something in Oscar's ear that earned her a smile. Oscar laughed and pointed at the TV, obviously explaining the game to her. It was obvious they were interested in each other.

Natasha's phone vibrated against her leg. Again. She peeked at it. Text number six. She didn't have time to read it though because

Summer, Gavin's girlfriend and another friend from high school, squeezed into the chair beside her.

"They're a little overwhelming, aren't they?"

Natasha nodded. She'd been fielding questions and comments like this all night from everyone. Natasha suspected one or both of the boys had told everyone to play nice with Nate's depressed sister. Even Oscar and Gavin had stopped to console her because of her current living arrangements. She didn't know if it irritated her or pleased her.

Summer dug her elbow into Natasha's side. "Earth to Nat."

"Sorry," she mumbled. "I zoned out."

Her brain had been like Swiss cheese since the breakup. She couldn't remember if she was coming or going, alive or dead, happy or sad. The only thing she knew for sure was that she couldn't seem to move on, to get out of the funk she was in. She couldn't get over Brick.

As if on cue, the phone tucked under her leg vibrated. She closed her eyes and exhaled. Maybe she couldn't get over him because he wouldn't leave her alone. The constant barrage of texts and voicemails was getting to her, wearing her down.

Summer poked her in the side. "What's going on? You've been moping in the corner all night, staring at your phone and sucking on your wine."

Natasha shrugged. "It's Brick. He's bombarding me with texts and voicemails. He won't leave me alone."

Summer rubbed her leg. "I'm sorry, sweetie." She rested her head against Natasha's. "What are you going to do?"

"Sick my brother on him?" Natasha giggled.

Summer snorted. "Nate would gladly kick Brick's ass."

"He already did," Natasha muttered.

"What?" Summer squeezed her hand so hard it hurt. "You're kidding?"

"When they went to pick up my stuff, I guess Brick showed up, and they got into it."

"Shut up!" Summer laughed. "That sounds like Nathaniel. He is always coming to your rescue, he and Mason both." She looked at Tasha out of the corner of her eye. "Hey, did you know Mason is single?"

Natasha rolled her eyes. "Of course, I do. What does that have to do with anything?"

"Well, you're single, *he's* single." Summer grinned and wiggled her eyebrows. "Maybe there's something there?"

Natasha couldn't help it; she laughed. "I don't think so. Mason is my friend. That's it." Her phone vibrated, more than once. She pulled it out from under her leg. This time, Brick was calling. She hit the button on the side twice and stuck it back under her leg.

"Summer!" Gavin yelled from the other side of the room.

"Give me a minute!" Summer turned back to Natasha. "Don't let Brick get to you. Ignore him, block his number, anything to get him off your case. You deserve better, sweetie. Maybe that something better is Mason."

"You're being ridiculous." Natasha downed the rest of her glass of wine, got to her feet, and went into the kitchen. She grabbed the bottle from the counter and refilled her glass. She needed to get drunk and dull her senses so she didn't feel anything. Summer followed her, then stood right beside her, staring at her.

"You're both single, and you're both lonely," she said.

"How do you know Mason is lonely?" Natasha asked. "Did he tell you he was lonely?"

"I've known Mason for almost as long as you and yes, I can tell he's lonely." Summer stepped closer to Natasha and lowered her voice. "He's always the third or the fifth wheel, the guy who sits in the corner while the couples have fun. He's always got that mopey smile on his face, the one that screams 'I'm not happy, but I'm gonna fake it until I make it.' You know which one I'm talking about." She reached out and squeezed Natasha's arm. "It's the same smile you've had on your face for the last few weeks."

Natasha grimaced. "Gee, thanks Summer. I'm so glad you've got me all figured out." She crossed her arms over her chest, her wine glass dangling between two fingers. "You know that I just broke up with Brick three weeks ago. I am not ready for another relationship. Not right now. I need time to mourn the one I lost."

"Brick's an asshole," Summer said. "He always has been. I think you figured that out a while ago. You're just afraid to admit it's been over between the two of you for a long time. He's out of your life for good. You need to move on. Why don't you go after the good guy for a change?"

"Mason and I are friends; that's it. If there was ever a time for us, I'm pretty sure it's passed. I am nothing more than his best friend's sister. I'm not sure I've ever been anything more to him than Nate's twin sister. After everything I've gone through, I need time to get my life in order. I'm not in the mood to put myself out there to get rejected."

"You don't know that he'll reject you," Summer argued.

"He will. Trust me. Like I said, we're friends, nothing more. Besides, it would be pretty shitty of me to pursue someone a few weeks after dumping my fiancé. Besides, if Mason had feelings for me, he would have said something."

"Maybe he never got the chance," Summer pointed out. She pushed a hand through her hair and sighed. "There always seems to be someone in the way."

Natasha glanced into the living room, but everyone was engrossed in the game. She lowered her voice anyway. "I don't have feelings for Mason. If I ever did, it was some dumb fleeting moment back in junior high. There is nothing between us."

"Bullshit," Summer muttered. "You went out and found a guy who was the polar opposite of Mason because you had feelings for Mason, and it hurt you when he dated Allison. Finding someone who was so completely different from Mace was your way of saying 'F you' to the guy you really cared about."

Natasha rubbed a hand over the back of her neck and grimaced. This conversation irritated her. "I don't want to have this discussion anymore. Can we change the subject, please? I ... I just can't talk about this anymore."

Summer rubbed Natasha's arm. "I'm sorry, Tash. I'll back off."

"Thank you." Natasha rubbed her forehead; she could feel a headache coming on.

Gavin let out a loud whoop, drawing Summer's attention away from Natasha. She squeezed Natasha's hand, skipped out of the kitchen, and leaped into her boyfriend's arms, giggling as he kissed her neck.

The phone in Natasha's back pocket vibrated again. She yanked it out and looked at it. It was Brick. Again. She had just enough time to shove it in her back pocket before Nate appeared at her side, grabbed her hand, and dragged her into the living room.

"Come on, sis. Remember when we used to watch the Mariners as kids? Come watch with us. It'll be fun, just like old times."

Natasha took a huge swallow of her wine and glanced at Mason out of the corner of her eye. "Sure, fun. Just like when we were kids."

Chapter 6

Mason

Once the Mariners lost, the party was over. Oscar and Vera left to get something to eat, followed by Summer and Gavin. After a call from Brooke, Nate's assistant manager at the bar, Nate left to deal with a bar-related emergency, leaving Mason home alone with Natasha. He had no idea where she was; like everyone else, she had disappeared after the party broke up.

It didn't surprise Mason that everyone had disappeared, leaving him to clean up the mess. He was always on clean-up duty, especially since he was the odd man out. Everyone else had a significant other or was working on getting a significant other, except for him. It left him to clean up messes, pay bar tabs, and act as the designated driver. Mason didn't argue; he was happy to help his friends, though it got a little old after a while.

He tossed the beer bottles in the recycle can, stacked the empty pizza boxes on the table, and turned off all the lights, except the one over the stove and the light in the small foyer. He checked his watch before he flopped down on the couch and closed his eyes. It was after eleven, and he was exhausted. He needed to go

— 43 —

to bed and get some sleep; he had a photography appointment early in the morning.

Mason knew he would need to move soon so Natasha could have her bed, but he was tired. He'd move when she told him to move. Besides, it gave him an excuse to spend time with her when she reappeared.

After a few minutes, he heard the faint sound of her voice, getting louder by the second. He pushed himself to his feet with a grunt and followed the sound to the small patio at the back of the house. The door was open a crack, and he could hear Natasha on her phone.

"I can't, Brick," she said. "I don't think you understand what you did to me. I will never get the image of you with that woman out of my head."

Mason moved the curtain covering the sliding glass door aside with one finger. Natasha sat on one of the rickety patio chairs, her phone pressed to her ear. He let go of the curtain and leaned against the wall, watching Natasha through the gap in the curtain. He hated to eavesdrop, but he couldn't help himself, not when it came to Natasha. Both he and Nate thought she wasn't talking to Brick; apparently, they were wrong.

"Brick, listen—." Natasha's mouth snapped shut, her lips pursed in a tight line. She squeezed her eyes closed, the porch light illuminating the tears sliding down her cheeks. Her entire body shook as she pressed the phone tight against her face. Mason couldn't tell if she was angry or hurt.

Maybe it's both.

"Goddamn it, Brick; shut up and listen to me!" Natasha yelled. Her voice echoed through the dark night and carried into the house. Even if Mason hadn't been eavesdropping, he would have heard that.

"You're always drunk. You're always sorry. And you always,

always say it won't happen again. But then, you do it again. And again. How long have I put up with this shit?"

She didn't speak for a few seconds, but her head shook from side to side as she listened to whatever Brick was saying on the other end of the phone.

"I don't deserve this," Natasha whispered. She cleared her throat and spoke louder. "I've been putting up with your shit for too long. I should have realized sooner that I don't deserve to be treated like I don't matter. I never deserved it. I need to be with someone who loves me, cares about me, and puts me first."

A sob tore out of her, the sound so heart-wrenching Mason felt the ache deep in his bones. The need to protect her, to shelter her from any more pain, overwhelmed him.

I'm going to kill Brick if I see him again.

"Don't do that," Natasha continued. "Do *not* throw that in my face again." Another sob escaped her, and she drew in a shaky breath. "He has nothing to do with this. With us. You will not drag him into this and try to deflect the blame off yourself. This is about *you* and the choices you've made in our relationship. I've been more than understanding, and I've tried to be patient. I've given more time and energy to this relationship than I should have. I can't do it anymore. I'm done. It's over. I'll return the engagement ring—."

Brick must have interrupted her because she abruptly stopped talking and rolled her eyes. She listened for a second before she spoke.

"I don't care what you do with it. Pawn it, sell it, give it to the bitch you were fucking. I do not care. I'm returning the ring, and then I do not want to see you again. Ever."

Natasha stabbed at her phone screen, screaming in frustration when it apparently wouldn't do what she wanted.

Mason shoved the door open, stepped outside, and snatched the phone from her hand. On the other end, he heard Brick curse.

He ignored it, hit the end button, and shoved the phone in his front pocket. He reached for Natasha, and she didn't hesitate to fall into his arms, her face pressed against his chest as heartbreaking sobs ripped through her. They fell to the couch after he led her inside and across the living room.

Natasha wrapped her arms around Mason, pressed her body tight against his, tucked her head under his chin, and let go. Her tears soaked the front of his shirt, but he didn't care. He held her, rubbed circles on her back, and murmured platitudes meant to comfort, anything to soothe her pain.

She clung to him like a drowning woman holding on to her rescuer. More than anything, Mason wanted to be her rescuer; he wanted to save her from everything and everyone who might hurt her. For now, he would be her friend and hold her until she got it all out.

Once the tears tapered off and the sobs became nothing more than the occasional heaving breath, Natasha twisted her head to look up at him. She gave him a weak smile.

"Thank you, Mason. You're a great friend."

"You're welcome," he whispered.

She took his hand and held it tight. "I don't know what I'd do without you. I love you, Mace."

Mason hugged her tight. "Love you, too." He kissed the top of her head and closed his eyes.

If only you knew how much.

—

"Oh my gosh," a loud voice squealed. "Aren't they just the cutest couple ever?"

"Shh," Nate hissed. "You're going to wake them up. And they aren't a couple, though they should be."

Mason opened his eyes, squinting to see in the dimly lit room. Nate stood behind the couch, smirking at him and Natasha tangled in each other's arms. Some girl Mason had never seen before stood beside Nate, also staring at them. Mason gave Nate a dirty look, waved his fingers, and mouthed, "Go away."

He glanced at Natasha. She was asleep, her red hair falling over her face and her fingers twisted in the hem of his shirt. It was the first time she'd looked content since she moved in with them.

"Comfy?" Nate whispered.

Mason glared at him and put a finger to his lips. Nate nodded, put his hands on the girl's waist, and pushed her toward his bedroom door. A high-pitched giggle burst out of her, the sound like nails on a chalkboard to Mason's ears.

"C'mon, Dottie, let's leave the happy couple alone," Nate whispered. He opened his bedroom door and ushered her inside.

Natasha stirred in Mason's arms. She stretched, her hand smacking him in the face. Her head popped up, and she squinted at him.

"Sorry." She looked around the dark living room. "What time is it?"

"It's okay," he replied. He pushed her hair away from her face before looking at his watch. "It's a little after two."

She nodded. "Wow. I was dead to the world; I haven't slept like that in weeks. Maybe I should sleep with you all the time." She giggled, put her hands on Mason's chest, pushed herself upright, and leaned against him. She bent over and kissed the corner of his mouth.

"Thanks again. Talking to Brick was rough. I appreciate you being there for me when I needed a friend." She kissed the corner of his mouth again before she climbed off him and disappeared into the bathroom.

Mason groaned, rolled to his side, and hugged the pillow to his chest. He willed the feelings and the inappropriate situation stirring in his pants to go away.

What the hell am I doing? What is Tasha doing?

This was too reminiscent of high school and their first two years of college. He'd consoled her after every breakup, the friend perpetually there for her. Then he'd wait around for Natasha to realize he was more than her twin brother's best friend, not just that skinny kid she'd known since first grade. He was someone who could love her like she'd never been loved before.

Mason's phone vibrated in his front pocket, making him jump. He sat up and yanked it free, immediately realizing the rose gold phone in his hand was not his, but Natasha's. He forgot he took it from her earlier and shoved it in his pocket. The screen showed a text message from Brick.

Mason shot a quick look at the closed bathroom door. Guilt tore through him, but it quickly dissipated. He was protecting Natasha; that was all. He took a chance and typed in a passcode— her birthday. The phone opened, so he checked the text message.

[Brick: I'm sorry, baby. Let's talk. Call me, please. I will do whatever I have to so you're happy. You name it, and I will do it. I want you back. I love you.]

Anger rushed through him. He wanted nothing more than to tear Brick apart piece by piece, slowly and painfully.

Why won't he let her go? Let her move on?

Another text popped up on the screen.

[Brick: I swear I won't mention Mason or his feelings for you again. I'm begging you to give me a chance.]

Confusion replaced the anger. How the hell did Brick know he had feelings for Natasha? It wasn't the first time he'd mentioned it. The only person Mason had ever told was Nate, and both of them had been holding onto that secret for going on twenty years.

Am I that obvious?

Maybe he wasn't as good at hiding his feelings for Natasha as he thought. It had been obvious to Allison, his former girlfriend, and Brick seemed aware of it as well. So much for keeping secrets.

His finger hovered over the messages from Brick. Natasha didn't need to see them. She needed space and time to heal. She needed to move on.

Natasha needed Mason.

The bathroom door opened, and Natasha stepped out, face freshly scrubbed and glowing. For once, she had a smile on her face, one that actually reached her eyes for the first time since her breakup with Brick. She opened the linen closet and started pulling out the sheets and blankets she used for the couch. She glanced at Mason out of the corner of her eye.

"Are you gonna get off my bed or what?" The blanket fell to the floor, so Natasha bent over to pick it up.

While she was preoccupied, Mason swiped left on the messages, hit delete, then he locked the phone. He held it out to Natasha with a forced smile on his face, pushing his anger, confusion, and guilt deep down inside himself.

"Yeah, sorry. Here's your phone." He pressed a chaste kiss to the top of her head. "I'll see you in the morning." He squeezed her shoulder and headed for his room, his heart thumping hard against his ribcage.

Chapter 7

Natasha

I shouldn't have come alone.

Natasha shifted uneasily and knocked on the apartment door again. She checked her watch; it was twenty minutes after four. Brick agreed to meet her there at four, after she left the theater for the day. Not that it surprised her, but he probably forgot.

Just as she turned to leave, the door flew open. Brick stood in front of her, hair a mess, sleep creases on his face, and wearing nothing but a pair of ratty sweatpants. He scrubbed a hand over his face. The smell of alcohol washed over Natasha every time he moved.

"I was asleep." His tone was accusatory, like they hadn't planned to meet, and she had shown up unannounced.

Natasha sighed and clenched her fists. "You knew I was coming. We talked about it."

Brick didn't bother to respond. He opened the door all the way, turned around, and stumbled back into the apartment. Natasha followed him.

She wrinkled her nose and attempted to breathe through

her mouth. The sink overflowed with filthy dishes, piles of dirty clothes littered the room, empty liquor bottles laid all over the tables, and ashtrays overflowed in several spots around the room.

Brick grabbed a stained t-shirt from a pile on the couch, held it to his nose, and inhaled deeply before he pulled it on. Then he dropped into his beat-up recliner and stared at her. Natasha opened her purse and took out the box containing the small diamond ring he had given her almost a year ago. She shoved aside one of the overflowing ashtrays and set the box on the table beside his chair.

"As promised, here's the ring." She gripped her purse tight with one hand and took a step backward, moving toward the door.

"So, that's it then?" Brick snapped. "You drop it off and leave? The last two years didn't mean anything to you? You can walk away from our relationship so easily?"

Natasha froze; she'd been afraid of this. Nothing with Brick was easy, and ending their relationship was no exception. She shook her head and met his eyes. "If you can fuck someone else without a second thought, then I can walk away without a glance back."

"Quit throwing that in my goddamn face. I made a mistake. If you'd let me explain—."

Natasha laughed, though this certainly wasn't funny. "Let you explain? Explain what, precisely? I caught you having sex with another woman in our bed; that is not a mistake. You didn't *accidentally* end up with your dick inside of her while she screamed her head off." She took a deep breath and fought the tears threatening to fall. "There is nothing for you to explain. I saw it with my own eyes. Shit, Brick, every time I close my eyes, I see it."

Brick sat forward in his chair and clasped his hands between his legs. He stared up at her, attempting to look endearing. She'd seen it before. "I love you, Nat. Please give me a chance to make it up to you. I'll do anything you want. Please, I am begging you to give me another chance."

Natasha shook her head. Dealing with Brick gave her whiplash. One minute he was an asshole, the next he tried to charm her into taking him back. But this time it wouldn't work.

"No, Brick. I can't. I'm done. I can't be with someone who has no respect for me."

Brick shot to his feet and before she could back away from him, he grabbed her upper arm. "Please, baby." His grip on her tightened. "Let's talk it out. I know we can figure it out if we try. After you didn't answer my text the other night—"

"What text?" Natasha interrupted.

"I sent you a message after we got off the phone. You didn't answer me."

Natasha shook her head. "I didn't get it." Knowing Brick, he was drunk and thought he sent it but usually he didn't. It happened when he was drunk.

"Well, I sent it."

"It doesn't matter if you sent it or not because I am done. I told you; I can't do this anymore. You don't love me, and I need somebody in my life who loves me. Somebody who puts me first. Somebody who doesn't treat me like garbage."

"Somebody like Mason?" Brick grumbled.

Natasha rolled her eyes. "I am done having this argument with you. It's not like you listen to me, anyway. I told you; Mason has nothing to do with this. Or with us. Absolutely nothing."

"Now who's lying? Mason has always been smack-ass in the middle of our relationship. I've been competing with him for years." Brick threw himself back in his chair, a loud crack coming from it when he landed in it. "Whatever. I know you claim Mason has nothing to do with this, but I know better. Whether or not you want to admit it, you compare every guy you date to your brother's best friend. I don't compare to Mason."

"You never tried." Natasha snapped her mouth shut so fast she bit the tip of her tongue. She pinched the bridge of her nose and exhaled slowly. "It's over, Brick. I'm sorry. You believe whatever you want to believe. It doesn't matter anymore." She spun on her heel, hurried to the door, and yanked it open.

"You're a little bitch," Brick yelled after her. "I don't know why I ever thought I loved you."

Natasha froze for a split second, then she stepped out of the apartment and pulled the door closed behind her. Her fingers trembled as she took her apartment key off the ring and shoved it under the doormat. Once she was in her car, she took her phone out of her purse and blocked Brick's number. She prayed he would leave her alone.

She gripped the steering wheel hard as she drove to her brother's bar, cursing under her breath. How dare Brick say those things about Mason. Mason had nothing to do with the shit show her relationship with Jason "Brick" Brickman had become. Brick needed somebody to blame, and that somebody was Mason.

Speaking of Mason, she needed to talk to him. If Brick really had texted her, that meant Mason deleted it, which he had no right to do. She was going to make sure he knew it, too.

—

Natasha let the door slam shut behind her, stomped across the bar, and sat on the barstool next to Mason. She dropped her purse on the floor and laid her head on the bar with a sigh.

"How did it go?" Nate asked.

Her head came up, and she glared at her brother. "How do you think it went? It was a shit storm. He begged me to take him back. When I said no, he got pissed off and called me a bitch. He said a bunch of other stuff, too. He was an utter and complete ass."

"You went alone?" Mason interjected. "You should have told me you were going. I would have gone with you."

"You are the last person who should have gone with me," Natasha snapped. She hadn't meant to sound so bitchy, but frayed nerves did that to a person. She cleared her throat. Might as well get this over with. "Mace, did I get a text from Brick the other night? When you had my phone in your pocket?"

As soon as the question was out of her mouth, she knew she was right by Mason's reaction that there had been a text, a text she never saw. Mason's jaw tightened, and his fists clenched on the top of the bar. He opened his mouth, then snapped it shut again.

"Tash, I was just—."

"Trying to protect me?" she asked. "When are you and my brother going to figure out that I can take care of myself? I'm a big girl, an actual grown-up. I don't need your help."

"You were upset. I thought it would be best if you didn't talk to him anymore."

Natasha slapped her hand down on the bar. "That's my choice, Mason. Mine. Not yours. Not Nathaniel's. Mine and mine alone. I appreciate that you thought you were helping, but you can't make those kinds of decisions for me. Trust me to do it on my own."

Mason stared at the top of the bar, his face tight and pinched. "Okay. I'm sorry."

Nate reached across the bar and took her hands. "Nattie, don't be mad."

Natasha shook her head and tried not to smile. Nate using her hated childhood nickname wasn't going to lighten the moment or cheer her up.

"Don't call me that," she muttered. "It's Natasha or Tasha. Pick one." She sat up straight, her shoulders back. "Look, I'm fine. I promise. I just want to forget today happened." She straightened her shoulders and took a deep breath. "Nathaniel Boris Garin, I demand you get me a drink. A glass of wine. Or maybe a bottle."

Nate made a face at her, but he did as she asked. After a few drinks and some food, maybe she would feel better. At least, that's what she hoped.

——

Natasha dropped the pool cue on the table and threw her hands in the air. "Four in a row, baby!" she yelled. "Beat that!"

Mason laughed and shook his head. "You're on a roll. I'm not even going to try." He reached for his scotch and soda, but before he could pick it up, Natasha snatched it, downed the remainder, and slammed it down on the table.

"I need another drink!"

"Um, no, I think I need another drink." Mason snorted. "And maybe you should have some water."

Natasha made a face and shook her head. "I'm fine. In fact, maybe I'll have a margarita instead of another glass of wine. Where's my brother?" She spun around, grabbing the table to steady herself.

Mason took her elbow and helped her sit at one of the nearby tables. "You're done," he said.

"You're such a party pooper," she mumbled. "You know, I don't need you to babysit me. I can take care of myself."

"I know," Mason said. He sat down next to her and took her hand. "I'm just looking out for you. I've been looking out for you for twenty years."

Natasha sighed. "Maybe I'm sick of you looking out for me." She scrubbed a hand over her face. "I'm sorry; that was mean." She pushed herself to her feet, wobbling slightly. "I'm going to the ladies' room, and then I'm going home."

Mason grabbed her hand. "You're not driving, right?"

"Of course not. I'll call an Über or something."

"I can take you," he offered.

"No offense, Mace, but I really don't want you to take me home. I need a break. From you, from Nate, from everybody." She spun around, grabbing the table again to steady herself before stomping down the hall to the bathroom.

Natasha took a minute to splash some water on her face before she returned to the pool tables. Mason had a beer, and sitting on the table in front of her seat was a bottle of water. She dropped onto the stool, took a sip of her water, and cleared her throat.

"You can't drive me home. You've been drinking," she said, pointing at Mason's beer bottle.

"I know," he replied. "I called you an Über; it should be here any minute." He pushed her purse across the table with a smirk. "I'm not going. I'm going to stay here and help Nate. Go home and get some sleep. Take a break from both me and Nate, just like you asked."

Natasha snatched her purse off the table and stood up. "Goddamn you, Mason." She leaned over him, the spicy scent of his cologne assaulting her senses. She forced herself to concentrate, to get the words out. "You're too damn nice. I hate it."

Mason's phone lit up. He glanced at it. "Your Über is here." He scrubbed his mouth with the back of his hand and didn't meet her eyes. "I'll talk to you later. When you're sober."

Natasha rolled her eyes, yelled goodbye to her brother, and pushed through the crowd out the door. Tears stung her eyes, and her heart thumped erratically in her chest. She wanted to scream.

What the hell is wrong with me?

Chapter 8

Mason

Mason couldn't blame Natasha for being pissed. As usual, his attempts to protect her and watch out for her, like he'd always done, had resulted in him overstepping his bounds and making Natasha angry.

It's just like high school all over again.

Sophomore year of high school, Natasha dated a transfer student, a football player named Reggie. To Mason's unending irritation, Natasha was completely enamored with Reggie. Natasha always went for the jocks, something Mason wasn't, at least not in the tenth grade. They dated for weeks and seemed like a good match, at least according to everyone in school. Except for Mason, who knew they weren't. Natasha played a part when she was with Reggie, acting like someone she wasn't.

A month into their relationship, Mason saw Reggie in a downtown restaurant with a pretty brunette woman in a University of Montana sweatshirt. They seemed far too friendly to be friends.

Mason told Nate, and the two of them confronted Reggie. Reggie brushed them off and told them they were idiots for

— 57 —

thinking he would cheat on Natasha. Mason kept pushing until Reggie blew up at him, screaming at him to back off. Mason took a swing, missed by a mile, and fell on his ass. Reggie laughed at him and walked away.

Mason went straight to Natasha, intent on breaking the news. To his chagrin, Natasha was furious with him. Reggie had already told her what happened; the girl Mason saw Reggie with was his cousin, visiting from college for the weekend. He felt like an idiot. Worse, Natasha was so angry, she refused to talk to him or Nate for weeks. She called them both overbearing and ridiculous.

Even after Natasha discovered the woman wasn't Reggie's cousin, but a former girlfriend, her anger with Mason didn't diminish. When Reggie broke up with her and started dating the former girlfriend, Natasha claimed it was because he couldn't deal with her brother and his best friend always being around.

This was too much like that. Mason knew Brick was the wrong guy for Natasha, but he couldn't convince her. Everyone knew Brick was an asshole, so why didn't Natasha know? Mason had her best interests in mind—always. He wanted to protect her, shield her from any harm or pain. He knew she could stand up for herself and take care of herself, but whenever he was around her, an overwhelming need to take care of her came over him.

After Natasha left, he switched to drinking water. It wasn't that he was drunk; he'd only had two drinks while he and Natasha played pool. But he wanted to drive home, so no more alcohol.

Business in the bar seemed to pick up during the last hour, so Mason slipped behind the counter to help Nate, taking over bartending duties while Nate bussed tables. Mason enjoyed helping Nate at the bar; he was good at it, and it was easy. Nate had been short-staffed off and on all summer, so Mason had helped several times when this happened. Hanging out at the bar allowed Natasha to get a much- needed break from both him and Nate at home, while it gave him a chance to think. It was easy to slip back into bartender mode; he could mix drinks in his sleep, and he enjoyed listening to the customers talk about their day.

It was after midnight when he finally left the bar. Nate had become preoccupied with one of his female customers, deciding to show her all his bartending tricks. Not wanting to be in the way, Mason said his goodbyes and took off.

He drove slowly through town toward home, taking his time. He wanted to talk to Natasha, but he wanted her to be sober. He had a feeling that wouldn't be tonight. She was probably out cold on the couch, as she'd had a lot more to drink than she normally did. So, Mason was in no rush to get home.

Their house was one of fifteen built on a small hill overlooking Lakeside. They'd been built to appeal to the married college students who came to Lakeside to attend the college, or those students not interested in dorm life. He and Nate moved into their house when they were in college, and neither of them saw a reason to move out after they graduated. It was a five-minute drive to Nate's bar and close to the photography studio where Mason worked. It was small but comfortable.

At least it had been when it was just the two of them; three people living there was a bit much. Nat liked to joke that they were like the three roommates on an old TV show his parents liked, *Three's Company*.

Mason parked in the empty driveway. He still felt bad about the text he'd deleted and wished he could take it back. He understood why Natasha was angry and hurt. If Mason could fix the situation, he would.

The lights were off in the house, and it was eerily quiet. If Mason hadn't sent her home in the Über, he would have thought Natasha wasn't there. He unlocked the door and stepped inside. Natasha wasn't asleep on the couch like he'd expected. Instead, he could see a light in the small backyard. He made his way through the house to the back door and slipped outside.

Natasha was on the steps at the end of the patio, hugging herself and staring down the hill at Flathead Lake. She had on his gray Lakeside College hoodie. It was huge on her; the sleeves hung down past her hands, and the bottom hem covered her thighs. Mason crossed the patio and sat down beside her.

"You know I've been looking for that sweatshirt," he said.

Natasha laughed quietly. "I took it weeks ago; it's comfy."

"It's okay," he whispered. He bumped his shoulder against hers. "Hi. I thought you'd be passed out on the couch."

"I guess I sobered up." She bumped into him like he'd done to her. "What are you doing home? I thought you were staying at the bar with Nate. You know, to give me space."

Mason chuckled. "The sarcasm is unnecessary. I came home. Nate was ... preoccupied."

"A woman?"

"Yeah? Dottie? That's her name, right? Isn't she the one who was here a few nights ago?"

"I think so. Do you think it's serious?" she asked.

Mason snorted. "I doubt it. When was the last time Nate had a serious relationship?"

Natasha giggled. "Um, never." She shook her head. "I didn't realize my brother was such a ladies' man. It's kind of weird, you know. To me, he's just my annoying twin brother who drives me crazy. I don't see him as somebody women want to date. I guess I don't know him as well as I thought I did."

Mason exhaled loudly. "You haven't been around much the last few years, Tash. People change."

Natasha rolled her eyes. "That's not fair; I was around. You're just upset because I've been living my own life without you and Nate interfering."

Mason scoffed. "That's not true, and you know it. You spent the last two years doing everything in your power to stay away from us."

"Yeah, you're right, I did." Natasha put her head in her hands. "And look where it got me."

Mason slipped his arm around Natasha and hugged her. "I'm sorry. I shouldn't have said anything."

"No, no, you're right. If I hadn't tried so hard to prove to everyone that I wasn't just Nate's twin sister, that there was more to me than that, I might know more about my brother's life. Shit, I might know more about him. I'm not joking when I say I did not know so many women wanted to date him."

"*All* the women want to date your brother." Mason chuckled. "Especially the college girls."

"Ew."

"Sorry. It's true, though. I swear he has a new woman every week. I can't believe Dottie has been around for more than a week. In fact, it's miraculous. And it's not that you don't know him well; it's just that Nate lives his own life on his own terms."

Natasha snorted. "Yes, he does. Especially since Daddy helped him buy the bar. That place *is* his life."

Mason tapped a finger against his chin. "Maybe that's why he doesn't have time for a relationship. Owning the Time Out takes all his free time."

"He uses the bar as an excuse not to get too close to anyone," Natasha said. "As soon as they want more, he moves on. He blames it on the bar. My brother doesn't want to get close to anybody."

Mason shook his head. "Not true. Nate has a lot of friends; he has you, Oscar, Gavin, your parents—"

Natasha patted his leg. "He has you."

"Exactly. Maybe he hasn't found the right woman yet," Mason suggested. "It takes some people a while to find the one person they want to be with for the rest of their life."

Natasha laughed. "And some people are like me. They find someone and discover too late he's an asshole."

Mason cleared his throat. "I'm sorry, Tasha. About everything.

I'm sorry Brick is an asshole, and I'm sorry I didn't let Nate kick his ass." He took her hand and held it tight. "And I'm really sorry for overstepping and deleting that text message. I shouldn't have done that. I wanted to protect you, but I should have known you knew what you were doing, and you can look out for yourself. Without my help. After twenty years, it's kind of force of habit to look out for you."

Natasha stared at the lake, illuminated by the moon, a frown on her face. "I can't say that I'm okay with what you did or that I'm not mad. I'm a big girl, Mace. I got myself into this mess with Brick, and I need to get myself out of it." She closed her eyes and pinched the bridge of her nose. "At least I hope I get myself out of it. I know you and my brother think you're helping, but I have to deal with this on my own. Brick is my problem." She shivered and wrapped her arms around herself.

Mason wrapped his arm around her and hugged her close, sharing his body heat.

"Why are you so nice to me, Mason Adler?" she whispered.

Because I've been in love with you since first grade.

Not that he said that out loud. Instead, Mason shrugged. "I don't know. I guess it's because you're my best friend's sister. And you're my friend. How could I not be nice to you?"

Natasha tensed and abruptly stood up.

"Do you have any hot chocolate in this place?" she asked.

"I don't know," Mason replied.

"Come on, let's go check the kitchen." She tipped her head toward the back door.

Mason nodded and stood up. He thought about taking Natasha's hand, but it wouldn't mean the same thing to her. Instead, he tucked his hands in the pockets of his jeans and followed Natasha inside.

Chapter 9

Natasha

Avery came through the door like a woman on a mission, her blonde curls flying behind her and a huge smile on her face. She kissed Natasha's cheek before she dropped into the seat across from her.

Avery and Natasha had been roommates during college, sharing an apartment off-campus. They hadn't been close at first, but as time went on, they'd become good friends. After Avery got involved with one of her professors—a man only a couple of years older than her—her world turned upside down. Fortunately, everything worked out in the end, but the ordeal had brought the two of them closer than ever.

"You look tired, Nat," she said. Avery was the only person besides Brick who called her Nat instead of Natasha or Tasha.

"Wow, hello to you, too," Natasha said.

Avery flinched and gave her friend a sheepish grin. "Sorry, sweetie. That was a pretty crappy greeting." She reached across the table and took Natasha's hand. "How are you?"

"I'm exhausted," Natasha replied.

Avery sat back, crossed her arms over her chest, and made a face. "I can't imagine why."

"Well, let's see." Natasha held up her hand and ticked off each point as she spoke. "I'm sleeping on a lumpy, uncomfortable couch. I'm living with two bachelors, one of whom is my brother, and the other is a guy I've known almost my entire life. My fiancé—sorry, ex-fiancé—cheated on me and is inexplicably pissed at *me* for breaking off the engagement. Oh, and my brain is a jumbled mess." Natasha took a sip of her coffee and shrugged.

"Understandable, after what Brick did," Avery said.

"It's not just Brick; it's Mason, too."

Avery's eyebrows shot up. "Mason? What the hell did Mason do?"

"Nothing specific. He's just being ... well, he's just being Mason." Natasha pushed a hand through her hair. "He's so goddamn nice. Overbearingly nice. So much so that I hate it."

Avery laughed. "No, you don't. It might irk you a little, but you don't hate it. Mason's your friend, and a good one at that. What you hate is that he knows you better than you know yourself."

"No, he doesn't," Natasha snapped.

"Yes, he does," Avery insisted. "He's been part of your life for what, something like eighteen years?"

"More like twenty," Natasha said. "Since first grade. Mason has always been there, you know? Wherever Nate was, Mason was right there, too. They were inseparable."

"I seem to remember you telling me you and Nate were inseparable when you were kids. If he and Mason were always together, doesn't that mean *all* of you were always together?"

Natasha chewed on the inside of her mouth and glared at her friend. "Yes," she admitted begrudgingly.

Avery smiled and shook her head. "Quit pouting and hear me out. Mason is Nate's best friend, right? But don't you think he's your friend, too? Maybe not your best friend, but he's your friend."

"Yeah," Natasha said. "Mason's my friend. He's probably one of my best friends."

Avery cleared her throat. "Has it ever occurred to you that maybe Mason wants to be more than your friend?"

Natasha raised an eyebrow. "Excuse me?"

"Think about it, Nat," Avery said. "Try to see Mason as someone other than your old friend from school, the guy you grew up with who lived down the street."

Natasha rolled her eyes. "I've been friends with Mason forever. Don't you think I would have noticed if he had some weird crush on me?"

Avery picked up her coffee, sat back, and took a sip. "Honestly, Nat, no, I don't think you would notice."

"What's that supposed to mean?" Natasha snapped.

"Hey, hear me out," Avery said. "I'm not saying anything bad about you. All I'm saying is maybe Mason did a fantastic job of keeping his feelings for you under wraps. From what you've told me, you were popular in high school and Mason was … not. Would you have dated him in high school?"

Natasha shook her head no. Not in a million years. Mason was her friend, but not her type at all. Back in high school, he'd been skinny, uncoordinated, nonathletic, and nerdy.

"And after high school, you kind of went your own way, right?"

"Yeah." The wheels spun in Natasha's head. *God, is Avery right? Is Mason harboring some long-standing crush on me?*

"Look, I'm just speculating here," Avery continued, "but maybe Mason is overbearingly nice for a reason." She shrugged. "It could be worth a conversation."

Natasha choked on her coffee and burst out laughing. "You think I should ask him? Wow, I can just hear that conversation. 'Hey, Mason, have you been harboring a super-secret crush on me for twenty years?' That's ridiculous, Avery."

Avery giggled. "You could start there."

"Okay, let's say he has had a crush on me. Then what?"

"Well, how do you feel about him?" Avery asked.

"What do you mean?"

"You heard me," Avery snapped. "How do you feel about Mason? Can you see yourself with him? Is there something there?"

"I just broke up with my fiancé, Avery!"

Avery rolled her eyes. "I know that, Nat. But that doesn't mean you're made of stone. You can't be completely oblivious to Mason. I mean, that man is desirable. *Hot.*"

Heat rushed to Natasha's cheeks. Avery was right; she wasn't oblivious to Mason or his looks. Or how incredibly sweet he could be. She closed her eyes and took a deep breath before she spoke.

"Okay, look, I have noticed how attractive Mason is. I'd have to be dead not to see it. Especially when he comes home after his run in that damn half-zipped sweatshirt, running shorts, and stupid man bun, all sweaty and breathing heavy. I'd be crazy not to notice. And maybe, just *maybe*, the fact that's he's so sweet bugs me because I actually like it. And I shouldn't."

"What do you mean you shouldn't?"

"Again, I just broke up with my fiancé. It's a little too soon to be swooning over some guy."

Avery reached across the table and squeezed Natasha's hands. "He isn't some guy, Nat; he's Mason."

"Yeah," Natasha whispered. "Or maybe the problem is, *he's Mason*. I've known him my whole life. Where's the excitement, the thrill of something—someone—new? Figuring out what they like, what they want, who you can be to them? Where's all that?"

"Maybe that's the thing. It might be nice to be with someone who knows you. Someone you don't have to pretend with or figure out. Someone who likes you for you, faults and all," Avery said. "Talk to him."

Natasha shook her head. "I don't know if I can. I mean, I'm not even sure Mason has feelings for me or that he wants to date me. This is all speculation. Mason has never said or done anything that makes me think he is interested in anything more than friendship. I thought we had a moment the other night. We were really opening up to each other, and there were these feelings bouncing around in the air between us, but then he told me he's nice to me because I'm Nate's sister."

"What? You're kidding, right?"

"I wish," Natasha said. "But it's true."

"You're not going to say anything to him, are you?" Avery asked.

Natasha shook her head. "I can't, Avery. I'm not in a good place right now. I don't think I could handle it if Mason rejected me. After everything I've been through the last few weeks, something like that would push me right over the edge."

Avery sighed, but she nodded. "I get it; I do. But my advice is still to talk to him. Ask him. Tell him you deserve to know how he feels. Once you know for sure, then you can decide what you're going to do. And I shouldn't have to tell you this, but if you need someone to talk to, I'm a phone call away."

Natasha sipped her lukewarm coffee and smiled at her friend. "Thank you. I can't tell you how much I appreciate that. Now, enough about me and my lousy life. Tell me how Jacob is, and how your new job is going."

A huge smile spread across Avery's face, and she immediately launched into a story about her new job and life with her professor, Jacob. Natasha listened, trying to smile and nod in the appropriate places as she sipped her coffee.

At least somebody is happy.

———

Natasha threw her backpack under the table and pushed the door closed behind her. Nate was on the couch with a pretty blonde snuggled up against him; Natasha wondered if it was Dottie. Mason was at the other end of the couch, as far away from the affectionate couple as possible. Open beer bottles and several bowls of popcorn sat on the table in front of them.

Mason turned to look at her, a desperate grin on his face. "Tasha! You're home."

"I am." She kicked off her shoes and tossed her coat on the chair beside her backpack.

"Come sit by me," Mason begged. He stared at her with puppy-dog eyes, blinking rapidly. She had to stifle a giggle.

"What are we doing tonight?" she asked.

"We're watching a movie!" Nate said. "Come watch it with us."

Natasha froze in place, then she spun around, with her hands on her hips. "As long as it's not a romantic comedy. I am not in the mood for any kind of rom-com. Actually, I'm not in the mood for *any* kind of romance." She glared at her brother and his best friend before she went into the bathroom and slammed the door.

She couldn't tolerate some cheesy romance, not with the mood she was currently in. Her head spun like crazy since she left Avery; she was equal parts angry and sad about the turn her life had taken. A month ago, she wouldn't have pictured herself where she was—no fiancé, sleeping on her brother's couch, and suddenly unsure of what her feelings for Mason were. This was all Avery's fault.

Natasha splashed cold water on her cheeks and changed into the sweatpants and t-shirt she kept stashed in the bathroom cupboard. After taking a few deep breaths and centering herself, she returned to the living room and headed for the kitchen.

The girl who had been sitting on the couch with Nate had her head in the refrigerator. She straightened up when Natasha entered the kitchen.

"Hi there," she said. "I'm Dottie." She stuck out her hand.

Natasha shook the girl's hand. "Hello. I'm Natasha. I'm Nate's sister."

Dottie bit into a piece of celery; her answer came around the crunch of celery in her mouth. "It's so great to meet you. Nate talks about you all the time. I heard about what happened between you and your boyfriend. I'm really sorry."

Natasha smiled stiffly. "Thanks." She cleared her throat. "Do you mind if I get in there?" She pointed at the fridge.

"Oh, yeah, sorry." Dottie stepped out of the way. "I'm done, anyway. I'll see you in the living room."

Natasha grabbed a bottle of water, took a deep breath, and went to join everyone else on the couch.

"So, what are we watching?" she asked.

"A horror movie," Nate said.

"I hate horror movies." She sat down next to Mason, her leg pressed against his, as she scooped a handful of popcorn from the bowl on his lap and shoved it in her mouth. Cued up and ready to play on the TV was the latest popular horror movie.

Nate and Mason both laughed. "You do not," Nate said. "You love them."

"Can't we watch another baseball game or something? That was fun when we did that the other night."

"There isn't a game on tonight, unless we want to watch the Yankees," Nate said.

"Yuck," Mason interjected.

Natasha noticed Mason avoided eye contact with her. Things had been awkward between them since the night they'd sat on the back porch and talked. Natasha did not know how or why things had gotten so weird, and she hated it. She wanted to fix it, but she didn't know how.

"There you go. No baseball games, little sister says no romance movies, so horror movie it is!" Nate grinned and hit play.

Natasha grabbed the blanket off the back of the couch and pulled it over her lap. She prayed the movie wouldn't be too scary. At first, it wasn't so bad; the movie depended on the jump scare tactic. She got through the first couple of scary parts without losing it, but when the set of hands came out of nowhere and clapped next to the mother's head, she lost it. A loud scream escaped her, and she hid her face against Mason's shoulder.

He tried to scoot away from her, but there was nowhere for him to go. Natasha wrapped her arms around him and inched closer to him.

"Get back here," she whispered. "You need to protect me."

Mason laughed, slid his arm around her waist, and put his hand on her hip. Natasha snuggled closer, the blanket clutched in her hands, pulled up next to her face. If anybody in the world could protect her, it was Mason.

Chapter 10

Natasha

Natasha laid awake after everyone else had gone to bed. Every few minutes, a ridiculous giggle would erupt from Nate's room. The thought of what might be going on behind Nate's bedroom door made her gag.

She rolled to her side, punched one of her two pillows a few times, and laid back down with the other pillow over her head. She stared at Mason's closed door and the dim light emanating from the crack at the bottom. He was still awake.

When had her world turned upside down? How did a guy she considered a friend suddenly become something more in her eyes? Was this a rebound thing, her heart screaming at her to find someone new to heal the deep fissure in her chest? Or were these new, bizarre feelings a product of Avery's suggestions? Who knew?

Natasha could make up all kinds of excuses for why she shouldn't get involved with Mason, why a relationship with him was a bad idea. Not that any of those reasons occurred to her as she laid on the couch, staring at his door.

Maybe it wasn't a bad idea. Mason was sweet, protective, and, of course, gorgeous. She could definitely do worse.

Another giggle, this one louder than the others, came from her brother's room. She pressed the pillow tight against her head, squeezed her eyes closed, and tried not to listen.

When Mason's bedroom door opened, Natasha's eyes popped open. She watched him tiptoe across the room, headed for the kitchen. He wore nothing but a pair of gray sweatpants, hung low on his hips; his feet were bare, as was his chest. Natasha dragged in a deep breath and let it out slowly, as she watched his delectable ass cross the room.

Delectable ass? What the hell?

She tossed the pillow to the end of the couch, threw off her blanket, and followed Mason to the kitchen. He had his head in the refrigerator and mumbled to himself.

"Hey, Mace," she whispered.

Mason jumped, his head connecting with the refrigerator, a quiet curse leaving him. He stood upright and rubbed his head.

"I thought you were asleep," he muttered.

As if on cue, another giggle came from Nate's room. Natasha pointed at her brother's door. "Who can sleep with that going on?"

Mason chuckled. "I can't hear it in my room."

"Lucky," Natasha mumbled. "I've been listening to it for an hour. I can't sleep."

Mason shifted from foot to foot and cleared his throat. "If you want, you could crash in my room; you can't hear anything in there. I'll throw my sleeping bag on the floor, and you can have the bed."

"I don't want to put you out—"

"You're not."

Natasha made a face, prompting Mason to shake his head and laugh.

"I swear. It's fine." He grabbed a bottle of water from the fridge and pushed the door shut with his knee. "Come on."

Natasha considered saying no, but the promise of a good—or at least decent—night's sleep beckoned. She followed Mason to his room. He threw his sleeping bag and pillow on the floor and pointed at the bed for her.

"I just changed the sheets yesterday, and there's an extra pillow you can use."

"Thanks." She shut the door, dropped to the bed, and pulled the blankets up to her chin. The scent of Mason surrounded her—leather and amber. He'd been wearing the same cologne since high school; any time she smelled it, she thought of him.

Natasha stared at the ceiling and tried to work up the nerve to talk to Mason about what she was feeling and, more importantly, how he felt about her. She wasn't sure she could sleep until they talked.

Talk to him.

She hated that tiny voice in her head, but it was right. So was Avery. If she was truly developing feelings for Mason, and maybe vice versa, they needed to get it out in the open and be honest with each other.

The truth will set us free.

She peered over the side of the bed. Mason was on his back, his long black hair spread out across the pillow, one hand resting on his stomach. Light snores were coming from his open mouth.

"Dammit," she muttered. The truth would have to wait for another day.

Natasha straightened out the blankets, adjusted the pillow under her head, and closed her eyes. As she drifted off to sleep, she promised herself she would talk to Mason sooner rather than later.

She slept better than she expected, straight through until the sun came up. Mason was gone when she woke up, but her brother was on the couch, arms crossed and staring at her as she emerged from Mason's room.

"Is there something you want to tell me?" Nate demanded.

Natasha rolled her eyes. "No. Mason slept on the floor, and I slept in his bed. He was kind enough to let me crash in his room because listening to my brother's latest conquest giggling all night made me nauseous."

Nathaniel had the good sense to look embarrassed. "Oh, god, I'm sorry," he whispered. He jumped off the couch and hugged his sister. "I swear I didn't mean to traumatize you."

"You're forgiven," she said. "Just try to rein it—and her—in, please."

"I will, I promise." Nate kissed her cheek. "Now that I have my explanation why you're in Mason's room, I can go to work. See you tonight."

———

The next few weeks were a blur. Natasha's vow to talk to Mason about his feelings—and hers—was far more elusive than she imagined. She couldn't seem to get a minute alone with him, despite every effort to get him by himself.

If he wasn't working, she was. His calendar was full of photo shoot after photo shoot, and when he wasn't doing that, his part-time job as an EMT at the small Lakeside hospital kept him busy, especially during summer. He'd gone from working two days a week to three days a week; it seemed more like a full-time job than something he did as a side job. Mason also stepped in to help Nate whenever he was short-staffed at the bar, which seemed to be several times a week.

As for Natasha, rehearsals for the theater's summer show were in full swing. Not only was she the theater manager, co-director, stage manager, and head of marketing, but she also had a part in the show. She did the menial work during the day and ran rehearsals at night. Most nights, she didn't get home until close to midnight and by then, Mason was sound asleep. If he wasn't home, he was at the bar, and she was asleep by the time he got home. Their lives were a revolving door of schedules.

Two weeks before the show's opening night, Natasha had a rare night off. Instead of going home like she should have, she stopped at the Time Out Bar and Grill to see her brother. As crazy as he made her, he was still her brother—her twin brother—and whether she wanted to admit it or not, she needed him. Maybe he could help her figure out a way to talk to Mason.

Of course, that meant telling Nate she might be developing feelings for his best friend. While she suspected her brother probably already knew—she could hide nothing from him—coming right out and telling him was a little scary. He could react one of two ways: utter, total, and complete anger, or he would love the idea. Natasha hoped for the latter.

She parked her car on the street and took a deep breath. The bar didn't look too crowded; the lot was close to empty, with only seven or eight cars parked with hers. She grabbed her purse and headed inside.

Natasha was right; the bar wasn't crowded. Most of the cars must have belonged to the staff. Nate was behind the bar, where he always was, chatting with a woman, of course. He waved when he saw his sister and gestured for her to join him.

"Hey Tash, you want a drink?" he asked when she sat down.

"Just water. With lemon."

Nate rolled his eyes, but he did as she asked.

"Am I interrupting anything?" Natasha whispered, tipping her head in the direction of the woman Nate had been talking to.

Nate laughed and shook his head. "No. Cecily's a friend. Things have been rough for her lately, and she needed someone to talk to."

"She's not one of your many conquests?" Natasha winked.

"Uh, no." Nate cleared his throat. "What are you doing here in the middle of the afternoon? No rehearsal?"

"No." She traced the rim of her water glass and contemplated how she would tell her brother about Mason.

Somehow Nate knew; he always knew. He leaned on the bar, took his sister's hand, and squeezed it. "Talk to me, Natasha Anne. What's going on? Is it Brick?"

Natasha bit her lip and shook her head. "Is there someplace quiet we can talk? Your office, maybe?"

"Come on." Nate tossed his rag in the sink, stopped to whisper something in one of the server's ears, and then slipped out from behind the bar.

Natasha followed him down the hall and up a short staircase to a small office tucked under the eaves at the front of the bar. He sat behind his desk, and she took a seat on the old recliner across from him.

"Okay, sis. What did you want to talk about?"

"Mason."

Nate grimaced. "I know it's hard living with two bachelors, but we're doing our best, I swear. Mason is having a hard time adjusting to you being around all the time, that's all."

"That's not what I'm talking about. Yes, living with a couple of bachelors sucks, but I'm getting used to it." Natasha took a deep breath. "Mason has been our friend for a long time."

Nate crossed his arms over his chest and raised an eyebrow. "Stop beating around the bush, Tash. What the hell is going on? Did Mason do something I should be concerned about?"

Natasha shook her head. "No. It's not anything like that."

"Then spit it out."

"I think ... I think I like Mason," Natasha blurted.

Nate was silent for far too long. When he finally spoke, there was a gleeful quality to his voice that threw Natasha out of whack.

"You like Mason? Like, you like, *like* Mason? As in, like him more than a friend, maybe like him like a boyfriend?"

"Could you say 'like' a few more times, please?" Natasha muttered. Nate just smirked at her. "Yes, I have feelings for Mason. At least, I think I do."

"You either do or you don't, Tash. I don't think there is really an in-between."

Natasha squeezed her eyes shut. "Except right now, I'm not sure how I feel. Mason is my friend, and he's been looking out for me. I'm noticing him in ways I never did before. But—"

Nate sighed. "There is always a 'but.'"

"But I just broke up with Brick. Those wounds are still fresh. So, yes, I might have feelings for Mason, but I'm not sure what to do about them."

Nate leaned forward and stared into his sister's eyes. He looked so serious she wanted to laugh. "Have you told Mason?" he asked.

"You sound like Avery," she mumbled.

"Have you?" Nate pressed.

"No, I haven't told him. I'm not even sure what to say." Natasha threw her head back against the recliner and groaned. "What am I gonna do?"

"You know what Mom says," Nate said. "Sometimes you have to do something you hate to know what you really want."

"Don't quote our mother at me," Natasha grumbled. "If I want a lecture, I'll call home."

Nate laughed. "Sorry. But sometimes our mother knows what she's talking about."

Natasha stuck her tongue out at him. "You didn't answer my question. What am I gonna do?"

Nate sighed, sat back, and crossed his arms over his chest. "Tell him, Tasha. He deserves to know."

Natasha sat back and crossed her arms over her chest,

mimicking her brother. "Why doesn't this bother you? I thought you'd lose your mind when I told you. You're surprisingly calm."

"I guess because it doesn't surprise me." Nate scrubbed a hand over his face. "And maybe I like the idea of you and Mason together. He's a great guy, and you're my sister." He leaned forward, his elbows on his desk, gazing intently at her. "He'd be good for you, Tash. You'd be good together."

"You think so?" she asked.

Nate nodded.

"Okay, great. How do you feel about talking to him about me?" She gave him her best sisterly smile. "Pretty please?"

"What is this, high school?" Nate chuckled. "I don't think I should talk to him. He needs to hear it from you. Not me."

Natasha slumped in her seat and put her hand over her eyes. "I know, I know. I just need to find the right time."

"There's never a right time," Nate said. "Get him alone and tell him."

"Or you will?" Natasha asked hopefully.

"Um, no." Nate shook his head and pointed at her. "That's up to you, my darling sister."

———

Easier said than done.

Getting Mason alone didn't get any easier after telling Nate about her feelings for his best friend. She didn't know why she thought it would.

"Earth to Tasha?"

"Hm?"

Nate shook his head and sighed. "I asked if you talked to Mason yet?"

"I'm trying, okay? Besides, it's only been a few days since I told you. I just can't seem to get him alone. Every time I try, something happens—people showing up to watch baseball on the big screen,

Mason getting called into work, a costume emergency at the theater. It's a never-ending stream of craziness around this place."

"He's going to be home tonight, and I'm going to be at work. I'm closing, so I won't be home until two or three in the morning. There's no baseball game, no distractions. Unless he gets called into the hospital, he'll be here. Talk to him tonight."

Natasha exhaled. "I can do that. At least I think I can."

Nate laughed. "Don't think about it; do it." He kissed the top of his sister's head. "I gotta go. Let me know how it goes." He grabbed his car keys and yelled goodbye over his shoulder.

Natasha got ready for rehearsal, determined to get home on time for once. She was out the door ten minutes early and had everything set up and ready to go by the time the other actors arrived. She ran rehearsal like a drill sergeant, keeping everyone moving, stopping only when necessary.

It felt good and, to her surprise, no one complained. In fact, when she called it a night, several of the other actors thanked her for a well-run rehearsal and getting them home early. Natasha drove home with a smile on her face about the compliments.

When she pulled into the driveway, Mason's truck was there. Natasha took a deep breath, grabbed her backpack, and climbed out of her car.

I can do this.

Chapter 11

Mason

Since the night of the horror movie, the inadvertent cuddling on the couch, and Natasha sleeping in his bed, she had acted weird every time the two of them were together. Mason kept hoping they could get a minute alone to talk, but it seemed like they were never by themselves.

A lot of that was his fault. He was swamped: weddings, family photos, and his part-time job as an EMT at the hospital kept him insanely busy. He'd even helped Nate at the bar a few times when he was short-staffed.

Maybe you're avoiding her.

"I'm not," he said out loud. He had officially lost it, talking out loud to himself. He'd gone off the deep end.

The sun hovered over Flathead Lake as Mason turned the corner and swung into the driveway. No one else was home; Nate was at the bar, and Natasha probably had theater rehearsal. He wasn't sure if he should be relieved or not. He knew he needed to talk to Natasha, but the thought terrified him.

It wasn't Natasha he was afraid of; it was the rejection. He'd known this woman almost her whole life, and he had been in love with her for years. A rejection from the perfect woman, the only woman who had ever mattered to him, would be devastating.

No other woman compared to Natasha. None of the girls he dated in high school held a candle to her. Not even Allison—a woman he thought he loved—could withstand a comparison to Natasha. Allison always fell short because Natasha was the standard he held all women to because in his eyes, she was perfection.

Once Allison discovered this painful truth, it was over between them. It was an ugly breakup: screaming, yelling, throwing things, and accusations he couldn't deny. He did his best to smooth things over, but there was no appeasing Allison. Mason broke her heart, and, in return, she verbally eviscerated him. He deserved every word and took it all to heart. He was a coward and an asshole who led on a beautiful woman, hurt her, and destroyed her. The guilt still lingered two years later.

Exhausted after working sixteen hours straight, Mason let these thoughts wash over him as he moved through the house on autopilot. They weighed him down, souring his mood. He showered and ate something, then threw himself on the couch, propped his feet on the coffee table, and let those depressing thoughts follow him into sleep.

Nightmarish, vague dreams about Allison and Natasha haunted him. The front door opening and the kitchen light coming on dragged him out of a restless sleep. He had no idea what time it was. He grunted as he pushed himself upright.

"Hello?" Natasha called.

"Hey," he responded groggily. "I'm in here, on the couch."

Natasha stepped into the living room and hit the lights. "What are you doing sitting in the dark?" she asked.

Mason grunted and covered his eyes with his forearm. "I fell asleep." He checked his watch, surprised to see it was only a little after ten. "You're home early."

"Rehearsal wrapped early." She took a deep breath and gazed at him. "Can we talk for a minute?"

Mason straightened up. "Uh oh, this sounds serious."

Natasha giggled, but it was shaky and off-kilter, not her usual carefree and calm giggle. Mason's stomach did a slow roll as Natasha sat down next to him.

"This is so stupid," she muttered. "I don't know where to start. Shit, I don't know what to say."

"You know you can tell me anything," Mason said. "What is it?"

Natasha visibly swallowed. "Have you ever had a friend that was more than a friend? Or maybe you wanted them to be more than a friend?"

Mason chuckled. "Oh, yeah." *I'm looking at her.*

"Did you tell them?"

He shook his head. "No, I didn't." He leaned forward. "What are you trying to tell me, Tash?"

Mason's heart pounded so hard, it hurt. What the hell was this? What was happening?

Natasha gnawed on her lower lip and looked up at him through her eyelashes. She took a deep breath and opened her mouth, but before she could speak, someone pounded loudly on the front door.

"Dammit," Natasha muttered. She shoved herself to her feet and headed for the door, but Mason caught her hand in his, stopping her.

"I got it," he said. Mason walked to the door, with Natasha right behind him. He yanked it open and came face to face with Brick, reeking of cigarettes and alcohol. He swayed from side to side and blinked rapidly as he looked up at Mason.

"What the hell are you doing here?" Brick slurred.

"I live here, asshole," Mason snapped. "What are *you* doing here?"

"I came to talk to my fiancée," Brick replied. "Get the hell out of my way."

"I'm not your fiancée anymore, Brick," Natasha piped up. She stepped out from behind Mason. "Go away."

Brick put one foot over the threshold and reached for Natasha, but Mason pushed her out of the way, stepped in front of Brick, and stuck out his arm, blocking the doorway. "No one invited you in. I suggest you leave."

Brick grunted, put his hands on Mason's chest, and shoved as hard as he could. While Brick was stocky and, at one time, strong, he was no match for Mason, who stood 6' 6" and weighed 250. He towered over Brick by at least five inches and didn't even stumble when Brick pushed him.

Mason spread his legs and set his feet. "I said it was time for you to leave," he repeated.

Brick narrowed his eyes. "You know what, Adler? Fuck off." He stepped to the left to get around Mason but when Mason reached for him, Brick ducked and squeezed under Mason's outstretched arm, elbowing him in the gut as he passed him. Brick lunged at Natasha, who tried to back away, but Brick grabbed her arm, and yanked her close. "We need to talk. Now."

Natasha tried to yank her arm free, but Brick tightened his grip, his fingers sinking into the flesh of her upper arm. A startled gasp left her.

Mason had seen enough. He grabbed Brick by the back of the neck and squeezed. "Let her go."

Brick released Natasha with a growl and swung at Mason, his fist grazing Mason's chin. It didn't hurt, but it startled Mason, causing him to lose his grip and stumble back two steps. Brick yelled and leaped at Mason, throwing himself against the larger man's chest, his body weight sending them both to the floor.

They grappled with each other while Natasha stood over them, yelling at them to stop. Mason finally shoved Brick off and onto the floor, but not before Brick landed several blows to Mason's face and chest. Once Mason could get his feet under him, he grabbed Brick by the back of the shirt and half-carried, half-pulled Brick out the front door. He threw him onto the gravel driveway.

"Get out of here. Now," Mason ordered. "If you ever touch Tasha again, I'll put you in the hospital. Stay away from her; I mean it."

Brick touched a finger to his bleeding lip and winced. He shook his head and staggered to his feet. "This isn't over."

"Oh, but it is," Mason said. "I promise you, if you come back, you will regret it." He turned his back on Brick and went back into the house. He slammed the door behind him and stood at the window until Brick got in his car and drove off.

"Tasha, call Sheriff Willis and tell her Brick is driving drunk through downtown. I don't want anyone to get hurt."

———

An hour later, after a visit from Sheriff Willis, a frantic phone call from Nate, and one melted ice pack on his rapidly swelling eye, Mason and Natasha were finally alone. Again.

Mason laid on the couch, a bag of frozen peas on his eye, his head propped on a pillow. Natasha sat down beside him and brushed his hair out of his face.

"Thank you," she said.

"You're welcome," he whispered.

"I was, uh, gonna tell you something before we were rudely interrupted," she said.

"Oh, yeah, I almost forgot." He took the frozen peas off his eye and dropped it on the coffee table. "So, what exactly were you going to tell me?"

Natasha took his hand and stared at his fingers as she spoke. "You've always been there for me, Mason. You were the best friend

I didn't know I had. Today proved that even more. Standing up to Brick like that—."

"Brick doesn't get to hurt you and get away with it." Mason looked down and whispered, "Nobody gets to hurt you and get away with it."

Natasha sighed and smiled. "Why are you such a good guy?"

Mason shrugged one shoulder and chuckled. "Thank my mom for raising me right."

Natasha laughed. "Trust me, I will next time I talk to her."

"You're stalling, Tash."

Natasha rolled her eyes. "Okay, fine." She exhaled and blurted, "Lately, I've been thinking that I might be ... well, I guess what I'm trying to say is that I've been feeling like you and I could be more than friends."

"What?"

She pulled her hand out of his and punched him on the shoulder. "You heard me."

Mason put his hand on Natasha's hip and pulled her close. "Are you telling me you have feelings for me? Real, honest-to-God feelings?"

Natasha nodded. "Y-yes," she stammered. "At least, I think I do. I can't fight them anymore." She made a face, and all Mason wanted to do was kiss her.

He swallowed, licked his dry lips, and tried to control his shaking hands. Natasha could probably feel the tremor where his hand rested on her hip. He pushed himself upright, stared into Natasha's stormy gray eyes, and squeezed her ice-cold hand.

"What do you think we should do about it?" he whispered.

"I guess that's what we have to figure out, huh?" she murmured.

The front door flew open and slammed into the wall. "I'm going to kick Brick's ass!" Nate shouted as he walked through the house entrance.

Natasha shook her head, mouthed "sorry" and pushed herself

to her feet. She turned to her brother. "No need, big brother. Mason already did."

Mason also stood up behind her, put his hand in the middle of Natasha's back, and whispered in her ear. "This isn't over, Tash. We have a lot to talk about."

"I know. And we will talk, I promise." She turned around, stood on her tiptoes, and kissed his cheek before hurrying across the room to meet her enraged brother.

Chapter 12

Natasha

A week after finally telling Mason how she felt about him, Natasha gave everyone at the theater a night off. They had been working hard and, with only a week and a half until the show, they deserved a day off. Of course, she still went to work; her job never seemed to end. She worked on the pile of paperwork she'd been neglecting, reached out to the local paper about advertising the show, and did some work on the theater's website. Giving everyone the night off was a great idea; not only was she grateful for the chance to get her neglected work done, but the prospect of a night off had her smiling all afternoon. Maybe she and Mason could finally talk about their feelings for each other.

On the way home, she stopped at the store and bought chicken, potatoes, and a salad. Before she moved in with Nate and Mason, it was unlikely a salad had ever crossed the threshold of the boys' small house. The thing she hated most about living with two bachelors—aside from sleeping on the couch and sharing a bathroom with two boys—was the lack of decent food in the house; it drove her crazy. A person could only eat so much cereal, frozen burritos, and Pop-tarts. If they weren't eating some kind of frozen food, they ate at the bar or got takeout—pizza, Chinese, or sandwiches from the deli. Natasha wanted actual food, and the only way to get it would be to cook it herself.

Once she was home, she dropped everything in the kitchen, changed into shorts and a t-shirt, put her headphones in, and went to work. Natasha danced around the kitchen barefoot while she cooked, lost in her own world.

Since she was intent on finishing the food preparation before Mason and Nate got home, she let herself get completely absorbed in what she was doing and, thanks to the music blasting in her ears, didn't hear the front door open and close. When a hand landed on her shoulder, she screamed and dropped the bottle of salad dressing in her hand. The plastic bottle bounced across the kitchen floor and slid to a stop beside the stove. She ripped the earbuds from her ears and spun around to yell at whoever scared the shit out of her.

Mason stood behind her, his hand pressed to his mouth in a poor attempt to stifle his laughter. His entire body shook, his face turned red, and tears formed at the corner of his eyes. He gulped and let out a laugh so loud, Natasha's eardrums vibrated.

She raised her hand to punch him, but Mason grabbed her wrist and held it comfortably tight. He took a step closer to her and trapped her between his rock-hard body and the kitchen counter. The jerk wasn't wearing a shirt, just that damn hoodie, unzipped to show off his chest, glistening with sweat. Her fingers itched to touch him, to flatten her hands on his chest and kiss him. Her entire body trembled at the thought.

Mason towered over her, staring down at her with his silvery-gray eyes. His tongue swiped across his lower lip. He released her wrist and put his hand on her waist, his fingers digging into her hip as he leaned over her.

"I think you owe me a kiss."

Time slowed; every second seemed to stretch into a minute as Mason moved closer. Anticipation heightened every sense, and longing twisted in her gut.

"I smell food!" her brother yelled, as he burst through the front door. "What's for dinner?"

Mason released her, shrugged, turned around, and made his way through the house, mumbling, "Hey, Nate," in his best friend's direction before he ducked into his bedroom.

"Shit," Natasha grumbled. She shot a death glare at Nate's back before she went back to making the salad. Her brother had impeccable timing. For the second time in a week, he had interrupted an important moment between her and Mason. She might kill him if he did it again.

—

After dinner, Nate left to pick up Dottie. Natasha sat on the couch and propped her feet on Mason's lap, who had been sitting there for a while. "What are you watching?"

"A World War II documentary." He glanced at her feet but didn't ask her to move them.

"That sounds boring," she mumbled.

"It's not boring," he scoffed. "The history of our world is interesting."

"I don't know why you didn't become a history teacher. You have an unusual obsession with world history." Natasha leaned over, plucked the water bottle from his hand, and took a drink.

"I didn't want to be a teacher," Mason replied.

"I know. Photography is your first love. But how fulfilling is it running someone else's photography studio in tiny little Lakeside, Montana? Senior pictures, the occasional wedding, family photos? Don't you want more?"

Mason made a face and shrugged. "I like my job. I like the studio. It frees me up to take photos of the things I really love:

Flathead Lake, Glacier Park, the mountains, all of it. I love it here. The unique beauty of this place is like no other. I might like history, but I think teaching would bore me to tears. I enjoy having the freedom to pursue my art."

Natasha nodded. "I get that; it's why I love working for the theater. I may have to do the mundane, managerial stuff, but I get to do what I love. I get to be an actor." She took another drink of Mason's water and handed it back to him. "Hey, how come you've never taken any pictures of me?"

The look of surprise on Mason's face made her laugh. He opened his mouth and quickly closed it again. He contemplated his answer before he said, "I mean, I have taken pictures of you. I probably have hundreds of pictures of you."

"Yeah, but I don't think we've ever done an actual photoshoot, have we?"

Mason frowned and stared off into space, his usual look when he was thinking way too hard. "I, uh, I don't know. Do you want me to photograph you?"

Natasha shrugged. "I need new headshots, and I'd love to have you take them. I mean, I've been meaning to ask you, but I kept putting it off."

Mason tipped his head to one side and raised his eyebrow. She hated it when he did that; it gave him this sexy, smirky look that made goosebumps rise on her skin.

She bit her lip and stared back at him. "What?"

"Why'd you put it off?"

She resisted the urge to squirm under Mason's scrutiny. She gave him what she hoped was a nonchalant smile. "I didn't want to bug you. You have better things to do."

Mason looked skeptical, but he seemed to accept her answer. "I would love to photograph you. Figure out a day that works for you, and I'll take them."

"Okay, I will." Natasha cleared her throat and reached for the remote sitting on the couch between them. "Let's watch something else."

Mason snatched up the remote before she could grab it and held it over his head, out of her reach. Natasha lunged for it, threw herself across Mason's lap, and stretched as she tried to get it out of his hand. He switched it to the other hand and twisted away from Natasha to keep it away from her. He slid to the edge of the couch as she struggled to climb over him. They both fell to the floor, with Mason landing on top of her.

"Oof, get off of me, you giant."

Mason shrugged. "Hey, you started it."

She giggled and plucked the remote out of his hand. "Yes, I did. And thank you."

"Oh, okay, I see how it's going to be." He chuckled and shook his head. "All right, you asked for it."

He slid his hands up her sides, just below her ribs, and tickled her. He tickled her until she squealed and squirmed, her arms flailing and her legs kicking. He didn't stop until tears fell from her eyes, and she begged him to stop.

"Give me the remote," he whispered.

Mason was so close that the tip of his nose touched hers and their breath mingled. Natasha licked her lips, put her hands around the back of his neck, lifted her head, and brushed her lips against his.

Mason's eyes widened. He stiffened and attempted to shift his body away from hers. When Natasha urged him closer, tightening her grip on the back of his neck and tugging him down, Mason slipped his arm under her and relaxed against her, his hips nestled between her legs. He kissed her, tentatively at first, in a slow and easy manner. Natasha sighed and pressed her hand against the small of his back. As the kiss deepened, the world around her faded into the background until the only thing was Mason and the kiss; it was the single most perfect kiss she ever experienced.

When it was over—far sooner than Natasha wanted—Mason rested his forehead against hers and exhaled.

"Was that okay?" he whispered. His lips slid up her jaw to her ear.

"It was perfect." She tangled her fingers in his hair, turned her head toward him, and caught his lips in another kiss. "Absolutely perfect." She wanted to stay in his arms all night, as the thought of all the things they could do made her blood boil.

If Natasha hadn't heard the familiar sound of her brother's laughter outside the front door, she would have stayed wrapped in Mason's arms all night. Instead, the sound of raucous laughter and high-pitched giggles echoed through the night air.

Mason groaned. "Shit, Nate's back with Dottie." He released Natasha and climbed to his feet. Then he leaned over, effortlessly picked her up, and set her on the couch. Before they separated, he gave her a quick peck on the lips.

Nate came through the door with Dottie on his arm. When he saw his best friend and his sister in the living room, a cheesy grin contorted his handsome face into a clown-like caricature.

"Hey, guys," Nate said. "Whatcha doing?"

"Just watching some TV while we waited for you to get back," Mason said. "I was ... uh, gonna grab us some more beers. Do you guys want one?"

"Yeah, that sounds great!" Dottie piped up. "Doesn't it, Nate?" She gave Natasha's twin a flirty smile.

Nate shrugged. "I guess so." He kissed Dottie's cheek. "Wait here, babe. I'll help Mace with the beers and grab us some snacks."

"Get me a glass of wine!" Natasha yelled after her brother.

Dottie dropped to the couch beside Natasha. "Hey Tash, how's it going?"

Natasha forced herself to grin at the overly exuberant girl and her casual use of Natasha's nickname. "I'm doing well," she replied. "How have you been?"

"Great." Dottie smiled. "Your brother is amazing. He's so funny and cute. I'm so glad we met."

"How did you two meet? I don't think Nate ever told me," Natasha asked. She was almost afraid to hear the answer. She'd discovered most of the women Nate dated had been picked up at his bar, and, from what Mason told her, he used every ridiculous, cheesy, stupid line imaginable to do it.

"At the bar." Dottie shrugged.

Natasha forced herself not to spout something rude and sarcastic; instead, she plastered a smile on her face and nodded.

"My sorority sisters dragged me in there when I turned twenty-one for a drink," Dottie continued. "Nate gave me a free margarita; it was love at first drink." Dottie burst out laughing. "He is awful cute, though, isn't he? But why am I asking you? You're his sister!"

Natasha laughed politely and glanced toward the kitchen. Not only had they interrupted her and Mason's first kiss, now she had to listen to the sorority girl fawn over her brother.

"Can I ask you a question?" Dottie continued. "Does Nate ever talk about me?"

Oh, good lord, what is this? High school?

Natasha kept her thoughts to herself. She shook her head and willed her eyes not to roll back in her head. "No, not really."

"Oh." The dejected look on Dottie's face almost made Natasha feel sorry for her. Almost.

Natasha leaned over the end of the couch. "Hey! Hurry with those drinks, would you?" she yelled. "And make sure they're cold."

Nate peered around the corner. "Maybe you should relax, Tash."

Natasha stuck her tongue out at him as he returned to the living room with two bags of chips and a container of dip. He set everything on the table, perched on the arm of the couch next to his sister, and ruffled her hair.

"What's up, Nattie?"

Natasha rolled her eyes at Nate's use of her childhood nickname, crossed her arms over her chest, and rested her head against the back of the couch. "Not much. How are things with you, big brother?"

"Great." Nate poked her in the side. "Why do you ask?"

She looked pointedly at Dottie, who was digging through her purse and not paying attention to Natasha and Nate at all.

"What?" Nate mouthed.

Natasha shook her head. "Later," she mumbled.

Nate shrugged and sat down next to Dottie. He put his arm around her and kissed her neck, making her giggle.

Natasha sighed. It shouldn't bother her that Nate was having fun with the younger woman, at least until he found out Dottie was falling for him.

Mason stuck a glass of wine in Natasha's face and sat down beside her. He bumped his knee against hers and smiled.

Her stomach flip-flopped, and heat rushed through her. She couldn't wait to recreate that kiss later.

Chapter 13

Mason

Mason splashed cold water on the back of his neck. He squeezed his eyes shut and tried to think of stupid, mundane shit to take his mind off the feel of Natasha's body under his. It had been hours since it happened, but it was going to take a cold shower to turn off these feelings.

It didn't help that he'd spent two hours sitting inches away from her, inhaling the scent of her strawberry shampoo and listening to her throaty laughter. He'd tried to sleep, but he couldn't stop thinking about their kiss, which led to him thinking about other things they could have done before Nate interrupted them. It took all his self-control not to invite her into his bedroom at the end of the night, but they weren't there yet, despite how badly he wanted it.

Mason wasn't sure *where* they were actually. Natasha told him she had feelings for him, but it had ended there. Were they dating? Were they not dating? He didn't know, and it drove him crazy.

He opened the bathroom door and tiptoed past a sleeping Natasha. Seeing her sprawled across the couch, with one leg hanging over the edge and the blankets kicked off, tempted Mason to wake her with a kiss and finish what they'd started. When he took a step toward the couch, Nate's door opened and his best friend came out, clad in just his boxers.

"Pants, dude," Mason whispered.

Nate jumped and swore quietly. "What are you doing out here? Ogling my sister?" He chuckled.

Mason scoffed. "No. It's not my fault she sleeps on the couch that I have to pass every time I go to the bathroom."

Nate put his hands up. "Okay, okay. I was only kidding. Sheesh."

"Why aren't you in there with Dottie?" Mason asked.

"Dottie left a couple of hours ago, and I needed a drink," Nate answered. "Not that it matters why I'm walking around my house in the middle of the night. You know, you look like you could use a drink, too."

"I need about a thousand of them," Mason muttered. "I'm going to bed." He spun around and stomped to his room. He wanted to slam the door, but he didn't want to wake up Natasha.

"Dammit," he muttered under his breath.

———

Mason had been on edge since he and Natasha kissed. He hadn't been able to get a second alone with her since then; Nate was always around when they were home. Neither of them had been home much, anyway; Natasha was working a lot to get ready for an upcoming show at the Lakeside Thespians Dinner Theatre, while he had been busy with several weddings and family photo shoots. They hadn't even set up Natasha's new headshots because of their conflicting schedules.

Any time they were together, the sexual tension between them tore him apart. He longed to take her into his arms and kiss her. Hell, he wanted more than that. He couldn't sleep, and his concentration was shot. He lived on coffee and energy drinks for the time being.

Their discussion about Natasha's feelings hadn't changed anything. Kissing her hadn't changed anything. She was still the unattainable woman torturing him with her presence.

Mason was determined to end his constant questions and the incessant wondering about where he stood with Natasha. He needed to suck it up and talk to her, tell her he reciprocated her feelings, and find out if they could try to make a relationship between the two of them work. If he was going to continue living in the same house with her, he had to know the truth.

"Earth to Mason!" A loud knock on the bar top pulled him out of the fugue he'd fallen into. He was so lost in his own head he forgot he was at the bar with a drink in front of him.

"What the hell is up with you, bro?" Nate asked. "You haven't been yourself for more than a week. You're all moody and contemplative."

"And you've been reading your word-of-the-day emails again, haven't you?"

Nate narrowed his eyes. "Stop trying to change the subject. What is going on with you?"

Mason took a deep breath. "I kissed Tasha," he blurted out.

Nate dropped the cloth he used to clean the bar on the floor and stared at Mason. "You what?"

"I kissed your sister," Mason repeated. He picked up his drink and downed it in two swallows. He coughed and winced as the alcohol burned his throat.

The grin on Nate's face almost split it in half. "It's about damn time."

"You know, most guys want their best friend to stay *away* from their sister," Mason said.

Nate laughed. "Most guys don't have you for a friend, either. You're a good guy, Mace. I'd be crazy not to want my sister with you."

"Would you feel the same way if you knew she has feelings for me?"

"She finally told you?" Nate asked.

"You knew?"

Nate snorted. "Of course I knew. She's my sister. Tasha talked to me, told me she liked you, and asked my advice. I told her to talk to you."

Mason sat up straighter, downed his drink, and glared at Nate. "Did you tell her how I feel about her?"

"No, I didn't. She needs to hear that shit from you, Mace, not me." He leaned on the bar and looked his friend in the eye. "Besides, I wouldn't do that to you. You and my sister need to work this out on your own. I'll be a sounding board, to both of you, but that's it. I am not playing middleman. We're not in high school anymore."

"If I recall correctly, you didn't help me in high school either," Mason pointed out.

Nate nodded. "You're right, I didn't. I didn't think you two should have gotten together back then. Tasha was still figuring out who and what she wanted to be. I think she would have broken your heart if you had dated in high school."

Mason narrowed his eyes. "You don't think she'll break it now?"

"I don't." Nate leaned on the bar. "My sister has spent a lot of time figuring out who she is. By the time we were in high school, she was sick of being 'Nate and Nattie.' Distancing herself from me—which meant distancing herself from you—gave her a chance to figure out who she was without me. Without us. She needed that. She learned a lot about herself, and she learned some hard lessons. I don't know if she's got it figured out yet, or if she knows who she is or what she wants. Tasha just has to figure out how to go after what she wants and get it."

"So maybe I won't be her brother's annoying best friend anymore?" Mason said.

"Eh, I don't know. She still might think you're annoying." Nate winked. "Wait, when you kissed her, she kissed you back, right?"

"Yes, she did. But we haven't really talked since it happened."

Nate rolled his eyes. "You need to talk to her."

Mason glared at Nate. "Don't you think I know that? I haven't had a chance. Life keeps getting in the way. *You* keep getting in the way. It's crowded in that tiny house; whoever said three is a crowd wasn't lying."

"Nah, three's company, bro. It's fun."

Mason threw a balled-up napkin at Nate's face and laughed. "I need to talk to her because I can't keep living in the same house with her, not knowing what's going on between us."

"Are you going to tell her how you feel?"

Mason nodded. "Yeah, I have to. She told me how she feels, so I owe it to her to be honest about my feelings for her."

"Thank God," Nate said. "And it only took eighteen years."

Mason grimaced. "Twenty. Thanks for reminding me how much time we wasted."

"It'll be fine. You'll see. I think everything will work out." Nate poured Mason another drink. "When are you gonna talk to her?"

Mason shrugged. "I don't know. I should probably wait until after her show opens. She's been so busy—"

"Hey, you know what?" Nate interrupted. "The theater is having their opening night party here at the bar. I'm giving them the back room for the night. You could come by the bar and talk to her then. If everything goes well with the show, she'll be in a good mood. It would be the perfect time to talk to her."

"That's a great idea." Mason rapped his knuckles on the bar. "I think that's what I'll do."

Nate's impossibly huge grin seemed to grow even wider. Mason shook his head and laughed. Who knew his best friend would encourage him to date his twin sister?

—

Mason spent the next week planning. He ordered flowers, planned to be off work from the hospital that night, and then convinced Natasha he wasn't going to be at her show because he had to work. He decided he wanted to surprise her instead, showing up at the party with flowers and sweeping her off her feet. At least, that was how he imagined it.

He prayed it worked.

Unfortunately, Natasha was angry with him for ditching her on opening night; their other friends, Summer and Gavin, and Oscar and Vera, planned on attending. Avery would be there as well. Nate couldn't make it because of staffing issues at the bar, and Mason had her convinced he wouldn't be there. Even though she hadn't come out and said it, it pissed her off he wasn't coming.

The day of the show, she asked Mason again if he would be there. He had just returned from work and she was at the kitchen table doing paperwork. When he reiterated for the tenth time that he couldn't attend because of work, she'd crossed her arms and glared at him. "First, my brother ditches me, and now you."

"Tash, I can't. It's summer, and the hospital is short-staffed. I'm on duty."

The way her face fell broke his heart, but he stuck to his guns. "I'm sorry. I know you're disappointed."

She gave him a weak smile and shrugged. "It's okay. I understand. At least Avery will be there." She rose to her feet.

"Tash, I swear I'll make it up to you," Mason pleaded.

Natasha shrugged and nodded, but she wouldn't meet his eyes. "I have to get ready." She disappeared into Nate's bedroom.

An hour later, Natasha emerged from her brother's bedroom in full makeup, with her auburn red hair loosely curled and pinned up so it framed her face. She had on a tight white tank top and short little shorts that emphasized her figure, fitting for the part of a cheerleader in the *Mean Girls* musical. Mason's breath caught in his throat, and he couldn't tear his eyes away from her.

"You look amazing," he said.

Natasha smiled, though it didn't reach her eyes. She didn't say anything as she gathered her things to take to the theater. Mason almost told her the truth just so he could see her smile.

He knew she was angry, and he hated to be deceptive, but when he showed up at the party later that night, he wanted her to be surprised.

She finished shoving everything in her backpack, grabbed her dress off the back of the bathroom door, and headed for the door.

"Good luck tonight!" Mason called after her.

Natasha froze with her hand on the doorknob. "Break a leg," she said. "You're supposed to say break a leg." She walked out without looking back.

—

Mason was on his way out of the door when his phone rang. He fully intended to decline the call, but when he saw it was Mr. Ward, his boss, he had to answer. Mr. Ward had been out of town for weeks—in Missoula with his grandchildren—so they had never discussed Mason buying the business; in fact, Mason thought he forgot.

So, instead of declining the call, he answered.

"Hello, Mr. Ward."

"Mason, how are you?"

"I'm doing well," Mason replied. "How's Missoula?"

"Wonderful." His boss cleared his throat. "How are things at the studio?"

"Busy as usual. Are you planning on coming back to Lakeside soon, sir?"

"That's why I'm calling," Harry explained. "I'm not coming back to Lakeside. The movers will clear out my house next week. I had my lawyer draw up papers to transfer the business to you."

Mason froze, unable to take another step. He wasn't sure he'd heard Harry correctly. "With all due respect, Mr. Ward, I appreciate the offer, but we haven't discussed price or anything like that. I'm not even sure I can afford to *buy* the business from you."

Harry chuckled. "My lawyer will deliver the paperwork to the studio on Wednesday. Look it over, and then we'll talk."

"Um ... okay. I'll ... I'll do that," Mason replied.

Once they'd said their goodbyes, Mason climbed in his truck and stared out the window. He could just see the lake through the cluster of houses, and his heart thumped in his chest. If this was for real, his life would change forever. Owning his own photography studio, even in tiny Lakeside, Montana, would be the dream come true.

He refused to get his hopes up, as he hadn't even seen the paperwork yet. More than likely, it would be out of his reach. Everything he'd ever wanted in life had been out of his reach. Why would this be any different?

Mason put the car in gear, but his enthusiasm for the surprise he'd planned was gone. Natasha was one of those things in his life that had always been out of reach, and nothing had changed. Chasing after her was an unattainable dream. He glanced at the bouquet on the passenger seat. A sense of dread crept over him—maybe this was a mistake.

He backed out of the driveway, but he second-guessed himself all the way to the theater. By the time he parked in the back of the lot, he had talked himself in and out of talking to Natasha about his feelings for her. When he stepped out of the truck, he still didn't know what he was going to do, but he squared his shoulders and went inside anyway.

Maybe I'll let fate decide.

Chapter 14

Natasha

The show was a phenomenal success, better than expected. A full house packed the theater, the crowd was into it, and the theater's owner was ecstatic. Natasha couldn't have been happier. The only thing that would have made it better was if Mason could have been there.

She regretted being angry with him; it wasn't his fault he had to work. Mason would have been there if he could have. As soon as she saw him, she planned to let him know she wasn't mad that he wasn't able to be at her show. Nothing could kill her good mood.

Once the final curtain fell, Natasha hurried to the dressing rooms to grab her stuff. She planned to duck out early so she could set up for the party.

Thanks to Nate, the opening night after-party was being held at the Time Out Bar and Grill. Natasha arrived first so she could get everything ready. Grateful for a minute alone, she took a second to duck into the bathroom. She smoothed the skirt of her forties-style, blood-red dress, checked her tightly curled hair, and carefully re-applied her makeup in the mirror. She'd spent a lot of time getting her look perfect, and the result pleased her.

She desperately hoped Mason would show up for the party. She sent him a text inviting him, hoping he would know it meant she wasn't angry anymore. He responded with a thumbs up, and nothing else. It wasn't a yes, but it also wasn't a no. She didn't even know what time he got off work.

It wasn't long before the cast and crew arrived, so Natasha shifted into hostess mode, greeting everyone and directing them to the back room of the bar. Once she had everyone settled and mingling, she went out front to thank her brother again for the use of the back room for the party. The crowded bar was no surprise; it was always busy. Nate worked his butt off to make this the most popular bar in Lakeside, and he succeeded. Natasha stepped behind the bar and tapped Nate on the shoulder.

When he turned around, she threw her arms around him and hugged him. "Hey, thanks for letting us use the bar for our after-party," she said.

"You're welcome," Nate replied. He kissed her on the cheek. "Anything for my sister, but I have some bad news. Trista is out sick, so I'm shorthanded. You're gonna have to help." He shoved a tray of drinks into her hands. "Take this back there, will you? And, if you need anything, I'll do my best to get it to you. I called another server to come in, but I haven't heard from her. We're swamped thanks to the pre-Labor Day crowd."

"I'll help with my party," she offered. "Almost everything is back there anyway—appetizers, food, bottled drinks—so we're good. I'll get any other drinks we need. Don't worry about anything." Natasha kissed Nate's cheek and headed for the back room with the tray balanced on one hand.

Fifty people packed the room, spread out across the remodeled back patio. Last summer, Nate remodeled the bar to make more room for indoor events. He'd had the back patio enclosed and turned into a sprawling room, with tables, chairs, a small bar in the corner, and a restroom. It was the perfect spot to host a party. Natasha set the drinks on the table, then she went to the sound system, plugged in her phone, and started the music. Before she knew it, people packed the dance floor, and the alcohol flowed. She made several trips back and forth to the front of the bar, keeping everything and everyone stocked with their favorite drinks. After a couple of trips, her friends volunteered to help, giving her the chance to hang out with everyone.

Just after eleven, Natasha saw Mason come through the door. She stood on her tiptoes and waved at him. His silver-gray eyes landed on her, and a grin spread across his face. He hurried across the room, wrapped an arm around her waist, and kissed her temple. He pulled his other hand out from behind his back and handed her a bouquet of a dozen pink carnations.

"My favorite!" She kissed him on the cheek. "Thank you! How did you know?"

"Seriously? I've known you for twenty years. What kind of friend would I be if I didn't know what your favorite flower is?" He hugged her close. "The show was magnificent. And you were fabulous."

"Wait? Were you there? I thought you had to work?"

Mason shrugged. "Please don't be mad, but I lied; I wanted to surprise you. I wouldn't leave you hanging like that."

Natasha hugged him tight, her cheek pressed to his chest, his heart pounding in her ear. "Thank you, Mace. I appreciate it more than you know. You are amazing."

Mason blushed and cleared his throat. "There was no way I could disappoint you. Hey, can I steal you away for a minute? I need to talk to you."

Natasha's stomach flipped. She nodded, so Mason took her hand and led her outside.

Should I be nervous?

Once outside, Natasha leaned against the porch railing and tried to act like her heart wasn't trying to pound its way out of her chest. She swallowed past the lump rising in her throat. "Okay, what's up?"

"I wanted to talk to you," Mason said. "About you and me."

She'd expected this, but that didn't quell her nerves. Even though she had told Mason about her growing feelings for him, and they had kissed, they hadn't really talked about what that meant, if it meant anything. They'd never talked about Mason's feelings.

Natasha took a deep breath and nodded. "It is probably time we talked, isn't it? There's a lot of air to clear."

Mason nodded. "I agree. We need to talk."

Natasha dropped into a chair on the patio and folded her hands in her lap. "So, you and me, huh? Are we ... are we a thing now?"

"You sound like you think that's a bad thing," Mason said.

Natasha shook her head. "No, I don't think it's a bad thing. I want to talk about us. We *need* to talk about us."

"Oh? Is this going to be more of the 'I have feelings for you, Mason' discussion, or are we going to figure out what we both want to do? I know what I want from you, Tasha. What about you? Do you know what you want?"

"I think I know what I want. I was just afraid to admit it. In fact, I fought it like crazy, but I don't want to fight it anymore." She stood up, stepped close to Mason, and put a hand on his chest, her finger circling the button on his shirt. She looked up into his mesmerizing gray eyes and smiled. "I like the thought of us together, Mason; I think it's a good thing."

Actually, she loved the thought of her and Mason together. She could picture them together for a long time, if not forever, but she wanted to take her time, make sure it would last. No rushing into it headlong or doing something stupid.

Her words brought a smile to his face. "Really?"

"Yes, really."

Mason slid an arm around her waist, brushed the hair from her face, and pulled her close. "You don't know how long I've waited to hear you say that." Mason rested his chin on the top of her head. "Are you sure about this? About us?"

Natasha nodded. "I am. I promise. But—"

Mason released her with a sigh. "There's always a but, isn't there?"

Natasha stood on her tiptoes and pressed a lingering kiss to his lips. She took his hand and squeezed it. "Hear me out. My breakup with Brick is still kind of fresh and honestly, sometimes it still hurts. I want to do this, but I want to take it one day at a time, see where it takes us. Are you okay with that?"

Mason nodded. "I've waited twenty years; I think I can wait a bit longer."

Natasha snorted. "Twenty years? No pressure though, right?"

"No pressure," Mason whispered.

"How about you kiss me to seal the deal?" Natasha asked.

Mason lifted her off her feet, his lips on hers. He kissed her until she couldn't breathe. Kissing Mason could easily become her new favorite thing. Reluctantly, she pulled away.

"We should go inside before people come looking for me."

Mason groaned and set her back down. "Fine. But you're going home with me tonight."

Natasha burst out laughing. "Okay, if you insist. I'll go home with you tonight." She kissed him again. "Come on, let's go inside."

—

The party was a tremendous success. Everyone ate, drank, and partied way too hard. As for Natasha, she had too much to drink. Her celebratory mood had as much to do with the success of the show as it did with her new relationship with Mason. For the first time in a long time, Natasha let loose.

By the end of the night, walking turned out to be a chore, as did staying upright. She leaned on Mason as they made their way up the sidewalk to their front door. He propped her against the wall while he unlocked the door, then he put his arm around her and helped her inside.

Once Mason set her on the couch, Natasha kicked off her shoes and stretched out. Mason got her a bottle of water and sat on the floor. Natasha ran her fingers through his long, black hair, twisting the strands around her fingers.

"I love your long hair," she murmured. "When you grew it out in high school—."

Mason rested his cheek on the couch next to her leg and smiled. "You told me you hated it."

"I lied." Natasha giggled. "I lied about a lot of stuff in high school. And maybe some things in college."

"Oh, really?" Mason raised an eyebrow. "What exactly did you lie about?"

Natasha closed her eyes and giggled again. "I lied when I told you Courtney Johnson didn't like you."

What am I doing? Too much alcohol, and I can't keep my mouth shut? she thought.

Mason chuckled. "Jealous?"

"Yes," Natasha whispered. "I didn't want you to date anybody. Nobody was good enough for you."

Natasha never told anyone about Courtney Johnson. Back in high school, Courtney had a crush on Mason. When she'd approached Natasha in math class to ask her about Mason, Natasha lied and told Courtney that Mason wasn't interested in dating anyone. She'd then told Mason that Courtney didn't like him. Natasha couldn't imagine the two of them together, so she made sure it didn't happen.

Mason stared at her, the intensity of his gaze boring into her soul. She took a sip of the water, but she couldn't swallow past the lump in her throat.

"Nobody was good enough for me?" Mason whispered.

Natasha considered lying, but she'd already gone too far. Might as well strive for honesty. "Not as far as I was concerned. The thought of you with anybody else always rubbed me the wrong way. I didn't think anybody would understand you like I did."

Mason turned to face her, his chin resting on the couch cushion. "You're the only woman in the world who has ever understood me." He cupped her face with his large hand, his thumb brushing her cheek. He kissed her, his lips soft against hers.

Natasha sighed and rested her head on his shoulder. "Take me to bed."

"I thought you wanted to take things slow?" Mason said.

"Maybe I changed my mind," she whispered.

Mason laughed. "Maybe you've had too much to drink."

She giggled again. "I had a lot of wine."

"And a couple of margaritas, and those five or six shots when you swore you could drink Ted under the table." Mason brushed her hair away from her face. "You need sleep."

"I need *you*," Natasha responded.

She wanted Mason, needed him. The desire was an ache in her soul she couldn't contain anymore.

Mason climbed to his feet, then he helped Natasha off the couch and led her to his bedroom. Her heart pounded in anticipation, sobering her up. He stood beside the bed as she stretched out across it and stared up at him, waiting. Instead of stripping off his clothes like she hoped, Mason grabbed the blanket from the end of the bed and pulled it up to her shoulder before lying down beside her. He brushed her hair off her face and kissed her forehead.

"Go to sleep, Tasha. We have all the time in the world."

Natasha sighed and closed her eyes. "All the time in the world," she whispered before she dozed off.

Chapter 15

Mason

Mason woke up alone. He was on one side of the bed while the other side was empty, the blanket thrown off and the pillow rumpled. He scrubbed a hand over his face, pushed a hand through his hair, and shoved himself to his feet. Mason opened the bedroom door and saw the living room was empty.

"Tasha?" he called.

Silence.

Great. I take her to bed and wake up alone the next morning. Did I already screw it up?

Nate's bedroom door opened, and he poked his head out. "She's not here; I don't think she came home last night. The couch was empty when I got home around three." He stepped into the living room, pulling his bedroom door closed behind him. "Did she talk to you?"

"She was here last night." Mason headed for the kitchen, Nate right on his heels.

"What do you mean 'she was here?'" A grin spread across

Nate's face. "Wait a minute. Was she in your room?" The grin changed to a grimace. "Ew, don't answer that."

Mason didn't look at his best friend as he pulled the stuff for coffee from the cupboard. "She was in my room, but nothing happened. She had a lot to drink last night. I took her in there, covered her with a blanket, and we both went to sleep. Then I woke up alone."

Nate leaned against the counter and crossed his arms. "My sister slept in your bed last night. Does that mean what I think it means?"

"It means we're figuring things out," Mason said.

"Are you a couple or not?"

Mason nodded. "We're taking it slow, though, so don't make a big deal out of it, okay?"

"But it is a big deal. Isn't it?"

Mason laughed. "For me, yes. And I guess for her, too. She's still hurting from the breakup with Brick, so she doesn't want to rush into something new."

"Understandable." Nate clapped him on the back. "I'm glad to hear it, bro. I always thought you two were meant to be."

"Nate?" The woman's voice echoed through the house. "Where'd you go?"

Mason raised an eyebrow. "That didn't sound like Dottie," he whispered.

Nate shook his head. "It's not; Dottie and I broke up a couple of days ago. She was too young for me." He shrugged. "You know I'm not in any hurry to settle down. Dottie was getting too serious. Don't worry; I let her down easy."

"Nate!"

"Be right there," he yelled. He turned back to Mason. "About my sister—"

"Is this where you tell me if I hurt her, you'll kill me?" Mason asked.

"I think you already know that." Nate chuckled. "Seriously, though, she's my sister, and she's trusting you with her heart. Don't break it." He spun around and darted through the living room, back to his bedroom.

"No pressure," Mason muttered under his breath.

Once the coffee was done, he poured himself a cup and returned to his room. He didn't feel like meeting Nate's latest conquest, so he'd hide in his room and watch TV until she left. As he sat down on the bed, he glimpsed a piece of paper stuck between the pillows. It was a flyer that had probably been stuck on the front door, or maybe his car window. Scribbled on the back was a note from Natasha.

> *Mason-*
>
> *Sorry I had to leave! I had to get down to the theater and take care of last night's box office receipts. I'll talk to you soon, I promise!*
>
> *Tash*
> *P.S. Thank you for being a gentleman last night. You were right, of course. I was too drunk for us to do anything.*

Mason smiled to himself. At least he hadn't screwed things up. He'd made the right decision last night, despite certain body parts insisting otherwise. It hadn't been easy to turn Natasha down, do the right thing, and be a gentleman. In fact, it had sucked, but he knew in the end, it was what had to happen. He was glad he'd listened to his head and not his groin, for he and Natasha had plenty of time to figure things out.

—

The large manila envelope sat in the center of the table, beckoning Mason to open it. He'd been sitting on the couch for almost an hour, staring at it, afraid to open it and shatter his dream of owning the photography studio.

He hadn't told anyone about the proposed deal between him and Harry Ward, fearing he'd jinx it if anyone else knew. But now that the papers were here, he regretted not talking to Nate about it. Despite his age, Nate was a shrewd businessman who'd grown a tiny bar with no customer base into a thriving business in less than five years. If anyone could give him sound business advice, it was his best friend.

As if on cue, the front door slammed. Nate tossed his keys on the kitchen table, grabbed a bottle of water from the fridge, and plopped on the couch next to Mason.

"What are you doing?" he asked. "I texted you like ten times, and you never answered. Tasha's meeting us at the bar in an hour."

Mason nodded at the envelope on the table.

Nate glanced at it, raising his eyebrows. "What is that?"

"It's a proposal from Mr. Ward. He wants to sell me the photography studio."

"What?" Nate scrambled to grab the bulky envelope but stopped. "Why didn't you tell me?" He glanced at Mason, hand poised and waiting for his friend's permission to rip it open. When Mason nodded, Nate tore open the envelope and dumped the papers out.

"You read it," Mason said. "Tell me what it says. How much is Harry asking?"

Nate was silent as he skimmed the paperwork, taking him too long read, as far as Mason was concerned. After several minutes, Mason punched him on the shoulder.

"What does it say? How much does he want?"

Nate laid the paperwork on the table. "Nothing."

"What? You're mistaken. Read it again."

"I read it more than once, bro. Harry doesn't want anything. All he wants is a legally binding agreement that you will keep the studio open in Lakeside for at least one year. After the year is up, you are welcome to sell it, close it, whatever you want to do. He said the best thing about owning the studio has been the reputation he has built in this town and the relationships he has established. He doesn't want to drop it like a hot potato when the business is flourishing."

Mason sagged against the back of the couch. The studio was his; all he had to do was keep it open for a year. Given that he had no plans to go anywhere, it couldn't have been a better deal.

"What do you think?" Mason asked.

"What do I think?" Nate said. "I think it's crazy. But I also know Harry. He's struggled since his wife passed away. He doesn't enjoy being away from his kids and grandkids, so this gives him a way out. If you didn't work for him, he'd close up shop and move. He probably wouldn't even bother selling it, just hang a closed sign in the window and walk away."

"So, should I do it?"

Nate nodded. "It's a once-in-a-lifetime opportunity. If you don't take advantage of it, you'd be stupid. Hell, if you don't do it, I might call Harry and tell him I'll take it off his hands. I think I know a photographer who could run it for me." Nate winked.

"Hilarious." Mason took a deep breath and slowly exhaled. "Where do I sign?"

—

"Where are we going?" Natasha asked.

"You'll see," Mason said.

Natasha made a face. "I don't like surprises, Mace. You know that."

"I'm not trying to surprise you, I swear. The place is off the beaten path. We have to walk."

"Am I going to get all hot and sweaty? If so, any photographs you take won't look so great."

"We won't have to walk far; it's not too far off the road." Mason turned down a dirt road two miles out of town and followed it for another mile. He parked in an enormous field and gestured for Natasha to get out of the truck.

Natasha jumped out of the truck, hiked her backpack higher on her shoulder, and dropped her sunglasses into place. "Which way?"

Mason pointed at a small hill two hundred yards away. "There's a small meadow that butts right up to the lake on the other side of that hill. The beach is gorgeous. It's a great place to get some nature shots for your portfolio. And mine. Come on."

"You better pray it's worth it," she grumbled. "I hate hiking."

Mason forgot Natasha didn't love the outdoors; she didn't like hiking, camping, or anything like that. None of that interested her, which always amused him since they lived in one of the most beautiful states in the union. He loved exploring, especially around Lakeside and Flathead Lake.

While hiking, Mason took Natasha's hand and helped her climb over a fallen tree and maneuver past some overgrown shrubs. He kept hold of her hand as they hiked toward the hill in the distance.

"It will be worth it, I promise," he said.

The two of them had been dating for a little over three weeks, and it had been the best three weeks of his life. Because they lived together, they were together constantly. Mason loved every minute. But, as Natasha requested, they were taking things slow, easing into a relationship twenty years in the making. As far as Mason was concerned, they could move at a snail's pace as long as Natasha belonged to him. He'd been patient for twenty years, so he could be patient a while longer until she was ready.

It took twenty minutes to reach the small beach and meadow.

Mason grinned as Natasha froze in place, her mouth comically hanging open as she took in the lake's beauty. It was quiet here: no boats charging past, their wake sending waves on the shore, no people clamoring for a spot on the beach, no kids yelling, or college students catcalling. The sun reflected off the crystal-clear water, and the green of the trees appeared brighter and more vibrant.

Mason took everything in with a photographer's eye—the contrasting colors in the grass and leaves, the pink-and-purple flowers, and the blue sky. Natasha would look even more gorgeous than usual against the backdrop of the lake. He pulled out his camera and dropped his backpack to the ground. He quickly snapped a couple of pictures of Natasha, since she wasn't looking.

"Hey! I wasn't ready!" She made a face and flipped him off.

Mason snapped another photo before lowering the camera. "Those make the best shots."

Natasha trudged across the meadow and dropped her backpack beside his. She spun around, her back to him, and looked over her shoulder. Her eyes were hooded, the smile on her face demure yet alluring at the same time. It had his stomach dropping to his toes and his upper lip sweating. He took another picture before he grabbed her and kissed her.

"We aren't going to get many pictures taken if you stop to kiss me after every shot," she said when he released her.

Mason sighed. "I know. You just looked so irresistible, and now that I don't have to hold back—" He shrugged. "Besides, I enjoy kissing you."

"I enjoy kissing you, too," she whispered. "But before we get completely distracted, let's get the new headshots done. Then you can kiss me all you want."

Mason chuckled. "Sounds like a good plan."

They spent the next hour taking a multitude of photos. Mason couldn't get enough of Natasha—she was unbelievably photogenic. Of course, he was biased; he found her beautiful no matter what.

Once he finished photographing Natasha, he took a few minutes to walk along the edge of the lake with his camera in hand. Every inch of Flathead Lake, especially the area around Lakeside, was stunning; he could spend hours and hours taking photos of the area. In fact, he had spent hours doing just that, losing himself in the lake's beauty.

"Mason!"

He hurried back to Natasha. She must have had more in her backpack than the little bag of makeup he'd seen her take out earlier, because when he got back to her, he found her sitting on a large blanket with sandwiches, two small bags of carrots, and juice boxes spread out in front of her.

"What's this?" he asked.

Natasha grinned and held up a sandwich. "Peanut butter-and-jelly."

Mason couldn't hold back the laughter. "My favorite! Thank God it's not bologna." He tucked his camera into his backpack, sat down beside her, plucked the sandwich out of her hand, and took a huge bite.

"This is delicious," he mumbled around a mouthful of food.

He devoured everything Natasha handed him, then stretched out on the blanket, with his hands clasped behind his head and his eyes closed. After a few minutes, Natasha laid down next to him, her head on his arm.

"What are you thinking about?" she asked.

"That this weather won't last much longer," Mason replied. "Now that Labor Day is over, the cold weather will head our way."

"That's what you're thinking about?" She giggled. "How romantic."

Mason chuckled. "Sorry. I'm not so great with the romance stuff, but I'll work on it."

"You could start by kissing me," she whispered.

He turned to face her, their knees touching. Mason dug his fingers into her hip, took her chin in his hand, and tipped her head back so he could stare into her eyes. He slid his hand up her side and into her hair, pulled her close, and kissed the corner of her mouth.

"Is that all you got?" Natasha asked, her breath warm against his skin.

Mason wrapped an arm around her back, the tips of his fingers brushing the skin between the waistband of her shorts and her t-shirt. He swiped his tongue across her bottom lip. Natasha opened her mouth, and his tongue brushed against hers. She opened her mouth more, allowing him to fully explore hers. His tongue moved over her teeth and lips, his nose brushing against hers as the kiss deepened. Natasha pulled out the rubber band holding his hair away from his face, twisted her fingers in his hair, and tugged slightly to pull him closer to her.

A tiny groan from Natasha sent a spark shooting through him, settling deep in his gut and causing an ache inside him he couldn't ignore. He rolled Natasha to her back, his knee between her legs, the kiss becoming something more, something stronger, something he didn't think either of them could fight.

Natasha wrapped herself around him, arms and legs, until he could barely tell where she ended and he began. He lost himself in the kiss, the world around him fading to a blur of colors and sounds that meant nothing as long as he was in her arms.

This was what he had wanted all his life, what he needed all of his life. She was his; she had always been his, she would always be his. Mason would do whatever it took to keep this woman by his side.

Chapter 16
Natasha

Natasha moaned and sank into the blanket as Mason's weight settled over her. This felt *right*, like it was meant to be, like it was the only thing in the world she had ever wanted or needed.

She closed her eyes and let herself go, let herself forget about everything and everyone. There was just Mason.

As the kiss deepened, Natasha's fingers itched to touch Mason's bare skin, to feel his tanned, taut body naked against hers. They'd been dating for three weeks, and Mason had been a perfect gentleman at her request. His touch ignited something in her, something that only he could satisfy. Natasha needed it, and she didn't want to wait any longer. The temptation was too great.

She shoved the unbuttoned flannel he wore off his shoulders and tugged it down his arms, tossing it aside. Mason's eyes widened, and a low grunt left him as Natasha traced the muscles in his back through the thin gray t-shirt he wore.

"I thought we were waiting," he whispered.

"I don't want to wait anymore, Mace. I want you. All of you."

Mason smirked. "Does that mean what I think it means?"

Natasha poked him in the shoulder. "Yes, you ass. Are you gonna make me say it?"

Mason nodded.

"Fine." Natasha twisted her fingers in Mason's hair and pulled, dragging him close so she could press her mouth against his ear. "I want you to make love to me, Mason."

Mason growled deep in the back of his throat, an animalistic sound that made her ache inside. Mason slipped his hand under the edge of her shirt and pushed it up her stomach, stopping halfway, his fingers dancing over her stomach that were not quite tickling, but sending delightful pings of desire traipsing through her. Natasha moaned, and Mason pulled the shirt all the way off, leaving her in just her bra.

Goosebumps rose on her skin as Mason's hands caressed her waist, goosebumps that had nothing to do with the cool air. A shiver danced along her spine. Natasha wrapped a leg around the back of Mason's thigh, slid her hand under his t-shirt, and coaxed him out of it.

Natasha kept her fingers tangled in Mason's hair, using them to hold him close as his mouth was on hers. They kissed, their bodies intertwined together, as his feverish body heated her from the inside out. When she moaned, Mason moaned in response. When she moved, Mason moved with her, their connection never breaking.

Mason moved to her neck, nipping at her skin and licking over the new love bites that marked her skin. His lips roamed over her body, over her breasts, down her stomach, and across her hips as he unbuttoned her shorts and slid them down her legs. Natasha kicked off her shoe, giggling when one shot up into the air and landed two feet from her head.

Mason chuckled and rose to his knees. "Let's try not to knock anybody out. What do you say?"

Natasha nodded and silently watched him remove her other

shoe and her socks, then he pulled her shorts off and dropped them on top of her shoes. He caressed her leg for a moment before leaning down to kiss a trail up her legs, stopping to knead, lick, and suck her inner thighs.

This was a side of Mason she hadn't known existed. Sure, she had fantasized about him occasionally; after all, she was only human, but she never imagined those fantasies would come to fruition. She never imagined timid, good-guy Mason would be a bold, take-charge kind of lover.

When he bit her inner thigh, so close to where she desperately wanted him, Natasha threw her head back and thrust her hips forward, chasing Mason's sinful mouth. She wanted his mouth on her, needed to feel him devouring her, feasting on her.

Mason grabbed her hands and held them at her sides as he worked his way up her nearly naked body—kissing her stomach, licking her breasts, his tongue dancing over the lace covering her nipples. He nipped and sucked at the sensitive skin of her neck before he caught her lips in his and pushed his tongue into her mouth.

"Mason," she gasped when he eventually pulled away. "Jesus, I never imagined."

Natasha trembled, her body slick with sweat, and her breath tearing in and out of her throat. She dug her fingers into his hips, desperate to keep him close.

Mason slid his hands up her back, unhooked her bra, and added it to the growing pile of clothes.

"God, Tash, you're so beautiful," Mason murmured. "I want you so bad."

Natasha nodded and tugged on his hair. "I want you, too."

Mason took her breast in his mouth and, to her surprise, sucking not so gently. The shock of the pain mixed with pleasure made her hiss and arch her back, her hands fisting in the blanket beneath her. She'd never felt like this, never been this turned on by anyone, ever.

Mason released her and scrambled to his feet. He fumbled for his wallet, pulled a condom out, and stuck it between his lips. He yanked off his shorts and tossed them aside before dropping to his knees in front of Natasha. He dragged her lacy pink panties down her legs and threw them over his shoulder. He tossed the condom on the blanket next to her head, licked his lips, and stretched out, hovering over her. Then she couldn't see his face anymore because it was between her legs, his tongue and two fingers deep in her pussy. She screamed, the pleasure overwhelming her. There was no way she could hold back; gasps and moans escaped her as her body spasmed. Natasha let herself go, let herself get lost in the intensity of the feelings racing through her, with every muscle tightening as she came into Mason's mouth.

He held her, lapping at her wet center, his finger brushing over her swollen bud until she collapsed in a boneless, out-of-breath mess. When she could somewhat breathe again, Mason grabbed the condom, ripped it open, and slid it down his length. He pulled her legs around his waist and eased into her, eyes closed, not moving.

Natasha put her hand on his chest. "Don't stop, Mace. I want this. I want *you*."

That must have been all he needed. Mason gripped her hips, hard, his fingers digging into the flesh, and he slammed into her repeatedly. He whispered how beautiful she was, how much he wanted her, needed her.

Tangled together with bodies moving, hips thrusting, lips crashing together, and their breath mingling, the insane pleasure coursed through them as they raced toward their finish. Her name rumbled from Mason's chest as he came, his head thrown back and his long, black hair ruffled by the wind. Natasha dug her nails into his thighs as she writhed beneath him, her walls clenching around him and milking his cock dry.

Mason collapsed on top of her, his weight shifted to one side so he didn't crush her. He sighed and closed his eyes.

Natasha turned to face him, tracing his jawline with the tip of her finger. "That was amazing," she whispered. "I'm not sure it's ever been like that with anyone." She kissed his cheek. "Thank you."

Mason wrapped an arm around her and pressed a kiss to her temple. "You should always be treated like that. Worshipped, treasured."

"Sometimes I can't believe you're real." She giggled. "You're too good to be true."

A breeze blew through the meadow, whistling through the trees. Mason sat up and pushed a hand through his hair. "It's getting cold," he muttered.

The air had chilled, and the sun was low over the lake. As soon as she sat up, the cool air hit her flushed, hot skin, sending a shiver racing down her spine. She trembled and wrapped her arms around herself. Every year, she forgot how quickly the weather turned in Montana: warm during the day and cold at night.

"We should get back before it gets too dark," Mason said.

Natasha nodded, grabbed her clothes, and pulled them on. Mason did the same, rushing to cover himself as the wind picked up.

Once he was dressed, he climbed to his feet and held out his hand. "Come on."

Natasha took it and let him help her up. He pulled her into his arms and held her tight. She pressed her face against his chest and hugged him back.

They separated and quickly cleaned up their things, shoving everything into the backpacks. Mason held her hand as they hiked back through the woods to his truck parked alongside the road. He opened the door for her, helped her inside, and kissed her cheek before jogging around the front of the truck to the driver's side. He held her hand as they drove back to their place.

Natasha rested her head against the seat and closed her eyes. The hum of the tires on the road, Mason's warm hand wrapped around hers, and the dark night lulled her to sleep. For the first time in a long time, she was at peace.

—

The peace didn't last long. Their driveway was full of cars when they pulled in; it looked like they parked half the town in front of their house. Mason had to park three houses away.

Natasha jumped out of the truck and was immediately hit by the sound of loud, bass-filled music filling the night sky, pulling all the energy in the neighborhood toward their small house. Every light was lit, and the doors were wide open. People spilled into the yard.

"What the hell is this?" she yelled.

Mason shook his head. "Who the hell knows? Maybe Nate got bored?"

Natasha felt bad for their neighbors, forced to endure whatever was happening at their house. As they passed, Natasha saw their shy, introverted neighbor peering out her window with an irritated look on her face.

Mason took Natasha's hand as they made their way through the people clustered around the front door. As soon as they were inside, Mason called for Nate, but it was unlikely Nate had heard anything over the music. Mason must have spotted Nate, because he tightened his grip on Natasha's hand and dragged her through the crowd and into the living room. Nate stood in front of the TV with Oscar and Gavin.

"Mace! Tasha! You're finally home! Where the hell have you two been?" Nate said.

"Out," Mason grumbled. He swirled his finger in a circle. "What is all this?"

Nate made a face. "It's a party."

Mason sighed. Natasha squeezed his hand and smiled at her brother. "We know it's a party," she said, summoning every ounce of patience she had. "The question is, why is it here and not at the bar?"

"Oh, well, it started at the bar," Nate explained, "but then it kind of followed me home." He shrugged. "Who am I to say no?"

Natasha shook her head. "Are you ever going to grow up?" she asked.

Nate leaned over her, a huge grin on his face. "Nope."

Mason rolled his eyes and ducked into his bedroom. Natasha followed him.

"Hey, are you okay?" she asked.

"Yeah," Mason replied. "Nate drives me crazy sometimes. I wasn't expecting to come home to a party. I thought maybe we could hang out and watch movies or something."

Natasha stepped into his arms and rested her head on his chest. "I had a great time today. Don't let Nate and his partying attitude ruin it; we might as well go out there and join the madness."

Mason laughed and kissed the top of her head. "You're right. I'm being stupid. Let's go join the party."

Natasha linked her arm through Mason's and let him lead her back out to the party. Her mom always said to make the most of an unpleasant situation. While the party might not be bad, it wasn't ideal. They might as well have fun.

As soon as they emerged from the bedroom, the teasing began. When she kissed Mason on the cheek, Oscar yelled, "Get a room!" And when she glanced at Mason over her shoulder, Gavin started making kissing sounds, his eyes wide, and a delighted smirk on his face.

I think I need a drink.

Natasha excused herself to go to the kitchen to make margaritas. Being teased was no fun; if it continued, she needed a drink. Or two. Nate followed her and leaned against the counter beside her with a huge, cheesy grin on his face.

Natasha dropped the bottle of margarita mix on the counter and yanked open the freezer. She refused to look at her brother. "What is it you find so amusing, Nate?" she asked, with her head in the fridge.

Out of the corner of her eye, she saw her brother shrug. "Oh, you know. My best friend and my sister, that's all."

She shook her head; Nate's amusement astonished her. "Isn't it supposed to bother you I'm dating Mason? I thought brothers *didn't* want their sisters dating their best friends?"

Nate snorted. "Are you kidding? I've been waiting *years* for this moment."

Natasha jerked her head in his direction, margarita mix splashing onto the counter as she turned to stare at her brother. "What do you mean, *years*?"

"You know. Years. No pressure or anything, but you are the woman Mason has been waiting for his whole life. There isn't anything on earth that man loves more than you. No one, and I mean no one, can hold a candle to you. He has been in love with you since we were kids." Nate grabbed a chip out of the bowl on the counter and shoved it in his mouth, chewing loudly with his mouth open.

Natasha took a deep breath. *Years.* She pushed a hand through her hair. Nate had to be joking. There was no way Mason had been in love with her since they were children.

Love.

Jesus, that was another thing. Was Mason really in love with her? And if he was, why hadn't he ever said anything to her? Her head spun.

"So, what you're telling me is that Mason has—" She couldn't finish the thought.

Apparently, Nate could. "—has been in love with you for most of his life," Nate said.

Natasha could only stare at her brother, unsure how to deal with this information. While she'd known Mason liked her, had in fact liked her for a while, she didn't know he'd been in love with her for years. Or that he saw her as some kind of "ideal" woman. That was a lot of pressure.

She spun the top off the tequila bottle and took a huge gulp. It burned and made her eyes water, but she didn't care.

Nate stared at her, mouth agape. "What the hell, Tash?"

"I need a drink," she snapped.

Nate plucked the bottle from her hand. "I don't think you need it straight from the bottle. What is wrong with you?"

"Nothing," she snapped.

Her brother raised an eyebrow, glanced over his shoulder at the people in the living room, and then took a step closer to his sister while lowering his voice.

"Are you okay?" he asked.

Natasha snorted. "Of course, I'm okay."

Nate narrowed his eyes and crossed his arms over his chest. "Don't you think I know when you're lying? Talk to me. What's wrong?"

Natasha pinched the bridge of her nose. "I guess I didn't realize Mason has had feelings for me for ... for a while. I always thought I was nothing more to him than your dumb twin sister."

Nate laughed and shook his head. "Sometimes you are so *thick*, Tash. Mason has loved you since we were six years old. How have you not seen it? How have you not realized that, for Mason, you are the only woman in the world? The perfect woman in one tiny, fiery, redheaded package."

"That's not fair," she whispered. "How am I supposed to live up to that?"

"No one is asking you to live up to anything," Nate said. "You and Mason are together; that's all that should matter."

"You don't get it, Nate." Natasha pushed a hand through her hair. "I have always had to live up to other people's expectations. Mom and Dad expected me to be like you: smart, business-savvy, and focused. They expected me to find a nice guy, settle down, run a business. I disappointed them when I decided to be an actress—"

"That's not true."

Natasha held up her hand. "Let me finish. I have spent my whole life trying to do what everyone expects me to do. Being what someone else wants or needs. I did it for our parents during high school. I did it for Brick after we started dating; hell, I did it for every guy I *ever* dated. And now, I have to do it again with Mason. It's not fair; it's not what I want."

"I don't think Mason expects anything of you," Nate said.

"You know what? I need to talk to Mason." She straightened her shoulders and gave her brother her best smile. "Could you please tell your best friend I'd like to speak to him for a minute?"

"Tasha—"

She pursed her lips and promised herself she wouldn't swear at her brother. "Please, Nate. Could you get Mason? I *need* to talk to him."

Nate nodded and did as she asked. At least some things were simple.

Hopefully, it's that easy with Mason.

Chapter 17

Mason

Nate came out of the kitchen like someone had lit a fire under his ass. He headed directly for Mason, grabbed his friend's arm, and pulled him away from the group surrounding him.

"You need to go talk to Tasha. Now," Nate said, his voice low so only Mason could hear him.

Mason glared at his friend. "What did you say to her?"

"Nothing." Nate shrugged. "Well, something, but I didn't think it was a big deal. Something about you being in love with her for years and that she has always been your ideal woman. I don't know. I think she's panicking."

Mason swore under his breath. "Jesus, Nate, you told her I've been in love with her for *years*? We've been dating for three weeks. I better talk to her." He pushed past Nate and made his way to the kitchen, elbowing people out of his way.

Natasha was in the corner of the kitchen, arms crossed over her chest and gnawing on her lower lip. Mason had barely set foot in the kitchen before she leaped across the floor and got in his face.

— 129 —

"Have you really been in love with me your entire life?" she asked.

The unmitigated anger in her voice caught him off guard. "Wh-what?" he stammered.

Natasha took a step back. "I asked if you have really been in love with me your whole life. According to Nate, you've loved me since you were six."

Mason nodded, nothing more than a tip of his chin, but it was more than enough to tell Natasha that yes, he had loved her since he was six. Her face fell, and it ripped his heart in two. He took a step toward her, but she put her hand up and stumbled back, her ass hitting the counter.

Natasha nodded. "Okay. That's, uh, wow. That's a lot to deal with. When you said you waited twenty years for me, I thought you were joking. Good lord, Mason. Twenty years?"

"Let me explain," Mason said.

"Can I ask you a question?" she blurted out before he could say anything else.

"Of course you can," he said.

"Do you even love *me*, Mace? Or do you love the *idea* of me?"

Mason's stomach flipped, and bile rose in the back of his throat. "I don't know what you mean."

Natasha took a step closer, her shoulders back, chin raised. "Sure you do. Do you love *me,* or do you love some version of me you've created in your head? The unattainable woman, your best friend's sister, the girl engaged to another man: is that who you love? That woman? Or me?" She stabbed a finger into her chest.

"You, Tasha," Mason replied. "I love *you*. I have loved you for a long time."

Natasha snorted and shook her head. "How can you be so sure? I don't think you even know the real me."

Mason froze, his fists clenched at his sides as a flicker of irritation sparked through him. If anybody knew Natasha Garin, it was him. He took a deep breath and paused before he spoke. "That's funny, Tash. Because I don't think you know the real you."

"What did you say?"

"You heard me," Mason said. "For years I've watched you try to fit the girlfriend mold of whoever you're dating. You acted however they wanted you to act. I never saw you be *you*. It makes me sick to think about you spending the last two years burying the real you so you could stay with a guy who never loved you or appreciated you. Shit, not just the last two years. You've wasted years chasing after something, sorry, *someone* to make you whole."

The light in her eyes dulled. "At least I didn't spend most of my life afraid to tell the woman I love how I feel."

Mason balked and flinched. "That's not fair," he whispered. "I waited for you. While you worked your way through Reggie, and Dave, and Mike, and Bobby, they broke your heart. I waited while Brick tore it to pieces. I gave you space. You had a chance to figure it out. I waited until you were ready. I waited until you knew who and what you wanted. I waited for you to figure out I was Mr. Right."

Natasha scrubbed a hand over her face. "You know what? Maybe I don't know what I want. Or who I want. Maybe you aren't Mr. Right, Mason. Maybe you're just *Mr. Right Now*." She spun on her heel, ripped open the closet to snatch out her jacket and backpack, and was gone, out the front door and rushing past everyone.

The silence was deafening. All conversation had stopped; even the music wasn't playing. Mason didn't want to turn around; he didn't want to see the sad, pity-filled looks on the faces of his friends. Instead, he dug his keys out of his pocket and walked out the front door.

—

Mason drove around the block several times, but he didn't see

Natasha anywhere. She couldn't have gotten far, not on foot. Lakeside was a small town; there weren't a lot of places she could go.

He pulled off the road and parked in the lot of the local grocery store. He grabbed his phone and quickly typed out a text to Natasha. He stared at it for several minutes before he deleted it and tried again.

[Mason: I'm sorry.]

He waited; his heart pounded when the three little bubbles appeared. After a few seconds, they disappeared. Five minutes went by, but Natasha didn't respond. He tossed his phone on the passenger seat. She needed time to cool off.

Mason closed his eyes and rested his head against the back of the seat. He screwed up, and he knew it. With Natasha and his feelings for her, he didn't always think straight; it had been like that for years. He reacted with emotion rather than thinking before he opened his mouth and inserted his foot.

Natasha's words repeated over and over in his head.

At least I didn't spend most of my life afraid to tell the woman I love how I feel.

She was right, to an extent. He had spent years afraid to tell Natasha how he felt about her. Mason had convinced himself that she wouldn't want him because he *was* Mason, her brother's best friend. Her friend. And definitely not her type. During high school, Natasha had gone for the big, strong, alpha male types: guys who played sports and ruled the school. That wasn't Mason. He didn't hit his growth spurt until the summer before senior year. He left to spend a month with his father and his new wife, returning to Great Falls six inches taller and sixty pounds heavier thanks to the growth spurt.

For the first time, girls paid attention to him, but not the girl he wanted. He could have done a circus act in front of Natasha, and she would still ignore him. She wanted anyone but Mason, regardless of what Mason or Nate thought.

Not that Natasha cared what they thought or bothered to hang around long enough to find out. She fell off the radar, avoiding her brother and Mason as if they had the plague.

Mason probably saw her three or four times over the next year. He knew Brick proposed, thanks to Nate, but that was the extent of his knowledge of Natasha's life.

However, the torch he carried for Natasha never extinguished. She was always there, always on his mind. But he kept his distance, waiting for things to change.

Then she'd stumbled through their door, and his entire world imploded.

Mason scrubbed a hand over his face. There was no use sitting here rehashing the past, the mistakes he'd made, and the opportunities he'd let get away. He put the truck in gear and turned it toward home.

—

The party was over by the time he got back to the house. The only cars in the driveway were Nate's and Natasha's. It gave him a glimmer of hope that she had come home.

Nate was in the living room, trash bag in hand, picking up empty cans and bottles. He glanced over his shoulder when Mason shut the front door, but he returned to cleaning when he saw who it was.

"She's not here," Nate said.

"Have you heard from her?" Mason asked.

Nate nodded. "She texted me. She went to Avery's. She wants to be left alone. Said she needs some time to think."

Mason leaned against the wall, crossed his arms, and shook his head. "I fucked up."

"You both fucked up." Nate tied off the bag, looked around

the room at the remaining mess, grimaced, and pulled another bag out from under the sink. "My sister is a strong woman. It took her a while to figure it out and even longer to get out of that goddamn relationship with Brick, but she did. She's spent most of her life trying to be what everyone else wants: our parents, one boyfriend after another. Now that she's finally figuring out who she is and what she wants, it scares her to think she might have to conform to *your* idea of the perfect woman."

"I didn't ask her to do that," Mason interjected.

"No, you didn't. And that's her fuck-up. She assumed you wanted to change her, mold her into something she wasn't. You need to talk to her. She needs to talk to you. You two can figure this out. I know you can, if you talk it out."

"I know that," Mason said. "Does she?"

"She will." Nate sat on the couch, holding the bag between his knees. "I feel kind of responsible for this."

Mason crossed the room and sat beside his best friend. "Why? You didn't do anything."

"Oh, but I did." Nate sighed. "I like the idea of the two of you together. A lot. I've been pushing it. I wasn't helping either of you, but I was encouraging the relationship. Maybe I should have played the middleman and done my best to mediate your relationship. I think my input might have been helpful."

Mason snorted. "That's weird." He could only imagine the level of uncomfortable those kinds of conversations could have reached.

Nate burst out laughing. He dropped the trash bag on the floor and fell back against the couch, his hands over his face. "Oh, Jesus! What did I just say? Can you imagine?"

Mason chuckled. "Um, I'm trying not to."

Nate patted Mason on the shoulder. "Look, it will all work out. Tash needs some time to process shit, that's all. Give her some space."

"I've been giving her space for years, Nate. Maybe I'm sick of waiting."

Nate raised an eyebrow and stared at his best friend. "Are you serious? After all this time, after everything you've gone through, after finally getting the girl, now you're going to say you're done. Just like that?"

"No, it's not 'just like that.' I've been waiting for your sister since I was six. I waited through idiot boyfriend after idiot boyfriend, and I waited until I was the man she wanted. Or at least the man I thought she wanted. Problem is, I'm not sure I am the man she wants. Maybe I really am just Mr. Right Now. The rebound boyfriend, not the guy she's supposed to end up with."

"Do you really think she's using you as a rebound thing after Brick? Have some fun with an old friend, then move on to something better or improved?"

Mason shrugged. "I don't know anything anymore." He shoved himself to his feet. "I'm tired. I'm going to bed. We can talk about this more tomorrow when I can think straight."

"Mace, wait."

Mason ignored Nate, went into his room, and quietly closed the door. He fell into his bed, fully clothed and shoes on. He was suddenly exhausted and wanted to sleep for a week.

———

"So, she's still at Avery's?" Mason asked.

"Yeah," Nate answered. He tossed his keys on the kitchen table and sat down across from his best friend.

Mason groaned and dropped his head to the table, banging it on the flimsy wood. "How am I supposed to fix this?" he mumbled.

"I don't know if it's up to you to fix it, Mace. I think this one is on Tasha."

Mason rubbed a hand over his face, wincing at the rough stubble under his hand. "What is that supposed to mean?"

"My sister created this mess. She's got you wrapped around her little finger, and she knows it. She's known it for years. I think she took advantage of your feelings for her and, dare I say it, I think she might have used those feelings to her advantage."

Mason's head came up off the table, and he glared at Nate. "That's a pretty shitty thing to say about your sister."

Nate sighed and shook his head. "I know. Trust me, I feel like shit saying it." He cleared his throat. "Are you sure she didn't know you were in love with her? You never told her after you guys started this dating thing?"

"No, I didn't tell her," Mason muttered. "It's not really the best way to start a relationship. 'Hey Tasha, I've been in love with you for roughly twenty years. No pressure though.'"

"If you had just told her—"

Mason groaned. "Don't start that crap again."

Nate smacked his hand on the table. "I am gonna start this crap again." He leaned over the table, face drawn tight, brow furrowed, fists clenched. "You've been sitting on your ass for far too long. You could have told her in high school or college, or any time in between."

"There was always someone else, Nate. Your sister bounced from guy to guy throughout high school and college. Every time she broke up with one, I was there, picking up the pieces, being the friend she needed. Then she'd brush me off and move onto the next guy, leaving me in the dust, again." Mason shot to his feet, irritation fueling his need to move. "I dated Allison because I was tired of waiting for Tasha."

"Yeah, we both know how well that went," Nate snapped. "It lasted what, ten, eleven months before she realized you were head over heels in love with another woman? And while you were with Allison, trying to get over my sister, Tasha ended up with Brick, the world's biggest asshole."

Mason swung around, his finger in Nate's face. "That was not my fault."

Nate planted his hands on the table and stared at Mason. "No, you're right. It wasn't your fault. But maybe you could have stopped it. Jesus, you keep blowing it with my sister, and it pisses me off. If ever there were two people in this world who belonged together, it's you two."

"Don't you think I know that?" Mason asked. "But I'm not the only one who blew it. Instead of falling for the guy standing right in front of her, the guy who stood up for her, gave her a shoulder to cry on, and supported her when she needed it, she kept hooking up with idiots who walked all over her and broke her heart. We both screwed up."

"I just hope you two can fix it. Because that's my sister, Mason, and as much as I care about you, if push comes to shove, I'll pick her over you every single time. It would be a shitty choice, a damn near impossible choice, but one I'll make if I have to. And it will be my sister."

Struck speechless at Nate's declaration, Mason swung around and stalked away, angry tears clouding his vision. He was almost to his room when he hit the corner of the coffee table with his bare foot.

"God dammit!" he yelped. The pain radiated up his leg, forcing him to hop a couple of feet on one foot. His fist connected with the wall beside his bedroom door, as all his anger and frustration boiled to the surface and exploded in a rain of drywall dust and paint chips.

Chapter 18

Natasha

"Go away, Avery," Natasha mumbled. She shoved her head under the pillow and pulled the blankets up to her chin. She didn't want to talk to her friend, her brother, to anybody.

"I'm just leaving you some water and a couple of ibuprofens," Avery whispered. "I have a feeling you're going to need it."

Natasha half-expected Avery to say something more, to lecture her, or maybe agree with her, something, but she heard the door to the spare bedroom click closed. She waited until she was sure Avery wasn't lurking outside the door, ready to burst back in and talk, before she pushed the pillow to the floor and struggled to sit up. The stupid blankets twisted around her stupid legs, and the fight to untangle herself had her in tears. She swiped at her eyes with the corner of the bedsheet, grabbed the water and pills, then downed them in two swallows.

She leaned against the headboard, eyes squeezed shut as she prayed not to vomit. This was by far the worst hangover she'd had since college. Unfortunately, this hangover didn't come with memory loss; she remembered every detail of the previous day, from the photo shoot to the lovemaking, ending with the colossal fight witnessed by five or six dozen of Nate's closest friends.

Just thinking about the fight made heat rush to her cheeks and her heart race. It mortified her they'd fought in front of all those people, and that she'd said the things she said and Mason had said the things he'd said. Maybe she would stay in this room forever, then she wouldn't have to show her face to her friends ever again.

Not only was Natasha embarrassed, but she was pissed and hurt, too. Mason intentionally hurt her feelings, saying things he knew would rip her apart and destroy her. The man was intimately connected to her life, knew everything about her, even her dirtiest secrets, her heartbreaks and pain, and he'd thrown it in her face to hurt her.

Of course, she was no angel. She'd done the same to him, mocking him for not telling her how he felt about her all these years. She'd wanted to hurt him, to make him feel like she felt.

What were they doing? Why were they purposefully trying to hurt each other, lashing out, intent on causing pain? They were friends.

Or were they?

They'd crossed the line friends shouldn't cross; once that line was crossed, there was no going back. Natasha had known that going in, and so had Mason. Their fight the previous night meant the end of not only their so-called relationship, but the end of a twenty-year friendship.

The thought terrorized her and caused an ache deep in her soul, an ache she didn't think would easily heal.

"Oh, god," Natasha moaned, as realization hit her. She rolled to her side and pulled the blankets tight around herself. There was only one reason the end of her friendship with Mason could hurt so badly.

"Am I in love with Mason?" she whispered to herself.

—

Avery left her alone for the rest of the day, sneaking in to leave a sandwich around noon and again with a cup of tea about three. Natasha mumbled thank you both times, but she didn't move.

Her phone went off intermittently, but she didn't bother looking at it. Not now; maybe later, if her mood improved.

Around five, Natasha dragged herself out of bed and made her way down the hall to the bathroom. She could hear the TV playing downstairs and the quiet, murmured voices of Avery and Jacob. For a split second, she considered going downstairs, but she quickly changed her mind. She wasn't sure she could handle hanging out with the happy couple or the inevitable questions that might arise.

When she'd called Avery, after storming out of Nate and Mason's house, she'd kept her explanation to a bare minimum. The less said, the better. Somehow, Avery knew, and she didn't pry. She was a good friend.

Once she'd used the bathroom and washed her face, she returned to the bedroom. Natasha sipped the lukewarm tea and gnawed on the peanut butter-and-jelly sandwich as she checked her phone.

She had missed calls from Nate, Summer, and even her mother. There were two from Mason, and they had both come late last night. Had he really given up so quickly?

Natasha hit the button, held the phone to her ear, and waited. It only rang twice before he answered.

"Hey, sis. How are you?" Nate asked.

Natasha could tell he was being careful, weighing his words, feeling her out.

"I'm okay," she replied. "I ... uh, I wanted to apologize for last night. The fight, in front of your friends. It was stupid, and it shouldn't have happened. I'm sorry."

"Apology accepted. Where are you?"

"I'm at Avery and Jacob's," she explained. "I'm okay, I swear. And I really am sorry."

Nate sighed. "I appreciate the apology, Tash. The fight certainly has created quite the rumor mill around the bar, though."

"Great," she muttered. "Why does this feel like high school all over again?"

"Can I ask you a question, Tash?" her brother asked.

"I suppose," she said.

"What are your intentions with Mason?"

Natasha snorted. "What are you? His mother?"

"Natasha."

She froze at the tone of her brother's voice. He was serious.

"I ... I don't know. At first, I thought maybe we could be friends with benefits, you know? Then I thought maybe we could date, have fun, maybe see if it took off. Nothing serious, though. I wasn't ready for serious, or at least I didn't think I was ready for serious."

"Are you ready now?"

"I don't know," Natasha whispered. "Do you think I screwed everything up?"

"Maybe," Nate said. "You've known him for twenty years. Not only is he my best friend, but he's your friend, too. You didn't think some friends-with-benefits thing might affect that friendship?"

"I didn't think about that." She sighed. "Or maybe I did, but I ignored the potential shit show it could cause. I haven't exactly been thinking clearly lately."

"Can I ask you another question?" Nate said.

Despite the urge to say no, Natasha mumbled, "Yes."

"Did you really not know?" he asked.

"Know what?" she inquired, though she suspected she knew what Nate meant.

"You didn't know Mason was in love with you? All these years, everything he's done for you: being there time and time again, standing up for you, giving you a shoulder to cry on, all of it. You didn't know?"

Natasha sighed. This was the question she'd been asking herself all night. Had she known Mason was in love with her? Did she know it and choose to ignore it?

"Maybe I knew," she admitted. "But I think I ignored it. Because everyone kind of expected me and Mason to end up together, you know? You remember how Mom and Dad joked about it, and our friends thought it was funny to tease us and call us a couple? I so badly wanted to believe Mason was nothing more than a friend, so I ignored the hints I saw that showed he might want more. After a while, he was just Mason. If I needed a friend, I knew I could count on him. It never occurred to me he might read more into it."

"Even after you started to date?" Nate asked.

"No," Natasha snapped. "I didn't say that. The problem is, I didn't think. My heart led me, not my head. I was stupid."

"I'm going to sound like a broken record, but you need to talk to Mason. And you need to decide what you want from him. I know what he wants from you, and I think you do, too. Now you have to decide if you're willing to give him what he wants."

"You make it sound so easy," Natasha said.

"I know I do. And I also know it's difficult. Talk to him, Tasha. Don't leave this hanging between the two of you. You'll regret it if you do."

Natasha heard a faint crash through the phone, and then Nate cursed under his breath. "I gotta go. I hired a new server, and I think my glassware may be in trouble. If you need me, you know where to find me. I love you, sis."

"Love you too, Nathaniel." Natasha disconnected the call and tossed the phone on the bed. She leaned over, her head in her hands. Just thinking about talking to Mason made her stomach queasy. She threw herself back on the bed, one arm over her eyes.

Tomorrow. I'll talk to him tomorrow.

———

Tomorrow turned into two days and then three, and before Natasha knew it, it had been a week since she'd been home. Avery told her she could stay as long as she wanted. Even Jacob encouraged her to take her time deciding what she wanted to do.

She went back and forth to work and avoided the bar. She met Nate for lunch at Roselli's and got him to bring her some clothes. He was nice enough not to push her on the Mason issue. When she was at Avery and Jacob's, she hid in the bedroom, pretending to sleep when she was really moping. Work was her safe space; since the busy summer season had ended, the theater was empty all the time. She could hide out in her makeshift office at the back of the stage or pretend to clean the prop room or costume closet. Anything to avoid thinking about Mason.

Saturday night, she was in her office at the theater, supposedly finishing up paperwork when what she was really doing was reexamining the last twenty years of her life, going over every moment of time she'd spent with Mason. She realized at two in the morning how much she had ignored, intentionally and unintentionally.

Every time she broke up with one of her so-called boyfriends, Mason was there to pick up the pieces. He'd take her out for ice cream, order her favorite—chocolate with rainbow sprinkles—without even asking her what she wanted. Mason would listen to her talk, let her ramble on and on about the mess her life had become, and he never judged. He listened.

"Nat!"

Hearing her name being called in the empty theater made her jump. She shoved herself to her feet and stepped out of her office onto the black stage.

"Hello? Avery, is that you?"

"Where the hell are you?" Avery shouted. "It's so damn dark in here I can't see my hand in front of my face."

"Hold on!" Natasha took two steps to the right and hit the switch on the wall, illuminating the stage in the fluorescent light.

Avery stood at the bottom of the stairs leading to the stage, shielding her eyes with her hand.

Natasha smiled at her friend. "What are you doing here? It's late. I thought you'd be home by now."

"Jacob has a late class, so I thought I'd find you." She held up the plastic bag in her hand. "I stopped by the bar. Nate sent food; he said you probably hadn't eaten all day."

Natasha nodded. "He's right. Come on up. We'll eat in my office."

Avery hurried up the short set of stairs and across the stage. She ducked into the office and took a seat. "It's creepy in here when it's dark."

Natasha laughed. "I like it. I guess after spending so many years on stage, I'm used to it. The quiet of an empty theater is what I like the most. It lets me think."

Avery pulled food from the bag while Natasha grabbed waters and plastic utensils from a stash in the corner. "Oh, and how's that working for you?"

Natasha sighed as she sank into her squeaky office chair. "I don't know. I still don't know what to say to Mason. And every day that goes by makes it harder. He's going to think I don't care or that I don't want to fix this thing between us."

"Do you want to fix it?" Avery asked.

Natasha nibbled on a French fry and stared at a spot above Avery's head. "Yeah, I do. But it's weird, you know. Mason's supposedly in love with me, but sometimes I'm not even sure he knows me."

Avery narrowed her eyes. "I'm not so sure about that."

Natasha opened her mouth to protest, but Avery held up her

hand. "Hear me out. Mason's always been around, right? I'd be willing to guess Mason knows you better than you know yourself."

"That's not possible," Natasha protested.

"Can I ask you a question?" Avery said. "Or maybe a couple of questions?"

"Yeah, of course."

"Does Brick know you don't like beer?"

"That's a weird question." Natasha snorted.

"Just answer it."

"Um, no, he doesn't. I guess I never told him I don't like beer."

"Okay," Avery continued, "does he know your favorite ice cream? Does Brick know you love baseball, but you don't like football? Does he know your favorite movie is *For the Love of the Game*? Does he know you didn't learn to drive until you were seventeen? Or that you've wanted to be an actress since you were a little girl? Does he know any of that stuff?"

Natasha swallowed the French fry that had turned to a lump in her mouth. "I ... I don't know. I don't think so. Why are you asking me these things?"

"Does Mason know?"

Natasha snorted. "Of course, he does. How could he not know? We've known each other forever."

Avery sat back and crossed her arms over her chest. "Nat, I haven't known you as long as Mason, but I know all that about you. I also know that you change when you date somebody. You try to mold yourself into someone you're not in order to please the guy you're with. You *act* like the girlfriend they want."

"I ... I do not." The words came out in a whisper, as if the words knew they weren't true even as they left her mouth. Natasha put her head in her hands and before she realized what was happening, her life and the boyfriends in it flashed through her head.

Reggie, her high school boyfriend: he wanted the beauty queen, the popular girl, the girl that made all the other guys envious. Natasha turned into exactly that, spending money on clothes, makeup, her hair and nails, anything to impress Reggie. He dumped her for a former girlfriend, the prom queen.

Mason picked up the pieces, reminding her that there was more to her than her looks.

Next up was Mike, a college sophomore, looking for the cute girl who was mature enough to deal with him. That lasted just a few months, even after Natasha did everything in her power to appear mature and sophisticated: ignoring her same-age friends, purging her room of her childhood memories, redecorating it into a sophisticated room fit for a college student. Mike broke up with her because she was too young.

Once again, Mason had been there, comforting her when she needed him most. He helped her unpack her stuffed animals and posters, even rehanging her favorites on her bedroom walls.

It had been the same with Dave and Bobby, guys who never really knew her, never appreciated her for her. Because she never showed them the real her. Natasha gave them what they wanted; she became the girl they wanted. And when those relationships were over, it was Mason she turned to for comfort.

Brick was the worst. His dislike of her twin brother and his jealousy of Mason—something she'd never understood until now—forced her to push both of them away. She'd hidden herself away in a dark depressing apartment, determined to make her relationship with the selfish jackass work; Natasha was sure she could make it work if she just tried harder to be what Brick wanted. In the end, it hadn't mattered what she did. Brick didn't love her and probably never had.

After finding Brick in bed with that co-ed, when she'd gone to her brother's looking for sanctuary, it had been Mason she'd really wanted to see. Because Mason would make it better.

Mason made everything better.

Over the last twenty years, she had ignored the one man

in her life who would have given her the world. She kept him at arm's length and convinced herself that he was only a friend, nothing more.

Mason was always there whenever she needed him. For the longest time, she believed it was because of Nate, because he was her twin's best friend, and he was looking out for his best friend's sister. But the more she thought about it, the more she realized Mason was there because *she* needed him. It wasn't out of obligation to a friend or a misguided need to be the good guy; Mason looked out for her because he cared about her.

Because he loves me.

"Oh my god, Avery, I'm an idiot." Natasha brushed at the tears trickling down her face. "What have I done?"

Avery put her hand on her friend's arm and squeezed gently. "Nothing you can't fix."

"I have to go."

Natasha snatched her car keys off the desk and grabbed her backpack. She checked her watch. Hopefully, he was home.

Chapter 19

Mason

Mason hadn't seen Natasha in a week, not since the fight that had ended in the utter and complete devastation of his hopes and dreams. He'd done his best to distract himself: working long hours at the studio to facilitate the ownership change, and even picking up a couple extra EMT shifts, along with running every morning and sometimes late at night. He'd shove his earbuds in, playing his music at deafening levels in order to drown out his thoughts.

Tonight was no exception. He worked until almost nine before he headed home, ignoring Nate's texts suggesting he join him at the bar. Ten minutes after he got home, he was out the door again, the rhythmic pounding of his feet on the pavement in sync with the rhythm playing in his ears. The combination temporarily pushed all thoughts of Natasha and his screwed-up life out of his head.

Mason ran until his heart pounded, sweat ran down his face and chest, and his lungs were on fire. It was almost eleven when he unlocked the sliding glass door and stepped inside. Mason headed straight for the fridge; he needed water. The light barely illuminated the small room as he flipped it on over the kitchen sink. He grabbed a water, twisted off the top, and tossed it in the trash. Then he downed the entire bottle standing in the middle of the kitchen.

He unzipped his sweatshirt and yanked the earbuds from his ears before he tossed the empty bottle in the trash can at the end of the counter. He had only taken a couple of steps toward his room when he noticed her.

Natasha sat perched on the edge of the couch: head down, elbows on her knees, red hair hanging in her face. One of her legs bounced up and down, a nervous tic she had developed when she was anxious. She clasped her hands together between her legs, gripping each other so tight her knuckles were white.

Mason froze, stopping short of actually stepping from the kitchen into the living room, almost as if there were an invisible barrier between him and Natasha. She looked up, and they stared at each other from across the room, neither of them speaking. The tension was thick enough to cut with a knife.

"Hi," Mason said. He couldn't think of anything pithier than that. His brain froze along with his body.

"Hi," she replied. Natasha licked her lips and rubbed her hands together repeatedly, two other nervous habits she'd gained over the years. "I'm sorry if I startled you."

Mason took a step into the living room, just over the threshold from the kitchen. "I wasn't expecting you."

Natasha laughed, the sound hollow. "I almost didn't come in. I sat in the car for fifteen minutes talking myself into coming in here. Then I get inside, all set to talk to you, and you're not here. I almost left a dozen times."

He inched closer. "But you didn't."

"I should have. I wasn't sure you'd even talk to me." Natasha squirmed in her seat. "But Avery convinced me we needed to clear the air. Along with a few dozen phone calls from my brother."

"Okay, let's clear the air. You first." Mason nodded at her.

Natasha took a deep breath before speaking, then she let the words out in one long exhale. "I've behaved horribly. I've treated you horribly."

Mason shook his head before she even finished speaking. "It's okay—"

"No, it's not," she interrupted. "It's most definitely not okay. And I won't let you excuse my behavior, not anymore. I embarrassed us in front of all those people, some of them complete strangers. I can't believe we said those things to each other. We are two of the stupidest people on earth."

"I agree with that."

"Well, that's good." Natasha pushed herself off the couch and took two steps toward him. Her arms were crossed, hugging herself, protecting herself, and closing herself off because she felt vulnerable. He'd seen her do it dozens of times. She didn't look at him; instead, she stared at a spot on the floor between his shoes.

"I'm sorry," she whispered. "I freaked out. When I found out you had been in love with me for years, it screwed me up. I can't live up to the image of me you've created in your head. I'm not some woman to put on a pedestal and compare with every other woman on earth. I'm just me. I want someone who wants the real me, someone who sees the real Natasha Garin."

Mason shook his head, a smile teasing the corners of his mouth. "I know the real you, Natasha," he said. "I've seen you at your best, and I've seen you at your worst. I remember you in your unicorn t-shirt and bright purple shorts that you wore every day the summer after fifth grade. When you were so sick you had to sleep on the bathroom floor, covered in one of your grandmother's quilts, I was there. I've seen you falling down drunk and stone-cold sober. I know you can kick your brother's ass at Scrabble, but you let him win because it makes him feel good. You love chocolate ice cream with rainbow sprinkles, especially after a breakup. I know you had a pixie cut and braces in sixth grade."

Natasha blushed and shook her head. "Mason—"

"Let me finish." He closed the distance between them, cupped her cheek in his hand, and forced her to look up at him. "On prom night, you looked so gorgeous it made my heart stop. And when we graduated high school, you were all nervous and giggly, telling Nate you were going to call him Nathaniel because Nate sounded too immature." Mason took a deep breath, drinking Natasha in as she stared up at him. "You are the only woman I have seen for twenty years, even when I tried not to. I've seen you enough to know I am in love with you, Tasha. I love every single thing about you."

"Stop," Natasha murmured. A tear slid down her cheek.

Mason shook his head and slipped his arm around her waist. He pulled her flush against him and brushed a kiss across her lips.

"I can't. Not until you know that I'm in love with you. The real you. The woman you are when you're not pretending to be someone else. I don't need you to be something you're not because you are what I want."

Natasha grabbed the front of his hoodie and pulled in a breath so ragged, Mason felt it in his core.

"Say that again."

Mason rested his forehead on hers and closed his eyes. "I am in love with you. Since we were six years old, I have been in love with you. I love everything about you: all the good and all the crazy, even all the stuff that makes me insane. It doesn't matter because I love you. No matter what."

Natasha rested her cheek against his chest. "I always thought you and I would be friends forever. Even when we gave this dating thing a shot, I wasn't sure it would last. I didn't know what you wanted in a woman; I didn't know how to act to make you fall for me. I thought I had to act a certain way to get you to love me when all I had to do was be myself. I needed to stop pretending to be something I wasn't."

"And now?" Mason asked.

"I don't need to put on an act to earn your love," Natasha said. "I can be me."

"I want you to be you," Mason said. "That's all I ever wanted. *You*. Not a version of you that you create to make me love you. Just you."

Natasha nodded. "I can do that. I want to do that. I'm done pretending to be someone I'm not." She looked up at him, her eyes filled with tears. "I love you, Mace. I'm sorry it took me so long to realize it. But I love you."

Finally, after all these years, it felt as if a weight lifted from his shoulders with her proclamation. He slipped his hand into her hair and tilted her head back. The smile didn't leave his face even as his lips met hers. Her mouth opened to let him in, his tongue sliding against hers as their breath mingled and their bodies pressed together.

Mason lifted her up, her legs sliding around his waist while her arms were around his neck. The kiss deepened, the passion between them fueled by the years of denying their true feelings. Mason crossed the room in three long strides, hit the bedroom door with his shoulder, and stepped inside. His lips never left hers as he lowered her to the floor and kicked the door shut.

—

Mason rolled over, opened one eye, and checked the clock on the bedside table. Two a.m. Natasha slept soundly beside him, nothing visible but the top of her head, tendrils of red hair spread across the pillow. He eased out of bed, careful not to wake Natasha, pulled on his sweatpants and t-shirt, and slipped out of the bedroom. Nate sat on the couch with the TV on, sound down low, and the remote in his hand. He grinned at Mason.

"Hey, bro. Is that my sister's car outside?" Nate asked.

Mason nodded and pointed at his bedroom door over his shoulder. "Yeah. She's asleep."

Nate chuckled quietly. "Does that mean what I think it means? You guys made up?"

"We did," Mason said. He sat down on the opposite end of the couch. "I think we might be in a good place. Are you okay with that?"

Nate snorted. "Do you even have to ask? I'm definitely okay with it. Who wouldn't want their best friend dating their sister?"

"Just about every guy in the world." Mason chuckled. "But, seriously, you are okay with it, right? I don't want this to affect our friendship."

"It won't. If you hadn't fixed this whole thing," he gestured at Mason and the bedroom door, "that would have affected our friendship. This is a good thing. You and Tash belong together; you always have. I'm glad you finally figured it out." Nate put his hands on his knees and pushed himself off the couch. "Now, I'm off to bed. I thought you weren't ever going to come out of there. I've been waiting for over an hour."

Nate slapped his friend on the shoulder, muttered good night, and disappeared into his room. Mason shook his head and smiled. Hopefully, Nate's feelings wouldn't change.

Mason's bedroom door opened, and Natasha poked her head out the door. "Hey."

"Hi," Mason whispered. "I thought you were asleep?"

"I'm hungry. Do we have any ice cream?"

"I think so. What do you want? Chocolate with rainbow sprinkles?"

"Oh, no." Natasha laughed. "That's breakup ice cream. Do we have any vanilla and chocolate syrup?"

"I think we do," Mason said. "Why don't you go back to bed, and I'll get the ice cream?"

Natasha skipped across the room and put her hands on his

shoulders. "Don't take too long." She kissed the corner of his mouth before spinning around and returning to the bedroom.

"Oh, I won't," Mason whispered at her departing form. "I'm not wasting another minute of my time with you."

THE END

Book Club Questions:

1. Why do you think the author chose this particular book title? If you could pick a different title for the book, what would it be and why?

2. Do you think Natasha knew about Mason's feelings for her from the beginning?

3. What, if anything, did you dislike about Natasha? What did you dislike about Mason?

4. Should Mason have told Natasha how he felt about her years before? Would it have affected the outcome of their relationship?

5. Should Nate have intervened in the burgeoning relationship between his friend and his sister? Or was he right to let them figure it out?

6. Who was at fault for the fight? Natasha or Mason?

7. Would you forgive Natasha if you were Mason? Or vice versa?

8. Do you think Mason and Natasha were meant to be together?

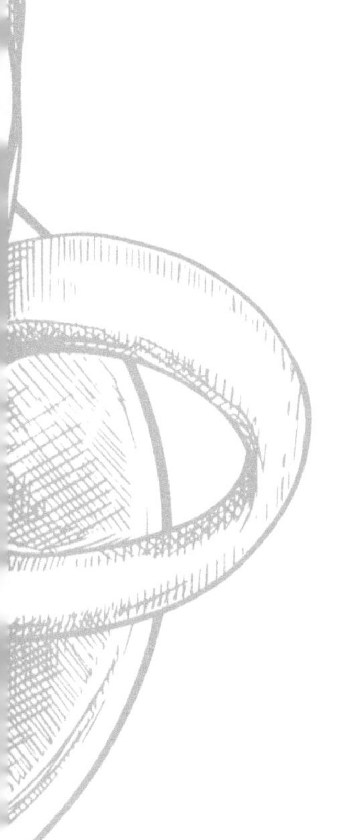

Right Kind of Wrong

Dedication

To the bookworms and coffee fanatics. You are my people.

Chapter 1

Nate

A noticeable energy filled the room, a mixture of anticipation and excitement. Nate approached the table, eyeing the eight-ball perched precariously near the corner pocket and the cue ball in the center of the table. He contemplated his shot, envisioning it in his head.

He leaned over, lined up the pool cue to ensure the correct angle, and took a few practice strokes to gauge exactly how hard he needed to hit the ball for an exact strike. The room fell silent, the only sound the faint hum of the overhead fluorescent lights.

Nate dragged in a deep breath, relaxed his shoulders, and tapped the white ball. It rolled smoothly across the green felt and hit the eight ball, which dropped into the corner pocket with a satisfying thud.

An eruption of cheers and applause exploded around him as he dropped the cue on the table and raised his arms above his head.

"There it is!" he shouted. "Whoo-hoo!" He spun in a circle, laughing at the shocked faces of his competitors.

A chorus of boos echoed back at him. He flipped off the

— 161 —

crowd as he headed back to the bar. Why anybody bothered to play pool against him, he'd never know. He couldn't lose.

Nate stepped behind the bar, grabbed a water from the cooler, and chugged it. He did a quick check of the bar to make sure his servers were on the floor and the customers were being helped.

A cute brunette sat on a stool across from him and smiled. He dropped the empty water bottle in the recycling bin and smiled at her as he leaned on the bar.

"Hi, I'm Nate," he said.

"I'm Mary," she said. "That was a great game of pool you played. Do you practice a lot?"

He nodded. "Every day. It's not too difficult when you own the place."

Mary propped her chin on her hand, her grin widening. "Wait? You own this place? Really?"

He smirked. "Yes, really."

"That's cool."

"I've never seen you in here before," Nate said. "Do you go to Lakeside College?"

"Yes. I'm getting my masters in anthropology," she explained. "I got my bachelor's degree from U of M, though."

"So, you're new in town." Nate tapped his fingers on the bar and gave her his best smile. "What can I get you to drink?"

"How about a White Claw? Raspberry?" she replied.

He did his best not to roll his eyes. Why did every girl who came through the door of the Time Out Bar & Grill have to be so cliché?

"Do you have your ID?" he asked.

Mary giggled, took her ID out of her back pocket, and set it in front of him. Nate examined it, looking for the telltale signs of a fake.

She narrowed her eyes and acted offended. "It's real, I promise." She sat up straighter. "I'm twenty-three."

He raised an eyebrow. "Twenty-three, huh?" He squinted at her license and turned it in the light, catching the holographic image in the corner.

"You're right, it is real," he said, holding it out to her.

Mary took it from him, her fingers brushing his. Nate grabbed a White Claw from the cooler, popped it open, and handed it to her.

"So, *Mary*, do you have a boyfriend? Girlfriend? Significant other?"

"I'm single," she said. "How about you?"

"Oddly enough, I am single, too." Nate chuckled. "Why don't you hang out here for a while, and we'll get to know each other?"

"I think that sounds like fun," she replied. "Lots and lots of fun."

———

Nate held Mary's hand loosely in his as they tiptoed through the living room and out the front door. They stepped outside, and he shut the door behind them. Mary shivered and snuggled up to him.

"It's cold," she muttered.

"Because it is October in Montana. It won't be much longer until we have snow." He glanced down at her bare legs and back up. "It's time to put the shorts away."

Mary rolled her eyes. "I like my shorts." She kissed him on the cheek. "Call me later?"

He shrugged. "If I have time."

"Maybe I'll stop by the bar after my class this afternoon. We can have lunch."

Nate shook his head. "We're closed today, so no lunch. Look, you're cold. Go get in your car."

She gave him a funny look before she hurried down the driveway to her car parked on the street. She waved at him as she pulled away from the curb. He raised his hand in a half-assed wave and opened the door.

"New girlfriend?" a voice said behind him.

Nate jumped, smacking his elbow on the doorknob. "Ouch. Damn it, Tasha, don't sneak up on me."

Nate's twin sister, Natasha, put her hands up and giggled. "I wasn't! Sheesh."

"What are you doing up so early?" he asked. He stepped inside and kicked the door closed.

"It's not that early. It's after seven," Natasha replied. "I have a full day at the theater. I assume you are up early because you had to say goodbye to your new girlfriend."

He sighed and rolled his eyes. "She's not my girlfriend. She's a girl I met at the bar last week."

"How long is this one going to last?" Natasha asked.

"I don't know. Not much longer." Nate shrugged. "Why don't you worry about your relationship with Mason and stay out of my business?"

His sister stuck her tongue out at him. "My relationship is fine, thank you. Make me some coffee while I get dressed. Mason will be out soon."

Mason was Nate's best friend, roommate, and Tasha's boy-friend. He had been friends with the Garin twins since they were kids. The three of them grew up together. Mason had been in love with Natasha their whole lives, but it wasn't until recently that the two of them started dating. Nate was thrilled for them.

Even though he was happy that his best friend and his sister were together, seeing his sister walking around in Mason's T-shirts, or watching them hold hands or cuddle, was weird. Worse than any of that, Nate despised hearing the two of them through the thin bedroom walls.

It had gotten so bad; he had to talk to Mason about it. It was the most unbelievably awkward conversation he'd ever had with his best friend. Just thinking about it again made him want to scrub his brain out with bleach.

Nate started a pot of coffee and took a pop tart out of the box in the cupboard. He ripped open the package and ate it while he waited for the coffee to finish.

Mason came into the kitchen, dressed for his morning run in shorts and a zipped-up hoodie. He had his long, black hair pulled into a bun at the back of his head, and his shoes were in his hand. He sat at the table to put them on. "You're up early," he said. "Where are you going?"

Nate talked around a mouthful of pop tart. "Work. We're deep cleaning the bar, so we're shut down for the day. I have the staff coming in to do a deep dive into every nook and cranny. I need to grab some cleaning supplies on my way in, and I wanted to get an early start." He grabbed a cup from the cupboard and tossed it to Mason, who caught it with one hand.

"Hey, you want to go get dinner with us tonight?" Mason asked. "Bring a date." He grinned as he poured coffee into the cup and grabbed sugar packets and creamer. "What's her name this week?"

Nate scowled. "I'm not seeing anybody right now."

"Bullshit," Tasha yelled from the other room. "What's-her-name just left." She came around the corner, dressed in jeans and a sweater, hopped onto the counter, and sat down, her legs swinging. Mason stepped between her legs, slid his arms around her, and kissed her with a loud smack.

"We're not serious," Nate insisted.

"You're never serious," Natasha muttered.

"You took the words out of my mouth, babe." Mason glanced at him. "What's wrong with this one?"

Nate sighed. "Nothing. I don't know. Maybe I'm tired of the dating scene."

Mason snorted. "Or have you finally blown through all the women in Lakeside?"

"Wow, you're hilarious," Nate deadpanned. He grabbed his car keys and phone off the table by the front door. He couldn't stomach another minute with his sister and Mason. "I'll let you know about dinner."

He slammed the door harder than intended and almost dropped his phone, juggling it briefly before securing it, only to have it go off right away. It was a text from Brooke, his assistant manager, making him grunt in frustration. She was running late for work.

It's going to be a long day.

The sound of banging drew Nate's attention to the house next door. His neighbor stood on her front stoop, staring at her door. Her blonde was piled on top of her head in a messy bun, her too-large glasses perched on the end of her nose, and her oversized sweatshirt hung to the middle of her thighs. A backpack sat on the ground by her feet, and she scowled, marring her pretty face.

"Are you okay?" he yelled.

His neighbor jumped and shrank into her sweatshirt. She nodded her head so hard her hair fell out of her bun, the soft curls framing her face.

Nate walked a few feet onto her front lawn. "Are you sure?" he asked.

"Yes, thank you," she replied, pushing her glasses up her nose. She spoke so quietly he barely heard her.

He shrugged, continued across the lawn, and got into his car. He started it, but he didn't leave right away. Instead, he watched as his neighbor pushed open her window and wiggled through it, her shoe falling off and landing in the dirt as she kicked and squirmed. Nate shook his head and chuckled. What the hell was she doing?

It occurred to him that he didn't know her name, and they'd

never spoken. She kept to herself and avoided any contact with anyone in the neighborhood. Mason was wrong. He hadn't met and dated *all* the women in Lakeside.

Not yet, anyway.

Chapter 2

Faith

Coffee spilled over the edge of the cup onto Faith's hand, burning it. She cursed under her breath, dropped her backpack on the ground, and put her cup on the windowsill. The front door swung closed behind her while she worked on getting the lid on the cup nice and tight—something she apparently hadn't done earlier. After she double-checked that the lid was actually in place and her coffee wouldn't spill, she picked up her backpack, opened the front pocket, and reached for her keys.

They weren't there.

Faith closed her eyes, and immediately the image of them on the table between two stacks of books popped into her head.

"Dammit," she muttered.

She wiggled the doorknob, knowing it was no use. She always locked it when she walked out the door. Always. She banged her fist against the door.

She jumped when she heard someone yell, "Are you okay?" from across the lawn.

It was one of her neighbors, not that she bothered to look up.

She kept her head down and nodded so hard her stupid hair fell out of the loose bun she'd put it in.

"Are you sure?" he asked.

Faith swallowed down her nerves. "Yes, thank you," she called without looking up. She pushed her glasses up her nose.

At first, she wasn't sure he heard her, but after a few seconds, his car door opened and closed.

Thank God.

She didn't have the strength to deal with some guy swooping in to rescue her, and she didn't need anyone else to solve her problems.

The window next to the door was open about an inch, just enough for her to get her fingers in and push it open. It wasn't a big window, but there was room for her to climb through it.

"Okay, here goes nothing," she mumbled under her breath.

Faith shimmied through the window. Her shoe slipped off, but that wasn't a problem. At least she wouldn't be walking around outside without it, since it was on the porch. The pile of books under the window tipped over, and the lamp fell off the table and hit the wall, but she made it inside. Heathcliff stared at her disdainfully from his perch on the kitchen counter. Her cat had no patience for her antics.

Once she had her keys in hand—and her fingers wrapped around them for good measure—she stepped outside, re-locked the door, and grabbed her things, including her shoe. She checked her watch.

Yep, she was definitely going to be late for work.

Sure enough, Faith walked through the front door of the library ten minutes late. Caroline Stover, her boss, and friend, watched her as she stumbled in, set her things behind the desk, and dropped into her chair.

"Rough morning?" Caroline asked.

"I locked my keys in the house and had to climb through the

window to get them," she replied, poking at her glasses again. "So, yeah, a little rough."

Caroline snorted and covered her mouth with her hand.

"Don't laugh at me," Faith mumbled.

Caroline shrugged. "I'm sorry, but I'm picturing you wiggling through a window. You're so tall, it must have been a treat."

Her friend was right. She was tall—six feet, to be exact. It had been an issue her whole life and one of the many, many reasons things had been difficult for her as a child.

Faith closed her eyes and smiled. She probably looked like a total klutz and completely ridiculous as she wiggled through her window. A giggle escaped her.

"It wasn't easy." She shook her head. "I can't believe I had to do that."

"You need one of those rock things where you hide your keys," Caroline said.

Faith nodded. "I'll order one from Amazon. Now, can we please stop talking about it and get to work?"

Caroline laughed. "Sure. It's not like there won't be something else to talk about later today."

She rolled her eyes. "As much as I'd like to argue with you, you're probably right."

———

She sat on the floor in the back room surrounded by books, paper cuts on her hands, dust in her hair, and an ache in her neck from looking down for the last two hours.

There was no place she'd rather be.

If someone told her ten years ago she'd be a librarian in a small town in Montana, she'd have laughed at them. Working as a librarian was a dream, but she never thought she'd get there. It required a college education—a master's degree—and when she was younger, she didn't know how she was supposed to get one of those. According to three different foster parents, a counselor at one of the five different high schools she attended, and three of her four case managers, foster kids rarely went to college. Her dream of being a librarian was unlikely to come to fruition. If she hadn't met Professor Hudspeth, she wouldn't be doing what she loved.

"Faith?"

"Back here," she yelled.

Caroline came around the corner. "How's it going?"

She smiled. "Aside from being covered in dust and having about thirty paper cuts, it's going great. I'm almost done sorting the books from the back room. They've been entered into the system. Next up is organizing and tagging the ones we're keeping and donating those we don't want anymore."

"By donating, do you mean 'taking them home?'" Caroline asked.

Faith shook her head and laughed. "It's not my fault one perk of my job is rescuing books that need a home."

"Your place isn't big enough to hold all those books."

She shrugged. "I just need some bookcases."

Caroline rolled her eyes. "There aren't enough bookcases in the world. Anyway, I came up here to see if you were done. It's after six."

Faith pushed her glasses up her nose and squinted at the clock on the wall. "It is? I didn't realize it had gotten so late."

"A few of us are going out for drinks," her boss said. "Would you like to go?"

She shook her head. Caroline asked her this question every Friday. And every week, her answer was the same. "No, but thank you for thinking of me. I have to go home and feed Heathcliff."

Caroline crouched beside her. "You know, you need to get out there and socialize. Make some friends."

"I have friends," she protested.

"You have me," Caroline murmured. "And your cat. You need more people in your life."

Faith must have looked as horrified as she felt, because Caroline smiled gently and squeezed her shoulder.

"Maybe next time."

She waited until Caroline was gone, then she got to her feet and brushed off her hands and jeans. She collected her things from the drawer in her desk and said goodbye to Josie, the evening librarian. Next to the back door was a large bag filled with books they had taken out of circulation. She picked them up, carried them to her car, and put them in the back seat. More books to add to her collection.

Faith didn't need friends. She had books. They were more than enough company.

Chapter 3
Nate

"Nate! Phone! I think it's your girlfriend."

The bar phone clattered on the counter as Brooke dropped it, then she grabbed the bucket of soapy water and headed for the back room.

"Thanks," he muttered after her, though she probably didn't hear him. He propped the phone between his head and shoulder. "Hello?"

"Hey, it's Mary."

He closed his eyes and took a deep breath. Mary wasn't his girlfriend. He never used the word girlfriend when referring to the women he dated; he hadn't used that word since Elle. He might never use it because of her. Besides, he didn't have the energy for a relationship. They were friends, *not* girlfriends. He devoted all of his free time to the Time Out Bar & Grill.

"Hi," he mumbled.

"You didn't answer your phone." Her voice was sharp and biting.

"I don't have it on me," he explained. "I'm *busy*."

"Oh, okay. Well, I thought we could go to a movie tonight or something," Mary said. "Are you free?"

Nate pinched the bridge of his nose. The last few days, he'd gotten the feeling it was time to move on. When the women wanted more—more dates, more commitment, more *anything*—he broke it off. Love was complicated, and he struggled with it more than most people realized. He didn't want or need it screwing up his life again.

"Listen, Mary, we need to talk."

The breakup took less than two minutes; Nate was better at breakups than relationships. He usually stayed friends with the women he broke up with, a necessity when he owned a popular bar in a small college town. He couldn't afford to alienate anyone.

Brooke, who had reappeared while he was on the phone, stared at him as he hung up, shaking her head.

"What?" he grumbled.

"Are you ever going to find a woman?" she asked.

"Are you?" Nate snapped.

She narrowed her eyes. "We're not talking about me. We're talking about you. When are you going to stop making your way through the girls in this town and find yourself a woman?"

He chuckled. "I find plenty of women."

"Yeah, a new one every week. Don't you want someone to love?"

Nate scowled. "Have you been talking to my sister? Because this sounds a lot like a conversation she and I had recently."

Brooke sighed. "No, I haven't been talking to Natasha. We both care about you, though, so we want to see you happy."

"Who says I'm not happy?" he protested. "I'm having fun."

"There's more to life than parties and girls."

He rolled his eyes. "You know what? If I want to talk about my love life, I'll be sure to seek you out. Okay?"

His assistant manager laughed. "You're a piece of work, you know that, right?"

Nate winked. "It's why all the women love me."

"Not all of us, sweetheart," Brooke shot back. She took a deep breath. "I need a break. I'm going to run down to The Percolator for coffee. You want anything?"

"We have coffee here."

"No, we have thick, black goo made by you. I want real coffee made by a trained barista."

Nate made a face. "I'm good."

Brooke dropped her apron on the bar and grabbed her coat off the barstool. "I'll be back in ten. Stay out of trouble."

He threw a towel in Brooke's direction, but she was too far away to hit. Her laughter followed her out the door.

"Am I ever going to find a woman?" he muttered under his breath. "What a stupid question." He turned on the stereo in the corner and punched the volume button until the speakers shook and the window rattled. The music drowned out the constant barrage of annoying questions his brain threw at him. Maybe it would drown out Brooke when she came back.

———

It had been a long, weird day. After Brooke harassed him about finding love, he moped around, wondering if he was destined to be alone forever. He'd dated tons of women, but none of them made him want anything serious. His relationships—if they could be called that—got shorter with every girl who came along.

He parked on the street in front of his neighbor's house. The driveway was only big enough for two cars. After his sister moved in, they established the "last one home parks on the street" rule. To his permanent irritation, he was almost always the last one home. Late nights were one of the many hazards of owning and running a bar.

Nate was at the front door before he realized he had left his cell phone in his truck. He turned around and jogged back, taking a shortcut across his neighbor's lawn.

It was dark and because he stared at the ground as he headed across the lawn, still contemplating the shit show his love life had become, he didn't see his neighbor until it was too late. He slammed into her, hard enough to make her stumble back a few steps. The bag she had in her arms flew into the air, hit the ground, and burst open, books flying everywhere.

"Oh, shit! I'm sorry," Nate apologized. He dropped to one knee and scooped up several books. His fingers brushed against hers as they reached for the same book, an electric shock jolting him at her touch.

His neighbor yanked her hand back, wincing as if a snake had bitten her. He stared at her, seeing her for the first time.

She was tall, almost as tall as him, with legs that went on for miles. Her blonde hair hung to her waist, her clothes were too large as if she was hiding in them, her glasses were on the end of her nose, and she had a scowl on her face. How the hell had he never noticed her? He couldn't take his eyes off her as she stomped around the yard, grabbing books.

Nate got to his feet and grabbed some books near his feet. He walked across the lawn, stepped in front of her, and held them out to her with a hesitant smile.

She mumbled, "Thank you," took the books, and stacked them with the others.

"Are you okay?" he asked.

"I'm fine." She nodded, her voice barely above a whisper. She didn't look at him as she spoke, then she abruptly spun on her heel and rushed up the lawn to her front door.

"At least let me help you," he called after her.

"No, really, I'm fine," she yelled over her shoulder, even though she jostled the books in her arms as she struggled to unlock her door. "You... you have a good night." She stepped inside and slammed the door closed behind her.

"Perfect," Nate mumbled. "Now women are literally running away from me." He ran a hand through his hair and continued to his car. "Just perfect."

He got his phone and jogged back across his neighbor's yard, glancing at her window as he passed it, wondering if he'd catch another glimpse of her before he went inside. The curtains covering the window made that impossible.

"Hey," Mason called over his shoulder as soon as Nate stepped inside. He was on the couch with an open box of pizza in front of him, a beer, and the baseball game on TV. Exactly what he wanted.

Nate tossed his keys on the table by the door. "Where's Tash?"

"She went out with Avery," Mason answered.

He grinned. "So, I'm off the hook for dinner?"

"Yeah. I know you're upset since you were so excited to go out with us." He shook his head and chuckled. "Grab me another beer, will ya?"

Nate washed his hands and dried them on the towel hanging off the stove, then he opened the fridge, grabbed two beers, and returned to the living room. He handed a beer to Mason, took a slice of pizza, and sat down.

Mason glanced at him. "I need to talk to you," he said.

Nate shot his friend a dirty look. "I swear to God if you mention my love life, I will lay you out flat." He took a huge bite of pizza and chewed aggressively while staring at Mason.

"I'm not going to discuss your love life. Not to mention, your love life is the *last* thing I want to talk about." He put his beer on the table, grabbed the remote, and hit mute. "Me and Tasha are moving out."

The pizza in Nate's mouth was suddenly nothing but a lump of cold dough and congealed cheese. He forced himself to swallow it and took a drink of his beer to wash it down.

"You're... you're moving out?" Nate asked. "Both of you? Together?"

"Yes, both of us." Mason snorted. "We found a place on the other side of town, on the lake. A townhome. You know Van Brooks, right?"

Nate nodded.

"It's his wife's place. She lived there before they got married. Her father owns it and wants to rent it out," Mason explained. "I signed the lease agreement this afternoon."

"Oh. Um, wow." Nate sat back against the couch. "Okay."

"I know it's out of the blue," Mason said. "But Tasha and I have been talking about moving out for a couple of months. You know as well as I do this place is too small for the three of us. We're packed in here like sardines, tripping over each other, bumping into each other." Mason raised an eyebrow. "Overhearing things we don't want to overhear."

Nate exhaled and nodded. "Yeah, I get it. I do. It's weird, though? It never occurred to me you'd move out. I guess I never thought about it."

"We can't be roommates forever," Mason said. "We're not college students anymore, so it's not like we need to live together to save money. The bar is doing great, and the photography studio is picking up steam. We're adults; it's time we moved on to bigger and better things."

"Shit, that sounds scary." Nate chuckled. "But you're right. It probably is long past due for you and Tash to get your own place." He held out his hand. "I'm happy for you guys, bro. Seriously."

Mason shook Nate's hand and smiled. "Thanks." He narrowed his eyes and leaned close to his friend. "You're sure you're okay with this?"

He nodded. "Yeah, I am. My sister loves you. You two are great together. And I can finally have the bachelor's life I was meant to live. It couldn't be more perfect."

Mason grinned and slapped Nate on the back. "I told Tasha you'd be happy for us." He picked up his beer and unmuted the television.

"Yeah," he muttered. "Happy."

Chapter 4

Faith

Faith couldn't see where she was going, not only because it was dark, but because the bag of books she struggled to carry blocked her view and her glasses had slid down to the end of her nose, as usual. She prayed she wouldn't stumble like she'd done on multiple occasions, even when she had nothing obstructing her line of sight.

She headed across the lawn, holding the bag in one arm while she attempted to find her keys in the bottom of her backpack. Just as her fingers closed around them, somebody slammed into her, hard enough to make her stumble back a few steps, the bag in her hand tumbling to the ground and bursting open, books flying everywhere.

"Oh, shit, I'm sorry!"

It was Faith's neighbor, the cute one with the short, brown hair, blue eyes, perfect, sexy stubble, and confident gait. Faith figured his good looks were the reason he had a new girlfriend every week. He dropped to one knee at the same time she did and picked up several of the books. His fingers brushed hers as they both reached for the same book, an electric shock jolting her. She yanked her hand away, jumped to her feet, and snatched up the scattered books. When she turned around, her neighbor stood in front of her with books in his hand.

"Thank you," Faith whispered. She refused to make eye contact with him as she gingerly took the books from him and stacked them with the others. She scooped them up and got to her feet.

"Are you okay?" he asked.

She nodded. "I'm fine."

Hoping not to embarrass herself any further, she quickly picked up another book off the sidewalk, spun on her heel, and hurried to her front door, jostling the books in her arms as she battled with the lock.

"At least let me help you," he yelled after her.

"No, really, I'm fine. You... you have a good night." She shoved open the door, stepped inside, and slammed it closed behind her.

Faith tossed the books into the basket by the door, which was already overflowing, and turned on the lights. She pressed her hands to her flushed cheeks. That was the first time she'd spoken to her cute neighbor. He had smiled at her several times, though it was likely more out of politeness than anything else, and she was pretty sure he was the one who had called to her this morning.

Sometimes, she imagined responding to his smiles, flirting with him a little. But that was a dream. If she couldn't make eye contact with him, how could she flirt with him?

Faith shoved herself away from the door with an irritated sigh, pulled off her oversized sweater, and tossed it on the table. She grabbed two of the books off the pile she'd dropped in the basket and examined the spines as she made her way to the kitchen. She'd make some tea and lose herself in one of the new-to-her books for a few hours. It would take her mind off her run-in with her neighbor. He'd probably already forgotten about it.

———

Faith shivered, tucked her blanket around her legs, and snatched her cup off the table, hoping the hot tea would help her warm up. Unfortunately, it was empty.

Fall in Montana brought cooler weather. The weather changed quickly here, and winter swooped in every year, taking her by surprise. Lakeside, Montana, had been her home for six years, and she still hadn't adjusted to the sudden changes in temperatures. Faith couldn't believe there were people here who wore shorts and T-shirts when it was sixty degrees outside. She put on two pairs of socks in the middle of summer.

She picked up Heathcliff and put him on the floor, then she kicked off the blanket and grabbed her empty cup. A loud knock on her front door startled her. Her book fell to the floor, and the cup dropped from her hand onto the coffee table, landing on its side next to her battered copy of *Pride and Prejudice* and the newest Stephen King novel. Nobody ever knocked on her door, except salespeople or someone delivering food, especially at eight in the morning.

Faith jumped off the couch, but her feet tangled in the blanket on the floor and caused her to stumble forward, so she smacked her knee on the corner of the glass coffee table. Heathcliff darted out of her way and escaped into the bedroom.

"Ow," she mumbled under her breath as she limped across the living room to her front door. She balanced on one foot and rubbed her sore knee while she looked through the peephole.

Her neighbor, the cute one she'd collided with the night before, stood on her front stoop, with a cocky smirk on his perfectly chiseled face and his blue eyes flashing with what looked suspiciously like glee. He acted like he belonged there, casually leaning against the rail, a book in his hand.

Faith ducked, forgetting for a second that he couldn't see her. Her breath caught in her throat, and she felt like she was choking as her heart tried to pound its way out of her chest.

This can't be happening.

What the hell was she supposed to say to him? She wasn't sure she could talk to him. Scratch that. She *couldn't* talk to him. She didn't know how to have a conversation with a man. Shoot, she could barely talk to people outside the library.

She glanced in the mirror hanging on the wall to her left and wasn't happy with what she saw—disheveled, dirty blonde hair pulled up in a messy bun, too big glasses that slid down her nose, no makeup, baggy, comfortable clothes, and the look of perpetual confusion she always had on her face.

For a second, she considered not answering the door, but another knock—louder than the first—made her realize she had to open it. She suspected her neighbor would stand there knocking until she opened it and talked to him. Faith took a deep breath, unlocked the door, and opened it far enough to stick her head out.

Her neighbor grinned. "Hi."

The word coupled with his dazzling smile, casual confidence, and gorgeous face almost knocked her off her feet. "H-hello," she squeaked out. Faith cringed as the words left her, and heat rose in her cheeks. Why did she have to sound like a scared mouse? If she was lucky, the floor would open up and swallow her.

"Hi," he repeated.

"C-can I help you?" she asked. Damn it, still squeaking like a mouse.

"I think you dropped this," he said. He held up a book.

"What?"

Good lord, why am I such an idiot?

He laughed and shook his head. "Remember last night, when I crashed into you and your books went flying? I think this is yours. My roommate found it on the sidewalk this morning in front of your house."

Faith reached out and took the book with two fingers, careful not to touch him, remembering the weird shock that rocketed up her arm when they'd touched last night. "Thank you."

She gripped the book in one hand and tried to close the door with the other, but her neighbor stuck his hand through the gap and blurted, "My name is Nate."

Faith eyed him warily, but she reached out and grasped his hand. There were callouses on the pads of some of his fingers, but his grip was bold and confident. It was probably her imagination, but she thought he held onto her a few seconds longer than necessary.

"I'm Faith," she whispered.

Nate's grin widened as he leaned against the doorjamb. One hip jutted out, his brilliant blue eyes sparkling. "It's nice to meet you. I wanted to apologize for last night. I wasn't watching where I was going."

She stepped back. Being close to Nate overwhelmed her, like standing next to the sun. She grabbed the doorknob and squeezed it until her hand hurt.

"It's okay. I... I'm okay. No harm done." She held the book up and wiggled it. "Thanks again. It was, uh, nice to meet you." She slammed the door before Nate said anything else.

Faith thought he would knock again, and if he did, she didn't know what to say to him. She held her breath and leaned against the door. She didn't move or breathe until she felt like her lungs might burst, then she dragged in a deep, cleansing breath and peered through the peephole.

Nate was gone.

Thank God.

Chapter 5

Nate

Nate spent the night thinking about his run-in with his neighbor. He wasn't sure if it was his imagination or what, but there had been some crazy jolt to his system when they'd touched. It stayed with him. He'd woken up with her on his mind.

As soon as he showered and dressed, he headed for the kitchen. Sitting at the center of the table was a book. Nate picked it up and flipped it over to read the back.

"Hey, Mace, where did the book come from?" he yelled. "The one on the table. It doesn't look like your normal World War II read."

Mason stuck his head out of his bedroom door. "I found it on the sidewalk by the street when I went for my run. I don't know how it got there."

"I do," Nate replied. "I'll be right back."

He ran out the front door with the book clutched in his hand before Mason said anything else. He jogged down the driveway and across the lawn, sliding to a stop in front of his neighbor's door. He pushed a hand through his hair and knocked a quick double tap. Then he stepped back, crossed his arms over his chest, and waited.

To his surprise, the conversation with Faith didn't go as he expected. Maybe it was because he'd grown accustomed to sweeping women off their feet, easily charming them with a smile and a wink, but that hadn't happened this time. In fact, she seemed more interested in getting rid of him than chatting with him. The death blow had come when she slammed the door in his face, something that had never happened to him.

That must be why she stayed on his mind. He thought about her on his way to work, while he prepared the bar to open, and even now as he worked, surrounded by attractive women.

How was it he hadn't noticed Faith before? He had no clue how long she'd lived next door, didn't know her name, or anything else about her. He'd seen her coming and going from her house, not that he'd paid much attention. He might have smiled at her once or twice, but he was a friendly person. Things like that happened without him thinking about it.

Natasha came through the front door of the Time Out Bar & Grill and waved at her brother as she made her way through the crowd. She sat on the bar stool across from him, propped her head on her hand, and smiled.

"Hey, big brother," she said. She loved to remind him he was a few minutes older than her.

Nate returned the smile and filled a glass with Sprite. He set it in front of her. "What are you doing here?" he asked.

"Can't I come say hi to my brother?"

He shook his head. "No, because you're the queen of ulterior motives. So, what's up?"

Natasha traced the rim of her glass with her finger. "Mason said he told you we're moving out."

Nate nodded. "He did."

"You're okay with it?" she asked.

"Why wouldn't I be?"

Natasha shrugged. "I thought living alone might, I don't know, bother you."

"Are you kidding?" he said. "I get to walk around in my underwear again, watch what I want on TV, and eat what I want. Plus, I won't have to watch my sister and my best friend making out. Which, by the way, grosses me out."

Natasha laughed and her cheeks turned a light shade of pink. "Sorry about that. I'll tell you what. We'll keep it under control until we move out, okay?"

"Thank God," Nate muttered.

"So, I... uh, heard you broke up with that girl. Mary?" Natasha said.

"You and Brooke have been talking about me, haven't you?" He sighed.

"Yes, but only because we worry about you." She sipped her Sprite. "Are you okay?"

"Yes. Why wouldn't I be?"

She shrugged. "I don't know. I guess... well, it worries me that it doesn't bother you when you break up with someone. It's like it's no big deal."

"It isn't a big deal," he replied. "I only dated her for a couple of weeks."

"You never date anybody for more than a few weeks. Why are you opposed to settling down or dating one woman?" she asked. "What happened that made you afraid to let someone into your life?"

For a split second, Nate considered telling his sister about Elle, spilling his guts and telling her everything he'd held back for the last six years. It might be a relief to tell her about the woman who ripped out his heart and stomped it into oblivion.

"I guess—" He stopped when Natasha leaned forward with an

expectant look on her face. He took a breath before he spoke. "I guess I'm not ready to settle down."

"I worry about you," his sister muttered. "Especially with us moving out and leaving you alone."

"Well, don't," he said. "I'm fine. You and Brooke need to stop fussing over me like you're my mother or something."

"Yeah, well, I'm your sister. I think I get to worry."

"There's nothing to worry about. My life is amazing—I've got my bar, I've got my friends, and I've got you. Quit worrying that I'm wasting my life and I'll never be happy. I'm only twenty-seven—"

"We're almost twenty-eight," Natasha interjected.

Nate threw his head back and laughed. "Okay, twenty-eight. Let me live my life. I'll figure it out when I need to figure it out. For now, I'm enjoying myself. Besides, I think I'm done with the serial dating for a while. The stuff you and Mason said about me dating all the women in Lakeside, it kind of hit home. So, I'm taking a break. At least until the right woman falls in my lap."

Or I run into her and almost knock her down.

Natasha clapped her hands and grinned. "Yay! I'm glad to hear that."

"Tell me how you really feel," he grumbled.

Brooke appeared at his side. "What are you glad to hear?" she asked Natasha.

"My brother is going to take a break from dating until he finds the right woman," his sister explained.

Brooke threw her head back and laughed. Her entire body shook, and she couldn't catch her breath. "Oh God, are you serious?"

"Yes, I'm serious." Nate rolled his eyes and crossed his arms over his chest.

Brooke stopped laughing and stepped into Nate's personal space. "Wait a second. What's wrong with you? Are you sick?" She pressed the back of her hand to his forehead, which made Natasha cackle with delight.

He batted Brooke's hand away. "I'm not sick. What's wrong with not dating?"

"For normal people, nothing. For you, sweetie, it's weird."

He rolled his eyes. "You know what? I'm going to excuse myself from this conversation because you're both annoying me. I'm gonna go do some paperwork before I head out for the night. You still good to close?"

"I got it, boss." Brooke winked at him and crossed her arms over her chest.

Nate clapped her on the shoulder and headed upstairs to his office. Halfway up, he glanced back at the bar. Brooke and Natasha had their heads together, talking. Natasha caught him looking and waved at him. He gave her a tight smile before continuing upstairs.

———

For the first time in months, Nate went home alone on a Saturday night. It was a refreshing change to drive home in silence instead of making small talk with a woman he barely knew. Not that he couldn't have found someone; there were plenty of women at the bar more than willing to do anything for the chance to be with him. He wasn't interested. Taking home a different woman week after week had gotten tiresome. He needed a change.

As he turned the corner onto his street, he saw his neighbor crossing her lawn. He pulled to a stop in front of her house and jumped out of the car.

"Faith!" he yelled.

She froze and turned slowly to stare at him as he hurried to her side.

"Hi, there," he said when he caught up with her.

Faith stared at the ground, clutched the book in her hand, and muttered, "Hello."

Nate took a deep breath and inched closer. If only she'd look him in the eye. She wouldn't make it easy on him, though. He touched her arm, and she recoiled, stepping back as if he'd shocked her. He jerked his hand back and stuck it in his pocket.

"Would you like to get a cup of coffee with me sometime?" he asked.

Faith looked confused. She opened her mouth, then closed it again.

"Please, say yes," Nate insisted. "I was thinking we could get to know each other better. I mean, we've lived next door to each other for quite a while, and I only recently learned your name."

"I don't know," she mumbled.

"I promise, no pressure, just coffee." He smiled, hoping he didn't look too eager, or he'd scare her away.

Faith's eyes narrowed, and she sighed. "O-okay, I guess. Coffee sometime. Sure."

Before he could say another word or ask her when she wanted to go, she muttered, "Goodbye," turned on her heel, ran to her door, unlocked it, and darted inside. Nate heard the lock click into place.

At least he got her to agree to the date. He whistled as he made his way across her lawn and up his driveway. He couldn't quite wrap his brain around what he'd done. Three hours ago, he told his sister he didn't want to date anymore. Then he asked his neighbor out.

Inside, he tossed his keys on the table and stepped into the kitchen. Mason and Natasha stood at the counter, scooping food onto plates. Mason glanced at him.

"Why are you grinning?" he asked.

"What?" Nate mumbled.

"You're grinning." Mason chuckled. "I know that look. Did

you find some poor, defenseless woman unable to resist your charms as you walked to the front door?"

He grinned and shrugged. "I... uh, I asked our neighbor out for coffee."

Mason narrowed his eyes. "Which neighbor? The woman two houses down? Dude, she's married."

Nate shook his head. "No way! Jesus, Mace, like I'd hit on a married woman." He punched his friend on the shoulder and then pointed helpfully toward Faith's house. "The one who lives right next door."

"Wait, the girl who wears glasses, always has her nose buried in a book, and scurries away like a scared mouse any time anyone talks to her?" Natasha asked. "That neighbor?"

"Yes, that neighbor," Nate replied. "Her name is Faith. That book you found? It was hers. I ran into her a couple of days ago, I mean literally ran into her, which sent her books flying. I returned the book Mace found and introduced myself. Just now, when I pulled up, she was outside, and on impulse, I asked her out."

Mason laughed. "She is *so* not your type."

"Oh, really?" Nate snapped.

"Don't get defensive," Natasha interjected. "Mason is right. She isn't really your type."

"And what exactly *is* my type?"

"Nate—"

He put his hand up, cutting off Mason's protest. "I can't believe this is a serious question. Why do I have to have a type? What's so wrong with me being interested in a woman who goes against my social norm? It might be nice to go out with someone who wasn't half-drunk the moment I met her. I'm tired of meeting women at the bar. Or how about this? I think she's sweet, and I'd like to get coffee with her sometime."

Nate pushed past his sister and best friend and stalked across the living room to his bedroom. He slammed his door; the sound ricocheting through the house. He ignored Mason and Natasha's shouted apologies by turning on the TV in his room and turning up the volume.

The thing was, he wasn't angry with them, not really. They were only voicing the questions lurking in the back of his brain as soon as he asked Faith out. She wasn't his type, not anywhere close, but he'd asked her out. He wasn't sure why, but the second he saw her outside, the idea popped into his head, and once it was there, he couldn't shake it loose.

For the first time in a long time, Nate had experienced the twist of nerves in the pit of his stomach as he waited for Faith's answer. It was an eternity before she'd reluctantly agreed. He suspected she'd said yes to get him to go away.

She had been on his mind since he'd returned her book to her. There was something about her—her reserved smile, the way she clutched her book like it was a lifeline, even how her voice was so low and soft, forcing him to concentrate if he wanted to hear her. Those things fascinated him, and he needed to find out more about her. Tomorrow, he'd talk to her and schedule their coffee date.

Chapter 6

Faith

Faith dropped her backpack and slid to the floor. She wrapped her arms around her legs and rested her head on her knees.

"What the hell just happened?" she muttered to herself.

Somehow, she'd agreed to a coffee date with her adorably cute neighbor. Nate. His name was Nate. It wasn't her fault, really. She hadn't been able to think straight with those intense blue eyes of his boring into her, staring into her soul. She only wanted him to stop looking at her as if he was memorizing her, so she said yes, her mouth getting ahead of her common sense. Now that she was alone, she regretted it.

When had her life turned into a cheesy romantic comedy? Guys who looked like Nate, guys who could have any girl they wanted, didn't go out with girls like her. They didn't act interested in her or ask her out for coffee.

Maybe it was a joke, or he lost a bet with one of his friends or somebody at his bar. That was probably the reason he asked her out.

Faith got to her feet and looked out the window next to the door. Her front yard was empty. She threw the deadbolt and slipped the chain into place before she went to the kitchen, where she took a cup from the cupboard to make tea. She leaned against the counter, with Heathcliff weaving between her legs while she waited for the electric kettle to warm the water.

"I can't go out with Nate," she said out loud. Heathcliff looked up at her and meowed before he disappeared down the hall.

The thought of a date with her neighbor terrified her. How the hell was she going to get out of it?

Faith was painfully shy, had been since she was a child. It was why her nose was always buried in a book. It was her way of hiding in plain sight. If she went out with Nate, she wouldn't know what to say, how to act, and she wouldn't be able to function like a normal person. Not to mention the stares of the other coffee shop patrons, judging her, wondering how and why he was with her. It would be nothing short of embarrassing for both of them.

A million reasons not to go out with him ran through her head. But the one that stood out more than any other was her inexperience with men. She hadn't dated since high school, and that had been a brief, disastrous relationship during her senior year. It left such a nasty taste in her mouth that she hadn't dated since, making it nine years since she had been on a date. Faith kept her heart locked down, refusing to let anyone in, aside from a few close friends. It was easier to protect herself when she didn't open herself up to heartache.

It would be for the best if she stayed home with her cat and her books. They never let her down.

There had to be a way out of it. While she couldn't deny there was a physical attraction, she wasn't prepared to date Nate. Forget that she could get lost in those blue eyes of his or drown in the perfect pitch of his voice. The attraction was purely physical, nothing more. She'd come up with some excuse to not have coffee with him—dead grandparent, sick cat, or maybe she'd claim she was sick.

She couldn't go out with Nate, even if it had the potential to be a perfect date. Tomorrow, she'd tell him the date was off.

For the third morning in a row, Faith was late. To make matters worse, she discovered she was out of coffee, which meant a stop at The Percolator. It was becoming a habit she couldn't break. On her way out the door, she grabbed her latest read off the kitchen table and shoved it in her oversized purse. Halfway down the sidewalk, she looked down and realized her slippers were on her feet. With a sigh, she turned around and went back inside.

Five minutes later, she had on shoes instead of slippers and was on her way to the coffee shop. Unfortunately, half-asleep college students desperate to wake up filled The Percolator, so the line stretched from the counter to the door. Faith got in it, opened her purse, and pulled out her book. It would be a while before she got her coffee.

As she inched forward, she heard the door open, and someone got in line behind her.

"Hi there," a deep voice said in her left ear.

Faith jumped, squeaked like a mouse, and dropped her book. She bent down to get it, but a hand reached past her and snagged it first. She stood upright and came face to face with Nate.

He wiggled his fingers in a cute little wave and put her book into her hands. "Good morning."

She clutched it tight and stared at him.

He chuckled and pointed at his chest. "Nate," he said. "Your neighbor."

"I know who you are," she blurted. She immediately regretted it; she hadn't meant to sound so harsh. She closed her eyes and exhaled. "Sorry. Um, hi."

She spun around and held her breath, hoping he wouldn't try to talk to her or expect her to have a conversation with him.

The line moved, and she moved with it. She put her book in front of her face, but she couldn't concentrate on it. Once she got to the counter, she ordered her coffee, but before she could pay, Nate reached around her and dropped a twenty-dollar bill in front of the barista.

"I got it," he said. "Mine and hers. Large Americano, hot, no cream or sugar. Keep the change."

"You didn't have to do that," Faith whispered.

Nate's smile dazzled her. "Just so you know, this doesn't count as our coffee date." He took his drink from the barista, nodded at Faith, and left.

"Do you know that guy?" the barista asked as she handed Faith her drink.

She shrugged. "He's... he's my neighbor," she mumbled.

"He's cute," the barista said.

She nodded, then she turned around and bolted out the door.

Outside, she looked up and down the street, but Nate was gone. She got into her car, started the engine, and drove to work, chastising herself for the entire drive.

Was Nate flirting with me?

Faith couldn't tell when someone flirted with her. In fact, she was oblivious to it. Not that it happened often, if ever.

She pulled into her parking spot behind the library, grabbed her things, and headed inside. She tripped on the edge of the concrete stairs leading up to the door and almost dropped her coffee. Some of it sloshed over the side of the cup when she hit her elbow on the door as it swung closed. She cursed under her breath.

"Good morning, Faith," Caroline called from the front counter.

"Hello," she yelled back. Once she stashed her things in her desk drawer, she headed out front.

Caroline stood on a stepstool in the non-fiction section a few feet from the main checkout counter. She balanced a stack of books on one arm and returned them to the shelf with the other. She hummed a nameless tune under her breath as she worked.

"Do you need some help?" Faith asked.

Caroline jumped, the books in her hand tottering precariously.

She put them down and shook her head. "Yeah, don't scare the crap out of me."

Faith giggled. "Sorry."

"It's okay. Anyway, I'm good down here."

"Well, if you need me, I'll be upstairs, shelving books." She turned to go.

"Will you check the workrooms while you're up there?" Caroline asked. "Several study groups were here late last night and there are books everywhere."

Faith nodded and headed to the second floor. Workrooms suitable for small study groups lined one side of the library's second floor. Shelves of reference books filled the other side of the expansive room. Sure enough, two of the rooms had books stacked haphazardly on the tables, as well as some on the floor.

Faith grabbed a rolling cart from behind the desk and pushed it into the first room. Her mind drifted as she stacked the books on the cart.

Nate surprised her when he bought her coffee this morning. While she'd planned to cancel their date, she never got around to it. Instead, she'd done her best to avoid running into him. She looked outside for his car before she left, didn't get out of her car until she made sure no one else was around, and even then, she ran to and from her front door. She had been avoiding him, hoping if she didn't see him or talk to him, the date wouldn't happen.

Maybe he was being nice.

Except, men—people—weren't nice to her. Faith could count the number of people who treated her with kindness over the years on one hand. None of them were of the male persuasion. She had a deep-rooted suspicion of anyone who did anything for her, stemming from her shitty childhood and a mother who was better at manipulating her child than raising her.

Faith closed her eyes and took several deep breaths, a trick her therapist told her to use when her anxiety got the best of her.

Any time she thought about her mom, her anxiety skyrocketed. Today was no exception.

She set the pile of books in her arms on the table and sat down. It had been a while since she thought about her mother. The woman hadn't been a part of her life for almost ten years. When Faith was twelve, she'd been put in foster care. For the next four years, she had bounced from group home to group home, with occasional visits from her mother, and even one attempt to move back home that lasted less than a week. At sixteen, she emancipated herself, and the day after graduating high school, she packed her measly belongings into a thrift store suitcase and bought a bus ticket to wherever the money in her pocket would take her. It turned out to be Missoula, Montana.

Faith lived in Missoula for six months until chance brought her into the path of Margaret Hudspeth—Maggie, for short. Maggie was a professor at Lakeside College. She had been spending the summer in Missoula teaching at the University of Montana. Maggie frequented the coffee shop where Faith worked, and they struck up a friendship. When she told the professor about her dream of becoming a librarian, Maggie offered to help her in any way possible. The next thing she knew, Faith was in Lakeside, working as an assistant librarian-in-training and going to school for free. She owed her new life to Maggie, and she was beyond grateful for everything her new friend helped her achieve.

After she graduated from Lakeside College with a master's degree in Library and Information Sciences, Faith stayed in Lakeside. She loved the little town and the Flathead Lake area. After six years, it was her home.

Faith got to her feet. Enough reminiscing, she had work to do. After work, she had big plans to hide in her house and read her book.

Chapter 7

Faith

*M*ission accomplished.

Faith avoided Nate all weekend. It wasn't difficult; she stayed inside and didn't leave, not even when Caroline called and suggested they go to Kalispell for dinner and a movie. By Sunday night, she had no doubt he'd completely forgotten about the coffee date.

Monday started off on the right foot. For once, she made it out of the house on the first try—keys, shoes, clothes, and purse where they were supposed to be. Nate's car was in front of her house, a normal occurrence after the girl Faith suspected was his sister moved in with them. Thankfully, he wasn't anywhere to be seen. She hurried down the sidewalk, quickly got in her car, and started it, but when she tried to put it in drive, the gear-shift wouldn't move. She tried again, but still nothing. She shut off the car.

"Shit." Faith rested her forehead on the steering wheel and tried not to cry. This wasn't happening. She'd spent what little money she had saved on new tires three months ago. If something was wrong with the damn thing, she couldn't afford to fix it.

A tap on the window made her jump. When she turned her head to see who it was, Nate wiggled his fingers in a tiny wave. She sighed and opened the door.

"Car trouble?"

Faith bit her lip and nodded. She swallowed and said, "Yeah. I don't know what's wrong with it, but I'm going to be late for work."

He tipped his head toward his truck. "Come on, I'll give you a ride."

She thought about saying no, but she needed to get to the library. Caroline was on her way to Missoula for the day, leaving Faith in charge. She *had* to get to work. Worrying about her car would have to wait. She grabbed her things and followed him to his truck. He unlocked it with the remote on his keys and opened the passenger door for her. She glanced at him out of the corner of her eye and pulled herself into the truck. Nate shut the door, jogged around the front of the vehicle, and got in.

"I, uh, I'm sorry," he said. "I don't know where you work."

Faith clutched her hands in her lap and stared at them. "The library," she whispered.

He shook his head and chuckled under his breath.

"What?" she asked.

"Nothing," he replied.

She rolled her eyes. She knew she gave off stereotypical vibes— the books, the glasses, the bun in the hair—it screamed "librarian." It hadn't occurred to her how strong those vibes were until Nate laughed at her. Heat rushed to her cheeks, and she squeezed her hands together so tight her knuckles turned white. Faith felt the weight of his gaze on her, but she stared straight ahead, chewing on the inside of her cheek.

He cleared his throat. "I shouldn't have laughed. I'm sorry."

"You're full of apologies, aren't you?" she muttered.

He shook his head and hit the button on the door to roll down the window a few inches, letting the cold air into the truck's cab. "Yes, I am. I'm sorry I don't know where you work and that I laughed."

Faith sighed. "First, there's no reason for you to know where I work. We're neighbors who know nothing about each other. Second, I know I scream 'librarian' when you look at me."

"Actually, I figured you were a librarian because you obviously love books," Nate explained. "You always have one in your hand, you have stacks of them in your house, and when I ran into you, I knocked a bunch of books out of your arms. It seemed logical. It has nothing to do with how you look."

She peeked at him out of the corner of her eye. He was so relaxed. He drove with his wrist propped on the steering wheel, the wind from the open window tousling his hair, and he had a pleasant smile on his face. She couldn't see his eyes behind his dark sunglasses, which made it hard to figure out what he was thinking.

"Coffee?"

"Wh-what?"

"Let's get some coffee," he said.

Without waiting for her to answer, he made an abrupt right-hand turn and drove down Adams Street. He parked in front of The Percolator, shut off the engine, and jumped out. Faith reached for the door, but Nate was already there, pulling it open and holding out his hand. She took it and let him help her out of the truck. He slammed the door before she could grab her purse.

"My purse—"

"I got it," he said. "Don't worry about it."

Inside, they got in line behind the usual college students and people commuting to Kalispell. Faith hung back, standing behind him until he turned around, took her by the elbow, and guided her to stand next to him.

At the counter, Nate smiled at the barista and ordered himself a large Americano and a large hot vanilla latte.

"How did you know to order that?" Faith asked after he paid.

Nate smirked. "I overheard you the other day. You seem like someone who has a routine and stays consistent."

"You remembered what I ordered?"

He shrugged and, to her surprise, his cheeks turned pink. They stepped to the side to wait for their drinks.

"I don't always order the same thing," she murmured.

He looked at her, one eyebrow raised. "So, I got it wrong?"

Faith shook her head. "No. But sometimes I order tea, or something with caramel; once I even tried their pumpkin spice latte." She shrugged. "I thought you should know I'm not completely predictable."

Nate didn't have time to respond because the barista set their drinks on the counter. He grabbed both of them and carefully handed her the steaming hot drink. He held the door open and as she passed him, then he put his hand in the middle of her back and guided her to the truck. A tingle ran down her spine.

They were both quiet as Nate drove through town to the library. Faith directed him to the back parking lot when they arrived. He pulled into a spot close to the door and, to Faith's chagrin, parked next to the library's student worker, Paisley, who was still in her car.

She reached for the door handle, but he put his hand on her arm, stopping her. "I know an excellent mechanic. I'll talk to him."

She rubbed her forehead and sighed. "I don't know," she mumbled.

"Why don't I pick you up when you get off and take you home? Kane can stop on his way home and look at your car. Sound good?"

"You don't have to do that."

"Do you know someone who fixes cars?" Nate asked.

Faith froze, realizing she didn't know anyone. She reluctantly shook her head. "No, I... I don't know anybody."

"Well, Kane owes me a favor. Let me help you. Please?"

"Okay," she mumbled. She didn't have a choice; she needed her car. "I'm off work at six."

"I'll be here."

She opened the door, gathered her things, and jumped out. Nate shouted goodbye after her, but she slammed the door and cut him off. She ran to the back door of the library, digging through her purse for her keys.

Paisley met her at the door. She looked over her shoulder at Nate's truck, then she leaned close to Faith and whispered, "Was that the guy who owns the Time Out Bar?"

"Yes," she replied. "He's my neighbor. I had car trouble this morning, so he gave me a ride to work."

Paisley's eyes widened. "Nate is your neighbor? Lucky."

"Yes," she said. She closed her eyes. "Is he still there?"

"Yep." Paisley giggled. "I think he's waiting for us to go inside."

"Dammit." Faith's hand shook as she put the key in the lock. It took three tries to get it unlocked. As soon as the door opened, she darted into the building.

"Are you okay?" Paisley asked.

Faith leaned against the wall. "No. I don't know how to talk to him. He makes me nervous." She pinched the bridge of her nose.

Paisley patted her arm. "He is extremely attractive. He makes my friends nervous, so I understand why he makes you nervous. But he's human, just like anyone else. You should ask him out on a date." She turned and walked away.

Faith leaned against the wall and closed her eyes. How could Paisley be so nonchalant about something like that? There was no way she'd ask Nate out, not in a million years. Thinking about it made her want to vomit, as did the thought of riding home with him and letting him help her with her car.

How was she going to get out of that? The better question was, how the hell had she gotten herself into this situation?

Chapter 8

Nate

"Thanks, Kane. I appreciate it. I'll see you in an hour." Nate ended the call and tucked his phone in his front pocket. He turned around and bumped into Brooke. She grinned at him.

"You're leaving?" she asked. "Did your truck break down?"

"No," he replied, dragging out the word. "Why?"

"Because I heard you ask Kane to meet you at your place," she said. "Why else would you need a mechanic?"

He crossed his arms over his chest and glared at his assistant manager. "You were eavesdropping?"

Brooke grabbed a tray, opened the cooler, and took out several bottles of beer. "Maybe a little. So, did your truck break down or not?"

"You saw it in the parking lot, so you know it didn't." Nate picked up a cloth and wiped down the bar so he didn't have to look at his assistant manager. She had an uncanny knack for getting information out of him. "My neighbor's car isn't working. I'm helping her out."

"By asking Kane to come to your place? That's a bit more than helpful. Why doesn't she take it to his shop?" Brooke put her hands on her hips and smirked. "Or is this you making a move on some poor, unsuspecting female? I thought you were done with dating for a while? Or is your neighbor one of the few women in this town you haven't dated?"

"Stop it," Nate grumbled.

"What?"

"Don't make assumptions," he snapped. "I feel bad for her and I want to help."

Brooke put her hands up and took a step back. "Okay, fair enough. Are you coming back after you help her?"

He could almost hear the quotation marks around the word "help." He rolled his eyes. "Aw, sarcasm. Shocking, especially from you." Nate checked the clock on the wall. "Yeah, I'll try to be back by eight."

Brooke nodded, took the tray loaded with beers, and walked away. He dug his keys out of his pocket and headed for the door.

Ten minutes later, he parked at the back of the library. He kept the truck running and the heat on. Fall in Montana was chilly, and in the last few days, the temperature had dropped. He'd noticed Faith wearing a heavy sweatshirt this morning, so he wanted it to be warm for her.

At 6:03 p.m., the door opened, and she walked out. She stopped, looked around, and when she saw Nate in his truck, her shoulders slumped before she trudged across the lot. He jumped out and jogged around to open the door for her.

"Hi," he said.

"H-hello," she whispered as she climbed in and folded her hands in her lap.

"How was your day?" he asked once he was back in the truck.

"Um, it was good, thanks," she mumbled. "How was yours?"

Nate shrugged. "Not bad. I have to go back to work after Kane looks at your car, so it's not exactly over."

"You mentioned Kane earlier. He's a mechanic?"

"Yeah. He's a friend of mine, and he owns Lakeside Automotive. He agreed to stop by on his way home from work."

Faith shook her head. "Oh, no, he doesn't have to do that. I don't want him to go out of his way for me."

"I told you he owes me a favor. It's okay."

As they came around the corner, he saw Kane's car in front of his house. He parked behind him and got out. They met at the truck and shook hands.

"You're early," Nate said.

"My last customer showed up ten minutes ago. So, I thought I'd head over," Kane replied.

"Great." Nate turned to Faith, who had gotten out of the truck while they talked. "Kane, this is my neighbor, Faith. It's her car."

Kane raised a hand. "Hey, there. What's wrong with it?"

"My check engine light came on," she explained. "And when I put it in gear, it won't move."

"Have you noticed any unusual noises?" he asked. "Does it make a weird grinding or whining noise? Especially when you're speeding up or slowing down?"

Faith nodded. "I've heard both sounds, whining and grinding."

"Can you pop the hood?" Kane asked.

She went to her car, unlocked it, and got in. Nate heard a clunk, and the hood opened a few inches. Kane propped it open and leaned down.

"Nate, you got a flashlight?"

"Yep." He grabbed one from behind the seat in the truck and tossed it to Kane.

Kane looked under the hood, then he lay on his back and slid under the car. After a few minutes, he crawled out and stood up. "I'm not positive, but I think it might be your transmission. I need to take it to my shop to get a good look at it. I'll have one of my guys come tow it down there tomorrow, if you want?"

"How much is that going to cost?" Faith asked.

"I won't know until I get it in the shop," Kane said.

"Um..."

"I'll pay to have it towed," Nate interjected.

Faith shook her head. "You don't have to."

"Will you excuse us?" Nate said to Kane. He took Faith's elbow and guided her up the sidewalk a few feet from her car.

She shifted from foot to foot and twisted her hands in front of her. "You shouldn't have offered to pay," she mumbled.

"I want to help," he insisted.

Faith moved to protest, but Nate held up his hand. "I know you don't want my help. I don't know if you think I'm insincere or that I have some ulterior motive, but honestly, I don't. One neighbor helping the other. I'll cover the towing charge, and that's it. I swear."

She wouldn't make eye contact with him; instead, she stared at the ground. After a few seconds, she muttered, "Okay," so quietly Nate had trouble hearing her.

"Great. I, um, need your car key," he said, holding out his hand. "I'll give you a ride to the library until it's fixed."

Faith sighed as she took her house key off the keyring and handed her car key to him. "I don't work tomorrow," she whispered.

"Okay, no ride tomorrow," he said. "Hold on while I talk to Kane. I'll be right back."

Nate jogged down the sidewalk, gave Kane the key, and made plans for him to pick up the car the next day. They said their goodbyes, and Kane got in his car and left. When Nate turned around, Faith was gone. He saw light through the window by the door. He considered going to the door and knocking, but he decided against it. Obviously, she didn't want to speak to him, or she'd have waited. Maybe she needed a break, so he would give it to her. He returned to his truck to go back to work.

—

Nate stayed until the bar closed and waited for the parking lot to empty before he left. He wasn't in the mood to talk to anybody. He drove home in silence, lost in his thoughts.

At home, he had to weave through a maze of boxes to get to the couch. He turned on *Sportscenter* and stared at the TV without really comprehending what was on the screen.

Mason stuck his head out of his bedroom door and smiled at him. "Hey, how's it going?"

"Great," he muttered. "Why are you up so late? It's almost two."

"I'm reading," Mason replied. He stepped out and pulled the door closed. "Dude, you don't look so good. Are you sick?"

Nate snorted. "No."

Mason sat next to him and stared at him until Nate shifted away from him.

"Knock it off," he snapped.

Mason grinned. "I'm not doing anything."

"You're doing that thing where you stare at me until I crack. Like you did when Melody Olson cheated on me in high school, but I didn't want to talk about it." Nate crossed his arms and glared at his best friend.

"Or when Elle got married," Mason mumbled.

Nate recoiled. They didn't talk about Elle. It was an unwritten rule. She was off-limits.

"Watch it," he sneered.

"I'm sorry," Mason replied. "But you've been kind of mopey. Right now, you look like your dog died."

"Fine, I'll tell you what's bothering me, but you cannot laugh, and you *cannot* tell my sister."

Mason sat back and nodded. "Okay."

"Our neighbor? I don't think she likes me." Nate explained what happened earlier, starting with Faith's car trouble and ending with her disappearing into her house without a word.

"Wow," Mason said when he finished talking.

"See? She doesn't like me."

Mason chuckled and shook his head. "Has it occurred to you she might be shy?"

"What?"

"Shy, Nathaniel. I know you don't come across many of them down at the bar, but they exist. I don't know much about her, but I get the impression she's shy. She never makes eye contact with anybody. She's lived next door for years, and none of us have talked to her, and she keeps to herself. Getting attention from you is probably overwhelming."

Nate raised an eyebrow. "I'm not overwhelming."

"Not to the college girls hanging out at Time Out on the weekends, but to the quiet, shy woman living next door? Yeah, you are." Mason shrugged. "You're used to women falling for any line you feed them. You never have to work to get the girl. This time you might. Give her time, she'll come around."

"I think I like this woman," he murmured. "She's not like anyone I've ever dated before."

Mason grinned. "Then you should wait for her."

Nate scrubbed a hand over his face. "I'll wait. But it's weird. I've never done this before."

Mason clapped him on the back. "Welcome to the real world, buddy. It sucks."

Chapter 9

Faith

The tow truck was at her house at seven a.m. on the dot. Faith heard the telltale beep as it backed up and positioned itself in front of her car. She peeked out the window and saw Nate standing on his lawn, watching as they loaded her car onto the flatbed and drove away.

Nate glanced at her house before he climbed into his truck. She didn't bother to open the door. Instead, she returned to the living room, pulled the blanket from the back of the couch over her legs, and opened her book.

It was impossible to concentrate on the words on the page, not when Nate kept invading her thoughts. She couldn't understand why he was being so nice to her. Maybe it was a cruel joke.

It wasn't like it hadn't happened before. Growing up in the foster care system and bouncing from home to home had taught her the only person she could trust was herself. After her emancipation at sixteen, she'd lived in a local shelter owned by friends of her former case manager. They allowed her to stay in a tiny, closet-sized room in exchange for helping around the shelter—cleaning, laundry, even lawn work. Faith studied hard and kept to herself, intent on leaving Texas as soon as she graduated high school. The only friend she had was the niece of the owner, a girl named Connie, who was a year younger than her.

Three months before the end of the school year and Faith's escape from Texas, Connie found out Faith had a crush on a classmate. What followed was a whirlwind romance orchestrated by Connie, a romance that left Faith crying on her bedroom floor after a public break-up and shaming session used to remove her from his life. Only after being completely humiliated, she learned he'd only asked her out because Connie dared him to, and he kept dating her because he wanted to get her into bed. Her refusal to have sex with him led to her public humiliation.

Ever since, a deep distrust lingered, coloring her perception of any man's attention, making her convinced no one genuinely cared for her. While she desperately wanted Nate to be different, history had taught her it wasn't usually the case.

Faith closed her eyes. She needed to stop thinking about him. It was her day off, and as much as she loved her job at the library, she enjoyed the days she got to hang out at home with nothing to do but read her books and relax with Heathcliff.

Forty-five minutes later and several chapters into her book, there was a knock on her door, followed immediately by Nate calling her name. Faith closed her eyes and wondered if it was possible to ignore him.

"I know you're in there," he yelled. "You might as well open the door. I'm not going anywhere until you do."

She contemplated not getting up, but she was sure Nate intended to follow through with his promise to stand out there until she acknowledged him. With a sigh, she shoved the blanket off, put her book on the table, and walked across the living room to her door.

A grin spread across his face when she opened it. "Hi," he said.

His smile intoxicated her, which drove her crazy. She didn't want to fall under his spell. He was all wrong for her.

"Hi," Faith replied warily. "What are you doing here?"

Nate held up a drink carrier loaded with five precariously balanced drinks. "Can I come in?" he asked.

"Why?"

"It will only be for a few minutes. I promise," he said. "Give me ten minutes and then, if you want me to leave, I will."

Her first instinct was to close the door, but his smile, coupled with his sparkling blue eyes, made him irresistible. Faith stepped back and gestured for him to come in.

As she closed the door behind him, she had to swallow back the urge to vomit. Nate was in her house, walking toward her kitchen. He pushed a stack of books out of his way and put the drink carrier on the table. He appeared calm, confident, and as if being there was the most natural place for him to be. She inched closer, curious about what he was up to.

"Since I haven't been able to convince you to go get coffee with me, I brought the coffee to you," Nate said. "I remembered you like different things, so I got a variety—black tea, that pumpkin spice thing you mentioned, a vanilla latte like you had yesterday, and a caramel macchiato. The black coffee is mine." He removed each drink from the carrier as he described it and lined them up on the table. Then he sat down and smiled at her.

Faith's smile spread across her face as she shook her head. "You're crazy," she murmured.

Nate chuckled. "I know. Anyway, I thought you'd be more comfortable here, away from the crowds of people."

It shocked her that he apparently knew what she wanted all along. It would be easier, a date away from public scrutiny. The least she could do was give him a chance. She eased into the chair across from him, reached over, and picked up the caramel macchiato.

Nate took the black coffee and leaned back, sprawled in his seat like he belonged there. "Does that mean I don't have to leave?"

"You don't have to leave," Faith replied. She grabbed her sweatshirt off the back of the chair and pulled it on, burying herself in its oversized comfort, like a security blanket. Taking a deep, cleansing breath did nothing to stop her shaking hands or pounding heart. She sipped the coffee and peered at Nate over the top of the cup.

His eyes drifted around the house. "You really have a lot of books," he said.

Faith laughed, and a blush heated her cheeks. That was an understatement. Every inch of space was merely another place to put her books. Books overflowed everywhere—her tiny bookshelf, her kitchen table, the coffee table in the living room, and multiple baskets around the house. She meant to get rid of the ones she'd already read, but it never happened.

She pointed at herself. "Librarian, remember? Yes, it's cliché, but I love to read."

"I think it's refreshing," he said.

"Oh?"

Nate rubbed a hand over the back of his neck and shrugged. "The last few girls I dated, well, I'm not sure they ever read a book, unless it was for school. Books and reading weren't their thing."

"Those are my *only* things," she mumbled. "They have been my entire life. It was how I escaped from reality when I was younger and life wasn't... well, so great for me. Books are the one thing that makes me happy."

Nate rested his arms on the table, his complete attention on her. She didn't know how long she could handle those baby blue eyes staring at her or listen to his rich, full voice without fainting or possibly dying. It was hard to believe he was in her kitchen at her table, talking and listening to her as if it were the most natural thing in the world. Like he belonged there.

He looked around with an appraising eye. "You need more bookshelves."

"I know," she agreed. "But I don't have time to get any." Faith took a sip of her coffee and cleared her throat. She might as well make the best of their impromptu date. Not that she was good at this kind of thing, but there was nothing wrong with trying.

"Wh-what about you? What's your *thing*?" she asked.

He laughed, the sound filling the room. Nate made a cute "I'm concentrating" face before he answered.

"You know what? I thought I knew what it was, but lately, I'm not so sure." He looked at the top of his coffee cup and lowered his voice. "I studied business in school, and I own arguably the most popular bar and grill in a hundred-mile radius, but I don't feel … fulfilled. Sometimes, it feels like something is missing or, I don't know, off. I wish I knew what it was, but I don't have a clue."

He seemed so vulnerable that without letting herself think about it, Faith reached over and squeezed his hand, startled when that crazy electric jolt rushed up her arm. Nate must have felt it as well because his smile faltered the tiniest bit, replaced briefly with a look of confusion. It passed quickly, and his smile returned.

"I should go. I need to get to work," he whispered. "I'm sorry I barged in here and forced you to drink coffee with me."

She grinned. "It wasn't so bad. I… I enjoy talking to you."

"That's good to hear." Nate got to his feet.

Faith narrowed her eyes. "Why?"

"Because I plan on taking you out for a proper date," he said as he walked to the front door.

She jumped up and followed him, intent on telling him she didn't need another pity date. Before she could, he stopped and turned to her with that damn smirk on his face.

"And I will give you a ride to work until Kane fixes your car. That was our deal, right?" Nate winked at her, threw open the door, and bounded down the steps. Halfway across the lawn, he looked back and yelled, "See you tomorrow!"

Faith closed the door, then she pressed her hands to her warm cheeks.

Did we just have our first date?

She wasn't sure if that counted as a date, but she knew she couldn't wait to see him again.

Nate

Nate wasn't looking forward to telling Faith about his conversation with Kane. Her car repairs would cost almost $2000. Not that he was surprised. Every day that passed without a phone call from Kane made him worry that the cost had reached astronomical numbers and was too expensive to fix. By the time Friday rolled around, Nate wondered if it was even fixable. Now he had to deliver the bad news, and based on what he'd gleaned during their drive-to-work conversations this week, Faith couldn't afford a bill that large.

The music from the party at his house followed him as he trudged across Faith's lawn and up her sidewalk. After he tapped on her door, there was an enormous crash, and the cat meowed before Faith opened the door with her glasses propped on her head, sweater hanging to her knees, and mismatched socks. Nate bit his tongue and smiled. Faith was chaotic in a way he found utterly adorable. The more time he spent with her, the more he liked her.

"Um ... hi," she mumbled. Her brows furrowed, and she

gnawed on her lower lip. "What are you doing here? Did I leave something in the truck?"

Nate shook his head. "No."

"Oh, well, I didn't expect to see you until Monday. What's up?"

"Can I come in?" he asked.

Faith nodded, a bit too vigorously, which sent her glasses flying off her head. Nate reached out and snatched them mid-air before they hit the floor. He handed them to her as he stepped inside and shut the door.

"I talked to Kane about your car," Nate said. "He apologized for having it so long, but he had some family issues come up this week." He cleared his throat. "Anyway... he said it's uh... well, it's going to cost two grand to fix."

Faith's mouth dropped open. She snapped it closed, and tears welled in her eyes. Abruptly, she spun around and darted into the kitchen. She grabbed a napkin off the counter and pressed it to her face. Nate stood back and waited.

After a few minutes, Faith straightened up and turned back to him. "I'm sorry about that," she whispered. "I didn't expect that."

"It's a lot."

"It's more than I have," she said. "A lot more." She exhaled shakily. "I don't know what I'm going to do."

Nate took a step closer. "We'll come up with something."

Faith sighed and looked at the floor. "You've already done so much. I can't ask you to do anything else."

He stepped into the kitchen, caught her hand in his, and gently squeezed it. "I want to help. You're my friend. At least, I'd like to *think* you're my friend."

She nodded and her shoulders relaxed. "You're so sweet. What did I do to deserve a friend like you?"

Nate chuckled. "Ran into me with a bag of books."

Faith wiped her face and tossed the napkin in the trash. "I guess that was a good thing, huh?"

"I think it was," he whispered.

Faith pulled her hand from his, went to the sink, filled a glass with water, and quickly downed it. When she turned back to him, she seemed steadier and more balanced.

"I'll figure out how to get the money," she said. "Or I'll buy a bike."

Nate laughed. "You will not be riding a bike in the winter."

Faith shrugged. "Then I guess I'll call my neighbor to give me a ride." As soon as the words were out of her mouth, she blushed and looked down. "That was a joke."

"I know." He rocked back and forth on his toes for a second, knowing he needed to leave. He wanted to stay, but he wouldn't unless Faith asked him to. When she didn't, he clapped his hands together once and turned to leave. "I guess I'll go."

She followed him, standing back as he opened the door and stepped outside. The music from his house hit them immediately. The party was in full swing. He turned back to Faith.

"Would you like to come over? We're having a going-away party for my sister and Mason. They're getting their own place. BBQ, beer, and baseball on the TV. Why don't you join us?"

She shook her head before he finished talking. "I... I don't think so."

"Are you sure? It'll be fun."

"Would it count as our date?" she asked with a grin.

"Absolutely not," Nate scoffed. "Our first date will not be with a bunch of my drunk friends and my *sister*."

Faith giggled. "I'm not getting out of that date, am I?"

"Nope." Nate reached out, grabbed her hand, and gave it a gentle squeeze. "I'll talk to you later." He stopped with his hand on the knob. "Last chance?"

"No, really. I'm good. I'll see you on Monday."

Faith locked the door behind him. He stood on her porch for a few minutes, his head resting against the door, wishing Faith trusted him, wondering for the millionth time in the last week how he *could* gain her trust. After a few minutes, he strode back across the lawn to his house.

The music thumped in the center of his brain, making his eyes throb. He opened the door, the blaring music smacking him in the face, along with the noise of thirty people talking and laughing. Someone had already started a beer can pyramid on the kitchen table, and the baseball game played on the TV, competing with the other noises in the room. His friends shouted his name, and his sister waved at him from her perch on Mason's shoulders.

Nate waved back before he grabbed a plate and loaded it with food. Then he squeezed onto the couch between Oscar and Gavin. He watched the game without paying attention—neither team was his favorite—and thought about Faith. As much as he liked these people, right now, he wanted to be with her.

"Why are you making that face?" Natasha asked as she plopped down on the coffee table in front of him.

He sighed. "What face?"

"Your sad, grumpy face. If anybody should want to party louder than anybody here, it's you," she said. "By the end of the month, you'll have this place to yourself, and you can turn it into the bachelor pad you've always wanted."

Nate raised an eyebrow. "Who said I wanted a bachelor pad?"

"What single guy doesn't want a bachelor pad?" Natasha laughed.

"This one."

"You're funny." Natasha giggled, messed up her brother's hair, then bounded to her feet, and shouted Mason's name.

Gavin gave him an odd look. "You're not pumped about finally having this place to yourself?"

He shrugged. "Not really, no."

"But you'll be able to bring home any girl you want, judgment-free," Oscar added.

Nate sighed. "Yeah, well, I'm kind of sick of the 'dating a different woman every week' thing."

Gavin's eyebrows shot up. "Our resident ladies' man doesn't want the job anymore? Or did you finally date every woman in Lakeside?"

"You guys need new jokes," Nate muttered. "For the record, I haven't dated *every* woman in Lakeside, and yes, I think I'm sick of being a ladies' man. I want to find a nice girl to date, you know, for more than a few weeks."

Gavin slapped him on the back. "Good for you."

"Why does that sound condescending?" Nate asked.

Gavin didn't answer because somebody on the TV hit a home run, distracting him. With his friend's attention on the TV, Nate got up, dumped his half-full plate of food in the trash, and grabbed a beer from the fridge. He returned to the couch where he sat sucking on it, watching the chaos around him.

After the game ended, he snatched another drink and moved to the chair in the corner. When Natasha walked past him, he grabbed her arm.

"Can I ask you something?" he asked.

"Yeah, sure. What's up?"

He explained what he wanted to do. She stared at him for a few minutes, tapping her finger against her chin. "Yeah, I think it's a good idea. In fact, it's a great idea." She narrowed her eyes. "Who knew you were so romantic?"

He kissed his sister on the cheek, whispered, "Thanks," then slipped out the front door and jogged across the lawn.

Chapter 11

Faith

I should have gone.

Faith had chastised herself ever since Nate left, wondering why she hadn't gone to the party. Not because she wanted to meet new people, but because she would have been with Nate. And he obviously wanted her to go. If only she could let go of the ridiculous notion that Nate's friendship was based on ulterior motives.

An hour later, her doorbell rang. Now that she was friends with Nate, it rang more than it had the entire time she'd lived there. With a sigh, she pushed herself off the couch, went to the door, and peered out the window.

It was Nate.

Faith smoothed her hair before opening the door. He smiled at her.

"Hi," she murmured. "Wh-what are you doing here?"

"Do you want to watch a movie?" he asked.

"A movie? But what about your party?"

"Eh, I can hang out with those idiots any time. Besides, it's not really *my* party, it's my sister's party. And Mason's."

A strong, crisp breeze rattled the windows and made her shiver. Did Nate really want to give up an evening with his friends to spend time with her? She almost told him no, but something about the earnest look on his face made her decide differently. Another blast of cold air hit her, so Faith gestured for him to come in and close the door.

He walked past her into the living room, looking around for a few seconds until he found what he was looking for. He pointed at her TV remote.

"May I?" he asked.

Faith nodded.

Nate snatched up the remote, turned on the TV, and quickly flipped through her streaming services, which didn't take long since she only had a few. He sat on the edge of her couch and pulled up a movie.

She smiled when she saw what it was.

"*The Princess Bride*?" She couldn't believe that was the one he chose. It was one of her favorites; she had seen it more times than she could count.

He grinned. "Yeah. I saw the book on your kitchen table. It looked like you'd read it a lot, so I thought maybe you liked the movie, too."

"I *love* the movie," Faith replied.

"Great! Why don't you come sit by me and we'll watch it? I promise I won't bite." He winked at her, and her heart skipped a beat.

Half an hour later, they were side by side, watching the movie and eating from a bowl of popcorn balanced on the couch cushion between them. Faith shoved herself into the corner of the couch, but it wasn't big enough for her to get too far away from him. The only thing separating them was the bowl.

She concentrated on the movie, but sitting next to Nate unnerved her. He wore low-slung jeans and a tight white T-shirt, so tight it emphasized his biceps and taut abs. His fingers occasionally brushed against hers when they both reached for popcorn, and his infectious laugh echoed through the room. Faith watched him more than the movie. She couldn't help but wonder what it would be like to sit beside him with his arm around her, the two of them cuddled close together. It was easy to picture.

Unnerved by the direction her thoughts had turned, she jumped to her feet. "Would you like some hot chocolate?"

"Hot chocolate?" Nate mumbled.

"Yes," she replied. "I make fantastic hot chocolate. Trust me, you'll love it. I'll be right back."

She hurried to the kitchen and pulled ingredients from the cupboards. Every few seconds, she snuck a look at Nate. He was so relaxed, and sure of himself, sprawled over her couch like he'd been there forever, like he belonged. Meanwhile, she was a bundle of nerves, shaky and on edge. Faith envied him.

She propped herself against the counter, hugging herself as she tried to control her breathing. The hot chocolate was an excuse to get away for a few minutes so she could pull herself together. Nate probably thought she was insane or, more likely, he wondered what he had gotten himself into. Faith was willing to bet he was planning his escape.

The boiling milk interrupted her musings, drawing her attention away from her feelings of inadequacy.

The shot of Irish cream she added to the hot chocolate would calm her frazzled nerves. She prepared two mugs, topping both with a healthy dollop of whipped cream.

Nate gave her a heart-stopping smile when she reentered the room. He jumped to his feet to move a stack of books from the coffee table to the floor, making room for the popcorn bowl and both mugs. He took a mug, hissing when he touched the hot cup, and put it on the table beside the popcorn.

When they sat down, he was right next to her, his leg pressed against hers, one arm on the back of the couch, his hand close but not quite touching her. The smell of his cologne wrapped itself around her and pushed its warm scent into her nose, fogging her brain. She needed a distraction, and fast.

Faith raised her mug and sucked in a deep breath. The dark chocolate and whipped cream mixed perfectly to slice through the fog and clear her mind. She glanced at Nate out of the corner of her eye.

"Um ... Faith." He chuckled and tapped the side of his nose. "What?"

Nate's hand landed on her leg as he leaned into her. "Here," he whispered. The pad of his thumb swiped across the tip of her nose. He held it up and showed her the whipped cream she must have gotten on her nose when she shoved her face into her drink.

Faith couldn't take her eyes off him as he pushed his thumb between his lips and sucked on it. Heat pooled in the pit of her stomach, and an indescribable need roared through every nerve ending. She opened her mouth—probably to say something stupid—but she snapped it closed as Nate moved closer. His fingers danced down her back, and he slipped his arm around her waist. His mouth was a breath away from hers. He was going to kiss her, and in that moment, there wasn't anything she wanted more than to feel his lips against hers.

The crash was loud enough to make them both jump. It ruined the moment and broke them apart. His foot had bumped the stack of books he'd put on the floor, which hit another stack of books, followed by the end table, knocking over the precariously balanced lamp and sending it crashing to the ground. It shattered into pieces.

Ten minutes later, they stood at Faith's front door. Once they cleaned up the mess and the broken glass was in the trash, Nate looked at the clock and declared it was late and he had to get up early. Faith stared at the floor and shifted from foot to foot with her lower lip caught between her teeth and her hands clenched at her sides. She wondered if he'd kiss her before he left. Actually, she hoped he'd kiss her before he left.

Instead, he grabbed her hand, gave it a quick squeeze, and mumbled something that sounded vaguely like, "I'll see you later" before he disappeared out the door.

"Bye," she whispered.

Chapter 12

Nate

As soon as the door closed behind him, Nate took off at a dead run across the lawn, like his ass was on fire. The strangest feeling had overcome him.

Doubt.

He had always gotten the girl. There had never been a question of if or when, never. Any girl he ever wanted fell head over heels for him.

Until Faith.

God, he'd wanted to kiss her when they'd stood in front of her door. He wanted to reignite the spark the broken lamp put out, but Faith stared at the floor and shifted nervously, acting like she wanted nothing more than for him to leave. She wouldn't make eye contact with him. So, he left, turned tail and ran, his confidence in his ability to win over a woman shaken.

Nate opened his front door, darted inside, and slammed it behind himself, harder than he intended. Everyone was gone, except for Mason and Natasha, who was sprawled across the couch with her mouth open, light snores coming from her.

"Shh," Mason hissed, pointing at Natasha. "She's asleep."

"Sorry," Nate mumbled. He kicked off his shoes, went into the kitchen, grabbed a beer from the refrigerator, and drained it in a few swallows. He took out another one and dropped into a chair at the table.

Mason sat down across from him. He glanced at Natasha, leaned on the table, and said in a low voice, "What's wrong? I thought you were with the neighbor. Faith, right?"

"I was." Nate shrugged.

Mason chuckled. "Honestly, I didn't expect you home tonight. At least not at... what?" He checked his watch. "Shit, eleven-thirty. I figured you'd be staying the night."

"Faith isn't like that," Nate snapped. "She's... she's different. Hell, I'm not even sure she likes me."

"You're joking?" Mason shook his head. "None of your usual moves worked? Hard to believe."

"Believe it, buddy," Nate muttered. He leaned on the table, his head in his hands. "I can't figure her out. It's not like it usually is with a woman I'm interested in. It's not—"

"Easy?" Mason finished. He ignored the dirty look Nate gave him. "You know what, Nathaniel? Maybe she's not like the women you're usually interested in. In fact, I'm sure she's not. You're going to have to work for this one. But think about this: *if* you win her over, this might be the real deal. Especially for her. You need to be careful, and you need to be sure of what you're doing. Otherwise, you'll break her heart."

Nate nodded. Mason was right. Faith was different, and if he won her over, it wouldn't be like the other women he'd dated. Faith could be the *one*. His head spun with the possibilities.

"I'm gonna go to bed," he said, pushing himself away from the table. As he passed his sister on the couch, he turned back to Mason. "Are you leaving Tasha on the couch?"

"Hell, no. She's never sleeping there again." Mason jumped to his feet, bounded across the room, scooped Natasha up, and threw her over his shoulder.

"Hey," she mumbled sleepily. "What the heck?"

Nate laughed and headed for his room. Natasha had slept on the couch for months after a nasty breakup, until she and Mason finally got it together and realized they were in love. As much as he joked about how *icky* they were, Nate appreciated his sister finding love with his best friend. They were perfect for each other and meant to be a couple.

Once he was in his room, he peeled off his clothes and dropped onto the bed. He actually had to get up early, that's why he called it a night. Cecily Devereaux was coming to the bar in the morning to discuss his expansion plans for the Time Out Bar & Grill. If she liked what she saw, he was going to ask her to invest in the business. Nate had been working on this for months, though he had kept it to himself. Expanding the bar was a dream he hadn't thought possible until Cecily expressed an interest in his expansion plans. She was a sharp businesswoman, in charge of a multi-million-dollar company, and if he wanted to convince her to give him a lot of money, he needed to be on top of his game.

Instead of falling asleep, he stared at the ceiling, thinking about Faith, going over every move, word, and little thing he had done. Nate made himself crazy figuring out what he did to make her uncomfortable.

He couldn't get her out of his head—her soft skin, her sweet voice, and how insanely beautiful she was, though she didn't seem to know it. When he closed his eyes, all he saw was her, and all he thought about was how her lips would feel moving against his.

"Screw it," he muttered under his breath. He tossed the blankets aside, grabbed a pair of sweats and a T-shirt off the floor, and yanked them on. He threw open his door, stalked through the house, slipped on the old tennis shoes he kept by the door, and went out his front door. Nate ran across the lawn and up her porch steps. Without hesitating, he pounded on her door, not relenting until she opened it.

Faith's hair hung down her back, and she wore a baggy T-shirt, oversized boxers, and thick, wool socks pulled up to her knees. He saw more of her than he'd ever seen before, fanning the flames of his desire. She squinted at him, her eyebrows drawn together, her mouth in a tight, irritated line.

"Nate? What the heck?"

It was the only thing he let her get out before he crossed the threshold and grabbed her, his hands on her face, cupping her cheeks. He kissed her gently, his lips moving against hers.

Faith gasped and put her hands on his wrist, but she didn't resist, didn't pull away. In fact, she leaned into him, and her mouth opened. His tongue slipped into her mouth. God, she tasted like hot chocolate.

He groaned as he wrapped an arm around her waist, pulling her flush against him. Her hands slipped hesitantly around his neck, and her fingers slid up into his hair as the kiss deepened.

When they broke apart, they were both breathing heavily and staring into each other's eyes.

"That's how I should have said good night," Nate murmured.

—

After kissing Faith two more times, Nate returned to his place, crawled into bed, and slept better than he'd slept in weeks. Not even the worry about his upcoming meeting with Cecily could kill his good mood. He woke up with a smile on his face, and it stayed there. He grinned at the barista who made his coffee, grinned at the guy taking forever to cross the street and making him late, and smiled at Brooke when he walked into the bar.

"What's with you?" Brooke asked.

Nate shrugged one shoulder. "I'm just in a good mood."

"Okay," Brooke said, drawing out the word. "Why?"

"Because I am," he muttered, rolling his eyes.

"There's something you're not telling me." She stared at him until he wanted to squirm. He refused to let her ruin his good mood, though.

"Yep," he replied, smirking. He poured himself a cup of coffee from the pot behind the counter. "Don't bother digging for information because you're not getting it."

"Fine." Brooke crossed her arms. "Are you ready for this? Cecily will be here any minute."

Brooke was the only person who knew about his plan to expand the bar. She'd helped him put together a business plan to present to Cecily, even sketching the way the bar would look with the expansion. She cared almost as much as he did.

"I'm going to run upstairs and make a phone call," he said. He drank the rest of his coffee and put the cup in the small sink.

"Did you not hear me when I said Cecily is going to be here any minute?"

"Yes, I heard you," he mumbled. "Fine, I'll wait. You know what? I think I need more coffee."

As he poured himself a cup from the pot behind the counter, Cecily breezed in, her husband, Lincoln, and their dogs in tow. Nate shook both Cecily's and Lincoln's hands, then petted both dogs. Whenever Cecily came in, she had her Shih Tzu, Sebastian, with her. He was the inspiration for the pet area Nate planned to build at the back of the bar, including covered seating and a small play yard for the dogs.

Cecily Devereaux was Lakeside's resident "rich girl." She lived in an immense house on an island in the middle of Flathead Lake with Lincoln and their dogs. While she wasn't originally from Montana, she had adopted the town as her own after moving there when she was a teenager. She'd been receptive to Nate's ideas about expanding the Time Out Bar & Grill because she loved Lakeside and wanted to be a part of making it a vacation destination.

Once everyone had coffee and the doughnuts Brooke brought, Nate laid out his plans for expanding the bar. Cecily was all business, asking questions and jotting notes in a small notebook she'd pulled from her purse. Occasionally, Brooke interjected an important piece of information or pointed out something on her drawings.

"This looks amazing," Cecily said when Nate finished speaking. "Your sketches are fabulous, Brooke."

She grinned. "Thank you."

"So, what do you think?" Nate asked.

"This is a brilliant plan," Cecily replied. "If you don't mind, I'd like a few days to go over everything."

Nate nodded. "Absolutely."

"Great." Cecily got to her feet and ordered Sebastian and their other dog, Sadie, to her side. They immediately obeyed. Lincoln attached their leashes while Cecily gathered everything and put it in her bag.

After everyone left, Nate went upstairs to his office, dropped into his chair, and grabbed the phone. He dialed Faith's number from memory. She answered on the first ring.

"H-hello?"

"Hi," he breathed. "How are you?"

"I'm okay," she replied. "You?"

"I'll be better if you say yes to a date tomorrow."

Faith laughed, an enticing, breathy laugh that made Nate's stomach twist oddly.

"Does that mean yes?" he asked.

"Yeah. I mean, yes. Yes, I'll go on a date with you tomorrow."

Nate exhaled. He'd been holding his breath, waiting for her answer, sure her it would be no. Now that she'd agreed to go, he could relax. He knew exactly what they were going to do. He needed to make a phone call.

Chapter 13

Faith

When she woke up the next morning, she'd convinced herself that Nate kissing her senseless at her front door while she was in her pajamas couldn't possibly be real. Then he called her, and before she knew what happened, she had agreed to go on a date with him. A date meant going out in public, and the thought terrified her. How was this her life?

She texted him several times in a thinly veiled attempt to get him to tell her where they were going. He didn't fall for it, keeping her guessing.

Late Sunday afternoon, Nate knocked on her door. She took a deep breath and willed her hands to stop shaking as she unlocked it.

"Hi." Nate's smile blinded her. He leaned against her door frame, calm and casual, incredibly handsome in a pair of jeans and a dark green button-down shirt. He straightened and held his hand out to her.

"Shall we?"

Faith nodded and took his hand. This was it, the *date*. She still couldn't believe she was going out with Nate, or that she'd kissed him, or that he wanted to spend time with her. She didn't understand what he saw in her.

As usual, Nate opened the passenger side door and helped her into the truck. Despite her repeated protests over the last week, he *always* opened her door and helped her in and out of the truck. He said his mom would "beat his ass" if he wasn't a gentleman.

They drove down U.S. 93, turned right on Adams, and parked in the lot by Volunteer Park. He jogged around the front of the vehicle and helped her out, then he tucked her hand into the crook of his elbow and kissed her temple.

Heat rushed to her cheeks. She could get used to this.

"Where are we going?" she asked.

"I wanted to show you something," he said. "I think you'll like it."

They crossed the street, then Nate stopped in front of a small storefront at the corner of the building. "Here we are." He pointed at the sign on the building.

Faith stepped back to read it. "Turn the Page," she mumbled. "What is this?" She eyed him suspiciously.

"Come on. I'll show you." Nate opened the door and gestured for her to go inside.

When she stepped across the threshold, the smell of new books assaulted her. She froze, astonished at what was in front of her. It was a large space, unbelievably so, considering the size of the storefront. Overflowing bookshelves crowded every available inch, signs pointed to every imaginable genre, and stacks of books covered the tables placed in various locations, their themes placed on signs prominently displayed in the center of the table. At the back of the store, a wrought iron staircase spiraled up to another level.

Faith's jaw dropped as she turned to look at Nate. "I didn't know there was a bookstore in Lakeside."

He raised his eyebrows. "Surprise!" He chuckled. "I thought you might like it." He looked around, then yelled, "Vera!"

A pretty brunette came around the corner and made her way toward them. She was ethereal, gorgeous, and when she hugged Nate, a surge of jealousy and intense inadequacy washed over Faith.

"Faith, this is my friend, Vera. She owns this place. Its grand opening is in two weeks, right?"

Vera turned her brilliant smile on Faith. She grasped Faith's hand and said warmly, "It's nice to finally meet you." She looked over her shoulder and yelled, "Oscar! Come meet Nate's girlfriend."

Faith's heart skipped at the word "girlfriend." Was that who Vera thought she was? Should she correct her? After all, she *wasn't* Nate's girlfriend; they were friends, nothing more. She sneaked a glance at Nate, but he seemed nonplussed at the comment.

A short, stocky man appeared from the stacks, carrying several boxes. He set them on the floor, dusted off his hands, and joined them. He slipped his arm around Vera's waist.

"Oscar, this is Faith," Vera said.

"Nice to meet you," he said.

She smiled shyly. "It's nice to meet both of you."

Vera's smile was so warm and inviting it instantly put Faith at ease. "I understand you're a book lover?"

She nodded. "I guess I am. I'm a librarian at the town library."

"That's why you look familiar." Vera laughed. "I love the library! I spent countless hours there during college. Well, come on. I'll show you around."

"O-okay," Faith stammered. She looked at Nate, and he gestured for her to follow Vera.

For the next two hours, Faith followed Vera around while Nate trudged after them, laughing at her obvious delight when she discovered something new. He carried her books and even got her and Vera coffee from a small coffee bar at the back of the store.

When they emerged from the bookstore, Nate carried two

overstuffed bags of books tucked under his arms, and Faith couldn't stop smiling and giggling. Vera insisted Faith return for the grand opening as she and Oscar waved goodbye from the door. She readily agreed.

Giddy with excitement, Faith bounced on the balls of her feet and talked nonstop about the bookstore and everything she had experienced. She had fallen in love with Turn the Page, and she couldn't wait to return. When they got to his truck, he set the bags on the ground and pulled her into his arms.

"Did you have fun?" he asked.

"Yes! It was amazing. Thank you!" Her heart pounded and her cheeks were hot. How had her life changed so much in such a short time?

Nate kissed the corner of her mouth. "You're welcome," he whispered. He scooped up the bags and put them in the truck. "Let's go get some food. Lugging around those books made me hungry."

Once they were in the truck, on impulse, Faith reached over and took Nate's hand. His eyebrows shot up, but he quickly recovered, replacing his look of surprise with a smile. He drove with one hand while holding Faith's hand tightly with the other.

———

At work on Monday, Faith couldn't stop talking about Vera's bookstore. She went on and on about every little corner of it until Caroline interrupted her.

"Wait a minute. How did you get into the store before it opened? I thought it didn't open until next month?"

She shrugged. "Nate went with me."

Caroline stopped dead in her tracks and turned around to look at Faith. "*Nate*? The same Nate who owns the Time Out Bar & Grill?"

Faith nodded.

"Why did he take you?" Caroline asked.

"Um... well, he, uh, he knows the owner. They're friends," Faith explained.

Caroline narrowed her eyes. "That doesn't explain why he took you there before it opens."

"We're friends," she whispered.

"You're friends with Nate? Since when?"

Faith exhaled loudly, blowing her hair off her forehead. "He ran into me one night in my front yard. The next thing I know, he's asking me out for coffee."

"What? When? Why didn't you tell me?" Caroline actually looked hurt.

"I'm sorry," Faith murmured. "It's just... well, I didn't want to go out with him."

Caroline's eyes widened. "Why didn't you want to go out with him? He's attractive, funny, owns his own business—"

"I know all that," Faith said. "I guess, um, I thought he felt bad for running into me. But then he helped me when my car broke down. He did this really cute thing with a bunch of different drinks from The Percolator, and he watched *The Princess Bride* with me. His idea. He finally won me over, so I went out with him."

"Are you going out with him again?"

Faith nodded, heat rushing to her cheeks. "I want to. I really like him, and I had so much fun at the bookstore." Her eyes dropped to the floor. "Life experience has taught me that the people I care about end up hurting me. I don't want that to happen with Nate." Tears welled up in her eyes. She brushed them away, but she didn't look up. She couldn't stand the thought of Caroline looking at her with pity.

Caroline hugged her, taking Faith by surprise.

"What was that for?" she murmured.

Her friend shrugged. "Just because." She cleared her throat. "Why don't we get some work done? Tell me more about the bookstore while we shelve the new books. Let's put some flyers up around the library to get the word out."

"Yeah, that sounds great," Faith said. "I'll see if Nate can ask Vera if she has any."

She followed Caroline down the hall. Her friend was being too nice. It hadn't been hard to recognize her hug for what it really was: sympathy. Faith had grown used to things like that growing up in foster care. She didn't want people feeling sorry for her. That was her biggest fear with Nate: that it was a front because he thought she was pathetic, or he pitied her. She couldn't bear it if that was the case.

Chapter 14

Nate

Three weeks.

Nate had been dating Faith for more than three weeks, and somehow, he'd kept things quiet and low-key.

Since their first date, they had spent a lot of time together. Not only was he driving her to work every day, but they'd gotten pizza at Roselli's, she'd made homemade macaroni and cheese for dinner, he'd hung out at her place and watched a football game while she read a book, and one Friday night he fell asleep on her couch after working at the bar. They'd exchanged hellos, and then he'd rested his head on the back of the couch, closed his eyes, and the next thing he knew, he was out. Faith had thrown a blanket over him, and when he woke a couple of hours later, she'd been sitting on the floor reading.

It was the best thing to happen to him in years, and he was terrified he was going to mess it up.

"When do we get to meet the mysterious woman next door who captured the heart of our resident ladies' man?" Natasha asked.

Nate glared at his sister, willing her to shut up. He didn't want to explain his relationship with Faith to his friends.

He chuckled and shook his head. "Never. You'll scare her away." He might have laughed, but he certainly wasn't joking. His core group of friends—his sister, Mason, Oscar, Gavin, Vera, and Summer—were a raucous bunch. Loud, crazy, and fun-loving. Faith was shy, quiet, and kept to herself. She wasn't used to being around a group of people like his friends.

"Vera and Oscar got to meet her," Mason argued.

"Vera isn't loud and scary," Nate retorted. "Or sarcastic and sassy." He looked pointedly at Natasha.

His sister stuck her tongue out at him as she poured herself another beer. They were at the bar, eating Nate's food and drinking his beer after spending the day moving Mason and Natasha's things into their new place.

"What about Oscar? He's loud and scary," Natasha quipped.

Nate sighed. "He behaved himself because Vera told him if he didn't, she'd kick his ass."

"Seriously, when do we get to meet her?" Summer asked.

"She's really shy." Nate rubbed his forehead. "I don't want to scare her away. I promise you'll get to meet her. Eventually."

"Doesn't she live next door to you? Next time we're over at your place, let's walk over and say hi," Gavin interjected.

Nate glared at his friend. "I will kill you," he warned. "Don't you dare go over there."

Gavin laughed. "Okay, okay. This is serious, isn't it? You really like this woman."

He nodded. "Yeah, I do." He liked her more than any of his friends—except maybe Mason—realized.

Summer leaned on the table and stared at Nate, her eyes boring into him. "Have you slept with her?" she asked.

"Whoa, Summer," Natasha yelled. "TMI!"

"It's a legitimate question," Summer said. "Look, we know

Nate is a ladies' man. We've seen the women he's paraded in and out of his place. None of those 'relationships' lasted more than what—a few weeks, maybe a month? The common denominator in all of those encounters was they started out in the same place. The bedroom. So, again, it's a legitimate question. Are you having sex with her?"

The group groaned collectively, acting appalled that Summer was asking these questions. Except Nate suspected they wanted the answers.

"No, no, wait." He raised his voice to be heard over his friends. "It's okay." He cleared his throat. "Look, not that it's anybody's business, but no, I am not having sex with Faith, even though we've been dating for three weeks." He took a deep breath. "That's not... I'm not in this to get laid. I genuinely like this woman. I'm not rushing into anything."

Everyone was shockingly quiet, staring at him like he'd grown another head. Mason smirked. His sister had a sappy smile on her face, and everyone else looked shocked.

Nate wasn't surprised; it shocked him as well. Faith had wormed her way into his heart like no other woman ever had. He hadn't felt this way since Elle. And somehow he'd messed that up. He had no intention of doing that again.

"Well, now I've heard everything," Gavin muttered. "I think I need more beer." He grabbed the pitcher and filled his glass.

Soon, the conversation moved on to other things, things that fortunately were not his love life. It was a relief because he didn't enjoy having it scrutinized.

He glanced at his watch, wondering if he could escape from his friends, take some food over to Faith's place, and hang out with her for a while. He grabbed his phone to text her.

[Nate: I might get away early. Do you want me to bring dinner over?]

[Faith: Sorry, but I'm working late. The librarian who works the evening shift is sick.]

[Nate: Okay. Can I come over when you get home?]

[Faith: Yes. I'll be there by 9:30.]

Nate shoved his phone in his pocket and refilled his beer. He still wasn't sure where he stood with Faith. He liked her and he thought she liked him, but it wasn't like it had been with other women. Those had been easy; those women had let him know from the onset they were interested and *wanted* to have sex with him. Faith was an enigma. While he thought she enjoyed his company, sometimes it was like pulling teeth to get her to go out on a date with him. Even though he'd told his friends they hadn't met Faith because they'd scare her away, the truth was she resisted every time he suggested meeting them.

And sex, well, he didn't know where they were on that subject. Not that he wasn't interested in sex with Faith, but there was something holding her back. Because he liked her so much, he had no intention of pushing her into anything she didn't want to do.

Two hours later, everyone was gone except Mason and Natasha. He sat at the table with them, nursing his beer, his thoughts constantly turning to Faith. He was antsy, checking his watch every few minutes, counting the minutes until he could see her.

Natasha rapped her knuckles on the table. "What is up with you? I've never seen you like this."

"Neither have I," Mason added. "You're not acting like yourself."

"I'm fine," Nate scoffed. "I'm... I don't know—"

"In love?" his twin asked.

"No," he muttered. "I'm... I'm not in love."

Natasha patted his arm. "You know what? You deserve love. You've been alone for too long. I worry about you."

"I'm *fine*," Nate repeated.

"I know you're fine," Natasha said. "But you're better with Faith in your life. You are aware of that, right?"

He nodded, then checked his watch. "I need to go. I want to take a shower before Faith gets home from work." He pushed his beer away and stood up.

"Are you okay to drive?" Mason asked.

"I drank half a beer," he replied, pointing at his glass. "I've been nursing it for hours." He kissed his sister on the top of the head and slapped Mason's shoulder. "Have fun in your new place. I'll see you later."

"Don't do anything I wouldn't do," Mason yelled after him.

"I hate you guys," he yelled over his shoulder as he walked away.

Once he was in his truck, Nate rolled his window down. It was cold outside, especially now that it was moving into November. But he needed the cool air to clear his head. His sister filled it with all kinds of ideas, things he didn't want to think about. He wasn't in love; he couldn't be. He'd only known Faith for about a month, not long enough to fall in love with her.

Besides, it wasn't love. He wasn't good at love. Elle had let him know that in no uncertain terms. She'd been clear when she broke up with him that he was a selfish, no-good piece of shit who didn't know how to love anybody but himself. So how could he possibly be in love with Faith?

Chapter 15

Faith

Her life was crazy. Crazy in a good way.

If someone told her six months ago that she would be in a whirlwind romance, the kind she'd only read about in romance novels—the insta-love, no slow burn kind of romance—Faith would have said they were crazy. Most days, it was like a dream and didn't seem real.

She'd had been dating Nate for almost a month. They spent most of their free time together, doing everything from dinner dates in Kalispell to watching TV. Well, he watched TV while she read a book.

Nate drove her to work every morning and picked her up every night until the mechanic finished fixing her car. Even if he wasn't opening the bar, he got out of bed and drove her to work, and he took a break to pick her up if he was at work.

Once she worked out an acceptable payment plan with Kane, it had still taken a couple of weeks for him to fix her car. The part he needed had to be ordered, and he had to go to Missoula to pick it up. When he'd messaged her it was ready, she was surprised at the disappointment that rushed through her. She'd gotten used to spending that time with Nate every day, and now it was over. When she'd texted Nate to ask him if he'd take her to pick it up, he'd responded with a sad face emoji, which made her laugh.

Faith convinced herself that since she had her car back, she wouldn't see as much of Nate as she had when it was in the shop. She was wrong.

When he dropped her off at the auto shop, he'd smirked at her and said, "Don't think because Kane fixed your car that it gets you out of spending time with me." Then he'd kissed her until she thought her heart might pound out of her chest.

Every day, it astonished her he wanted to be with her. She expected him to change his mind at any minute, realize he'd made a mistake, and bail.

Faith hadn't expected to see him after she took Josie's evening shift at the library, especially since he'd spent the day helping his sister and Mason move, but he'd been at her door less than five minutes after she got home. He'd swooped in, pulled her into his arms, and kissed her.

Nate released her and followed her into the kitchen. His quiet, melancholy mood was strangely out of place. He was usually in a perpetually good mood.

"Hey, you don't have to park on the street anymore," Faith pointed out.

"Yeah," he muttered. "I guess I don't." He rocked back and forth, staring at the ground. "Anyway, I only wanted to say hi. I'm sure you're tired after working all day." He gestured at the door over his shoulder. "I'm gonna go. See you later?"

"Yeah, of course," she replied.

"Good night," he whispered. He walked out, shoulders slumped and head down.

After emptying her backpack and changing into a pair of flannel pajama pants and an oversized sweatshirt, Faith headed back to the kitchen. She couldn't get Nate off her mind. He wasn't his usual cheery self, and she wasn't sure why.

Because his sister and best friend moved out.

She stopped dead in the middle of her kitchen. Of course. Nate was alone. He and Mason had lived next door to her for years. Then Natasha moved in, filling the little house even more. But now everyone was gone, and he was alone. How could she be so stupid?

She grabbed a shopping bag from under the sink, loaded it with mugs, milk, hot chocolate mix, whipped cream, and her bottle of Irish cream liqueur, then she put on her slippers, grabbed her keys, and hurried out the door. It was cold out, colder than it had been when Nate had come over. Goosebumps rose on her skin as she darted across the lawn and knocked on his door.

For a minute, she wondered if he had gone straight to bed; she couldn't see any lights on in the house. He yanked open the door, his irritated look changing to a hesitant smile when he saw her.

"Hey," he murmured. "What are you doing here? Is everything okay?"

Faith nodded, suddenly unsure of her impulsive decision to show up on Nate's doorstep. "I... I thought I'd make you some hot chocolate." She held up the bag and pointed at it.

His smile lit up the dark night. "That sounds amazing." He opened the door wide and gestured for her to come in.

She stepped into the front entrance. The house was like hers, though Nate's kitchen was to her left and the living room was through the foyer and around the corner. She emptied the bag, placing the things she'd brought with her on the table. Nate took a pan out of the cupboard, put it on the stove, then he sat at the table, watching her while she made the hot chocolate.

"Spoons?" she asked.

He pointed to a drawer next to the sink. When the mugs were full, and the whipped cream added, Faith handed one to him.

"Let's go sit on the couch," he said.

She followed him to the living room and sat at the opposite end of the couch from Nate. It was large, far bigger than hers, which meant there was at least two feet of space between them. They sat quietly, sipping their hot chocolate.

The house was empty, lifeless. No pictures hung on the walls, and no knick-knacks decorated the shelves. Of course, this had been the home of two bachelors before Natasha moved in, and she'd taken her things with her when she moved out today. She peeked at Nate out of the corner of her eye. He stared at the wall above the TV, silent.

"Are you okay?" Faith asked.

"Hm?"

"You don't seem like yourself," she said.

Nate gave her a half-hearted grin. "I'm sorry. Shit, this is the first time you've been in my house and I'm sitting here moping. You were nice enough to come over here and make me hot chocolate and..." He trailed off with a sigh and shook his head. "It's weird, you know? I've never lived alone. I lived at home with my parents and Tasha, obviously. While I was in college, I lived with Mason at the dorms, then here. Then my sister moved in with us. Now, they're gone and I'm by myself. Everything feels off-kilter."

Faith cleared her throat. "Don't you think you'll enjoy living on your own?"

He shrugged. "I guess I'll find out, huh?" He put his mug of hot chocolate on the coffee table and stood up. "I'll be right back." He darted into the bathroom and pushed the door closed.

She sat back and sipped her cocoa. It helped warm her a little, but it was freezing in Nate's house. She wandered back toward the kitchen, looking for the thermostat. It was in roughly the same location as hers.

No wonder she was cold; it hovered around sixty degrees. She jumped when Nate wrapped his arms around her from behind. She hadn't heard him come out of the bathroom.

"Are you cold?" he whispered in her ear.

She nodded. "A little."

He hugged her close and rested his chin on her shoulder. "Thank you for coming over. And making hot chocolate." He kissed her neck, and she relaxed against him. "Can I tell you something?"

"Sure." Faith closed her eyes, wondering what he was going to say. It scared her a little.

"I'm so glad I ran into you and knocked your books out of your hand. It was the best thing to happen to me in a really long time."

"Nate," she murmured. "You're crazy."

"Crazy for you." He chuckled. "And I like it."

Faith turned in his arms and rested her hands on his chest. "I like it, too. And if you're crazy, so am I." She closed her eyes, because she couldn't look at him. "Did you know before you burst into my life like the crazy ball of energy you are, I hadn't dated anybody since high school?"

"You're kidding."

She shook her head. "No, I'm dead serious. I had an unpleasant experience with a guy in high school, and it kind of scared me off dating. Apparently forever."

"What happened?"

Faith sighed. "Do you really want to hear this story?"

"Only if you want to tell me," Nate replied.

She closed her eyes. To her surprise, she did. "Can we sit down?"

"Sure." Nate led her to the couch and sat down beside her, his big, warm hand wrapped around hers.

"Okay," she murmured. "When I was in high school, I had a friend—if you could call her that—who set me up with this guy I had a crush on. I thought he liked me, you know? It turns out, this so-called friend told him I was easy, so he only dated me for sex. We had a public break up where I came off looking like a fool *and* a bitch. I haven't dated since. And since I'm being honest about my past, I haven't kissed a guy in nine years, and I'm a virgin." She threw herself against the back of the couch and put her hands over her face.

"Hey," Nate said. He grabbed her hands and pried them away from her face. "Faith, would you look at me, please?"

She looked up at him. As soon as she did, he leaned over and kissed her. "I'm sorry people suck. That guy sounds like a jerk."

"Yeah, he was." She stared at her hands folded in her lap, caught her lower lip between her teeth, and gnawed at it.

Nate ducked his head, forcing her to look at him. "What's wrong?"

Faith shrugged one shoulder. "Does it... does it bother you that I'm a virgin?"

He shook his head. "No, of course not. Why would it bother me?"

She snorted. "Um, maybe because you usually date women who are far more experienced than me? Or, I don't know, because *you're* more experienced than me. I'm a twenty-six-year-old virgin, and you, well, you've slept with every woman in town."

Nate rolled his eyes. "You know, I'm getting really tired of everyone saying that. I don't care that you're a virgin. I'm fine if you want to have sex or if you don't want to have sex. That's not what matters to me."

"Would you be mad if I didn't want to have sex?" she whispered. "Because I'm not sure I'm ready yet."

"Absolutely not," he replied. "I'll wait as long as you want. Forever, if you want me to."

Faith blushed. "Really?"

"Yes, really." He pulled her into his arms and hugged her close.

She closed her eyes and rested her head against his chest. God, she wanted to believe him; she really did. He seemed sincere, but she couldn't seem to push away the little niggle of doubt invading her thoughts.

What if he's lying to make me feel better?

Chapter 16

Faith

The next morning, Faith was still thinking about her conversation with Nate. Keeping the tears at bay had been almost impossible. Despite his assurances to the contrary, she had convinced herself he wasn't being honest. He probably wanted to spare her feelings, which is why he said he didn't care she was a virgin. Of course he cared. He was a man. It had to bother him.

After he walked her back to her place and kissed her good night, she'd gone to bed, but she hadn't been able to sleep. Her brain wouldn't let her.

Sunday, she was on her own because Nate worked a double shift at the bar. She cleaned the house and organized her books, which didn't go exactly as planned, but she put several boxes of them in her extra bedroom.

Monday came and went without a call from Nate. She'd looked out the window several times, but his truck was nowhere to be seen. She texted him, but she didn't get an answer.

Tuesday, he showed up at the library with lunch, which made Caroline grin like she'd won the lottery.

Nate laughed as he and Faith sat down in the breakroom. "Your friend is funny. Is she happy to see me?"

She giggled. "She's just surprised. So am I. What's up?"

"Can't I come have lunch with you?" he asked.

"Yes!" she insisted, blushing. "Of course."

"I admit, I have an ulterior motive," Nate said. He reached across the table and took her hand. "I've got this big ... thing coming up. A project I'm working on. I'm afraid it's going to take up a lot of my time the next few weeks, so I won't be around much."

"Oh, um, okay," she whispered.

Was this the breakup she'd been expecting?

He squeezed her hand. "Hey, look at me. This changes nothing."

Faith nodded. "Sure, I understand."

Nate was correct; she didn't see him much over the next few weeks. She missed him terribly, and even though he swore it was this mysterious project of his, she couldn't help but wonder if this was because of what they'd discussed about sex and her virginity. She threw herself into work, staying late, doing whatever odd jobs Caroline needed done.

When she finally got a free night at home, Nate was once again working, so she organized the boxes of books she had stacked in the extra bedroom. She separated them into twenty piles, divided by genre and alphabetized. She ran out of steam when she found a box of old romance books she'd brought home a few weeks earlier. Faith had never been much of a romance reader, but curiosity got the best of her. She sorted through them until she found one that looked interesting. The next thing she knew, she'd read more than a hundred pages.

The book was racy and unbelievably sexy. As she read it, her imagination ran wild, and she couldn't help but picture Nate as the novel's main character. Images of him doing the things the guy in the book was doing to the female lead filled her head.

Headlights splashing across the window interrupted her.

This room faced Nate's house, and the window overlooked his driveway. She jumped to her feet, tucked a receipt in her book to hold her place, then she went to the window. To her surprise, she saw Nate getting out of his truck. He'd told her he had to close, which meant he didn't get home until one or two in the morning, sometimes later. Instead of going inside, he ran around the front of the truck and opened the passenger side door. Hands appeared with a plastic bag of what looked like food containers from the bar. Nate took the bag, then a woman jumped out of the truck, slung a large tote bag over her shoulder, and followed him to his front door. Just before the door closed behind them, Nate glanced over his shoulder at her place.

A deep pain settled in the center of her chest, and her breath caught in her throat. She snatched her cell phone off the floor and dialed Nate's number. It rang once, then went to voicemail. A few seconds later, a text popped up.

[Nate: Busy working. Can't talk. Call you tomorrow.]

Faith's grip on her phone loosened, and it fell to the floor. He lied to her. He wasn't at work. He was home and with another woman who looked like she was prepared to stay the night. She leaned against the wall, trying to catch her breath, but after a minute, all she could do was slide to the floor, put her head on her knees, and let the tears fall.

—

After a restless night spent tossing and turning, Faith finally fell asleep around five a.m. When her alarm went off, she grabbed her phone to shut it off, then she texted Caroline to tell her she wouldn't be in. She felt stupid calling out of work because of a *man*, but her heart was in a million pieces. There was no way she could focus enough to get anything done. Not that she told Caroline it was because of Nate; she claimed she had the stomach flu.

Then she shut off her phone, pulled the pillow over her head, and to her surprise, fell asleep. She didn't wake until a few minutes before noon. Her jaw ached from clenching her teeth, a pain that radiated into her head. She turned her phone back on and found not only a sympathetic message from Caroline offering to bring her 7-Up and crackers, but multiple missed calls and texts from Nate. Those she ignored.

Faith was about to text Caroline when her phone rang in her hand with a call from her friend.

"Hey, Caroline," she answered.

"You're not sick."

"Um, what?"

"Don't um, what me," Caroline snapped. "What happened? Is something going on with Nate? He called here and did not know you were sick. Which is weird, don't you think?"

"No," Faith mumbled.

"Did you break up with him?" Caroline asked.

"I don't want to talk about it," she whispered. "It's... he's... Nate's all wrong for me."

Caroline huffed. "I'm going to give you some advice, whether or not you want it. I think you're making a mistake. A huge mistake. Has it ever occurred to you that Nate is the right kind of wrong?"

"What does that even mean?"

"On the surface, you can try to justify that Nate is wrong for you, but you know damn well he's not," Caroline explained. "He is right for you, and you know it. Don't throw what you've got with him away."

"It's too late," Faith whispered. "Look, I have to go." She hung up without waiting for a response.

Her storybook romance with Nate really had been too good

to be true. He probably got tired of not having sex and found someone who would give it to him without the emotional attachment. Faith wondered if he planned to break up with her or if he thought he could keep seeing her while he slept around with other women. The more she thought about it, the angrier she got.

It took her a few minutes to drag herself out of bed, but she was finally able to get up, use the bathroom, and brush her teeth. In the kitchen, she filled the coffeepot with water and shoved a filter in it, but when she opened the tin where she kept her coffee, it was empty. Tears sprang to her eyes.

"Dammit," she muttered under her breath. "Dammit, dammit, dammit." She slammed the container down on the counter, scaring Heathcliff and sending him scurrying out of the room, most likely to hide under her bed.

She couldn't survive without coffee, not today, so she hurriedly put on her shoes, coat, gloves, and hat, grabbed her keys, and went out to her car. She glanced at Nate's house as she walked across the lawn. His truck was gone. It made her irrationally angry.

A light snow fell as she drove to The Percolator. It was beautiful, and it enraged her. She wanted the world to be ugly and horrid. Beauty had no place in a world that stole her only joy.

Her mood didn't improve when she got to the coffee shop. The line was incredibly long, so long she almost turned around and left, but she was desperate for a cup of coffee. She craved it, so she slipped in line, but kept her head down, staring at the floor, her hands shoved in her pockets.

A few minutes after getting in line, she glimpsed Nate's friend Oscar sitting at a table with another man who looked vaguely familiar. Faith didn't look up or make eye contact with Oscar, and she turned her body and pulled her hat down so he couldn't see her face. She prayed he didn't recognize her as the line moved and she got closer to their table.

"What time did Nate say to be at the bar tonight?" the man with Oscar said.

Her ears perked up at the sound of Nate's name. She squinted at the two men, pushed her glasses up her nose, and scrutinized the one she didn't know. She was pretty sure she'd seen him coming and going from the house next door in the last few years. Faith had met none of Nate's friends, aside from Vera and Oscar. Any time he suggested they get together with his friends or the people at the bar, she'd come up with an excuse not to go because she'd been too nervous to entertain the thought of meeting such important people in his life.

"Gavin!" the barista yelled, and the man with Oscar jumped to his feet, grabbed the coffee, and returned to his seat.

"How do you think he convinced her to say yes?" Gavin asked as he sat back down.

Faith's head shot up; then she quickly looked down and concentrated on what they were saying.

Oscar shrugged. "Who knows? I'm sure he charmed her in that way he has."

"Yeah, that's easy for Nate." Gavin chuckled and shook his head. "All he has to do is flash those baby blues at a woman, and she's falling over herself to give him what he wants. I didn't think he'd win her over, though. She's a tough nut to crack."

"From what Mason said, this has been in the works for a while," Oscar said. "He's been after her for some time, but he stayed quiet about it. Now that she said yes, he's ready to celebrate."

"Is she going to be there?" Gavin asked.

Oscar nodded. "Probably. I bet she's going to be around a lot now that this is a done deal."

Gavin laughed. "I wonder how Nate feels about that?"

"He loves it." Oscar snorted. "You know how he is." He checked his watch. "Hey, we better go. I'll be late. Vera has a bunch of work for me to do before opening day."

Faith inched away from the table, careful to keep her face turned away from Oscar. Not only did she not want him to know she'd been eavesdropping, she didn't want him to see the fresh tears on her cheeks. She waited until Oscar and Gavin were gone, then she wiped her cheeks with her gloved hands.

She ordered her coffee when it was her turn, forcing herself not to run once she had it in hand. Home was a million miles away. It surprised her when she parked in front of her house because she had no memory of the drive from the coffee shop. Her brain had shut down.

Once again, she looked over at Nate's place as she crossed the lawn. She couldn't believe she'd let herself fall for such a jerk, especially one who lived right next door. He'd only been biding his time with her until he got the woman he really wanted.

As she stepped through her front door, her phone pinged with a message. When she saw it was Nate, she deleted it without reading it, then she shut off her phone.

Maybe it was time to move.

Chapter 17

Nate

Nate shoved his phone back in his pocket. Faith wasn't answering her phone or any of his text messages. He'd been calling her off and on all morning.

It was still dark when he'd left the house to head to the bar for a seven a.m. meeting with Cecily. Her flight to New York was leaving Kalispell at nine, and she wanted to meet before she and Lincoln left. Nate and Brooke had worked until three in the morning, putting the final touches on everything they had for Cecily. Brooke had crashed on his couch, and they went back to the bar together.

Cecily breezed through the front door of the bar, her Shih Tzus—Sebastian and Sadie—decked out in matching sweaters and leading the way. It took less than an hour for Cecily to go through the paperwork. She'd dragged Lincoln to a back corner of the bar, where they conversed for about ten minutes. When they returned to the table, Cecily pulled a stack of papers from her bag, signed the bottom of one with a flourish, and pushed it across the table.

"I love it," she said. "All of it." She pointed at the paper. "Consider that an open checkbook. Whatever you need for the expansion, it's yours. Go through the paperwork, and when me and Lincoln get back from New York, we'll meet. But it's a yes."

Nate shot out of his seat with a shout, startling the dogs. He hugged Cecily and shook Lincoln's hand, then he grabbed Brooke and hugged her until she begged him to let her go.

An hour after she entered the bar, Cecily was gone.

The first person Nate called was Faith, but it went straight to voicemail. He texted her and asked her to call him as soon as she could.

After that, he called his sister and Mason, as well as all their friends. It was a relief to let the cat out of the bag and tell everyone what he and Brooke had been up to for the last few weeks. He made them all promise to join him at the bar for a celebration that night.

Once he'd talked to his friends, he tried Faith again. Straight to voicemail. Maybe she broke her phone. That thought prompted him to look up the library's number.

"Lakeside College Library, this is Caroline. How may I help you?"

Nate cleared his throat. "Um, hi, Caroline. This is Nate Garin. I'm a friend of Faith's. Can I speak to her?"

"Oh, Nate, hi. Uh, she's not here. Faith called in sick this morning."

"Sick?"

"Yeah, she said she had the stomach flu," Caroline said.

"Thanks." He hung up and immediately texted Faith.

[Nate: I'm worried about you. Call me, please.]

He tried not to worry about Faith as he made preparations for the evening's celebrations, but it wasn't easy. His mind kept drifting to her. Around three, he slipped into the back room and called her again.

"Hello?" She sounded odd, almost unsure of herself.

"Hey, I've been calling you," he said. "Are you okay?"

She took a deep breath. "Can you please stop calling me? I don't want to talk to you."

"What?"

"Don't call me. Don't text me. I don't want to talk to you."

"What the hell are you talking about?" he snapped.

"I'm glad I know the truth now."

"The truth? The truth about what? Jesus, Faith, are you crying? Tell me what's wrong. What happened?"

She laughed, a horrible, sad sound that made his heart ache. "You know what? I should have known better. I was stupid to think you cared about me or wanted to be with me. Was I some kind of consolation prize? Someone to kill time with until you got the woman you wanted?"

Nate closed his eyes and squeezed his phone. "You're not making any sense."

"You don't have to be nice to me anymore," she whispered. "Go back to pretending I don't exist." The line disconnected.

———

After the phone call, Nate bolted, running up the back stairs to his office. He was furious, the anger and the damn feelings he'd ignored rushing up out of nowhere and overwhelming him. He sat down behind his desk and stared at the wall, which was where his sister and Mason found him. Mason set three beers on the desk and took a seat while Natasha came around and perched on the edge.

"What?" Nate mumbled.

"Tell me what's wrong," she said.

"Nothing is *wrong*," he replied.

"Bullshit. Brooke said you've been up here all afternoon, acting moody and depressed. I think she used the word mopey." Her eyes narrowed. "You didn't break up with Faith, did you?"

"No." He sighed, rested his head against the chair, and pinched the bridge of his nose. "She broke up with me."

"What? Why?" Natasha crossed her arms and glared at him. "What did you do?"

He gave his sister a dirty look. "I didn't *do* anything. The last time I saw her, everything was great. Then, out of nowhere, she told me to leave her alone. Something about her being a filler girlfriend until I got the one I wanted. I don't know what the hell she's talking about."

"Filler girlfriend? Does she think you're seeing someone else?" Natasha asked. "Wait. Are you seeing someone else?"

"Tasha, give him a break," Mason said.

Nate laid his head on his desk, his voice muffled when he spoke. "I never should have let myself get close to her. I'm so stupid. I swore I wouldn't let another woman break my heart, and then this happens. God, I'm an idiot."

"What is he talking about?" Natasha demanded. "Who broke his heart and when?"

"Elle," Mason replied.

Natasha poked him. "The girl you dated in college? I don't understand."

Nate sat up, resting his chin on his hand. "Elle and I dated for two years. More than that, I think. Anyway, I thought we were in a good place. I decided to propose."

"What?" Natasha yelled. She slapped Nate on the arm. "You were going to propose to your girlfriend, and I am just now finding out about it? I am your sister."

"A sister who was conspicuously absent when we were in college and for a couple of years after," Nate snapped.

"Sorry," she whispered. "Go on."

"Anyway, I planned on proposing to Elle, but out of nowhere, she dumped me. No actual explanation, only a lame excuse about how we'd drifted apart because all I cared about was my bar. She didn't even do it in person. She sent me a text message in the middle of the day while I was at work. Six months later, she got married."

"Oh my God, Nate." Natasha threw her arms around him and hugged him. "I'm so sorry."

"You're choking me," he mumbled.

"Sorry." She released him, grabbed a beer, and paced the length of the room. "This explains so much. You turned into a man whore because someone broke your heart. So, you decided it was easier to fuck around with a bunch of women than it was to settle down with one. Right?"

"Thanks for the analysis, Dr. Freud," Nate muttered. "Unfortunately, you're right. I was afraid to get close to anybody."

"So, that's why, if a woman wanted more, you dumped her." She took a drink of her beer and grinned triumphantly. "You're not completely broken; you were protecting yourself."

"Will you quit acting like you've solved some big mystery, please?" Nate muttered while Mason laughed and snorted.

"I would apologize," Natasha said, "but I am ecstatic that I figured out why the hell you were sleeping around. Nobody wants a man whore for a brother."

Nate rolled his eyes. "This is not helping me."

Mason, who had been surprisingly quiet, suddenly spoke up. "Are you in love with Faith?"

Nate's immediate instinct was to protest, deny that any feelings existed. He opened his mouth, then he shut it again. He couldn't say that because it would be a lie.

He loved Faith. Jesus, he wanted to spend every second of every day with her, and even that wasn't enough. This breakup and her sudden refusal to see him wounded him to his core.

"Nate?" Mason prompted. "Do you love her?"

"Yes," he whispered, afraid if he said it too loud, it would somehow ruin everything. "Yes, I love her."

"Can I make a suggestion?" Mason asked.

"Yeah, of course."

"You need to tell her how you feel," his best friend said. "Lay it all out for her. It's the only thing that will save your relationship."

"I don't know—"

"Trust me, I know what I'm talking about," Mason interjected. He glanced at Natasha. "Take it from someone who almost blew it with the woman he loves. Be honest."

"Mason is right," Natasha added. "Go talk to Faith. Tell her how you feel and fix this. Do whatever you need to do."

Nate nodded, got to his feet, and grabbed his jacket. "You're right. I can't sit here and wonder what the hell went wrong. I need to talk to her and do whatever I have to in order to convince her not to break up with me."

Chapter 18

Faith

Nothing she'd done in her life was harder than telling Nate to leave her alone—not her emancipation at sixteen, not her move from Texas to Montana, not even going through six years of college to get her master's degree. The pain in her chest, in her *heart*, was almost unbearable. When she'd told him it was over, she'd cried, despite how hard she tried not to break down. Faith let the tears fall. She needed to get it out, get Nate out of her system, and if she had to do that with bucket-loads of tears, so be it.

For the last hour, she'd been on the couch underneath her warmest blanket with Heathcliff on her lap, tormenting herself by watching *The Princess Bride* and thinking about Nate. Occasionally, she yanked a tissue out of the box on the table and wiped her eyes. Since she'd never broken up with anyone, she had no clue how long the pain was going to last. A day, a week, a month, a *year*? Time stretched endlessly out in front of her.

The pounding on her door startled both her and Heathcliff. The cat launched himself off her lap, knocking over a stack of books on his way to her bedroom. Faith got up, wrapped the blanket around herself like a protective cocoon, and went to the door. Even though she thought she knew who was out there, she closed one eye and looked through the peephole.

Nate.

"I know you're in there, Faith," he yelled. "Let me in!"

Why was he out there, screaming to be let in? He didn't have to pretend to like her anymore. She let him off the hook. She pulled the blanket tight around her and took a deep breath before she spoke.

"Go away," she yelled. Faith rested her forehead against the cold oak door. "Please, Nate, just go away." The tears threatened to fall again. She felt them building up, ready to break free.

"No," he said firmly. "I want to know what happened. I want to know why you broke up with me, why you're pushing me away?"

"Can't you accept that it's over?" she asked.

"It's not over," he snapped. "Let me in so we can talk."

"Don't you get it? I'm setting you free. You don't have to keep pretending to like me. I'll... I'll be okay. Go back to your life, to the woman you really want." She choked back a sob. "Please, go away."

There was no response, only silence. A quick look out the peephole showed her that Nate was still on the porch, leaning against the railing, arms crossed, staring at her front door.

"Dammit," she muttered under her breath. "Why is he so stubborn?" She took a deep breath, turned around, and returned to the couch. Nate couldn't stay out there forever, especially with the snow falling and the temperature dropping. He'd go away, eventually. All she had to do was wait him out.

———

Faith hadn't heard anything from outside her front door in quite a while, more than an hour. The last time she'd snuck a peek through the peephole, Nate was still on the porch, arms crossed, his eyes on the ground between his feet. Frustrated that he wouldn't give up and go home, she'd kicked the door with her stocking foot, hard enough to hurt, and so loud that Nate's head came up.

"Faith?" he'd called.

She had ducked as if he could see her, just like the first time he'd knocked on her door. She'd grumbled at herself as she returned to the living room and picked up a book. Not that she could concentrate on reading.

The second time she got up, she had no intention of letting Nate know she was checking on him. He was probably gone anyway. The sun had gone down, and the temperature had dropped drastically. It was too cold to be standing outside someone's door.

Faith tiptoed to the door and leaned carefully against it, nothing touching it but the tips of her fingers. Before she looked, she closed her eyes and took a deep breath, sending up a silent prayer he wouldn't be there. Then she looked.

Nate was gone.

Her breath caught in her throat, and her stomach churned. As much as she hated to admit it, she was disappointed he wasn't out there. He'd given up too easily. At least it confirmed how he really felt about her. She was turning away from the door when she heard a thump. She looked again, and to her surprise, Nate was climbing to his feet. He must have been sitting on the porch, leaning against the door.

He paced around the small porch, stomping his feet and shaking his arms. She could just make him out in the light cast by the streetlight. He'd been out there for two hours.

He's going to freeze to death.

"So what?" she said out loud. "Let him freeze."

"Faith?" Nate leaped at the door and attempted to look through the peephole.

She slapped a hand over her mouth. He must have heard her. Faith bent over, her hands on her knees. This was ridiculous. If she didn't tell him to leave, he'd stay out there all night. Resolve rushed through her, so she lunged at the door and yanked it open.

Nate fell face-first through the door, landing on his hands and knees. Faith shrieked and stumbled back, her feet tangling. She would have fallen if Nate hadn't jumped to his feet and grabbed her, keeping her upright. She put her hands on his chest and tried to push him away, but his grip on her arms was too tight.

"Let me go!"

"Faith, listen to me."

"Get out of my house, Nate," she retorted. "Now."

"No," he barked. "Not until you tell me what the hell is going on. I'll leave once you explain why you broke up with me. Tell me what I did wrong, and then I'll leave. But not before." He released her, shut the door, and stood in front of it. "Talk."

Faith closed her eyes. She couldn't look at him, knowing what he'd done. All she had to do was get through this moment in time. Once she told him she knew the truth, he'd leave, and it would be over. She could go back to her quiet, boring life.

"I know what you did," she whispered. She ran a hand through her hair, pushing it away from her face. "I saw you bring that woman home last night."

"What?"

"Last night, Nate. I saw a woman get out of your truck and go inside with you. I called you right after I saw her and you said you were working. You lied."

Realization dawned in his eyes. "I didn't lie. You misinterpreted—"

Faith shook her head. "No, I don't think so. Then this morning at the coffee shop, I overheard Oscar and Gavin talking about you getting some woman to say yes, that you'd been after her for a while, and now that you had her, you planned to celebrate. Obviously, you were using me to kill time and now that you've got the woman you want, you don't need me anymore. I broke up with you before you could breakup with me." A sob escaped her. "I should have known it was bullshit. Someone like you, a guy who could have any woman he wants, would never be interested in someone like me."

"Is that what you think?" he asked. "That I only dated you until... until someone better came along?"

Faith nodded, unable to speak out of fear that the sobs would break free.

"God, I suck at this, you know," he mumbled.

Faith wasn't even sure he was talking to her. He shoved off his jacket as he walked away from her, stopping in the middle of the living room and tossing the jacket on a chair. The tips of his ears and his nose were red bright red. He wrung his hands together as he paced around the room. She wanted to tell him to get out, to leave her alone, but she couldn't seem to do it.

Nate abruptly stopped and looked at her. "Do you know what? I am awful at relationships. Awful. I haven't had a serious relationship in four or five years."

"But all those women—"

"None of those women I dated meant shit to me. But I could talk to them, charm them, get them to like me. It was easy. But you, well, you are the one woman I need to talk to, and I don't know what the hell to say."

"What are you talking about?" Faith sat on the edge of the couch and put her head in her hands.

"Do you know Cecily Devereaux?" he asked.

Everyone knew Cecily Devereaux. She was the richest woman in Lakeside, as well as one of the nicest. Faith had met her at a library fundraiser last year and immediately liked her. They didn't cross paths often, but when they did, Cecily was always kind.

"Cecily is investing in the bar," he explained. "We've been meeting off and on for several weeks. My assistant manager, Brooke, has been helping me put together a new business plan and handling the designs for the expansion. Brooke came home with me last night to put the finishing touches on our last presentation. That was who you saw getting out of my truck. Brooke and I are friends, nothing more. Trust me, I am *not* Brooke's type. Not even close."

"I ... don't understand," Faith mumbled. "Why didn't you tell me?"

"I didn't tell anybody, not even my sister or my best friend. I was afraid of jinxing it. But this morning, after Cecily agreed to invest, I called everybody and told them. They're all at the bar right now, celebrating. Which is probably what you heard Oscar and Gavin talking about this morning."

Faith sighed. Had she jumped to the wrong conclusion? She pressed her thumbs against her forehead and closed her eyes.

"Faith, look at me."

When she opened her eyes, Nate had kneeled in front of her. He took her hands, sending a shiver racing through her thanks to his icy hands.

"I should have told you this a while ago, but I was scared. I'm not anymore." He swallowed, his throat moving noticeably.

"Told me what?" Faith asked.

"I love you," he whispered, as if saying it too loud would somehow negate the words. "I swear, I will never do anything to hurt you. I promise."

"Really?" she breathed.

"Yes, really." Nate curled his fingers around the back of her neck, caught her lips in his, and kissed her. It was the kind of kiss she'd read about in books; the kind of kiss that made someone believe in love. Made her believe in him.

Faith was breathless when they broke apart. She clung to Nate, afraid if she let go, she would collapse.

"So, are you still mad at me?" he asked quietly.

Faith laughed. "Maybe a little. I wish you'd told me about the expansion and the meetings with Cecily. I understand why you didn't, but if I'd known, I might not have freaked out."

"I'll tell you what," Nate said. "I promise I will never keep anything from you again, ever."

"I like that promise," she murmured.

Nate kissed her again. "Hey, do you want to come to the bar with me and celebrate? I think it's time for my friends to meet the woman I love."

Faith blushed. She loved how that sounded coming out of his mouth. She could definitely get used to being the woman Nate loved.

Epilogue

Faith

The hum of laughter and the clink of glasses filled the air, mingling with the loud music drifting from the corner stage. The polished wooden floors gleamed under the new lights, fresh flowers adorned every table, and the sound of children playing outside drifted through the open doors. Faith smoothed her skirt and glanced around the crowded room. Despite knowing almost everyone there, her hands shook and her heart raced.

Nate was holding court behind the newly finished bar, laughing as he poured drinks and accepted congratulations from not only his friends, but his regular customers as well. He'd rolled up his shirt sleeves, his tie was already loose, and he was in his element. A smiled tugged at Faith's lips. There was something so effortlessly charming about Nate when he was like this, doing what he loved. She envied him. Even after all this time, being around his friends made her a little nervous.

"Do you think he'll stop for a minute and let someone else take over?" a voice said at her side.

She turned to find Cecily smirking as she sipped from a champagne flute. Faith laughed, her gaze returning to Nate. "After the work he's put into this remodel, he deserves to celebrate."

"Yes, he does," Cecily agreed. "It exceeded my expectations."

Faith felt a pang of pride at what Nate had done. The remodel and expansion of the Time Out Bar & Grill had been his labor of love for the past eighteen months, a project he'd given every ounce of his energy. Now, the popular bar looked completely different. Nate bought the empty property next door and turned it into a sprawling outdoor area stretching all the way to Flathead Lake. He'd installed a small play area for children, making the bar and grill family friendly during the day. Brooke and Cecily had also designed a pet-friendly area for the town's many dogs. Cecily's Shih Tzus, Van's Belgian Malinois, Soldier, and Brooke's Border Collie, Mitchell, were out there breaking it in right now.

As if he sensed her thinking about him, Nate looked up and caught her gaze. His grin widened and he winked, then gestured for her to join him.

"Will you excuse me?" Faith asked.

Cecily squeezed her arm. "Of course. I'll talk to both of you later." She turned and disappeared into the growing crowd.

Heat rushed through Faith as she walked toward Nate, her heart racing. Even after all this time, she still felt like a teenager when he smiled at her.

As she approached, he slipped out from behind the bar to take her hand and kiss her cheek. "Are you enjoying yourself?" he whispered in her ear.

"Yes, and I see you are, too." She giggled. "You're in your element."

"Yeah, I love this stuff." He glanced around. "Do you have a minute? I need to talk to you about something."

Faith nodded. "Sure. I think I can tear myself away from the crowd for a few minutes."

Nate chuckled because he knew being around so many people made her nervous, even though she had become friends with *his* friends. He took her hand, led her through the new section of the bar, out the back door, and down to the beach. A cool breeze came off the water, but it was warm enough outside that it didn't bother her. Summers in Montana were her favorite.

They sat on one of the new benches, holding hands. Nate was more fidgety than usual, glancing over his shoulder every few seconds, knee bouncing, and fingers tapping.

"If you need to get back to the bar—" She trailed off as Nate dropped to his knees in front of her. "Wh-what are you doing?"

"You know, I had an entire speech planned, practiced it for hours. I even stood in front of the mirror and said it. I'm not great with flowery speeches or stuff like that." He took a deep breath and stared up at her with his gorgeous blue eyes. "Before you came into my life, I was walking around with my eyes closed. I couldn't see what I wanted, what was right in front of me, not until I ran into you. Literally, ran into you. You changed my life, Faith."

She shook her head. Her heart pounded dangerously fast. This wasn't happening. Things like this didn't happen to her.

Except they did. Ever since Nate came into her life, good things happened to her. He'd changed her life as well.

He reached into his pocket, pulled out a small velvet box, and opened it to reveal a stunning sapphire ring. She swallowed past the lump rising in her throat. He removed it from the box, then he took her left hand and slipped it on her middle finger. She stared at it, then slowly raised her eyes to look at him.

"Will you marry me?" he murmured.

Faith opened her mouth, but nothing came out. She took a deep breath and tried again.

"Yes," she whispered.

Nate smirked and leaned forward, tilting his head toward her. "I'm sorry. What did you say?"

"Yes!" she repeated loudly.

His smile widened, then he jumped to his feet and yelled, "She said yes!"

Cheers erupted from behind them. Faith spun around to see everyone standing outside, watching them. She blushed and put her hands over her face.

Nate sat down beside her, took hold of her hands, and pulled them away from her face. He cupped her cheeks and kissed her until she couldn't catch her breath.

"I love you," he said when they broke apart.

"Forever?" Faith asked.

"Always and forever."

She smiled and rested her forehead against their clasped hands, then she looked up at him.

"I love you, too."

1. Faith and Nate are total opposites—introvert vs. extrovert, book-worm vs. social butterfly. What do you think draws them together, and how do their differences help them grow individually?

2. Nate is known as a ladies' man at the start of the story. How did your perception of him change as the story progressed? Did he surprise you?

3. Faith has built strong emotional walls due to past disappointments. How did her relationship with Nate challenge those boundaries—and were there moments you thought she might retreat for good?

4. There's a theme of people not being what others expect them to be—Nate is more than a flirt, and Faith is stronger than she appears. How does the story challenge stereotypes or assumptions we make about others?

5. What do you think *Right Kind of Wrong* is saying about the idea of "the one"? Is love about finding someone who's your opposite, your match, or a mix of both?

6. If this book were to continue into a sequel or a companion novel set in Lakeside, which character would you want to see find love next—and why?

Running
Wild

Dedication

Thank you to the people of Lakeside, Montana, for letting me manipulate your little town to fit my stories. Visiting Lakeside is like coming home.

Chapter 1

Teddie

Theodora "Teddie" Calloway shoved herself away from her desk and stretched. She hated the days she was stuck inside ordering supplies and running numbers. She preferred being outside working on the ranch, riding her horse, or helping with the cattle or the cherry harvest.

Teddie checked her watch. It was almost five, and she still had to talk to Wyatt about moving the cattle and check with Luke about the hay sales. Her day rarely ended at sunset.

Helping run one of the largest ranches in Lakeside, Montana wasn't an easy feat, especially as a woman and the daughter of a former military man. Fortunately, she was up to the task. In fact, she had been the one to get Cherry Ridge Ranch running in the black for the first time since her father took over thirty years ago, and she'd kept it there for almost four years. If the Colonel listened to her ideas, they might turn their small family fortune into an enormous family fortune.

Teddie looked out the large, glass window overlooking the cherry orchard and the barn. She loved the view, but she loved being outside even more, so she shut her computer down, grabbed her hat, and made her way outside, walking down the path along the side of the house and past the orchard. After she moved back to the ranch to work for Cherry Ridge, her father had the guest-house behind the main house converted into an office space. Two of the bedrooms and the main living area now served as offices, and the last bedroom had become a storage room lined with filing cabinets. It was where she spent most of her days.

She was almost to the barn when she heard her father yelling, so she slipped behind a tree to listen.

Her father, Colonel Everett Calloway, appeared to be involved in a heated discussion with Cherry Ridge's foreman, Wyatt Dawson. The Colonel's arms gesticulated wildly, and his shouting occasionally reached her ears. Wyatt stood with his arms crossed and his lips drawn together, the only outward sign of his irritation. Dark glasses covered his eyes, but Teddie was sure if she saw them, his steel-blue orbs would be flashing in anger.

"Take care of it, Dawson," her father shouted before spinning on his custom-made cowboy boots and stalking across the man-icured lawn toward the kitchen entrance. Teddie watched him go, wondering what ridiculous thing he'd demanded of his staff this time.

Intent on talking to Wyatt—and hopefully smoothing things over—she continued walking to the barn. She was almost there when a horn honked behind her. Turning, she saw her mother pulling her truck to a stop in front of the kitchen, the shop where she made and sold her different pastries, jams, and jellies, among other things.

Her mother rolled down the window. "Teddie! Come help me!"

Maggie was the heart of the Calloway family. She'd grown up in Montana and had been the daughter of a rancher herself, so she understood the struggles her daughters dealt with, especially from a man like the Colonel. She was calm, warm, and intelligent, with an eye for what worked and what didn't work for her small business. Her mother kept her grounded.

Teddie met Maggie at the back of the Ford pickup, and together they unloaded the supplies and took them into the shed.

"Are you going to bake a lot?" Teddie asked. "This is more than you usually order."

"Yes, it is." Maggie grinned. "I thought I'd use some of those frozen cherries to make room in my freezers. Cherry season will be here before we know it, and I need all the space I can get. I've got a list of new recipes I want to make: scones, muffins, even some cookies."

Cherry Ridge was a cattle ranch and a fruit farm—cherries, apples, and pears, though they had more cherry trees than anything. Nothing was better than a Flathead Cherry, and nobody in a hundred-mile radius turned a cherry into something that tasted like heaven the way Maggie Calloway did. Pies, jams, compote, dried cherries, muffins, scones, and a million other things. So many things that Teddie couldn't keep track of it all. Her mother was always in the kitchen, and a weekend didn't go by that she didn't sell out of whatever she made with her cherries.

"You know what? Will you make a pie for the ranch hands?" Teddie suggested. "They'll love it."

A smile spread across Maggie's face. "That is a wonderful idea." She patted Teddie's cheek. "You're good to those boys. I'm sure they appreciate it."

"I hope so." Teddie cleared her throat and glanced at the stable. "Do you need help with anything else?"

Maggie shook her head, already off in thought, planning her baking for the next few days. Teddie kissed her mother's cheek and resumed her walk to the barn. She didn't see Wyatt right away, so she headed for the opposite end of the barn to see her horse. By the time she slipped inside, Wyatt had emerged from his office and was talking to some of the ranch hands with his back to her.

She couldn't help but stare at him. Wyatt was cowboy through and through—broad shoulders wrapped in a navy blue button-down that clung to every muscle, including his powerful arms and a lean, muscular body formed from years of hard ranch work. She saw his dark brown hair curling under the weight of the Stetson on his head, one he wore more than he didn't. He was perpetually tan, thanks to working outside, and he wore the usual uniform of jeans and work boots. Wyatt had an easy, pleasant smile and a wickedly evil smirk that made her knees go weak. He moved with grace and purpose, like a wolf on the prowl, and when he looked at her, her knees trembled, her heart pounded, and she forgot how to breathe. The man had a body built for sin.

Wyatt had been her weakness since high school. He'd worked at Cherry Ridge for as long as she could remember, and she'd had a crush on him since she was a freshman and he was a senior. For years, she'd hung around the barn, hoping to get his attention.

Not that Wyatt gave her the time of day; Colonel Calloway had a strict "the staff isn't allowed to mingle with the family" rule, an ironclad law he wrote in their contracts. It kept everyone away from his daughters.

"What are you doing down here?"

Teddie jumped and gave Wyatt a sheepish grin. She'd been so caught up in her thoughts, she hadn't realized he was in front of her.

"I wanted to talk to you about moving the cattle," she replied.

Wyatt rolled his eyes. "Christ, not you, too. Everett just yelled at me about it. It's going to take a few days to get everything together, but I will do my best to bring the cattle down off the mountainside by the end of next week."

She narrowed her eyes. "What are you talking about?"

"Your father said he wants the cattle off the mountain as soon as possible," he explained.

"Did he say why?"

Wyatt shook his head. "You didn't know about this, did you?"

"No," Teddie snapped. "Why the hell does he want to bring them down early? We've never done that before."

"Hey, don't yell at me. It wasn't my idea. I wanted to wait until after Labor Day, when it's a little cooler."

"Which is what we usually do, so why does he suddenly want them brought down early?"

Wyatt sighed. "Do not yell at me for this, but he said something about selling them."

"What? No fucking way. We are *not* selling those cattle. We will lose our ass on them." Teddie clenched her fists and swore under her breath.

"I know. I told him that, but he wouldn't listen to me," Wyatt said. "You need to talk to the Colonel."

"I will." She stalked past Wyatt without another word, too angry to even think straight. She needed to find her father and figure out what the hell he was doing.

Teddie rounded the corner in time to see her father and mother driving down the road toward town. So much for talking to him. Maybe it was for the best; it gave her a chance to calm down first. Either she was a part of the business or she wasn't. He couldn't go behind her back and do something as stupid as selling their cattle. It wasn't right, and she intended to talk to him about it. Apparently, she'd have to wait until morning.

With a sigh, she went in the house. She needed a drink.

—

"Where are you going?" her younger sister, Tessa, demanded, standing in front of Teddie's Jeep so she couldn't go anywhere.

"I'm going to town," she replied, leaning out the window. "Do you want to go?"

A smile spread across Tessa's face. "Yes." She danced around the side of the Jeep, yanked open the door, threw her purse on the floor, and got in.

Tessa was twenty-two, a surprise baby who came along when Teddie was eleven. While Teddie carried herself with poise and responsibility—exactly the kind of obedience her father admired—Tessa spoke her mind, embraced her fierce independence, and let her fiery temper and wild streak shine through. She constantly clashed with their father because she refused to conform to his expectations. It wouldn't be long before her sister left Montana behind.

"So, why was Dad pissed off earlier?" Tessa asked.

"Language," Teddie mumbled.

Tessa scowled and tossed her phone on the cupholder between the seats. "I'm twenty-two, Teddie," she groused. "I don't have to watch my language."

"You won't say that if Daddy hears you," she said.

"Colonel Everett Calloway can kiss my ass," Tessa muttered.

Teddie smiled. "Uh oh, what did he do now?"

"Oh, not much, just told me I can't see Noah anymore." Tessa's expression changed, her eyes narrowing and her lips pursing. "He's not good stock, Tessa Jean." Her impersonation of their father was spot-on. "I wish he'd remember we're his daughters, not soldiers for him to command. He's been out of the military for what, almost thirty years?"

Teddie nodded. "Since Grandpa died and left him Cherry Ridge. His attitude won't change, though. Once a military man, always a military man. Now, he's a *rich* military man. Daddy has certain ... ideas about how things work. And he's stubborn. You know that."

Tessa rolled her eyes. "What am I supposed to do about him?"

"What makes you think I know how to deal with him?" Teddie laughed and shook her head.

Tessa sighed. "Oh, I don't know, maybe because you've been around him longer."

"That doesn't mean squat," Teddie muttered. "If it did, you'd be talking to Mom. She's the one who has been married to the man for thirty-five years. I don't know why you think I have it any easier than you do. Daddy controls me as much as he controls you. I don't fight him like you do."

"You should. It'll take some of the heat off me." She crossed her arms and stared out the window. "You know, it would be nice if you rebelled once in a while. I'm sick of carrying the load."

Teddie laughed and shook her head. For a brief second, she considered telling her sister everything, but then she came to her senses. She didn't need the added worry that Tessa would accidentally spill her secret to their father. This secret was one her father would never forgive.

Chapter 2

Wyatt

Wyatt watched Teddie stalk out of the barn, hellbent on finding her father. He felt like a snitch telling her about the cattle, but she was an integral part of the ranch, and he would not lie to her. It was the Colonel's fault for not informing her that he planned to sell the herd.

He wasn't sure why anything the Colonel did surprised him; he'd known the man since he was sixteen, and he hadn't changed one bit. Everett Calloway was demanding, pompous, and difficult to work with. Mostly, he let Teddie and Wyatt take care of the ranch, but now and then, he demanded something ridiculous of them. If he'd let his daughter run the ranch, the place would make money hand over fist.

Despite knowing how difficult the Colonel was to deal with, he'd applied for the head foreman position when it became available three years ago. The pay was good—phenomenal, really—way better than what any other ranch foreman in the Lakeside area received. With good reason. Working for the Colonel was a nightmare.

There were other perks as well, but Wyatt pushed that thought away and set to work feeding the horses, moving from stall to stall, letting himself get lost in his work. It eased his mind and calmed him. He was coming out of the second-to-last stall when he heard his name. He turned to see Luke Moreno walking toward him. Luke was young, in his mid-20s, cocky, but a solid worker.

"Sorry I missed the meeting. Mrs. Calloway asked me to help her get cherries out of the freezer," he said. "What was all that about with the Colonel?"

Wyatt sighed as he walked the length of the barn back to where Luke stood. "He wants us to bring the herd on the mountain down to the bottom pasture."

Luke shrugged. "Yeah, so. We always do that."

"He wants us to do it next week," Wyatt explained.

Luke laughed. "You're joking, right?"

"Unfortunately, no, I'm not joking."

"But that's like three weeks early," Luke muttered. "And this heat wave isn't supposed to break for another couple of weeks."

"I know," Wyatt said. "But he's the boss."

Luke shook his head. "Great. Well, shit. I guess I better enjoy my weekend. Look, I'm gonna head into town. Are you going to the Time Out tonight?"

Wyatt shrugged. "Maybe. I don't know yet. If I do, I plan on beating your ass at pool."

"I'll save you a seat." Luke smiled, tipped his hat, and disappeared through the barn door. Wyatt finished feeding the horses, then he closed up the barn for the night.

He walked outside and leaned on the fence overlooking the pasture. A run-in with both Teddie and her father made for an interesting day. They were so much alike it was scary, not that Teddie or the Colonel would ever admit it.

While he'd known Teddie since high school, he hadn't noticed her until a few years ago. She was a different woman when she returned from college and took over the ranch. She was tall, almost six feet, athletic, and strong from years of working on the ranch. Her honey blonde hair fell to her waist, though she usually kept it in a braid or ponytail. Her green eyes were sharp and observant, filled with quiet determination. She was practical, almost to a fault, but there was a softness to her that few people saw, and those who did thought it meant they could take advantage of her. Definitely not the case. He'd learned that the hard way.

Shortly after Wyatt took over as foreman, he and Teddie had a run-in, of sorts. It was the first time he noticed her as someone more than the Colonel's daughter.

The sun was barely up, the grass still wet with morning dew, when Wyatt spotted Teddie marching across the pasture with a fire in her step and her face etched in anger. She stopped in front of him with her arms crossed.

"You moved the boundary markers," she said.

He didn't bother to look up, just kept hammering, like he hadn't heard the accusatory tone in her voice.

"Good morning, Teddie," he said around a mouthful of nails.

"You shifted the line ten yards to the north."

"Yes, I did," Wyatt replied calmly. "The post was rotting, and the creek is shifting west. You know as well as I do that part of the field floods every spring."

Teddie huffed. "What I know is you didn't ask to move the line."

He took the nails out of his mouth and turned to face her. "I didn't realize I needed to run every fence post movement by the Colonel's daughter."

"Well, maybe you should."

They stared at each other for a long moment, the air between them buzzing with something more electric than the normal indifference they had for each other.

"Do you always get this worked up before breakfast?" Wyatt asked.

"Only when someone redraws the property lines—"

"That is not what I did," he snapped. "I moved the fence line ten yards to the north so I could dig a culvert to keep the pasture from flooding. It is right on the edge of the property line, not past it. Now, if you're done yelling at me, I have work to do."

"Why does everything have to be a fight with you?" she asked.

"I don't want to fight with you, Teddie. I'm trying to keep this place running, like you."

She rolled her eyes. "Fine, next time talk to me first."

"Next time, I will," he said.

Teddie stared at him a beat longer than necessary; then she turned, flipping her blonde hair over her shoulder as she walked away.

Wyatt pinched the bridge of his nose, shaking himself free of the memory. He was tired and ready to go home to his modest cabin at the north end of the ranch. He was halfway to his truck when he turned around, returned to the barn, and went into his office, where he had a fully stocked bathroom and a change of clothes in his bottom drawer. Wyatt cleaned up and changed, then he got in his truck and drove to town. He needed a drink more than he needed sleep.

The Time Out Bar & Grill buzzed with people, like it did most Friday nights. Lakeside College was back in session in less than two weeks, so the college students were coming back to town. Inevitably, their first stop was the hottest hangout in town, the Time Out. It was so busy that Wyatt had to park at Volunteer Park and walk to the bar.

The music hit him as soon as he came through the door. Last spring, the bar's owner, Nate, hired a former rock star to play at the bar—Max Caldwell. Max fell in love with Lakeside—along with Donna, the town sheriff—and ended up staying.

It took Wyatt a few minutes to find the Cherry Ridge crew. They'd commandeered a bunch of seats near the pool tables and were raising hell. It looked like everybody was there—Luke, Hank, Jed, Ty, and Nash, as well as both of the Calloway girls. That wouldn't go over well with Colonel Calloway. He had strict rules about his daughters fraternizing with the hired help.

Wyatt stopped at the bar and got a whiskey before he sauntered over to the group at the pool tables. Luke clapped him on the back before he went back to flirting with Tessa.

Teddie smiled at Wyatt and patted the stool next to her. He sat down and sipped his whiskey.

"Did you talk to your father?" he asked.

She shook her head. "No, my parents left before I had time to ask Daddy about the cattle. I'll talk to him tomorrow."

"Do you think he'll listen to you?"

Teddie snorted. "Does he ever listen to me?"

"Good point," Wyatt muttered. "He doesn't listen to me either."

She bumped her shoulder into his. "Guess we have something in common."

"Wyatt! You're up!"

He got off the stool, tipped his hat, and joined Nash at the pool table. He took the cue, noticing as he bent over that Teddie was watching him. Wyatt winked at her and hit the ball.

Chapter 3
Teddie

*H*e tasted like whiskey, the cheap, good kind that you could only get at the bar, the kind her father would never, ever have in his home. His kisses were wet, sloppy, and damn near perfect. The touch of his rough, calloused hands as they slowly drifted up her sides ignited a fire under her skin. Every inch of her burned with need for him, want and desire woven into every fiber of her being.

Teddie pulled away. "Let's take this somewhere else before someone sees us." She chanced a look around the bar, but she didn't see anybody she knew, at least not in the general vicinity. That didn't mean somebody wouldn't stumble on them in the back corner of the bar where they'd been hiding for the last half an hour, making out like a couple of horny teenagers.

This corner of the Time Out Bar & Grill was dark, buried in the shadows. The jukebox was only a few feet away; the beat of the song thumping in her head and pounding through her blood, filling her brain with all kinds of not-safe-for-work ideas. She'd been thinking about this—about him—all night, ever since he'd walked through the door. Teddie wanted to be alone with him, behind closed doors, in bed.

Wyatt nuzzled her ear with his nose. "Where exactly do you want to go?"

"My place?"

He snorted. "What about your father?"

She laughed. "That didn't seem to bother you two weeks ago when you snuck into my room."

"Yeah, well, I was a nervous wreck the entire time."

Teddie kissed the corner of his mouth and ran her hand up his thigh. "You sure didn't act nervous."

Wyatt closed his eyes and sighed. She bit her lip so she wouldn't laugh again. He couldn't resist her, and she knew it. He'd cave and go back to the ranch with her if she was persuasive enough.

"My father won't even know. Sneak in the back like last time." She pressed her mouth to his ear. "Come home with me. I want you in my bed."

He groaned, then his lips were on her neck, sucking and biting, marking her as he slipped his hand back under her shirt and cupped her breast, his thumb drifting over the nipple.

Teddie's back arched, pushing against his hand, her fingers gripping the waistband of his jeans in a vain attempt to pull him closer.

"I'm not leaving here alone," she whispered. She released his waistband and ran her hand over the front of his jeans, his arousal jumping under her touch, making him groan again.

Wyatt released her, pushing himself into the corner of the booth. "We can't leave at the same time."

Teddie grinned. She had him. "No, of course not. Besides, my sister came with me. I'll get her and we'll leave. I'll leave my French doors unlocked for you."

He smirked, the look making her want to fall to her knees. "Why can't I resist you?" he murmured.

She giggled, kissed him one last time, then she pushed herself out of the booth. "I'll see you in a while."

Teddie went in search of her sister, finding her on the dance floor with Luke, of all people. Great, another Calloway daughter socializing with one of the ranch hands. They were going to give their father a heart attack. She poked her sister in the side and gestured at the door. Tessa rolled her eyes, but she followed Teddie outside.

"We're leaving?" Tessa asked.

"Um, yeah, I have to get up early tomorrow."

To her surprise, Tessa didn't argue. She climbed in the Jeep, shut the door, and made herself comfortable.

Teddie saw it as soon as she rounded the corner and pulled into the driveway. At first, it was a giant, hulking shape in the distance. As they got closer, it took shape—an RV the size of a tour bus parked next to the barn.

Tessa sat forward in her seat and stared at it. "What the hell is that?"

"I do not know," Tessa replied.

"You don't... you don't think that monstrosity belongs to Mom and Dad, do you? Is that what they went to town to pick up earlier?"

"It couldn't be anybody else's," Teddie said. "Not unless a rock star moved into the barn."

"Oh my God, it's hideous. What were they thinking?"

Teddie parked at the head of the driveway. "Trust me, I'm going to find out."

The house was dark when they went inside, so they were careful not to make too much noise, going through the side entrance directly into the kitchen.

"Thanks for letting me go with you," Tessa whispered. "I needed a night out."

Teddie smiled and giggled. Tessa always needed a night out. She squeezed Tessa's arm. "You're welcome."

They separated in the kitchen, each going to their rooms in different parts of the house. When Teddie was in high school, her parents allowed her to move to the "other side of the house," as they called it. Instead of her room being upstairs and down the hall from her parents' room, she was downstairs on the opposite side of the house in what had once been a guest suite. It was a large bedroom with an en suite bathroom and a small sitting area. Teddie tried to lie to herself and say it was almost like having her own place.

When Tessa was home from school, Teddie spent a lot of time in her room. Listening to her father and sister argue about everything drove her insane. Inevitably, Tessa dragged Teddie into every conversation, using her as an example of everything Tessa didn't want to be: the daughter who came home from college to help run the multi-million dollar a year ranch, slept in her teenage bedroom, and followed Daddy's rules.

I don't follow all of Daddy's rules.

Teddie pushed the stupid RV parked outside out of her mind, grabbed a clean set of sheets from her closet, quickly stripped the bed, and remade it. Then she unlocked her French doors, peeled off her clothes, went to the bathroom, and took a shower to wash off the bar smell. When she was done, she went to the bed, sighing as she sank into its inviting softness.

On the other side of the room, one of the double doors opened, and Wyatt slipped inside. A smile spread across his face as he crossed the room, his nimble fingers swiftly unbuttoning his long-sleeved button-down, leaving him in a plain white T-shirt and his low-slung jeans. He kicked off his boots, and then he was on her, pinning her beneath him on the bed.

Yeah, I definitely don't follow all of Daddy's rules.

—

Teddie straddled the man sleeping in her bed, tugged the oversized shirt she wore—his, of course—up around her waist, and pressed a kiss to the center of his back, right between his shoulder blades.

Wyatt stirred, groaning as he glanced back at her. "Hey. What time is it?"

"Five," she murmured.

"Shit." He moaned and buried his face in the pillow.

Teddie laughed and ducked under his arm, forcing him to roll to his side so she could snuggle up to him. His heavy hand fell on her waist, and his knee pushed between her legs as he pulled her close, tucking her beneath his chin.

She sighed and rested her head on his chest, his heart thumping in her ear. She wanted to stay there forever.

"I should go," Wyatt whispered.

Before she could protest, he slid out from under her and picked up his boots and jeans. He quickly put them on, then he turned to her with a smirk on his face.

"I need my shirt."

Teddie laughed as she got up and kneeled in front of him. She grabbed the hem of the shirt and pulled it over her head, holding it out to him with what she hoped was an innocent smile on her face, even though she felt anything but innocent.

Wyatt shook his head, his blue eyes flashing, and snatched the shirt from her hands. He put it on, then he grabbed Teddie, lifting her off the bed. His hands were hot against her naked skin as he pulled her legs around his waist. His mouth covered hers, and he kissed her as if he had no intention of leaving.

"Don't go," she said, running her fingers through his hair, her lips drifting along his jaw.

Wyatt sighed. "I have to. If your father finds me in here, he'll kill me." He set her on the bed, kissed her once more, and then he was gone.

Teddie crawled back under the covers and stared at the door.

Unfortunately, he was correct; her father would kill Wyatt if he found him in Teddie's room.

Teddie put her hands over her face and groaned. What the hell was she doing? Of all the rules she and Wyatt decided to break, it had to be the one Everett Calloway was most adamant about.

—

Teddie poured herself another cup of coffee and went in search of her father. While she was still angry about the sale of the cattle, she'd calmed down enough to discuss it with him rationally. There was also the question of the RV. Everett was on the porch with Maggie, having breakfast. She slipped into the chair beside her mother and set her cup on the table.

"Good morning," Maggie said, reaching over to squeeze Teddie's hand. "You and Tessa were out late. Did you go into town?"

Teddie nodded. "To the Time Out."

Out of the corner of her eye, she saw her father roll his eyes. She ignored it.

"So, what's with the giant bus by the barn?" Teddie asked. "Did we adopt a rock star?"

Maggie glanced at her husband, then back at Teddie. "Your father purchased an RV. We... we're going to travel."

"Travel? In that?"

"Yes." Maggie looked at Everett and her daughter. "I'm going down to the shop. You two play nice." She patted Teddie's hand, kissed Everett's cheek, and left them to talk.

"Did you have something to say, young lady?" Everett asked.

"Yes." Teddie cleared her throat. "Why are you selling the cattle?"

"Who told you?"

"So, you're not denying it?" Teddie sighed.

"Yes, I'm selling the cattle. Now, who told you?"

"Wyatt. He told me yesterday."

Everett chuckled. "And you waited until today to ask? That's not like you."

"I needed time to calm down," she snapped. She closed her eyes and took a deep breath. "This will seriously hurt Cherry Ridge. I'm guessing you're selling them below market price, is that right?"

"Correct."

"Daddy, you understand that selling those cattle will cost us up to $500,000. Right?"

"I am aware."

Teddie jumped up, the chair wobbling slightly before righting itself. "Then why are you doing it? And why didn't you tell me?"

"I don't have to tell you everything," Everett muttered.

"I think you do. Because this ranch is my life. I gave up everything to come back here and help you run it. I need to be included in a major decision like this."

Everett pinched the bridge of his nose and sighed. "I hoped to put this conversation off for a while."

Teddie narrowed her eyes. "What conversation?"

Her father shifted uncomfortably and stared at a spot above her head for almost thirty seconds before he answered.

"I'm selling the ranch."

Her world tilted on its axis, the words "selling the ranch" ringing in her ears like the echo of a gunshot. She gripped the table to keep herself upright as her stomach twisted and vomit rose in the back of her throat. A sudden aching pressure exploded in her chest. She swallowed, but her throat was tight and raw.

"You're... you're selling Cherry Ridge?"

Everett nodded. "Yes. Your mother and I aren't getting any younger. We'd like to enjoy our remaining years without the burden of running the ranch. That's why I bought the RV, so we can travel and see the sights. Selling the cattle is the first step toward the end goal. I have a buyer for the cattle, and the same person is interested in purchasing Cherry Ridge."

"But... but this place has been in our family for generations. You *can't* sell it."

"This is for the best, Theodora. You never wanted this life, anyway. I'm giving you a chance at freedom, a chance to live your life like you've always wanted. I won't let you carry the burden of Cherry Ridge."

A dull roar filled her ears as he spoke until all she heard was the blood pounding through her veins. She had worked on the ranch since she was a little girl, learned every inch, bled for it, given up everything for it. Did he really think she could walk away?

"No," she murmured. Teddie cleared her throat. "You can't sell it. Cherry Ridge belongs to our family. It's my legacy. It's not a burden. You can't take it away from me."

"While I appreciate your sentimental ties to the ranch, I've made my decision. We're not discussing it any further." Everett checked his watch. "Now, if you'll excuse me, I have a meeting."

Teddie sank slowly back into her chair as he stalked off, shoulders stiff, fists clenched at his sides. An immense sense of loss fell over her, so deep and gut-wrenching she had to bite her lip to hold back the tears. Her father had destroyed her life and walked away like it was no big deal.

She allowed herself a moment to grieve—no longer—then she squared her shoulders and rose to her feet. It would be a snowy day in hell before she let Cherry Ridge go.

Not without a fight.

Chapter 4

Wyatt

Wyatt hurried down the hill behind the house, cut through the cherry orchard, and headed for the barn. On the way, he grabbed clean clothes from the truck so he could shower and change. It wouldn't be the first time he'd done it since he started seeing Teddie.

If someone had told him a year ago, he would be dating—and seriously in love with—his boss's daughter, he'd have laughed in their face. But, after a drunken one-night stand and the best sex he ever had, fast forward almost a year, and he was in a position he never imagined himself in.

The Calloway women were strictly off-limits; they always had been. He'd known that since he started working at Cherry Ridge when he was sixteen, and he never thought twice about it. That rule had not changed.

A half an hour later, Wyatt had showered and put on clean clothes, and he was at his desk with a cup of coffee in his hand, going over paperwork and worrying about getting the herd of cattle moved down the mountain. It made his head hurt thinking about it.

"I recognize that face," a familiar voice said from the open office door. "You're figuring something out and it's kicking your ass."

"Jesse? What the hell are you doing here?" Wyatt laughed as he pushed himself out of his chair and hurried across the room, hand extended.

They met in the middle of the room, exchanging a handshake and a quick hug. Jesse McBride was one of his oldest and closest friends. The two men had known each other for years, attending both high school and college together before returning to Lakeside. But they had gone to work for rival ranches; Wyatt at Cherry Ridge and Jesse for Remington Cattle.

"I'm here to look at the herd," Jesse replied. "Remington wants to buy them. Preston brought me because that idiot knows absolutely nothing about cattle. Since I was here, I thought I'd stop by and say hello. It's been a while."

They chatted for a few before Jesse shook Wyatt's hand and excused himself. Wyatt leaned against his desk, the headache roaring between his ears. A soft whinny drew his attention, reminding him he still needed to feed the horses. He left his office, grabbed a bucket, and went to work. It took him almost an hour to make his way down the stalls. By the time he got to the last one, he was ready for a cup of coffee.

"Hi," a voice whispered inches away from his ear, making him jump.

"Jesus Christ, Teddie," he huffed. "You scared the shit out of me." He put the bucket of oats in front of the chestnut mare in the stall's corner.

Teddie grinned. "Sorry." She stepped into him, pushed herself up on her toes, put her hands on his waist, and kissed him on the corner of the mouth.

"What are you doing in here?" Wyatt tried to sound stern, but he failed.

"I wanted to see you." She slid her arms around him as she stepped closer, her body flush against his.

"You're lucky your father didn't see you," he said.

"He won't," Teddie shot back. "I've gotten really good at this."

Wyatt chuckled and shook his head. They had both gotten surprisingly good at sneaking around over the last six months. He glanced at the stall door, then he cupped Teddie's chin in his hand, tilted her head back, and kissed her. What he really wanted to do was throw her in the hay and take her, a plan he was sure she would have been one hundred percent on board with, but he held himself in check by sheer force of will.

Teddie drove him crazy and made him throw his inhibitions right out the window, including the one about staying away from the boss's daughter.

"Stop that," she scolded, punching him on the arm.

"Stop what?"

"Stop overthinking this and us." She wrapped a hand around the back of his neck and pulled him back to her lips, her tongue drifting over his and sliding into his mouth. She pushed into the kiss, her breasts pressing against his chest, her body warm, supple, and soft.

Reluctantly, Wyatt pushed her away and took a step back. "Did you talk to your father about the cattle sale yet?"

She nodded. "Yes, and I have a lot to tell you. Why?"

"Because Preston Remington is here with their foreman to look at the herd."

"What? He's here?"

Wyatt nodded. "Yeah, Jesse stopped to say hello and mentioned why they were here."

"Shit. I gotta go." She darted out of the stall and took off at a run for the path that circled the house, leading to the converted guesthouse around the back.

He was glad he didn't have to deal with an angry Teddie. When she got mad, she became a force to be reckoned with. And she was absolutely fuming.

Ten minutes later, Jesse strolled into the barn.

"Well, that was interesting," he said.

"What was interesting?" Wyatt asked, grabbing his coffee off his workbench.

"I don't remember Teddie Calloway being such a take-charge person," Jesse explained. "I remember a quiet, mousy girl who had a massive crush on you in high school."

Wyatt laughed. "That was fifteen years ago. Don't mess with her. She knows her shit. Do you know she got the ranch running in the black for four years straight? I think she can run this ranch better than anyone. Teddie knows this place inside and out; she knows what works and what doesn't. She's smart when it comes to doing what needs to be done."

Jesse raised an eyebrow. "How long have you been sleeping with her?"

Wyatt spat out the coffee he was swallowing. "What are you talking about?"

"I have known you since we were kids, Wyatt. You can't fool me. You've got it bad for that woman."

"Is it that obvious?" Wyatt asked.

"Does she know?"

Wyatt laughed. "Dude, we've been seeing each other for months."

Jesse's eyes widened. "Does the Colonel know?"

"Hell, no! Do not say anything to him. Or to Preston. That asshole will go running to the Colonel and rat us out faster than he sucks down one of his stupid cigarettes."

Jesse held up his hands and chuckled. "Okay, okay. I won't say a word. I swear. But I gotta ask. Is it serious?"

Wyatt shrugged. "We've never talked about it. Do I want it to be serious? Maybe. And I think Teddie does, too."

The sound of voices coming toward them ended that conversation, which didn't bother Wyatt. He hadn't talked to Teddie about their relationship and where they stood, so he wasn't comfortable talking to Jesse about it.

Wyatt leaned against the wall and crossed his arms. "I don't suppose you have a few men to spare next week?"

"Why? What's up?"

"I'm bringing the herd down off the mountain, and I need a few extra hands," Wyatt explained. "If I have some extra men, I might keep people from getting overheated."

"Why don't you wait until it cools down?"

Wyatt rolled his eyes. "The Colonel wants them off the mountain ASAP."

Jesse chuckled. "Of course he does." He tapped his chin. "I can spare at least two ranch hands. Plus, me."

"You don't have to do that," Wyatt said.

"I want to," Jesse said. "Besides, we don't currently have any cattle, the hay is cut and stored, and my list of chores is short. I've got time."

Teddie marched toward him, Preston right behind her. Her tight lips and angry stance told him everything he needed to know. This was going to be interesting.

Chapter 5
Teddie

"Daddy?" Teddie called.

She slammed the door shut behind herself and propped her sunglasses on top of her head.

"Daddy?" she shouted again.

"In my office," he bellowed.

The Colonel's office was at the back of the guest house, in what had once been the master bedroom. As Teddie rounded the corner, she ran directly into Preston Remington. He caught her as she stumbled, one hand on her waist, the other gripping her upper arm. He smiled, his face inches from hers.

"Teddie. How are you?"

She sighed and disentangled herself from Preston's grip. "Hello, Preston. What are you doing here?"

"Discussing business with your father," he replied. "Nothing you need to worry about."

Teddie rolled her eyes. It didn't surprise her he hadn't told the truth. The man was allergic to it. Besides, he knew as well as she did that she understood the business better than her father, who was nothing more than a figurehead. Wyatt ran the day-to-day operations of the ranch, and she dealt with everything else. Everett discussing anything with Preston was laughable. She definitely knew more than a snotty trust fund baby did about running a ranch.

"What kind of business?" she asked, wondering if he would be honest with her.

Her father stepped out of his office. "I told you. Preston is interested in buying the cattle along with the ranch. But he wants to look at them first."

"They're still on the mountain," Teddie said.

"Not the ones in the south pasture," Everett replied calmly. "Why don't you grab the Jeep and take Preston out there?"

Her father had a glint in his eye, the one she knew meant he had been scheming and plotting. He'd had the same look when he encouraged her to move back home and work at the ranch. There was something he wasn't telling her.

"I have work to do," Teddie argued.

"It can wait," the Colonel said. "Go with Preston and check out the cattle. Maybe run it by Wyatt, because he knows the herd better than any of us.

She bit back the "No shit," on her lips and gave her father a dirty look before she followed Preston out of the office. She put her sunglasses on, pushed past Preston, and stalked toward the barn with Preston hot on her heels, chattering in her ear, the scent of tobacco floating from the cigarette he'd lit as soon as they'd left the guest house.

Fuming over her father's interference in what she felt was *her* ranch, she heard nothing Preston said. They were almost at the barn when he grabbed her arm and stopped her.

"What?" she snapped.

"I asked if you wanted to get lunch later," he said.

Teddie shook off the hand on her arm and stepped away from

him. God, she hated this. Preston had always had a crush on her, ever since high school. While he was nice enough—for a spoiled rich kid who wanted for nothing and whose father doted on him until his death three years ago—he wasn't her type, something he didn't seem to understand. For two years, he'd followed her around like a lost puppy, repeatedly asking her out, refusing to accept that she didn't reciprocate his feelings. After high school, they both went off to different colleges, and Teddie hoped he would move on. But now and then, Preston turned up, asked her out, she turned him down, and life resumed. Hopefully, this would be another one of those times.

"I don't think so."

Preston shook his head, chuckling under his breath. "Are you still playing hard to get?"

"I never played hard to get," Teddie snapped. "I am not interested in dating you."

"Your father said you don't have a boyfriend," he replied.

She rolled her eyes. "He told you that?"

He shrugged. "Maybe he thought you might go out with me."

Teddie pushed a hand through her hair and quelled the urge to yank it out in frustration. "Just because my father said it doesn't mean it's true. He knows nothing about my personal life. Or my love life."

Preston shrugged. "We'll see." He walked past her toward the barn, flicking his still lit cigarette butt on the ground.

She clenched her fists as she snorted, put her heel on Preston's cigarette butt, and ground it into the dirt. Out of the corner of her eye, she saw Wyatt and the foreman from Remington Ranch, Jesse McBride, leaning against the stable wall. Preston called Jesse's name. Teddie picked up the pace, arriving at the barn a few seconds after Preston.

"Thanks, Jesse," Wyatt said, shaking his friend's hand. "I appreciate your help. It will be tight, but I think we'll make it." He tipped his chin in her direction as she approached. "Ms. Calloway, what brings you out this early? Are you looking to ride your favorite stallion?" He winked at her, making her blush.

Teddie took a deep breath and glared at Wyatt. "I need the Jeep. I'm taking Preston and Jesse to look at the cattle in the south pasture."

Preston put his hand in the middle of her back and grinned at Wyatt. "Then we're going to lunch." He slipped his arm around her waist, pulling her tight against his side.

Wyatt nodded, an odd look falling over his face. "The Jeep is behind the barn. If you'll excuse me, I need to get back to work."

Teddie took a step toward him. "Wyatt—"

Wyatt didn't look at her; he just disappeared back into the stables.

—

Teddie, Preston, and Jesse were out on the southernmost part of the property for close to two hours, discussing the cattle and the sale of the ranch. She didn't agree with the terms, and she told Preston as much, a concept he had a difficult time grasping. He argued with her all the way back to the main house, doing his best to convince her it was in the best interest of everyone involved for the Calloways to sell their herd along with the ranch.

"We stand to lose thousands of dollars," Teddie argued. "I do not see how this is a viable option for us. I need to discuss this with my father."

As soon as Jesse parked the Jeep in front of the house, Teddie had the door open and her feet on the pavement. Preston jumped out after her and followed her up the porch steps to the front door, where she stopped.

"What are you doing?" she asked.

"I thought we could talk about it some more over lunch,"

Preston replied. He took a drag of his cigarette, blowing smoke in her face as he exhaled.

Teddie clenched her fists. His chain-smoking was getting on her nerves. "I don't think so. We've discussed all that needs to be discussed. I'm going to talk to my father and make sense of this nonsense, then I'll be in touch. Have a good day." She opened the door, stepped inside, and slammed the door in Preston's face.

She walked through the house, out the back door, and down the short path to the converted guest house. Her father wasn't inside, and when she called his cell phone, he didn't answer. She dropped into the chair at her desk and put her head in her hands.

Maybe it was a good thing the Colonel wasn't around. Teddie was still furious with him. She turned on her computer and ran the numbers. By the time she finished, she was even more frustrated.

If her calculations were right—and they usually were—they might lose close to $500,000 if the Remingtons stuck to their offer, which was far below the expected market value for both the ranch and the cattle. The ranch was worth millions, and Preston was lowballing them.

"My father has lost his mind," she muttered out loud as she pushed her chair away from the desk. Her head pounded from staring at her computer screen. She needed some air.

Teddie followed the path down to the stables, one of her favorite places on the ranch. She loved how quiet it was, the only sounds the gentle neighing of the horses and the rustling of them moving in their stalls. She stopped outside Wild Blue's stall and waited. It only took a second for the horse to notice her, a soft whinny leaving him as he put his head over the stall door and nudged her hand.

"Hey, Blue," she whispered, scratching his chin. "How are you, buddy?"

"He missed you."

Teddie jumped, her heart hammering in her chest. She rested

her forehead against Blue's broad face for a moment before she turned to the man standing beside her.

"I missed him." She wasn't talking about the horse, and she didn't think Wyatt had been either.

"How was lunch?" Wyatt asked.

She heard the jealousy in his voice, though she was pretty sure he tried to hide it. Why couldn't he understand he had nothing to worry about, no need to be jealous, because her heart belonged to one man and one man only? Not that she'd ever said the words. She'd never told him she loved him, thanks to the underlying fear of her father and what he would do to Wyatt if he found out. The fear was always there, creeping around the back of her mind, dictating everything she did.

"I didn't go to lunch." She stepped away from Wild Blue, put her arms around Wyatt, and rested her head on his shoulder. His familiar, warm, and comforting scent washed over her, making her heady with desire.

"You didn't?" he whispered.

"Nope." Teddie smiled at him, plucked the hat from his head, and ran her fingers through his hair, scratching at the short hairs on the back of his neck as she pulled him down to meet her lips.

That simple kiss ignited the spark. Wyatt's arms locked around her waist as he dragged her into his office and slammed the door shut, drawing a few startled neighs from the horses. Teddie didn't know whether to melt with need or giggle at the craziness of what they were doing.

He pushed her against the door, impatient and greedy, his mouth slanted over hers, devouring her like a starving man as he maneuvered his thigh between her legs, pressing it against her warm core.

His name was a curse on her lips as she fumbled to undo his belt and pull open his pants. Wyatt groaned as her fingers brushed his half-hard cock.

He reached around her and flipped the lock on the door, then he picked Teddie up and carried her across the room to his desk, balancing her on the edge. Wyatt tugged her shirt up, his hands sliding beneath it to cup her breasts, his thumbs tracing her nipples through her lace bra.

She moaned, her back arching and her head falling back as his lips drifted along the line of her throat. She shoved her hand into the waistband of his underwear and took hold of his length, stroking him gently. His hips thrust with the movements as he impatiently pulled at her clothes; her shirt and bra effortlessly removed and tossed aside.

Wyatt stepped back, his blue eyes darkening with lust as he watched her take off her boots. He helped her yank her jeans off, both of them panting with lust by the time she was free of the tight denim. He pushed open her thighs and stepped between them, his hand between her legs, his fingers teasing her, opening her for him.

Teddie pushed his jeans and underwear down past his ass, and she guided him into her, hissing as the burn of the stretch balanced her perfectly on the edge between pleasure and pain. She wrapped her arms around him, put her hands on his ass, and urged him to move. It was all hands, lips, her and Wyatt, connected in the most intimate of ways, his body flush against hers, his mouth on hers, kissing her senseless, swallowing her moans as she climaxed, the orgasm exploding out of her, consuming her, a never ending moment in time that she didn't want to end.

Wyatt's orgasm came shortly after hers, his whole body tensing and his blunt fingertips digging into her hips as he came. When it was over, he rested his head on her shoulder, his breath tearing in and out of his throat.

The knock on the door startled both of them. Her hand hit a box of paperclips, knocking them to the floor.

"Dawson? Are you in there?" Another sharp knock.

"Shit," Wyatt swore under his breath, pushed himself away from her, and yanked his jeans up.

Teddie jumped off the desk and scrambled to grab her clothes. Then she ran for the bathroom, shutting the door a few seconds before Wyatt opened his office door.

"Colonel Calloway," Teddie heard Wyatt say. "What can I do for you?"

Chapter 6

Wyatt

Wyatt buckled his belt, glanced over his shoulder at the now-closed bathroom door, then he yanked open his office door. "Colonel Calloway. What can I do for you?"

Everett pushed past him, marched into the office, and stopped in the middle of the room with his arms crossed. He glanced slowly around, his eyes stopping on Wyatt.

"You need to clean up in here," Everett muttered.

Wyatt sighed. "Yes, sir."

"Where are we with moving the cattle down from the mountain?" Everett asked.

"We're leaving the day after tomorrow," Wyatt explained. "Jesse McBride from Remington Ranch is going to help."

"How long will it take?"

"Two days at least," he replied. "Or three. And no, I can't do it any faster. I don't want to lose any cattle or chance anybody getting heatstroke."

Everett scowled. "Whatever. Get them moved ASAP." He stormed out of the office without another word.

The bathroom door opened, and Teddie peered out. "Is he gone?"

Wyatt nodded and leaned against the edge of his desk as Teddie came out, fully dressed.

"I'm going with you," she said.

"What?" he asked. "Going where with me?"

"To get the cattle," she replied.

"Absolutely not."

Teddie crossed her arms and scowled, the look on her face surprisingly like her father's. "What do you mean, absolutely not? This is my ranch. I go where I please."

Wyatt rubbed his forehead. Everett would lose his shit when he found out Teddie planned to join them when they went to get the cattle. But Wyatt wasn't about to argue with her. He wouldn't win, anyway.

"Alright, we're leaving at six a.m. sharp, day after tomorrow."

"I'll be ready." She went to the door, stopped with her hand on the doorknob, and looked back at him. "I'll tell my father so you don't have to. See you later."

"Bye," he mumbled as the door swung closed behind her.

———

Teddie was already outside the barn with Blue saddled when Wyatt came around the corner. She threw her backpack in the back of the truck with the other supplies, then leaned against it with that look on her face that made him want to rip off her clothes. It wasn't just the Colonel who wouldn't like Teddie going with them to round up the cattle. That woman was temptation wrapped up in tight jeans and a pair of cowboy boots.

Wyatt gave her a tight smile, tossed his duffle in the truck's bed, and hurried inside to get his horse out of her stall. He was going to stay as far away from Teddie as possible, otherwise, God only knew what he might do.

"You ready for this?"

He jumped, swung around, and glared at Teddie. She wasn't going to make it easy on him, that was for sure.

"What is wrong with you?"

"Nothing," he muttered.

"Something must be bothering you," she replied.

"I said nothing," Wyatt reiterated. "Are you set to go?"

She nodded. "I brought my tent, too, like you said."

"Good," he said. He took a deep breath and exhaled. "Thanks."

Teddie nodded and followed him out of the barn. Wyatt finished saddling his horse, then he asked everyone to gather around.

"Good morning, everybody," Wyatt said. "Thanks for being here. I know we usually do this after Labor Day when it's cooler, but the Colonel asked us to bring the cattle down early, so that's what we're going to do. I'd also like to thank Jesse and the crew from Remington Ranch for offering to help. You guys know the drill. Hank will take the road up the side of the mountain, and the rest of us are heading up on the horses. We'll camp at our usual spot tonight and start bringing the cattle down tomorrow. Questions?"

Wyatt wasn't surprised there weren't questions. He'd worked with this crew for several years, and they could do this with their eyes closed. The only newbie, so to speak, was Teddie. Not that anyone would dare say anything to her about it.

It took most of the day to get up the side of the mountain to their camping spot, less than half a mile from the cattle. Hank was there with the truck and the dogs, the tents set up, and two fires roaring. He'd driven the uneven, bumpy trail up to the campsite, a trail that wound around the mountain and couldn't be used to bring the cattle down. After they fed, watered, and tethered the horses for the night, everyone pitched in to help cook dinner. By the time they ate and cleaned up, the sun was setting.

Wyatt noticed Teddie walk off through the trees after everyone grabbed beers and took a seat. He excused himself, snatched two beers from the cooler as he walked by it, and followed her. He found her sitting on a rock, looking out over a valley that stretched to Flathead Lake, so he sat down beside her and held out the beer. She took it with a smile.

"Thanks," she murmured. She took a long swallow, then wiped her mouth with the back of her hand. "It's beautiful, isn't it?"

The valley unfolded below them like a painting, rolling fields and dense clusters of trees woven together like a tapestry of green and gold. Flathead Lake shimmered in the distance, reflecting the reds and oranges of the setting sun. Wyatt dragged in a deep breath, the crisp air clearing his lungs. Sometimes, he forgot to stop and take a breath. Fortunately, Teddie reminded him daily that there was beauty in the world and he needed to take time to admire it.

"It is," he said.

"Cherry Ridge is my favorite place in the entire world. I've loved it since I was a little girl. I know every inch of this place like the back of my own hands. I know I grumble and complain and say that I came back here after college because of my father, but I did it because I love this place. I can't imagine anybody taking care of it like I do." She glanced at Wyatt. "Like you do."

"Was that a compliment, Theodora?" he joked.

After a moment he said, "I love this place, too. I've worked on this ranch since I was sixteen, and I never want to work any-place else. You know, when I was younger, I used to dream about owning Cherry Ridge."

Teddie sighed and glanced at him out of the corner of her eye. "My father is selling it."

Wyatt wasn't sure he heard right. "What?"

"You heard me," she mumbled. "My father is going to sell Cherry Ridge. He said he doesn't want to burden me with it, and he is ready to move on and live his life. Or something like that.

That stuff with Preston wasn't just about the cattle. It's about the whole damn ranch."

"Are you fucking kidding me?" Wyatt shook his head. "Jesus, maybe I'll buy it."

Teddie bumped her shoulder against his. "You'd have to fight me for it."

He chuckled. "I know. I know you love this place as much as I do."

"Almost as much as I love you."

"Wh-what did you say?"

"I said I love you." She laughed and put her hands over her face. "I cannot believe I said that to you out here in the middle of nowhere with eight ranch hands back there waiting for us around the fire. That was not how I wanted to tell you I love you for the first time."

Wyatt took her hand and pressed a quick kiss to her cheek. "I love you, too." He glanced over his shoulder. "And I can't believe I'm saying this, but I should probably get back there around the fire."

"Yeah, you should," she agreed. "I may be in love with you, but I'm not ready for my father to find out. Not yet."

He sighed. "I know. Someday, we'll figure out how I can be good enough for the great Colonel Everett Calloway." He turned to go, but Teddie grabbed his hand.

"Hey. You're good enough for me, Wyatt, and that is what matters."

Wyatt squeezed her hand, then he got up and hurried back to the fire with the others. He had to work to keep the grin off his face.

She loves me.

Chapter 7

Teddie

Teddie stared at the top of her tent and the faint sliver of moon-light making shadows on the tent's walls. She still couldn't believe she'd told Wyatt she loved him. She'd been holding onto that information for weeks, scared to say it out loud because she didn't want to freak him out. When she imagined expressing her feelings to him, it was during some beautiful, candlelit moment. She certainly hadn't intended to tell him out in the middle of a cattle drive with more than half a dozen ranch hands lurking in the dark.

"So much for that idea," she mumbled to herself.

Teddie sat up, unzipped her tent, and peered out. The stars, undisturbed by city lights, shone almost as bright as the moon. Crickets hummed in the tall grass and the embers in the fire crackled on the other side of the campsite. A cool breeze rolled down the mountain, so she grabbed a blanket, wrapped it around her shoulders, and slipped out of the tent. There were four other tents besides hers; she was the only one who wasn't sharing.

One of the ranch dogs, Echo, looked up when she opened

her tent. He padded across the clearing and sat in front of her, his head tipped to one side.

She climbed out, patted Echo on the head, wandered across the campsite, and sat by the fire. Echo lay down beside her, while the other dogs—Kris and Scout—scooted closer to the fire. Teddie absentmindedly rubbed Echo's ears while she stared at the stars overhead.

Even though she hadn't told Wyatt she loved him in exactly the way she'd planned, she was glad she'd done it. Having him say it back to her was an unexpected, head-spinning development. A smile played at the corner of her lips.

Wyatt loves me.

Teddie closed her eyes and breathed deep, the familiar smell of the ranch, of outdoors, of *Montana*, filling her nostrils. God, she loved it out here; there was no better place on earth. How could her father think about selling the ranch?

"There has to be something I can do," she muttered out loud.

"Talking to yourself, sweetheart?" Wyatt said from behind her.

Teddie squeaked, slapping her hand over her mouth to keep it from turning into a full-blown scream, while the dogs growled in unison. She clutched the blanket around her shoulders tighter and swung around. He stood a few feet away in a pair of sweatpants, a thin white T-shirt, and cowboy boots. As soon as the dogs realized it was Wyatt, they wagged their tails.

She looked him up and down, suppressing a giggle. "What are you wearing? Sweatpants and cowboy boots? And what are you doing sneaking around?" she whispered. "I thought you were asleep."

"I couldn't sleep, so I checked on the horses," he replied. "I didn't bring my slippers, and I'm sure the hell not going to walk around barefoot. What are you doing up?"

She shrugged. "I can't sleep. Too much on my mind."

"You worried about tomorrow?" he asked.

Teddie shook her head and scoffed. "No. I can wrangle cattle in my sleep. I've been doing it for years. I have *other* things on my mind."

Wyatt crossed his arms and smirked. "Oh, yeah?"

She was on her feet in an instant and in front of him. "Yes. For instance, I just found out the man I love also loves me. I'm reeling."

He chuckled. "Reeling, huh? What does that look like?"

Teddie glanced at the tents behind Wyatt, stepped into him, and put her arms around his neck. "Like this." She caught his lips in hers and kissed him.

When they broke apart and she stepped back, he grabbed her hand and dragged her across the campsite to her tent. When the dogs tried to follow, he ordered them to stay, which they did.

Teddie crawled inside the tent with Wyatt right behind her. He dropped to his knees, zipped the tent shut, and grabbed Teddie's ankles, pulling her toward him until she was lying flat on her sleeping bag.

"What are you doing?" she whispered, kicking her feet.

"Shh," Wyatt hissed as he ran his hands up her legs, slowly caressing the inside of her thighs.

Teddie sighed and relaxed under his touch as his fingers drifted under the edge of the tight boy shorts she wore, his rough, calloused fingers sending shots of electricity through every inch of her body. A low moan slipped out of her as he brushed her rapidly heating center.

Wyatt stopped and leaned over her, one hand on either side of her head. "If you're not quiet, I'll stop," he whispered. "And believe me, you don't want me to stop."

Teddie nodded as he eased his fingers down the front of her underwear and gently caressed her.

"Okay?" he asked.

She nodded, afraid to speak, because she definitely didn't want him to stop.

Wyatt pushed her T-shirt up past her breasts and captured her nipple in his mouth. His tongue circled the now erect nipple as he continued his exploration of her warm center. When his finger slid into her while his teeth tugged at her nipple, she nearly lost it. He grinned against her skin.

He kissed his way down her stomach until he hovered over her. Teddie grabbed his head with both hands and forced him to look at her.

"Wyatt, no," she whispered, shaking her head. She knew if he did what she knew he was about to do, she wouldn't be able to keep quiet.

"Oh, yes, sweetheart." That gorgeous smirk was back. "Remember, be quiet." He winked, his eyes on her as he pulled off her underwear and tossed them aside. Then, he slowly licked her.

Another moan rose in her chest, so she slapped her hand over her mouth, barely able to contain it. Her head fell back, waves of pleasure washing over her as Wyatt went to work. His tongue slid into her, along with his finger. He moved them together, his finger crooking just right to hit that perfect, sweet spot. The orgasm built in the pit of her stomach, and then she exploded, heat rushing through her as she rode out the insanity of the climax. A quiet whimper escaped her.

Wyatt pulled away and once again hovered over her. "I told you to be quiet." He kissed her, the taste of her on his tongue making her dizzy with desire.

Teddie pushed at his sweatpants, desperate to touch him. He sat up and shoved them off, along with his boxers and T-shirt. She took him in her hand and caressed his hard length, causing his breath to catch in his throat. He closed his eyes, bit his lip, and groaned.

"Shh," Teddie murmured.

He grinned at her, then he kissed her, sucking her lower lip as he pushed her legs apart and settled between them, his cock nestled at her entrance. The kiss continued as he slowly entered her, inch by glorious inch.

Unable to control herself, she moaned Wyatt's name. He thrust deep into her, hard, deliberately. She almost lost her mind as she kept pace with him, thrust for thrust, her hips snapping up to meet his, her nails scratching at his back.

It didn't take long for the familiar tension to rise in her again, her climax building and building as she desperately choked back the scream of pleasure attempting to burst free.

Wyatt knew how close she was, because he put his hand over her mouth, and God dammit, he stopped the delicious movement of his hips. He wrapped his other arm around her back and held her close as he looked into her eyes.

"I want you to cum for me, baby. I want you to cum all over my cock."

His hips twitched, and Teddie thought she might faint from the overwhelming sensations coursing through her. Her eyes rolled back in her head, and she sighed against his hand. Wyatt pulled his hand away, put his finger to his lips, then he sat up on his knees, moving her so her hips rose off the ground to meet his. He pulled her toward him at the same time that he furiously pounded into her.

It only took several perfectly placed thrusts before she came undone, the tension uncoiling inside her and the undeniable bliss exploding through her entire body as she rode out her orgasm.

Wyatt stiffened, and then his own climax took him, eliciting a satisfied grunt from him. He fell forward, catching himself with his hands next to her head. He kissed her before he collapsed next to her.

"Fuck, Teddie, that was amazing," he whispered.

A shiver rushed through her, though she wasn't sure if it was because of Wyatt or the chill night air. He must have noticed, because he got up, maneuvered her into the sleeping bag, and zipped her up before putting his clothes back on. He kissed her forehead, whispered, "I love you," and then he was gone.

"I love you, too," she said after him.

Chapter 8

Wyatt

Wyatt was up first, before the sun, stoking the flames of the fire to start breakfast and make coffee. He couldn't help but glance at Teddie's tent now and then, wondering how she slept after he left her.

"Mornin' Wyatt," Jesse called.

He raised a hand and waved at his friend, then went back to making coffee. It was going to be a long day, and he wanted to get moving before the heat overtook them.

The tents slowly emptied as everyone got up, ready to start the day. Wyatt left Hank to deal with the coffee and breakfast to look for Luke and Ty. He found them saddling their horses under the trees.

"Good morning," he said. "Did you boys eat breakfast?"

"Yes, sir," Ty replied with a grin.

Wyatt liked Ty; he was young, barely twenty, eager to please, and smart enough to make a split-second decision if necessary. He knew he wouldn't have Ty around long because someone was bound to snatch him up for a foreman job.

"I want you two to take the dogs and go up the mountain. You need to make sure we've got a clear path to the cattle. Then check the herd. Get a head count and look for any injured or weak animals and calves. I think we had a few catch pregnant before we brought the bulls down. The rest of us won't be far behind."

Once Ty and Luke were on their way, Wyatt returned to the camp. Teddie was up and sitting next to Hank, sipping from a metal camping mug. He tapped her gently on the shoulder as he passed her, then he grabbed a cup and poured himself some coffee.

An hour later, everyone was on their horses headed up the mountain, while Hank stayed at the campsite to clean up. Teddie was right up front and ready to help. To Wyatt's surprise, she fit right in with the ranch hands, laughing and joking with them, eager to make friends. It was more than her father had ever done. Everett didn't even know any of their names.

She was good with a horse, too, not that he was surprised. Teddie grew up on the ranch and had been riding horses since she was a little girl. He wasn't remotely worried about her helping to bring the cattle down, because he knew she'd follow directions and work just as hard as everyone else. He'd always admired her work ethic.

Two-thirds of the way up the mountain was an alpine meadow, stretching out like a lush, green quilt dotted with purple and blue wildflowers. The smell of sweet clover and damp earth mixed with the overwhelming odor of the evergreen pines surrounding the meadow. The cattle moved as one, shifting restlessly and staring uneasily at the border collies.

Wyatt adjusted the grip on his reins and turned his horse to face the others. "We need to keep them tight," he said, eyes scanning the herd. "No stragglers. Let's move 'em out."

The ranch hands fanned out, pressing the herd together. Luke whistled, and the dogs moved as one, helping them push the cattle in the direction they wanted them to move. The animals' hooves churned up dust, while the occasional snort or sharp bark broke the mountain's silence.

Wyatt kept one eye on Teddie, who was off to the side, monitoring some of the more skittish cattle. Jesse and one of his ranch hands, Clay, followed Teddie to make sure no cattle lagged behind.

Wyatt led the way, keeping a steady pace. The descent down the mountain was slow work. Some cattle had a difficult time with the steeper parts, hesitating on the loose rocks. They moved slowly, keeping the herd safe from injury.

When they were a little more than halfway down, they reached a narrow pass, forcing them to slow down and push the cattle through three or four at a time. It was tough going; the cows were hesitant, snorting and agitated. Wyatt and the others guided them through carefully, talking low and steady until they were through the pass. The dogs and Teddie rounded up the few stragglers, returning them to the herd.

After they made it through, the land evened out, and the pace picked up. The cattle moved quickly, as if they knew the open pastures of Cherry Ridge were waiting for them. The tension eased in Wyatt's chest. They were almost home. Two or three more hours, and this would be over.

Moving the cattle stressed him out, especially in the heat of the day. Things had gone far smoother than he'd expected. They'd stopped frequently for water breaks alongside the creek that flowed down the hill, which helped keep the animals hydrated.

Wyatt dropped back until he was keeping pace with Teddie. "Not bad, Calloway."

Teddie laughed and smiled. "You're not half bad yourself, Mr. Dawson."

"I do my best, ma'am," he whispered. "You know, I love Cherry Ridge as much as you do. I've been working on this ranch for half my life. I don't want to see it sold any more than you do."

"Don't worry," she replied. "I'm not giving up that easy. Cherry

Ridge is my legacy, and I will not let it go. I'll figure something out. Nobody is taking this place away from me, not even my father."

Wyatt knew she meant it. He just hoped she didn't get hurt.

———

He parked behind the stable, grabbed his coffee, and climbed out of his truck. Wyatt scrubbed a hand over his face and hurried inside. There wasn't enough caffeine in the world to combat his exhaustion.

Working the ranch meant he didn't get days off. After bringing the cattle down the mountain and getting them to pasture, he and the other ranch hands had worked late into the night, checking for any animals that might have suffered wounds and counting the new babies that had been born while they were on the mountain. It looked like they'd lost about five, but they'd gained at least ten babies, maybe more. He'd planned on going back out today, but Hank had brought him the bad news that the truck was giving him trouble. He'd barely made it back to the ranch.

Wyatt hadn't wanted to waste any time, so he stayed until almost midnight working on the truck. He discovered cracked fuel lines and a corroded, leaking tank. Unfortunately, he'd been so damn tired he couldn't keep his eyes open. He headed home, deciding to fix everything in the morning.

He fed the horses, then he checked to see if there were any pressing issues he needed to deal with before he worked on the truck. After he called Hank to send him to town for parts, he poured himself another cup of coffee and headed outside.

He set to work, tearing it apart to replace the worn-out parts with new ones. The temperature spiked as the sun rose, its angry rays beating down on him, adding to his exhaustion. Sweat rolled down Wyatt's neck and along his spine, settling in the middle of his back, staining his shirt.

It took him almost two hours to change everything out, and

he made a mess, spilling gas on the ground beneath the truck. As soon as he got it out of the way, he'd soak up what he could with the bag of cat litter they kept in the garage, clean it up, and run it down to Kane's auto shop so he could dispose of it properly.

Wyatt started the truck, satisfied that he'd fixed the gas leak, pushed open the door, and jumped out. He stretched, groaning as the muscles in his back, shoulders, and legs screamed in protest. He was in good shape, but everybody had a limit, and he had just about reached his.

"Did you get that beast running?"

He looked up to see Jesse walking his way. He raised a hand and nodded, frowning when he noticed Preston strolling behind Jesse like he owned the place.

Jesse got to him first. "Sorry about this, but he insisted on tagging along, said he needs to talk to the Colonel. I don't know why he's following me down here. I told him Calloway is probably in the house."

Wyatt sighed and braced himself. He had never gotten along with Preston Remington. He was three years younger—the same age as Teddie—and they hadn't run in the same circles in high school. Preston came from money while Wyatt had been working since he was a kid. They weren't friends, and frankly, Preston annoyed him.

"Hot out today, isn't it?" Preston said when he reached them.

Wyatt rolled his eyes. Preston had just stepped out of an air-conditioned vehicle and there wasn't a drop of sweat on him. He didn't know what an honest day's work was. The man had done nothing more strenuous than raise a cigarette to his mouth.

"What are you doing here, Preston?" he asked.

Preston scowled. "I'm meeting with the Colonel. I have an offer for the ranch."

"Is Teddie involved in those discussions?"

"Why would she be involved?" Preston scoffed.

Wyatt sighed. "Teddie runs this place. She needs to be a part of any discussions you have about *anything* to do with Cherry Ridge."

Preston shook his head. "If her father wants her involved, he'll let me know."

"I don't think she'll like that," Wyatt countered.

"I don't care." Preston shrugged. He flicked his lit cigarette at Wyatt, whose eyes followed it as it arched, the glowing ember of red and orange tumbling through the air.

His shout of "What are you doing?" caught in his throat.

The cigarette bounced on the hard-packed dirt and rolled under the truck, right into the gas that had leaked from the busted fuel lines. Time stopped, and for a heartbeat, there was nothing. Wyatt turned, foolishly thinking he could stop what was about to happen. The gasoline caught the flame and then there was a loud whooshing sound, then—BOOM!

It was deafening, like a crack of thunder as it struck a tree. A thunderous shockwave tore through the ranch, rattling windows and sending a fiery plume shooting into the sky. The force of the explosion lifted the truck off the ground, shattering the windshield as the metal shell of the vehicle crumpled in on itself like paper.

Wyatt's eardrums exploded, and an immediate ringing filled his head as bright, hot, orange light blinded him and unbelievable, intense heat surrounded him. The world tilted on its axis as hell rained down.

Chapter 9
Teddie

*T*eddie was at her desk, head resting on her folded arms, half asleep, when the explosion rocked the guest house, rattling the windows and shaking the furniture. The shock made her fall out of her chair and hit the floor.

"What the hell?" she muttered, pushing herself to her feet.

She raced for the door, leaving it wide open as she burst through it and darted around the side of the house.

A hundred yards from the barn, before she had even emerged from the orchard, Teddie slid to a stop, frozen in place as she watched thick, black smoke rise into the sky. Shouts echoed in the chaos as men cursed and coughed, scrambling to get to their feet. An unrecognizable pile of burning metal sat in the middle of the gravel drive, flames popping and crackling, the heat so intense she felt it where she stood.

"Oh my god," she moaned, fear turning her blood to ice.

Horses neighed and kicked at their stall doors as the fire licked at the sides of the barn. The air was thick with smoke and panic as people ran around yelling, screaming, and crying.

"Ms. Calloway!" Luke yelled, running toward her. "What the hell happened?"

"I don't know." The need to panic built in her chest, but she pushed it down. She had to keep it together, take care of the ranch. "Luke, grab Jed and check on the horses. If they need to be moved out of the barn, take them to the pens north of the barn. Tell Hank, Ty, and Nash to get the hoses and put this fire out. Now."

"Yes, ma'am." He turned to go, but Teddie grabbed his arm. "Where's Wyatt?"

Luke swallowed and shook his head. "I haven't seen him."

She nodded. "Okay. Go! Go!"

Luke took off at a dead run.

"Wyatt!" Teddie screamed, looking everywhere at once.

Hand up in front of her face in a futile effort to keep the heat from licking at her skin, she circled the burning hunk of metal— what she suspected was the ranch truck, the one that constantly broke down. On the far side of the tractor, on his stomach, was a man covered in soot.

Teddie fell to her knees beside him and rolled him over, but it wasn't Wyatt, it was Jesse. His eyes rolled back in his head, deep coughs left him, and blood poured from his ears. She sagged in relief, but the fear was still there.

She pulled Jesse's head into her lap and called for help. Maggie appeared at her side a few seconds later.

"I got him, sweetheart," her mother said. "Where's Wyatt?"

"I don't know."

"Go find him," Maggie instructed.

Teddie nodded as she got to her feet, the tears threatening to fall. She held them off by sheer force of will as she turned in circles, desperately looking for Wyatt. She ducked around the people with buckets and hoses who worked to douse the flames before they reached the barn and the horses.

That was when she saw him lying motionless near the stable

wall, half buried under a pile of hay, a large bleeding gash above his left eyebrow, and various other cuts and bruises covered every inch of visible skin.

"Wyatt!" Teddie ran to his side, dropping to her knees beside him as tears poured down her face.

He stirred, a deep groan leaving him. He grabbed her hand. "Hey, it's okay," he murmured. "I'm okay."

"Jesus Christ, no you're not! You're bleeding! I... I thought you were dead. I couldn't find you, and when I saw Jesse, I thought it was you—" She sobbed, the tears blurring her vision.

"I'm sorry," he mumbled.

Only Wyatt thought to apologize for almost dying. He had to be the most selfless, amazing man she'd ever met. "If you had died, I'd have killed you myself."

He chuckled and shook his head, but the laugh quickly changed to a groan. He furrowed his brow, narrowed his eyes, pressed his lips tight together, and hunched his shoulders.

"You're not okay," she said.

"I'm not okay," he replied just before he passed out.

———

Sleep was elusive, not that she could have slept with Wyatt lying unconscious in his hospital bed, every wire imaginable attached to him. Teddie checked to make sure he was still asleep before she slipped out of his room in the ICU and headed down the hall to the vending machines. She didn't want to be gone too long; Wyatt was in and out of consciousness, and she wanted to be there if he woke up again.

The concussion he'd suffered was severe, along with a burst eardrum, multiple lacerations, and several burns. When the truck exploded, the blast threw him over ten feet, where he thankfully landed in a pile of hay bales next to the barn before he blacked out.

Jesse was in a room down the hall, but unlike Wyatt, he hadn't regained consciousness. His wife, Claire, had not left his side. They had crossed paths several times, meeting at the vending machines or the nurses' station. Teddie's heart broke for her. The doctors didn't have any answers; they weren't sure Jesse would wake up, and if he did, what condition he would be in.

"Theodora."

Her shoulders slumped at the sound of her father's voice. She'd avoided her father ever since Wyatt ended up in the hospital, refusing to speak to him. She slowly turned around, crossing her arms over her chest as she stared at him.

"Colonel," she said.

"How long has this been going on?" he asked.

Teddie sighed. "How long has *what* been going on?" she retorted, knowing full well what he was talking about, but still playing dumb.

Everett grabbed her arm and dragged her into the waiting area, away from the nurses' station. He dropped her arm and turned to glare at her. "Do not play dumb with me, young lady. You know *exactly* what I'm talking about. You and that ranch hand."

"Wyatt Dawson, your ranch *foreman*?"

Her father rolled his eyes. "Fine. How long have you and Dawson been together?"

She gritted her teeth. "I don't know. A while. A few months." It had been much longer than that, but she wasn't ready to tell him that.

"You know my rule—"

"Your archaic rule about the staff not mingling with your daughters? That rule? I am aware of it."

"You need to end it."

Teddie shook her head. "Absolutely not."

"I am not giving you an option," her father said. "End it."

His phone rang before she could reply. He yanked it out of his suit jacket and looked at it. "It's the insurance company." He gave her one of his "this isn't over" looks, turned away from her, and answered the phone. Teddie stared at his back for a minute before she walked away and returned to Wyatt's room.

According to the doctor, he was still in and out of consciousness, so she picked up her book and sat in the chair next to his bed to wait for him to wake up. Not that she read much, just stared at the pages, basically sleeping with her eyes open. She didn't know what time it was when Wyatt whispered her name. She got up so fast her book hit the floor.

"Hi," she breathed, falling to her knees beside the bed.

"Hey," he mumbled.

Teddie fought back tears of relief and pushed down her emotions, doing her best to keep herself calm. She took his face in her hands and kissed him, brushing a thumb over the bruise on the side of his face.

"Don't cry," he said, grabbing her hand and squeezing it. "I'm alive."

Teddie nodded and wiped the tears from her cheeks. She grabbed the chair, pulled up to the bed, and sat down with her feet tucked beneath her. She held Wyatt's hand and spent the next hour answering his questions—how the horses were, how much damage the buildings had sustained, who else had been hurt, and anything he wanted to know. When he finished asking questions, it was her turn.

"What the hell happened?"

Wyatt told her what he remembered, which was only until the truck exploded. By the time he finished, he had trouble keeping his eyes open. He dozed off with his hand in hers.

—

Later that day, the nurses, with Wyatt's help, convinced her to go home for a few hours to shower, sleep, and get some proper food in her body. They assured her that if anything changed, she would be the first person they called. Teddie reluctantly agreed.

Tessa greeted her at the door with a hug, holding her tighter than she ever had before. Then she took her sister's hand and led her to the dining room, where she had a plate of food and a cold bottle of beer waiting for her.

"You should have told me," Tessa scolded. "About you and Wyatt."

"I didn't tell anybody," Teddie replied. "I didn't want anybody to know."

"Because of the Colonel?"

Teddie nodded, her stomach churning at the mere mention of her father. She would have to face him again eventually, something she was not looking forward to. In fact, she dreaded it. She pushed the thought aside while she ate the sandwich and drank her beer, even though she had little appetite.

"Did you know he was going to go to the hospital?" Teddie asked between bites of food.

Tessa nodded. "On his way out the door, he quizzed me, wondering if I knew you were dating 'that ranch hand.' When I said no, he told me it didn't matter, because he was going to put an end to it. I wanted to stop him. That's a fight I do not *want* to relive."

Teddie shook her head. "You didn't have to do that."

"Yes, I did." Tessa exhaled loudly. "Not that it mattered."

Teddie had finished eating when the kitchen door slammed.

"Tessa!" their father roared. "Where is your sister?"

"Did he sound like that when you were fighting?" Teddie mumbled.

"Yep. Exactly like that," Tessa replied.

Teddie swallowed half the bottle of beer, handed it to her sister, and wiped her mouth with the back of her hand. She stood up and braced herself.

"I'm in the dining room, Daddy!" she yelled. She pointed at

the door on the other side of the room that led to a back hallway and mouthed, "Go."

For once, Tessa didn't argue with her. Instead, she got up and walked away, shaking her head and mumbling under her breath.

Everett Calloway strode through the door a minute later with his fists clenched and his brow furrowed, looking as if he was about to erupt in hellfire. Teddie sucked in a deep breath and braced herself for a tongue lashing.

He stopped in front of her, arms crossed, his face unreadable. "Well?"

"Well, what?"

"Did you end your relationship with Dawson?" he asked.

Teddie rubbed her forehead. "Do you realize you have not *once* asked how he is? He was injured in an accident on *our* ranch, and the only thing you care about is whether or not he is dating your daughter. He is tired and in pain, but instead of worrying about healing, he is worried you're going to fire him."

"Which is exactly what I'm going to do," Everett stated.

She could barely contain her anger, the need to lash out at her father overwhelming her. "Why, Daddy? Because he broke your archaic rule about dating one of the Calloway girls?"

"Not only that. He almost cost us everything. We were lucky to put the fire out before it reached the stables. The truck exploded, a truck he'd been working on—"

"It wasn't his fault," Teddie interjected. "Preston Remington dropped his cigarette."

Everett rolled his eyes. "I don't want to hear any excuses. Preston explained what happened, and it sounds like Dawson didn't clean up the gasoline, which ignited the fire. It wasn't Preston's fault."

"Jesus Christ, Daddy—"

"Do not swear at me, Theodora," he snapped.

"I cannot believe you are going to blame this on Wyatt." She sucked in a deep breath. "You're going to fire him because of what Preston did?"

"He blew up the ranch truck and almost killed my horses!"

"No. Preston did that by carelessly dropping a still-lit cigarette on the ground. But you are so dead set on this being the fault of the ranch hand dating your daughter that you refuse to accept the truth. You want a legitimate excuse to fire him, so you're grabbing onto this. You are so damn thick!"

The anger radiating from her father forced her back a step. "This discussion is over, Theodora. I am firing Dawson, and you *will* stop seeing him. Period." He turned to leave.

"You can't tell me what to do," she argued. "I am a grown woman."

"You live under my roof and you work for me, so yes, I *can* tell you what to do." He stormed out of the room.

"Not if I don't live under your roof," she muttered.

Chapter 10
Teddie

Teddie yanked open her dresser drawers, tossed her suitcases on the bed, and randomly threw stuff in them. She wasn't paying attention to what she grabbed—she didn't care—she wanted to pack so she could get out of the house. Once both of the suitcases were full, she picked up a duffle bag, took it into the bathroom, and threw her toiletries in it.

Fifteen minutes later, she had everything loaded in her Jeep, and she was on her way down the drive, heading for Wyatt's. He lived in a small cabin on the north end of the property, about five minutes from the house.

Under the mat in front of the door, she found Wyatt's extra key and unlocked the front door. She got her things from the car and went inside, locking the door behind her and dropping the key in a little glass bowl on the table. Teddie sat on the couch and stared off into space.

This shit flipped her life upside down. Her father was going to sell the ranch—the only home she'd ever known—and the man she loved was in the hospital. Everything was out of control.

"Maybe not everything," she muttered. She grabbed her laptop out of her backpack and opened it.

There had to be a way to save the ranch without selling it to the Remingtons—a loan or an investor. If she figured something out, some way to buy the ranch from her father, she and Wyatt could run it together.

Exhaustion washed over her, so she kicked off her boots and stretched out on the couch, a small throw pillow under her head. Within minutes, she was sound asleep.

—

Teddie was still at Wyatt's place when he came home from the hospital. Of course, he told her she was welcome to stay as long as she liked, even it meant forever. She wondered if he was joking, though she didn't think he was.

"What did Claire say?" she asked after Wyatt hung up his phone. "How is Jesse?"

"He's angry, hurt, pissed, and out for blood," Wyatt said. "Anybody would be after losing their hearing in one ear in an accident that never should have happened." He eased onto the couch beside Teddie and slipped his arm around her shoulder.

"How are you doing?" he asked.

"I'm fine," she replied, a little too quickly.

"Liar," he whispered, kissing her cheek. "It's been almost a week since the fight with your father. Are you going to call him?"

"No," she snapped.

"Hey, hey, easy. It was only a suggestion."

Teddie sighed, turning in his arms to lay her head on his chest. Wyatt kissed the top of her head and rubbed circles on her back.

She felt bad that he was comforting her because he'd only been out of the hospital for three days. The severe concussion he suffered was causing him debilitating migraines, and he still lived with the prospect of being fired.

"I'm sorry I snapped at you," she murmured. "All of this stuff with the ranch is putting me on edge. Every day I am not there is a day when my father might sell it right out from under me."

"What time is your meeting with the bank tomorrow?"

"Nine a.m. I'm nervous about it, though. I have nothing of my own to prove I can repay a loan large enough to purchase Cherry Ridge. I don't even own my Jeep, for Christ's sake. My father bought it for me. I have a few credit cards in my name, but shit, do I even have a job anymore? I work for the Colonel, and I walked out." Teddie abruptly stood up and paced. "I'm not sure I can do this, Wyatt. Am I capable of running the ranch by myself?"

"Honey, you run it by yourself now. What exactly does your father do?"

Teddie took a deep breath, prepared to spout off a list of everything her father did, and then froze. Nothing came to mind. She was in charge of the financial aspects of the ranch, management of the land, servicing the equipment and structures on the ranch, most of their business relationships, and the buying and selling of the cattle. About the only thing she didn't do was hire the staff, though she took care of the payroll and their employment records. They knew if they needed anything, they should come to her.

"I... I guess I run Cherry Ridge, don't I?"

Wyatt leaned forward with his elbows on his knees. "You are the one with the connections, right?"

She snorted. "Are you reading my mind? I was just thinking that."

"Well, are you?"

Teddie nodded. "Yeah, I am."

"You need to use those relationships, babe. You have the connections; people come to you when they want to work with Cherry Ridge. Reach out. See if you can scare up some investors or a co-signer on the loan to buy the ranch."

"I don't know—"

Wyatt shook his head. "No, that's not an answer. If you want to keep this place, your childhood home, then you don't have much choice. Put together a proposal and start asking around."

Jesus, he was right. This ranch was hers. She understood it better than anyone in her family. If her father wasn't willing to let her have it, then she'd buy it out from underneath him.

"Have told you I love you yet today?" she asked.

He smirked. "Only four or five times."

"Will you come to the bank with me?"

"I can't," Wyatt replied. "I'm meeting with the insurance inspector tomorrow."

"That's tomorrow? What time?"

"I think around eleven," he said.

"I'll be there. I'll be done at the bank by then, so I can meet you at the insurance office."

He reached for her hand, tugging her close. "You don't have to do that. I can go on my own."

"I'm not letting you face Everett Calloway alone. You and me together, right?"

"Yes."

Teddie kneeled on the couch beside him, ran her fingers through his hair, and kissed him.

"How's your head?" she asked.

He shrugged. "Okay. Why?"

"Let's go to bed," she whispered. "You look tired."

"Okay, but I'm gonna shower first."

She kissed him again. "I'm going to clean the kitchen really fast, then I'll be in."

When Teddie walked into the bedroom, Wyatt lay sprawled across the bed, wearing only a towel around his waist. She thought he was asleep until he held his hand out to her and gestured for her to join him.

She stripped off her T-shirt and jeans, eased onto the bed

beside him, and let him wrap her in his arms. He rolled to his side, caught her lips in his, and kissed her, a deep, probing kiss that made her toes curl. He slipped his hand into her hair, cupping her head and holding her close as the kiss deepened. Their legs tangled together as Teddie pulled the towel away from his waist and ran her hands over his naked body. She moaned when his hard cock brushed against her leg. She reached for him, her nails grazing the tip of his length, drawing an answering moan from him.

"Is this okay?" she murmured against his lips as she wrapped her hand around his shaft, sliding it down the length, her thumb teasing the tip.

A growl rumbled through his chest. "I'm good, baby." He pushed her hair off her neck, kissing it hungrily.

Teddie pushed him to his back, kissing a trail down his neck and over his chest. Her tongue darted out, swiping at his nipple, circling it. She continued down his stomach, taking her time, enjoying his small gasps and moans, his cock so hard it throbbed in her hand.

She took him in her mouth, her tongue tracing the slit, a shuddering moan escaping her as the velvety soft skin slid past her lips. Teddie wrapped her hand around the base, opened her mouth, and slowly slid it down the shaft, rubbing it against the roof of her mouth.

"Fuck," Wyatt groaned, his hands tangling in her hair as his hips rose off the bed, pushing himself deeper into her mouth.

Teddie hollowed her cheeks and sucked gently, cupping and fondling his sensitive sac as she pulled him deeper into the wet heat of her mouth. She moved back up the length, grazing him with her teeth before repeating the movement several times, each time taking more of his cock, opening her throat to accept his tight, controlled thrusts.

She climbed to her knees, adjusting her position so she

hovered over Wyatt, the new angle allowing her to swallow him completely, caressing his sac as he fucked her mouth.

"Jesus, babe, I'm gonna cum." His hands fell to his sides, clutching desperately at the blankets on the bed.

Teddie wrapped her hand around the base of his cock and squeezed, releasing him to look into his lust blown eyes.

"Then do it," she challenged, stroking his length several times before she took him back into her mouth, sliding him past her swollen, saliva-slick lips, her head bobbing as she pleasured him.

A low groan echoed through Wyatt's chest as his cock pulsed in her mouth and his balls drew up tight in her hand, which were the all-too-familiar signs he was about to cum. Teddie intensified her movements, deep-throating him, swallowing him down, the pressure of her constricting throat increasing his pleasure.

Wyatt trembled beneath her, his release accompanied by an obscene moan, his cock jerking as he came, his taste flooding her mouth. She moaned with him, her nose pressed against his curls, taking what he gave her, draining him dry.

When it was over, Wyatt's soft cock slid from her mouth, and she slowly kissed her way up his body. She stretched out on top of him, nuzzling her face into the space where his neck and shoulder met, inhaling the clean scent of his skin.

His fingers drifted lazily up and down her back, his breathing steady and even. Tears welled at the corners of her eyes, the fear she'd held at bay for days threatening to push itself to the surface. Teddie knew she should be relieved life hadn't thrown her a vicious curve ball and stolen Wyatt from her too soon, and she was relieved, but now and then, it snuck up on her, especially in a moment like this.

She pushed herself closer to Wyatt, though it was impossible—they were already skin to skin, limbs tangled together— but that didn't stop her from trying. She held back a terrified sob, not wanting him to know how close she was to losing it.

But he knew; he always did. That was why she loved him.

His arms circled her waist, and he rolled them over, the two of them chest to chest. He kissed her, then he tucked her head under his chin.

"I'm right here, baby," he whispered. "I'm right here and I'm not going anywhere. I promise."

Chapter 11

Wyatt

"Mr. Dawson, thank you for meeting me," Lloyd Adams said. The insurance company had assigned Lloyd to investigate the explosion and subsequent fire. This was the second time he and Wyatt had met; the first time had been while he was in the hospital, twenty-four hours after the fire, when he'd been less than coherent.

A sharp rap at the door drew Lloyd's attention. He excused himself, went to his office door, and stepped outside. Thirty seconds later, Teddie blew through the door, obviously irritated, with Lloyd right behind her, and took a seat beside Wyatt.

"Um, Ms. Calloway, it's... I don't think... it's not a good idea for you to be here," Lloyd stammered. "I'll speak with you after the investigation."

Teddie shook her head. "Thank you, Mr. Adams, but I'd like to sit in on this interview, if you don't mind."

"Well, your father—"

"Has entrusted me with managing Cherry Ridge," she

interjected. "That hasn't changed." She looked around the room. "Speaking of my father, where is he?"

Lloyd cleared his throat, took his seat, and shuffled some papers around. "I, uh, I thought Colonel Calloway was going to be in attendance, but it looks like he won't make it." He cleared his throat again. "Mr. Dawson, can you tell me about Preston Remington?"

Wyatt sat up straight, surprised that Preston's name had come up. When he'd told Lloyd about Preston and his cigarette when he saw him at the hospital, Lloyd kept bringing the conversation back around to Wyatt. He'd subtly hinted that because Wyatt had been fixing the truck prior to the explosion, it was his fault.

"Preston Remington?" Wyatt asked.

"Yes, sir," Lloyd replied.

Wyatt sighed. "Like I said before, Preston threw a lit cigarette, which landed in a puddle of gasoline under the truck that I was repairing. That caused the explosion and fire." He shifted in his seat. "Why are you asking?"

"I've talked to almost everyone working that day, and they all said that while Mr. Remington was on site, he was not working. Is that true?"

"Yes," Teddie answered. "Mr. Remington doesn't work for Cherry Ridge. I believe he was there to meet with my father."

Lloyd nodded and scribbled something on a notepad. "Okay, several of them also mentioned they believe Mr. Remington is a chain smoker, so it is possible the story you told me—"

"It's not a story, Mr. Adams," Wyatt snapped. "It's the truth."

"And that's what I'm trying to get to. The truth." Lloyd held his pen over the paper on his desk. "Tell me again what happened."

Wyatt went through it again, every second, from the minute he finished working on the truck to waking up in the hospital. He explained that he'd parked the truck in front of the barn, noticed it leaking gasoline, and hadn't cleaned up thoroughly before

Preston arrived. He told Lloyd about Preston carelessly tossing his lit cigarette toward the truck and how he had tried to stop it, knowing full well he couldn't. Then he explained his vague memories of the explosion, the fire, and his pain. By the time he finished, he was sweating profusely.

Lloyd nodded and scribbled something on the papers on his desk. "Thank you, Mr. Dawson. I appreciate your help." He got to his feet, shook their hands, and escorted them to the door.

Wyatt took Teddie's hand as they walked out. They were almost out of the building when someone called her name. They turned to see Preston striding purposefully toward them.

"Teddie, wait!"

"Keep walking," he muttered.

"No," Teddie replied. "If I don't talk to him, he'll keep following us and yelling."

"Preston," she said when he slid to a stop in front of them. "What are you doing here?"

"That insurance guy wants to talk to me." He shrugged and turned to Wyatt, smirking. "He probably needs my help to get Wyatt fired for setting your ranch on fire."

Teddie must have seen the look on Wyatt's face because she stepped between them. "Knock it off, Preston. We know whose fault it was that the truck exploded. Stop acting like you didn't do anything wrong."

"I dropped a cigarette, Teddie. I didn't set off a goddamn bomb."

Lloyd cleared his throat from behind them. "Excuse me, Mr. Remington. I'm ready to see you now."

Preston grumbled something incoherent, then he followed Lloyd into his office.

—

Wyatt slid into the booth across from Teddie, took off his hat, and put it on the seat beside him. He ordered a cup of coffee for himself and an iced tea for Teddie. When she returned from the bathroom, she kissed him on the cheek and sat down.

"I didn't get a chance to ask you yet. How did it go at the bank?" he said.

She sipped her drink, then set it down with a sigh. "Okay, I guess."

"That doesn't sound good."

"Well, they're willing to help me get the money for the ranch," she replied.

"Why do I sense a 'but' coming?"

"*But* they want a co-signer or an investor to sign off on it." She shrugged. "Who the hell am I going to ask? Anybody I ask will want a say in how to run the ranch, and I don't think I'm okay with that. I'm not sure what to do."

Wyatt reached across the table and took her hand. "Can I ask you a question?"

"Yeah, of course."

"If Cherry Ridge were gone, if your father sells it, what would you do? Where would you go?"

Teddie opened her mouth, then she snapped it shut and shook her head. "I... I don't know."

He squeezed her hand. "Then that answers your question. If you can't see yourself anywhere else or doing anything else, that means Cherry Ridge is where you're meant to be."

"But my father—"

Wyatt slammed his fist on the table, making her jump. "Damn your father. He didn't care about you when he decided to sell the ranch, did he? So, why should you care about him? Stop tiptoeing around what the Colonel wants and decide what you want. And *who* you want."

Teddie yanked her hand out of his and sat back. "What is that supposed to mean?"

He rubbed his forehead. "Look, babe, I know you love me. I do. But you are still afraid of upsetting your father."

"That's not true," she argued.

Wyatt held up his hand. "You've been staying with me for almost a week, right? Have you unpacked anything? Picked up the rest of your stuff from the main house? No. Because you're just biding your time until you can move back home."

"It's my *home*, Wyatt."

He sighed and rubbed his head. "I know. The question is, do you want it to be *our* home?"

"What?"

"Do you see us running Cherry Ridge together?" he asked, though he thought he knew the answer.

"I... I don't know," she whispered. "I won't lie. I have thought about it."

"Do you see us running it together as partners, or do you see yourself as the owner and me as your foreman? As your employee?" he asked.

Teddie opened her mouth, then snapped it shut. That was all the answer he needed.

"I don't know," she repeated.

"I was afraid you were going to say that." Wyatt pulled a box out of his pocket, opened it, and set it on the table. "I've been carrying this around in my pocket for more than a month, waiting for the right moment, waiting until you were ready to tell your father about us." He shook his head and stared at a spot above her head. "When you told me you loved me on the mountain, I thought our moment had come, but then you said you weren't ready to tell your father. Tell me, have you told the Colonel you love me, or does he think we're just dating?"

Teddie swallowed, her eyes glued to the diamond and sapphire ring in the box. Tears welled in her eyes.

"Answer me, Teddie. Have you told the Colonel you love me?"

She slowly shook her head. "No, I haven't told him I love you. Not yet."

"When are you planning on doing that?" he asked.

"Wyatt," she whispered.

"So, you haven't told your father you're in love with me, and you still see me as your employee, not your equal? Do I have it right?"

"You're not being fair. I'm under a lot of stress right now." She gnawed on her bottom lip. "I don't want to add to it."

He nodded, his fingers tapping on the table, then he picked up the box with the engagement ring and shoved it in his pocket. "You know what? I'm gonna head home. I'm kind of tired, and I think a headache is coming on." He took out his wallet, dropped some money on the table, and then he stood up. "I'll see you later."

"Wyatt, wait," Teddie pleaded.

He stopped and looked at her over his shoulder. "I'd co-sign that loan for you, by the way. In a heartbeat. I've been saving every dime I've earned since I was sixteen, hoping someday I could buy a ranch of my own. It would be a dream come true if I could even be a part-owner of Cherry Ridge. I love that place almost as much as you love it. Hell, I love it almost as much as I love you. Nothing would be better than owning it with the woman I want to marry."

Teddie stared at him with tears sliding down her cheeks, but she didn't speak. Wyatt turned and left. It was up to her now. It was her decision to make.

Chapter 12
Teddie

She watched him walk away. She sat on her ass as the man she loved walked away and she didn't stop him.

Teddie wiped the tears from her face and finished her drink. Then she left, waving goodbye to the bar's owner, Nate, and his fiancée, Faith, on her way out. She climbed in her Jeep and stared out the window at Flathead Lake for almost half an hour, figuring out what she wanted to do—go home and have it out with her father or go apologize to Wyatt. She was still deciding what to do when her cell phone buzzed with an incoming message.

[Everett: I need to talk to you.]

Sighing, she quickly typed a response, then started the Jeep. She glanced at the phone she'd tossed on the passenger seat.

[Teddie: On my way.]

[Everett: Meet me in the office.]

It took her almost twenty minutes to drive to Cherry Ridge. As soon as she drove up the driveway, her mother came out of the house and waited for her at the top of the curve. She was barely out of the Jeep before Maggie descended on her and wrapped her in a hug.

"I've missed you," she whispered.

"I missed you, too, Mom."

Maggie held her at arm's length. "Where have you been staying?"

Teddie cleared her throat. "With Wyatt."

"Good, he needs someone to take care of him," her mother said. "How is he?"

"On the mend," Teddie replied. "Mom, did you know about me and Wyatt?"

Maggie shrugged. "I suspected the two of you were seeing each other, but I didn't want to interfere. I knew you'd tell me when you were ready."

"Did you tell Daddy?"

Her mother shook her head. "It's not my place to tell him. He needed to hear it from you, especially if you have feelings for Wyatt. Do you?"

"Yes, I do. I'm, well, I'm pretty sure I'm in love with him."

Maggie's smile widened. "I knew it!" She slapped a hand over her mouth. "Sorry," she mumbled through her fingers. "I'm happy that you found somebody to love."

"Thanks, Mom." Teddie took a deep breath. "Is Daddy in the guesthouse? He summoned me."

Her mother nodded. "He's waiting for you. Go easy on him."

Teddie laughed. "Excuse me? *Me* go easy on *him*?"

"Don't worry, I said the same thing to your father." Maggie hugged her again. "Come see me before you leave. I have a cherry pie for Wyatt." She turned and went back into her kitchen.

Next up was Tessa, who jumped on Teddie—literally—from

the porch. Tessa wrapped her arms around her sister and held her so tight she couldn't breathe.

"Thanks for leaving me alone with the tyrant," Tessa said. "He's been intolerable since you left."

"Shit," Teddie muttered. "Seriously?"

Tessa rolled her eyes. "Okay, maybe not completely intolerable, but difficult. I've been hiding out with Mom in her kitchen."

"Did he tell you what he's going to do?" Teddie asked.

"What do you mean? What is he going to do?"

"Sell Cherry Ridge," Teddie replied.

"Holy shit, what? He's going to sell the ranch? Can he... can he do that?"

"It's his ranch, Tess. He owns it, so he has the right to do whatever he wants."

Her sister crossed her arms and shot a dirty look over her shoulder at the guesthouse. "So, where does that leave us?"

Teddie grinned. "Homeless?"

"Ha-ha, you're funny. I'm being serious."

"So am I. And I don't know where that leaves us, but I'm going to find out." She patted Tessa's arm. "I promise I'll figure it out. I better go; Daddy is waiting."

"Good luck," Tessa murmured. "You'll need it."

Thanks to her pessimistic family, Teddie's nerves had ratcheted up tenfold. She marched down the sidewalk to the guesthouse, raised her hand to knock, then changed her mind, opened the door, and went inside.

Her father was at her desk, staring at her computer with an angry look on his face. He punched a few buttons on the keyboard, then shoved it away, muttering obscenities under his breath.

"Problem?" she asked.

Everett swung around, his look of anger moving from the computer to her. "It's about time."

"Daddy, you texted me less than thirty minutes ago. I was

in town, but after I got your text, I came straight here. What is the problem?"

"I need the ranch's financials for the last year," he said. "But I can't find them, and your computer is password protected."

"Yes, it is," Teddie said. "Why do you need the financials?"

"There is a buyer interested in Cherry Ridge, but he wants to see the financials before he decides." Everett got to his feet. "Can you get them for me?"

"I want to talk to you first."

Her father rolled his eyes. "About what?"

"About Cherry Ridge," she explained. "I'd like to make you a counteroffer."

"What? A counteroffer on the ranch? Are you serious?"

"I'm dead serious, Daddy. I want a chance to buy my childhood home before you sell it out from underneath me. Not only is this place my home, but it's my legacy, my *life*. I have devoted the last eleven years to Cherry Ridge. I know this place inside and out. I want the chance to take it over and make it mine. All mine."

Everett tipped his head to one side and narrowed his eyes. "Well, it certainly sounds like you mean business."

"Yes," she replied. "I do."

Her father slowly nodded his head. "Okay, I'll give you a chance to make an offer. I won't accept anything without letting you make a counteroffer. But I'm only giving you thirty-six hours. Does that sound fair?"

Without thinking about it, Teddie threw her arms around her father and hugged him. To her surprise, he patted her on the back. Everett Calloway wasn't one for affection, so a pat on the back was a big deal.

"Let me know when your counteroffer is ready, and we'll talk." He was almost to the door when he stopped, though he didn't turn around. "Are you planning on moving back home anytime soon?"

"I don't know," she murmured. "Are you still mad that I'm dating Wyatt?"

Everett's shoulders stiffened. "Maybe."

"Then, no, I'm not coming home. Not yet."

"Will you at least come back to work? There's a lot that needs to be done."

"Are you saying you need me?"

Her father sighed. "Theodora, don't test me."

"I'm sorry." She cleared her throat. "I'll be in tomorrow morning, first thing."

He nodded once, then he strode from the room without looking back.

Teddie dropped into the chair at her desk with a sigh. Everett Calloway was exhausting on a good day. She pushed a hand through her hair and got up. She'd say goodbye to her mom and sister, grab some clothes, and go back to Wyatt's. It was time to apologize to him.

—

She reached for the door handle, paused for a second, then instead of opening the door, she knocked. A few minutes later, the door flew open and there stood Wyatt with a strange look on his face.

"Why are you knocking?" he asked.

"I... well, I don't live here. I'm a guest."

Wyatt rolled her eyes, grabbed her arm, and yanked her inside. "Don't be silly. Get in here."

Teddie dropped her bag of clothes on the floor and followed him through the living room to the kitchen.

"You made dinner?" she whispered.

"Chili, cornbread, beer, nothing special. I thought you might be hungry, since you didn't eat breakfast or lunch."

As if on cue, her stomach growled, and Wyatt chuckled. "Sit down and eat."

"You're not mad at me anymore?"

He shook his head. "I wasn't mad at you, Ted. I'm angry with the situation and with the uncertainty of our future, and that you haven't told your father you love me."

"I just need a little time," she said.

"I know, and I'm willing to give it to you. But I won't wait forever. I love you, Theodora Jean Calloway, and I want to marry you. But I won't even think about that until the Colonel knows you're in love with me. Period."

Desperate to lighten the moment, Teddie smiled at him. "Did you just middle name me?"

Wyatt nodded. "I did." Unfortunately, he wasn't laughing.

She exhaled. "I *am* sorry, Wyatt. I know that's not what you want to hear, but I am sorry I haven't told my father. You know how difficult he can be, and with everything going on right now, I need to be careful. Once the ranch is mine, I will talk to him about us. I swear. Until then, please be patient with me."

"Once it's yours? Did you talk to your father about buying the ranch?"

"Yes," Teddie responded. "He agreed to let me make a counteroffer, and I'm going to do it."

"Does that mean you're going to get the loan from the bank?"

"I'm going to try."

Wyatt's eyebrows rose. "Who is going to co-sign for you?"

Teddie shrugged. "I don't know yet." She cleared her throat. "I know you offered, and I really appreciate it, but I'm not sure how my father will feel about that, and I don't want to ask you to do something like that. It's not fair to you. Please give me a chance to figure out what I'm going to do, okay? I need you to trust me."

"I can do that," Wyatt said. "But I need a promise from you?"

"Anything."

"After you decide what to do about the ranch, you'll tell your father about us."

"I promise," she whispered. She leaned over the table and kissed him. "I love you, Wyatt James Dawson."

He chuckled. "Did you just middle name me?"

Chapter 13

Wyatt

Wyatt sucked in a deep breath and scanned the area around the barn before he got out of the truck. The ranch hands did their best to clean up the mess caused by the explosion, but a big black spot remained in front of the barn, and there were scorch marks on the outside wall.

He wasn't just checking out what damage had been done, but he was also looking for the Colonel. Seeing Teddie's father wasn't exactly high on his list. In fact, he wasn't even sure if he should be there. The man had threatened to fire him.

"Oh, well," he muttered, pushing open the truck door and stepping out. "Here goes nothing."

Wyatt slammed the door and headed for the barn, skirting the black spot on the ground. He checked on the horses first, then he went to his office. Someone had straightened up his desk and cleaned the bathroom. He chuckled to himself and took a seat behind the desk. It was nice to have people who took care of him.

Once he caught up with what little paperwork he had to finish—mostly payroll stuff—he planned to check on the horses, take the ranch Jeep out to pasture to look over the cattle, and see if Mrs. Calloway needed any help with her cherries. It had been a few weeks since the harvest, and he hadn't checked in with her. He was usually a lot better about stuff like that, but he'd been distracted.

"Knock, knock."

Wyatt looked up. "Speak of the devil."

Maggie laughed. "You were talking about me?"

"No, but I was thinking about you. Well, you and your cherries. How are things going with the shop?"

"Pretty good. I mean, I've been busy, if that's what you're asking." She stepped into his office, crossed the room, and set a pie on the desk. "Teddie forgot about this yesterday."

Wyatt grinned. "You made me a pie? You know how much I love your pies." He got up, walked around his desk, gave her a one-armed hug, and kissed her cheek. "Thank you."

Maggie patted his cheek. "You're welcome. How are you feeling?"

"Okay," he replied. "I get a little woozy now and then, and I'm still getting headaches, but I'm good."

"You shouldn't be working," she scolded.

"I know, but this place won't run itself." He perched on the edge of his desk, crossed his arms, and looked down at Maggie. "So, you know about me and Teddie?"

Maggie nodded. "Of course I do. I'm not stupid. I knew my daughter had fallen head over heels for someone, I just didn't know who. After the accident, I was pretty sure it was you."

"And you're okay with it?"

"Yes. Why wouldn't I be? You're a good guy, Wyatt. One of the best. Teddie would be hard-pressed to find someone better."

Wyatt laughed and shook his head. "Can you tell Mr. Calloway that?"

"Trust me, I've tried. Even after more than thirty years together, that man doesn't listen to me." She sighed and gave him a weary smile. "I'll keep trying. Anyway, enjoy the pie. I need to get back to baking."

"Do you need any help?"

"Nope, Tessa is coming down to the kitchen. She's been learning to make all the stuff I make."

"Well, that's a surprise."

"Tell me about it. She loved helping me when she was a little girl, but when she hit thirteen, half her brain leaked out her ears and she became ... difficult." Maggie giggled. "Look, I better go."

"I'll walk you out." He walked with her to the barn doors, then they parted ways.

Wyatt walked back through the barn, stopping and checking on each horse. When he was done with that, he grabbed the Jeep keys off the hook by the door. Time to check on the cows.

—

The rain came out of nowhere, as it often did during Montana summers. One minute the sun was shining, the next it was pouring buckets of water. He was soaked by the time he got back to the Jeep from the pasture. Instead of switching to his truck, he drove the Jeep straight to the cabin. When he rounded the corner, he saw Teddie on his rain-soaked front porch. No big surprise, since she had called him about ten times while he was out in the pasture and sent twice as many texts. As soon as he shut off the Jeep, she darted down the steps and raced across the wet grass, stopping in front of him and staring up at him.

"Where the hell have you been?" she demanded. "It's been raining for an hour. I called you."

"I was in the south pasture with the cattle," he explained. "My phone doesn't work out there. What's wrong?"

"You've been out of the hospital for what, not even a week,

and you're out in the middle of a rainstorm with the cows? Have you lost your mind?"

"No." He chuckled. "Besides, I'm fine. You don't have to worry about me."

"Yes, I do. Jesus, Wyatt, I worry about you constantly, more so since the explosion. Dammit, don't scare me like that." She pounced on him, her mouth warm and hungry against his. His hands were on her before he could think, one hand cupping her cheek, the other in her wet hair, holding her to him.

Wyatt pulled her closer, flush against his chest, her heart beating in time with his. Teddie gripped his shirt, fisting the fabric and dragging him closer. The kiss deepened until they were both breathing hard.

The rain pounded down around them, drenching them both. Teddie's hair stuck to her face, her clothes plastered to her curves, and he couldn't stop drinking her in, not even as his mouth moved to her jaw, her neck, the raindrops on her skin like a sweet nectar.

Her breath hitched in her throat as she slid her fingers under the hem of his soaked shirt, her warm hands splayed over his stomach, and it burned somewhere deep inside him.

Wyatt gripped her hips tight, grinding against her. He kissed her again.

God, this woman was everything to him.

Teddie moaned, and something inside him snapped. He hauled her into his arms like she weighed nothing, her legs going around his waist, her breath warm against his throat. He turned around and pressed her back against the Jeep.

Wyatt didn't care that they were outside, or about the thunder or the lightning, or the mud on his boots. He wanted her, and when he kissed her again, it was with an ache and a hunger he'd kept buried.

"God, I love you," he murmured when he pulled away.

Teddie didn't say a word. She didn't have to. She knew what

kind of hold she had over him. He belonged to her, and they both knew it.

"Inside," she said.

His brain short-circuited.

Wyatt caught her lips in another searing kiss, and he moved, one hand gripping the back of her thigh as he carried her up the porch steps, the other around her waist. His shoulder hit the half-open door, opening it all the way. He stumbled inside, bumping against the doorframe, not that either of them noticed. Teddie kicked the door shut.

He set her on her feet and pressed her back against the wall, not gently, but urgently, nothing left to hold back his desire for her. Their lips met again in a messy, wet, teeth-clashing kiss. Her hand scrambled at the buttons on his shirt, yanking it open and shoving it off his shoulders. Her eyes dropped to his chest, and her breath caught in her throat.

His hands slid under her shirt, skimming her damp skin, up her ribs, and cupped her breasts. She gasped when his fingers brushed against her tight nipples; the sound swallowed by his lips on hers.

Both of their shirts hit the floor, and then there was nothing but mouths, hands, and a delicious friction, her chest against his, both of them slick with rain and flushed.

"Bedroom," he muttered, his voice so low and thick he barely recognized it.

Teddie nodded, her eyes dark and dazed.

Wyatt picked her up again, Teddie laughing into his mouth between kisses as he barreled through the house like a drunk on a bender. Once they got to the bedroom, he dropped her on the bed in the tangled sheets, then he stripped off her soaked denim jeans and underwear. He stared at her, drinking her in before he peeled off his own clothes and joined her on the bed.

He hovered over her, kissing her as one hand skimmed down

her side and between her legs. He couldn't wait. He needed her, wanted her more than anything he'd ever wanted in his life. His hunger for her burned deep inside him, insatiable and relentless.

Teddie moaned his name, arching into him when he settled between her legs and pushed into her in one long, slow, aching stroke that had them both trembling with desire.

It wasn't slow or gentle; it was need and instinct, their wet skin sliding against each other. Her hands fisted in his hair, dragging his mouth to her throat, while his grip on her hips left finger-shaped bruises.

They moved together like it was the most perfect union in the world, hell in the universe. Her nails dug into his back, both of them chasing the pleasure. Wyatt gave her everything she wanted, everything she demanded of him.

When Teddie came beneath him, her body tensing, her head thrown back, her walls clenching around his cock, drawing him in deeper, it pushed him right over the edge. He let go with a groan that echoed off the bedroom walls, and everything went white.

The rain still fell outside, quieter, softer than earlier. Wyatt pressed his forehead to hers and kissed the tip of her nose. He rolled to his back, keeping her close, their limbs still tangled together, his hand gently caressing her back.

Teddie sighed and rested her head on his chest.

"That was wild," she whispered.

Wyatt chuckled. "You bring the animal out of me."

"I didn't expect that. I was just going to yell at you, then make you a cup of coffee." She giggled and kissed his chest. "This was better."

Wyatt hugged her and closed his eyes. "Much better."

Chapter 14
Teddie

Teddie grabbed a cup of coffee from the kitchen, hoping to see her mother and her sister before she went to work. They weren't anywhere around, so she took her mug and went to the guesthouse. She slipped in as quietly as possible, praying she wouldn't see her father. Fortunately, he wasn't around either.

Two hours later, she still hadn't seen or even heard anyone, but she'd gotten caught up on paperwork, done payroll, and spoken to the bank, only to find out she wasn't going to be able to make her father a counteroffer unless she found someone to co-sign for her loan.

Wyatt's offer to help hung over her head, but she couldn't bring herself to ask him to do something so phenomenally huge and life-changing. The prospect of marriage was crazy enough, without throwing in a multi-million dollar debt to start off their lives together.

She needed some air, so she pushed herself away from her desk and went outside. She considered going to the barn to see Wyatt, but she went to her mother's shop instead. Being around Maggie always made her feel better.

Teddie walked through the cherry orchard, admiring the trees stripped bare after the cherry harvest. She tapped twice on the shop's kitchen door, pushed it open, and peered around the edge. The familiar scent of sugar and fruit surrounded her.

"Hey, Mom."

Maggie wiped the flour from her hands and smiled at her eldest daughter. "Hi, sweetie, what's up?"

"I came by to see what you're up to," Teddie replied. "How goes the pie making?"

Before Maggie could answer, Tessa came out of the refrigerator with a giant tub of cherries in her hands. "Hey, Ted, how's it going?"

"Tessa? What are you doing here?"

Her sister shrugged. "Mom is showing me the ropes."

"Really? You haven't baked since you were a kid," Teddie said. "I thought you didn't like it anymore?"

"I don't know. I've been down here helping Mom for the last few days, and I kind of like it."

"She's got a knack for it, too," Maggie added with a smile. "Oh, by the way, I took a pie down to the barn for Wyatt yesterday. Did he bring it home?"

"Oh crap, I forgot to take one for him, didn't I?"

Maggie nodded. "But that's okay. I got to say hi and check on him." She opened the refrigerator, took out a pitcher, and filled two glasses. "Here, try my cherry lemonade and tell me what you think."

"Thanks." She sat down at a small table in the corner and sipped the lemonade. "This is good."

"Tessa, will you excuse us for a few minutes?" Maggie asked.

"You know what, I think I'll go to town and pick up some

more sugar," Tessa said. She wiped her hands on a towel, tossed it on the counter, and then she was gone.

Maggie sat down across from Teddie. "Alright, what's wrong?"

She sighed. "What makes you think something is wrong?"

"I'm your mother," Maggie replied. "I can tell when something is bothering you."

"Did Dad tell you he agreed to let me make a counteroffer on the ranch?"

"Yes," Maggie said.

"Well, I can make the offer, but I won't have the money to back it up. The bank wants me to have a co-signer or find investors to front at least half of the money I need to purchase Cherry Ridge. I don't know how I'm supposed to find somebody to do that. Wyatt offered to help, but I don't feel right asking him to put up his entire life savings to help me buy this place. It's an enormous commitment."

"Do you think he's not ready for something like that?" Maggie asked.

"No," Teddie replied, dragging out the word. "I know he's ready to commit." She hesitated for a second, then blurted, "He wants to marry me."

She expected her mother to be more surprised or even emotional over the possibility of her daughter getting married, but she only smiled gently. "Sounds like he's okay with an enormous commitment to me."

"But how can I ask him to start our lives together with a huge debt hanging over our heads? That is so unfair to him."

Maggie got up and went back to the counter, where she returned to rolling out the dough for her pie crust. "Did you know I started the cherry shop in secret?" she asked.

"You did?"

Her mother smiled sheepishly. "Everett thought it was nothing more than a distraction." Maggie must have seen Teddie make a face, because she quickly said, "Oh, he never said that in so many words, but I heard it in his voice. He thought I needed a hobby, but I wasn't looking for something to pass the time. I wanted something that was mine. He indulged me by remodeling the staff kitchen and turning it into a little shop. I think he thought I'd get bored before too long."

Teddie laughed. "Daddy always said this was your hobby."

"I know." Maggie shook her head and laughed. "When I married your father, this ranch became my life, too. And even though I grew up on a ranch a lot like Cherry Ridge, I wasn't out chasing cows in the pasture. I was in the kitchen up to my elbows in flour and fruit in my apron pockets. Your grandmother taught me how to bake with the fruit we picked from the trees behind *our* house. The cherries were always my favorite. When we took over this place, those cherry trees were barely hanging on. I'm the one who brought them back to life."

"A lot of my memories from when I was little are of you in the cherry orchard taking care of your trees," Teddie murmured with a small smile. "And I remember helping you pit the cherries when I was little, my fingers stained red."

"Both you and Tessa used to help me." Maggie laughed. "Those are some of my favorite memories with you girls."

Teddie grinned. "Mine, too."

"Anyway, I started small, so small your father didn't even realize it was happening. I made pies for the farmer's market on Saturdays, then I added jams and jellies, cookies wrapped in twine and tucked in baskets. Next thing I knew, tourists stopped by on their way to Lakeside. Then it was locals who then became regulars. I started making more things, and before I knew it, the money was rolling in." Maggie paused and took a deep breath before she continued. "The shop does well, sweetie. Far better than anyone knows."

Teddie raised an eyebrow. "Oh?"

Maggie nodded. "Yes. But I've kept it to myself because I wanted to prove I could build something of my own, on my own, with no help. Just like you want to do with Cherry Ridge." She glanced up at her daughter, then returned her attention to the pie she was making. "I know what this place means to you, and how special it is."

Teddie swallowed, surprised at the swell of emotions rising in her.

"Please understand, I am not saying what I am about to say to undermine your father. But I have enough money saved from the shop to help you. I have enough to give you a real shot at buying Cherry Ridge. You don't have to lose the only home you've ever known because your father doesn't realize how much you love this place."

Struck speechless, Teddie stared at her mother for a long moment, the weight of everything pressing down on her. "You'd really do that? You'd give me the money?"

Maggie shrugged. "If you want to look at it that way. I see it as investing in your future."

Teddie jumped out of her seat, darted across the small kitchen, and threw herself at her mother. She hugged her while Maggie laughed and patted her arm with a flour-covered hand. When she stepped back, she had to wipe the tears from her eyes.

"Thank you, Mom. You don't know how much this means to me."

"No, I think I do," Maggie whispered, then she cleared her throat. "Let me get these pies in the oven, then we'll sit down and talk numbers. Pour yourself another glass of lemonade while you wait."

Teddie nodded and did as she was told. Her heart pounded in her chest, and her eyes kept leaking tears. She couldn't believe this was happening.

—

Teddie steeled her shoulders and knocked on her father's office door.

"Come in!"

She straightened her hair before she pushed open the door and stepped inside. "Hey, Dad, do you have a minute?"

Everett waved her in without looking away from the papers on his desk. Her father didn't have a computer on his desk; he liked to do things "the old-fashioned way."

Teddie eased into the chair across from him, clutching the folder with her counteroffer in her hands. She closed her eyes, willing the nervous rumble of her stomach to relax. It didn't help that her father took almost a full minute to put down the papers and look at her.

"What can I do for you, Theodora?"

She'd promised herself she wouldn't let her father get under her skin, no matter what he did or said. Using her full name was something he did to irritate her, especially when he was unhappy with her.

Teddie set the folder on her father's desk. "I brought you my counteroffer."

Everett opened the folder, glanced up at her, and then read every page. She kept still while he read; her father hated fidgeting. When he was done, he slowly closed the folder and folded his hands on top of it.

"This is impressive, Theodora," he said.

"Thank you," she mumbled.

He patted another folder beside hers. "I'm going to look over both offers, and I will let you know."

"That's it?" she asked.

Everett nodded. "Yes, that's it."

"Um, okay." Teddie got up and walked to the door. Her father cleared his throat, drawing her attention back to him.

"I'm serious, Teddie. This is superb work. I'm impressed with how much you put into this."

"Thanks, Daddy."

"I'll let you know by tomorrow," her father said.

As Teddie closed his door, her cheeks hurt from smiling. Her father didn't give praise often, so when he did, it meant a lot.

"Please let it be me," she whispered out loud.

"Let what be you?" an arrogant voice asked behind her.

She swung around to find Preston standing behind her with his sunglasses tucked in the front of his shirt and his baseball cap on backwards. His gum snapped repeatedly and annoyingly in his mouth.

"Preston! What are you doing here?"

"I came by to see your father." He narrowed his eyes. "He made it sound like you quit?" It wasn't a statement, but a question.

Teddie shook her head, her hair flying around her face. "No, I took a few days off. I needed to get my head on straight after everything that happened."

"Oh. Well, how's Wyatt?"

"On the mend," she replied. She smirked. "I think he's working today, if you want to say hello."

Preston made a face and shook his head. "I'm good." He pointed at the door behind her. "If you'll excuse me?"

Teddie stepped to the side and watched as Preston walked into her father's office without knocking. She rolled her eyes and walked away.

Now all she had to do was wait. It was going to be a long night.

Chapter 15

Wyatt

Wyatt flipped the pancake in the pan and checked the bacon in the cast iron pan, then he hit the button on the coffee pot. He had the plates on the table when Teddie walked through the kitchen door. Messy strands of her honey blonde hair framed her face, her eyes only half-open, wearing one of his thin T-shirts, barely skimming the bottom of her ass. She gave him a tired smile as she dropped into the chair at the kitchen table and poured herself a cup of coffee.

"Hi," he said, stopping to kiss the top of her head before he sat down across from her. "How'd you sleep?"

"I didn't," she mumbled. "I mean, I did, but not much. I'm so worried that Daddy will decide to sell the ranch to Preston instead of me. I cannot stop thinking about it."

Wyatt checked his watch. "Did he say what time he was going to let you know?"

Teddie shook her head. "No. Hopefully, he won't make me wait long."

As if on cue, her cell rang from the bedroom. She darted out of her chair so fast Wyatt had to grab it so it wouldn't fall over. He heard her speaking through the wall, but he couldn't make out what she was saying. He didn't like the look on her face when she came back to the kitchen.

"Uh oh, bad news?"

"It's not great news," she replied, tossing her phone on the table. "Daddy told Preston about my counteroffer, so late last night, Preston submitted a new offer. My father texted me about it last night, and honestly, I'm afraid I won't be able to compete with it."

"Did your father say that?" Wyatt asked.

"No. He hasn't gone over both proposals yet, but he wanted to let me know Preston submitted something new." She pushed her plate of food away and put her head on the table. "I'm screwed."

"Why do you think you can't compete with Preston's new offer?"

"Because it's Preston," Teddie muttered. "He probably offered an exorbitant amount of money that I can't match."

"Okay. Can you get a look at Preston's offer?"

Teddie's head popped up. "Hey, you know what? That's a good idea. I *can* get a look at it." She was on her feet again, headed for the bedroom.

A few minutes later, she emerged fully dressed. She kissed Wyatt on the head, mumbled, "See you later," and then she was gone.

"Bye," he muttered, eyeing her plate full of food. "Glad you enjoyed your breakfast."

Wyatt finished eating, took a shower, then he got in the truck and drove to the barn. When he walked into his office, Teddie was at his desk.

"Hi there," he said. "What are you doing at *my* desk?"

She held up a stack of papers and shook them. "I got Preston's offer off Daddy's desk and made a copy. I didn't want him to see me going over it, so I came down here." She grinned. "I hope that's okay?"

"Of course it is," he said. "Did you find anything weird?"

"Not yet."

"Let me know if you do. I'm gonna go feed the horses."

Teddie was still studiously looking over the offer when he finished feeding the horses, so he left her alone and made his way out to the pasture to check on the cattle. When he was done, he sent Luke and Ty to pick up hay while Hank and Nash cleaned the hay barn. After he'd finished all that, he returned to the barn. She was still at his desk, clutching the papers in one hand and gnawing on a pencil.

Wyatt leaned against the doorframe, watching her. "You're doing that thing where you chew on your pencil like you're punishing it."

She dropped the papers on the desk, along with her pencil. "I feel like punishing something. This updated offer *is* too good to be true, like I suspected. Supposedly, Preston got some new financial backers, making it possible for him to increase the purchase price. He also promised capital improvements to Cherry Ridge and that he will keep the current staff, including me *and* you."

"Really?" Wyatt stepped into the office, closed the door behind him, and crossed the room to the desk. He looked over her shoulder at the dog-eared papers with Teddie's notes scribbled in the margins.

"Yep. And there's more. He's going to lease the orchard to a nearby winery, but he promised to upgrade the equipment and housing on site, and he included a letter stating he and his investors plan on maintaining the ranch's legacy. But it's too good to be true. It's too... too *nice*. Preston isn't a generous person, and he doesn't care about legacies. Look what he did to his parents' ranch when his father passed away. He didn't give a shit about his legacy. The only thing he cares about is money."

"Let me see," Wyatt said.

She handed him the stack of papers, and he scanned it, brows furrowed.

"Where did these new investors come from?" Wyatt asked. "Do we know?"

Teddie shrugged. "According to the paperwork, it's a group of real estate investors out of Billings."

"I don't trust Preston," he mumbled. "You know what? Give me the names of the investors."

Teddie blinked. "What? Why?"

"I have a friend who works in agricultural financing in Missoula. He'll know if they're legitimate or not."

"I didn't even think about verifying the names," she whispered. "And you're willing to help me?"

"Of course I am. You're exhausted and stressed, Ted. Let me help you. Give me the names, and I'll call George."

Teddie jumped up and threw herself in Wyatt's arms, plastering his face with kisses. He chuckled as he hugged her.

"Thank you," she said.

"You're welcome." He kissed the tip of her nose. "I will not let Preston lie to the Colonel and get away with it. Or take this place away from you. Besides. I'd do anything for you."

"I don't deserve you."

"Yeah, you do." He hugged her close. "You deserve the world on a platter."

———

It took the rest of the day and into the evening for them to scour public records and for Wyatt to get the information on the investors from his friend. Once they had everything, it was far worse than they'd expected.

Wyatt grabbed one of the folding chairs leaning against the wall, put it next to his desk chair, and sat down. He spread the papers out on the desk.

"Alright, here's what George found out. These two investors, right here, these are names Preston used before in a land flipping scheme. This one is a shell company, and George can't find out any information about the owners. This guy is his cousin in Bozeman."

"Are you kidding?"

"I wish I were." Wyatt sighed. "And this one, he got himself blacklisted from a cattle co-op last year because he inflated the appraisal numbers."

"That asshole is selling a bunch of bullshit. It's a lie he's perpetrating to get my father's signature on paper. Once he does that, all bets are off." Teddie vaulted from her seat and paced the floor in front of the desk. "I need to talk to my father, convince him that selling to me is the best option."

"Well, go find him and talk to him," Wyatt said.

"I can't. When I went up to the house to get us food, I saw Tessa, and she said they took the RV to the other side of the lake to see how they like it. They won't be back until tomorrow."

"Then you've got time," he insisted. "Time to not only stop him from signing the agreement, but time to put together another proposal, a better one."

"A better one? How am I supposed to do that?"

Wyatt opened his desk drawer, took out the small velvet box, and set it on the desk. "Put together a proposal, including the money *your husband* is contributing, and explaining how the two of us are going to run Cherry Ridge together." He took Teddie's hands. "We can do this, you and me. You know we can. This ranch is your legacy, Ted, and together we'll make it the best ranch on Flathead Lake. This place will be *our* legacy, a place to raise our children, and someday pass on to our children." He grabbed the box and flicked it open. "So, Theodora Jean Calloway, will you marry me?"

Teddie nodded so hard her messy bun fell out of her hair. "Hell, yeah, I'll marry you!" She clambered into his lap, wrapped her arms around his neck, and kissed him, then she rested her forehead against his. "I can't wait to be your wife."

Wyatt took the ring out of the box and slipped it on her finger. "And I can't wait to be your husband. Now, let's get our offer put together, and then we'll go home and celebrate our engagement. Just you and me."

"That sounds amazing." She kissed him, her tongue sliding across his lips until he opened his mouth, her arms tightening around his neck, pulling him into her, her hips pressing into his.

Wyatt growled low in his throat. "If you don't stop that, we'll be celebrating right here on the desk."

Teddie giggled. "As fantastic as that sounds, let's get this offer done and go home. I want to spend some time with my fiancé."

Chapter 16

Teddie

Teddie parked her Jeep in front of the house. This was it, the moment of truth. Her father and mother had returned early this morning, and the Colonel had summoned her to his office.

Unfortunately, Preston had come, too. He'd parked his Mercedes in the circular drive.

She closed her eyes and took a deep breath. How in the hell was she supposed to keep her cool when Preston was here, the man who lied to get his hands on her family home? She exhaled and stepped out of the Jeep with her laptop bag in her hand. Her heart pounded as she walked through the orchard toward the guest-house, clutching the strap of the bag like it was a security blanket.

Tessa popped out from behind a tree. "Hey, Teddie."

Teddie stumbled back a few steps and glared at her sister. "Jesus, Tess, you scared the crap out of me!"

Tessa grinned. "Sorry. I saw you pull into the driveway, and I wanted to talk to you."

"Well, hurry. I'm going to talk to Dad."

"About buying the ranch?" Tessa asked.

She nodded, one eyebrow raised. "Yeah. Why?"

"Can I talk to you about something?" Tessa said.

"Sure." Teddie dragged the word out, curious about what her sister wanted.

"If you get your hands on the ranch, I want in."

Teddie snorted. "What? You've never wanted anything to do with the ranch before. Why now?"

Tessa pushed a hand through her hair and sighed. "In case you hadn't noticed, I've been spending a lot of time with Mom. She's been, well, she's been kind of showing me the ropes and how she runs her shop."

"I noticed," Teddie said.

"I'd like to keep it open, if you buy Cherry Ridge. People in this town love Mom's pies and pastries, and it makes good money. That's the only thing I am asking. Give me control of the shop. I can make it bigger, like a bakery or a jam empire. Whatever. Anyway, I don't think it's too much to ask."

Teddie nodded. "You're right, it makes good money. And I don't think it's too much to ask. Besides, the person who really loves it is the person who should run it. Right?"

A small smile teased the corner of Tessa's lips. "Yep."

"But this entire conversation will be for nothing if Daddy doesn't take my offer for the ranch, so I need to go. I have to stop him from taking Preston's offer."

Teddie tried to walk past her sister, but Tessa grabbed her and hugged her so tight she couldn't breathe.

"Tess, gotta go," she mumbled.

"Yeah, sorry. Go in there and kick Preston's ass."

Teddie nodded, squeezed Tessa's shoulder, and hurried through the orchard to the guesthouse. When she stepped inside, she heard her father and Preston talking and laughing.

"Shit," she muttered under her breath, stepping up the pace.

She paused outside the door for a second, then she pushed it open.

"Hi," she said.

"Theodora," Everett said. "You're late."

Teddie glanced at the clock. "I'm two minutes late. I stopped to talk to Tessa."

He gave her a curt nod. "Well, have a seat."

She did as she was told, her knees bouncing as she sat down and put her bag on the floor beside the chair. She grabbed one folder from the bag and slid it across the desk. "You need to look at this."

Everett glanced at it, then back at her. "What is this? Your counteroffer." He shook his head. "I'm sorry, but it's too late. I've accepted Preston's offer."

Teddie stared at her father, willing him to listen to her. "Please, Daddy, look at what's in the folder."

With a hefty sigh, Everett flipped open the folder and read the first page. He glanced up at her and Preston, then he read it again.

"Are you sure about this?" he asked.

Teddie nodded. "Yes, sir." She cleared her throat. "Wyatt has a friend in ag financing in Missoula. He helped us figure this out."

"Us?"

"Wyatt helped me," she replied. "We stayed up half the night connecting the dots. He wants to protect Cherry Ridge as much as I do."

"Protect Cherry Ridge from what?" Preston interjected.

"From you," Everett said. He closed the folder and tossed it across the desk to Preston, who opened it and skimmed the first page.

"I don't know about any of this," Preston muttered. "This is obviously an attempt to disparage me so she can buy the ranch out from under me."

"Oh, really?" Everett leaned over the desk with a look she

vividly recalled from her somewhat rebellious teenage years and, more recently, when he was angry with Tessa. Nobody lied to Colonel Calloway and got away with it. "Maybe I'll call Wyatt's friend myself?"

Preston's eyes widened as he looked between Everett and Teddie. "I... I don't think that's necessary. Besides, all of this is a moot point if Teddie doesn't have a counteroffer."

Everett turned back to her. "Alright, Theodora, do you have a counteroffer?"

"Yes." She removed another folder from her bag and handed it to her father.

He read through it, then he closed the folder. "This is more than your original offer. Do you have the money?"

"I have the money, Daddy," she said. "More than enough to buy Cherry Ridge. No investors, no strings. Just me and... and my husband."

Everett's brow furrowed, and he looked like someone pinched him. "Husband?"

Teddie held her left hand up and wiggled her fingers, showing him the diamond and sapphire ring on her finger. "Wyatt and I are getting married. We want to make Cherry Ridge our home, raise our children—your grandchildren—here."

"You're serious?" Everett said.

"I've never been more serious," she replied.

Everett stared at the top of his desk as he spoke. "I never wanted my children to feel obligated to run Cherry Ridge. My father didn't give me a choice; this place was mine whether or not I wanted it. I swore I wouldn't do that to you and Tessa. When I decided to sell the ranch, I thought I was setting you free."

"I'm not shackled to this place," Teddie explained. "I love Cherry Ridge. It's my home. I want to keep it that way."

"This is super sweet and all, but I have places to be," Preston interrupted. "Mr. Calloway, are you accepting my offer or not?"

She'd forgotten he was still sitting beside her. She folded her hands in her lap and waited for her father's answer.

Everett placed his hands flat on top of his desk. "I'm accepting Teddie's offer." He held up his hand before Preston could speak. "For a variety of reasons."

Preston opened his mouth to protest, but Everett pointed at the door. "Get out of my office. Now."

Everett waited until Preston had stormed out, then he opened the bottom drawer of his desk and pulled out a sheaf of papers. He dropped them on the desk.

"This is the contract to purchase Cherry Ridge," her father said. "I'm throwing it away."

"You're, you're ... what?" she stammered.

"I'm not selling you the ranch, Theodora."

"I don't understand," she protested. "I have the money. I told you I want it—"

"I'm giving it to you," Everett interjected. "As a wedding gift."

Teddie swallowed and fresh tears welled in her eyes. "I don't understand. I thought you wanted me to buy it."

Everett shook his head. "I wanted to know in here," he said, tapping the center of his chest, "that you really wanted this place. I told you, I don't want to burden my children with something they don't want. You proved to me you want Cherry Ridge, so it's yours."

"Just like that?" Teddie asked.

Her father laughed. "Just like that." He tapped his fingers on the desk. "I'm sorry I put you through that, but for years I thought you were only here because I asked you to come home after college and help. I should have known how much this place meant to you. I'm sorry I didn't."

Teddie smiled. "It's okay, Daddy. I understand. I guess."

Everett blinked, then a smile spread across his face. "I'll call my lawyer and have him draw up the paperwork to transfer the ranch to you. It will only take a day or two."

"Okay," she whispered, smiling.

"Why don't you tell Wyatt the good news?"

"Yeah, I will." She was halfway to the door when she turned around, went around the desk, and hugged her father. "Thank you, Daddy. Thank you so much."

"You're welcome," Everett whispered.

Chapter 17

Teddie

10 Months Later

It was Teddie's favorite time of year at Cherry Ridge, when the rows of cherry trees were in full bloom, their soft pink petals fluttering in the light breeze. That's why she chose mid-May for the most important day of her life, more important than any other day ever.

Her wedding day.

She'd decided to have her wedding right here on the ranch she'd fought so hard for, beneath the trees she climbed as a kid, the trees that gave Cherry Ridge its name. There was no better place to marry the man she loved than the place she called home.

Teddie adjusted the headband holding the veil in place on top of her head and fixed the curl that kept flipping the wrong direction and falling over her eye. Then she checked to make sure she wasn't standing on the edge of her dress.

She squinted as she peered down the row of trees. Folding chairs formed two neat rows on either side of an aisle strewn with cherry blossom petals. Coarse twine tied wildflowers to each chair back, matching her bouquet. Maggie insisted on helping with the decorations, and now the ranch looked like a spread in some country bridal magazine, only better, because it was her ranch and her mother who had decorated it.

Tessa stood beside her in a pale pink dress, holding both of their bouquets. She poked Teddie in the arm. "Are you okay?"

She nodded. "I'm a little nervous."

"Well, don't faint or something while you're walking down the aisle," her sister said. "I don't think I can catch you in front of a hundred people. But holy hell, that would be a crazy photo to have in your wedding album."

Teddie giggled. "First, it's more like thirty people, counting the photographer and the caterer, and half of them are people who saw me face plant in cow shit last week. I think I'm good."

Tessa smirked. "That's true. Can't top that."

The music started, a soft guitar solo, courtesy of Hank, who could play anything by ear. Tessa handed Teddie her bouquet, kissed her on the cheek, and started down the aisle.

Everett stood next to her in his dress uniform, pride and something that looked suspiciously like emotion shining in his eyes. He held out his arm, and she took it.

Teddie kept her eyes on Wyatt as they walked through the trees. He waited at the end of the aisle in front of the two tallest cherry trees in the orchard on a small, raised platform. He wore a long-sleeved white button-down shirt, a green vest, his favorite Stetson, and the biggest smile she'd ever seen on his face.

She made it to the front without tripping, taking Wyatt's hand as soon as she was close enough.

He grinned at her and whispered, "You're awful pretty when you're not yelling at me about the irrigation schedule."

"If you'd do it like I asked, I wouldn't have to yell," she replied.

Luke—who'd gotten himself ordained so he could be their

officiant—cleared his throat. Wyatt touched the brim of his hat with a smile.

"Ready when you are," he said.

Luke welcomed everyone and said a few brief words. He was charming and funny, just like Teddie knew he'd be.

"At this time, Teddie and Wyatt will exchange vows they have written themselves."

Tessa handed Teddie the ring she'd picked out for Wyatt. She smiled at him, took a deep breath, and clasped his left hand in hers.

"I love you, Wyatt Dawson. It didn't happen overnight, or like a bolt of lightning out of the sky, but gradually over time as I realized all the things that make you who you are. Like when you fixed the tractor without me asking, or stayed out in the pasture all night to help the cows give birth, or drove to Kalispell to get that flour my mom likes to use for her bread. You challenge me to be a better person and you don't take any crap from me. You stood by my side when things got tough and when I needed you, you were there. And somehow, through everything, I was lucky enough to find the man I love. I promise to fight for you no matter what. And if I need to fight with you, I'll do it, but only if you're being hardheaded. I'll laugh with you when the cows break the fence or cry with you when we have to put down our favorite horse. I promise not to micromanage your hay stacking if you promise to keep pretending you don't know where I hide my secret stash of chocolate in your office. And I promise to love you for the rest of our wild, crazy, messy lives if you promise to love me, too."

Wyatt laughed. "I promise."

Teddie slipped the ring on Wyatt's finger.

Luke chuckled. "Wyatt, your turn."

He cleared his throat, took Teddie's ring from his best man, Jesse, and squeezed Teddie's hand.

"I've been in love with you since the day you yelled at me to get my ass off your porch if I didn't plan on listening to what you had to say. And I knew I wanted to marry when you refused to give up the home you love. You are nothing but heart, Theodora Jean. I love that you don't back down, you don't give up, and you don't let anyone walk all over you—not even me. I will never try to tame you. I will keep your secrets, protect your dreams, and when the world gets too loud, I'll be your quiet place to hide. I promise to leave at least half of the last cinnamon roll for you and to always make sure you have a full cup of coffee. You are my best friend and the love of my life. I swear I will spend every day making sure you know how much you mean to me, even when you're yelling at me from the other side of the pasture."

Wyatt slipped the solid gold band onto her finger with hands still calloused from mending fences the day before.

When they kissed, it was a sweet, lingering kiss, even though the whole orchard was watching. They didn't give a damn.

Everyone clapped and shouted as they walked down the aisle past their friends and family. Someone whistled as Maggie dabbed the corners of her eyes. Everett's nod of approval meant more than anything he could have said.

"We did it," Teddie said with a smile.

"Yeah, we did." He kissed her forehead. "Now, let's go have a party."

———

The sun dipped behind the hills, leaving a gold haze over the ranch. The wedding crowd had thinned to the family, the McBrides, and the ranch hands. They'd gathered around the bonfire across from the barn, sipping drinks from small Mason jars. The flames crackled and popped, sending sparks into the clear night sky.

Teddie kicked off her shoes and padded across the grass, the hem of her dress gathered in one hand and a whiskey lemonade in the other. Wyatt stood by the fire, his vest long since taken off and his shirt sleeves rolled up to his elbows. He downed a glass of whiskey in two swallows. When he saw her, he held out his hand.

"Come dance with me, Mrs. Dawson."

She stepped into his arms without hesitation as a soft, slow tune played from the speakers hung on the outside of the barn. They moved together like they were one, her head on his shoulder, his hand resting lightly on the middle of her back.

Teddie looked around at the people she loved. Tessa and Luke were attempting to roast marshmallows over the fire, arguing about whether black or barely toasted brown tasted better. Her parents sat on a quilt by the fire with their legs stretched out, discussing their upcoming trip to Yellowstone in their new RV. Jesse and Claire danced a few feet from them while the other ranch hands sat around the fire talking.

"Ten bucks says you'll be out here tomorrow morning at six a.m., making a list of everything that needs to be done for cherry picking and worrying about the rain affecting hay season," Wyatt said. "And you'll probably still be in your dress."

Teddie laughed. "Twenty bucks says you'll be right next to me with coffee in your hand, taking notes."

They both took their responsibilities at the ranch seriously. There was never a day off, especially at this time of year. When they'd decided to get married in May, it was with the understanding that they'd postpone their honeymoon until later in the year. Teddie had joked they could wait until there was nothing to do, but then they'd never be able to go.

"Are you ready for this?" Wyatt asked.

"Yes. I've been ready for this my whole life. I'm right where I am meant to be with the person I'm supposed to be with. Together, we'll make this ranch greater than anyone imagined. Tessa has big plans for the cherry shop, and we've got the world on a platter. We can do anything we want."

"Anything?" Wyatt chuckled. "What are you thinking?"

Teddie pointed at the pasture in front of them. "What do you think of building a pen right there?"

"A pen for what?"

"Baby goats."

Wyatt shook his head. "Baby goats? Are you serious?"

Teddie nodded. "Yep. I *love* baby goats. They're adorable."

"Well, I guess we'll have to discuss that, won't we?" He wrapped his arms around her. "Maybe next spring. Unless we're busy with some other kind of baby."

She laughed, her face pressed against his chest. The world was hers. Whether it was baby goats or baby humans, she knew she could handle anything that came her way, as long as she had Wyatt by her side.

Book Club Questions:

1. The setting of Cherry Ridge Ranch plays a huge role in the story. How does the landscape—especially the cherry orchard—add to the mood, symbolism, or emotional depth of the story?

2. Teddie's sister Tessa chooses to stay on the ranch and run the cherry shop. In what ways does her arc mirror or contrast with Teddie's? What do you think of their relationship?

3. Let's talk chemistry and heat. How did the chemistry between Teddie and Wyatt evolve? Were there particular moments that stood out as a turning point in their relationship for you?

4. Teddie wanting to stay at Cherry Ridge isn't just about the land—it's about her family legacy. How does the ranch symbolize more than just a physical place for her? What does "home" mean in the context of this story?

5. Family plays a complicated role in the story: from Everett's pride to Maggie's quiet support. How do each of the family members influence Teddie, and which relationships are the most emotionally impactful?

Want to get all the latest info about Mimi Francis and her upcoming projects and events? Subscribe to her newsletter on mimifrancis.com for exclusive news, stories, and updates.

About the Author

Mimi Francis is a sassy romance writer known for her steamy tales of passion that leave readers breathless. When she's not crafting the perfect happily-ever-after, you can find her sipping margaritas and binge-watching Marvel movies or the TV show Supernatural. But her true loves (after her husband, of course) are her four Shih Tzus who keep her company as she spins stories that will make your heart race and your toes curl. Get ready to fall in love with her characters and the worlds she creates.

Discover more at
4HorsemenPublications.com

10% off using HORSEMEN10